Joseph Muenscher

The Book of Proverbs: In an amended Version

With an Introduction and explanatory Notes

SALZWASSER
VERLAG

Joseph Muenscher

The Book of Proverbs: In an amended Version

With an Introduction and explanatory Notes

1st Edition | ISBN: 978-3-75257-993-2

Place of Publication: Frankfurt am Main, Germany

Year of Publication: 2022

Salzwasser Verlag GmbH, Germany.

Reprint of the original, first published in 1866.

THE

BOOK OF PROVERBS,

IN AN

AMENDED VERSION,

WITH AN

INTRODUCTION

AND

EXPLANATORY NOTES.

BY

JOSEPH MUENSCHER, D.D.

GAMBIER, O.:

PRINTED AT THE WESTERN EPISCOPALIAN OFFICE,

1866.

PREFACE.

THE Exegetical labors of Biblical scholars in this country have hitherto been chiefly bestowed on the canonical and inspired books of the New Testament; and but little has been done by them to elucidate those of the Old. Accordingly, the common, as well as the learned reader of the Bible may find excellent helps to the understanding of the *Christian* Scriptures, but the former especially will seek in vain for works adapted to his wants on a large portion of the *Jewish* Scriptures. This is the more to be regretted, because the particular attention now directed to the study of the Old Testament in Seminaries of learning, Bible Classes and Sunday Schools, seems to require that Ministers and Laymen who are engaged in the religious instruction of the young, should have access to such works as are calculated to afford them the needed assistance in the explanation of that large and invaluable portion of the sacred volume. The following work is an humble contribution towards supplying the needed help in regard to the Book of Proverbs. This book has been almost entirely overlooked by Commentators, and yet it would be difficult to name one within the compass of the Sacred Scriptures more worthy the attentive study of the rising generation than this, for the obvious reason that much of it is addressed particularly to the young, while at the same time the whole of it is specially adapted to the formative period of life, and its precepts and monitions apply with peculiar force to those, whose inexperience exposes them to danger from almost every species of temptation. In the rendering of the text, it has been the aim of the writer not to depart unnecessarily from our excellent standard version. The deviations from that version are chiefly such as perspicuity and fidelity to the original seemed

to require. The renderings of other interpreters have in many
instances been given in foot notes, some of which will at least
be found suggestive.

The exegetical works which have been most frequently consulted, and from which the greatest assistance has been derived
in the preparation of this volume, are the following:—

MATTHEW POOLE.—Synopsis Criticorum. 5 vols. folio. London. 1671.

MATTHEW GEIER.—Commentaria in Prov. Sal. (Opera.) 2 vols.
   folio. Lugd. Bat. 1696.

JOHN PISCATOR.—Commentarius in Omnes libros Veteris Test.
   2 vols. folio. Herbor. Nassor. 1644-6.

ALBERT SCHULTENS.—Com. in Prov. Salomonis. 4to. Lugd.
   Bat. 1748.

GEORGE HOLDEN.—An Attempt towards an Improved Translation of the Proverbs, with notes Critical and Explanatory.
   8vo. London. 1831.

E. F. K. ROSENMUELLER.—Scholia in Prov. Sal. 2 vols. 8vo.
   Leipsic. 1829.

B. BOOTHROYD.—Version of the Proverbs in his New Translation of the Bible. royal 8vo. London. 1843.

GEORGE R. NOYES.—A new translation of the Proverbs, Ecclesiastes and the Canticles. 12mo. Boston. 1846.

MOSES STUART,—Commentary on the Book of Proverbs. 12mo.
   New York. 1852.

   Mt. Vernon, Feb., 1866.

INTRODUCTION.

I.

THE LIFE OF SOLOMON.

Solomon, (Hebrew שְׁלֹמֹה, Septuagint Σαλωμών, New Testament and Josephus, Σολομών, Vulgate, *Solomon*,) was the son of King David by his favorite wife Bathsheba, the widow of the faithful and heroic patriot Uriah. He was born in Jerusalem, B. C. 1035. The import of his name (*pacific*) is strikingly significant of the peaceful character of his disposition, and of his long, tranquil, and prosperous reign. High expectations were formed respecting him antecedently to his birth, in consequence of his having been the subject of the following remarkable prediction delivered to his father David. "Behold, a son shall be born to thee, who shall be a man of rest; and I will give him rest from all his enemies round about; for his name shall be Solomon; and I will give peace and quietness unto Israel in his days. He shall build a house for my name: and he shall be my son, and I will be his father; and I will establish the throne of his kingdom over Israel forever." (1 Chron. 22: 9, 10.) As soon as he was brought into the world, the prophet Nathan was commissioned to declare to David the divine favor towards the child, and to give him a surname expressive of that regard. "He called his name Jedediah (*i. e.* the beloved of Jehovah) because of the Lord." (2 Sam. 12: 25.) With regard to his early years and the education he then received we are not particularly informed; but it can hardly be supposed that a child of so much promise was neglected by such a man as David; and the youthful piety, the intellectual cul-

A

ture and literary attainments of Solomon, clearly evince
that both his moral and mental education were early and
carefully attended to. The will of God that Solomon should
be the successor of his royal father on the throne of Israel,
had been distinctly announced by the prophet Nathan. But
circumstances arose not long before the death of David which
rendered it necessary that some public demonstration should
be made in reference to that important matter, and that the
proper steps should be immediately taken by the king to
secure the succession to his favorite son. Those evils began
to develop themselves which are inseparable from Oriental
monarchies, where polygamy prevails, and where among
children from many wives of different ranks, no certain rule
of succession is established. Factions began to divide the
royal household and even the priesthood. Adonijah, the
eldest son of the king by his wife Haggith, relying on the
right of primogeniture which fell to him by the death of his
elder brothers Absalom and Amnon, directed his ambition
towards the throne, which he presumed would in the course
of nature soon become vacant. His pretensions were sec-
onded by Joab, whose counsel had heretofore decided many
of the principal measures of government, and whose influence
with the army, at the head of which he was placed, was with
great confidence relied upon. Abiathar, the high priest, also
espoused his cause, who necessarily from his official position
possessed great influence both with the priesthood and the
people at large. With the head of the army and the head
of the Church on his side, it is not surprising that Adonijah
felt quite sanguine of success; and becoming impatient of
delay, he invited his political and personal friends to a sumptuous banquet for the purpose of devising measures to secure
his succession. Intelligence of Adonijah's treasonable proceedings having reached the court of David, the king, by the
advice of Nathan and the solicitation of Bathsheba, resolved
on the immediate inauguration of Solomon. Accordingly he
instructed Nathan the prophet, and Zadok, one of the heads
of the priesthood, to place themselves under the protection
of Benaiah, the son of Jehoiada, the faithful commander of
his body-guard, and with a chosen band of reliable troops to

proceed forthwith to Gihon, a fountain near Jerusalem, where the people were accustomed to resort, and there anoint Solomon king. Adonijah, ignorant of his father's intentions, was not aroused to a sense of his guilt and danger, till the return of his rival to the city amid the acclamations of the multitude. He was still engaged in the ceremonial of the feast, exulting in the anticipated success of his schemes, when from the sudden change of affairs, he first learned that by his conduct he had rendered himself obnoxious to the charge of treason and usurpation. Impelled by his fears, he instantly fled for protection to the altar of daily sacrifice, which had been erected by David near the ark on Mount Zion,—the tabernacle of Moses being still in Gibeon. He hoped to find refuge at that sacred place from the doom which impended over him: for the sacred altar was a privileged place, not by the enactment of law, but by the custom of all nations. On being re-assured by a message from Solomon, he presented himself before the young king and did homage to him; who dismissed him with peremptory orders to keep himself quiet and secluded at his own house.

When David perceived his end approaching, overwhelmed with solicitude for the continued prosperity of that kingdom, which he had been the instrument under divine providence of raising to the highest pitch of grandeur and power, he gave a private audience to his son Solomon, and impressed upon him the necessity of a serious and fixed attention to religion and to the conscientious and upright discharge of the important duties belonging to his elevated and responsible station; assuring him at the same time, that this course of conduct was the only way in which he could expect to enjoy the approbation and continued support of the Almighty. (1 Kg. 2: 1–4.) He further gave him directions in regard to the course he should pursue towards certain influential but discontented and dangerous individuals, who would be near his person. He commended to his friendship and patronage the sons of Barzillai the Gileadite, in grateful acknowledgment of the kindness and hospitality received from that family during the rebellion of Absalom. Joab was the most fearless soldier of Israel; but his fierce temper

David had never been able to control. He apprehended, therefore, great inconvenience and hazard to his youthful successor, should this brave, but insolent, murderous, and disaffected leader be permitted to prosecute his ambitious schemes. David, accordingly, recommended Solomon to watch with the utmost vigilance the motions of his restless cousin, and on the first indications of disaffection, to put an end to his life.

Shimei, also, the son of Gera, was pointed out to Solomon as a profane and faithless wretch, who could not be trusted, and who had deserved the severest punishment for imprecating curses on his sovereign in the day of his adversity. David, indeed, had pledged his word to Shimei, not to put him to death; but this promise was not to be obligatory on his successor, should circumstances transpire to justify the infliction of the extreme penalty of the law upon him. Having thus provided for the security of the succession according to his wishes, the maintenance of the law, and of the dignity and prosperity of the national religion, David expired, having reigned forty years over the flourishing and powerful monarchy of which he may be regarded as the founder.

Solomon, the third and last of the Hebrew kings whose sovereignty extended over the twelve tribes of Israel, ascended the throne B. C. 1015, at the age of twenty years. He assumed the reins of government under the most favorable circumstances, with every conceivable advantage, and the most encouraging appearances and prospects. Soon after his accession the king was furnished at least with a plausible pretext, if not a clearly justifiable cause for removing the influential chiefs, against whom his father had warned him. Solomon has been severely censured by some writers for the course he pursued towards these men. But when viewed from the right stand-point, it will not, I apprehend, exhibit the aspect of tyrannical cruelty and barbarity which has been ascribed to it. The government of Israel at that time, like the governments of most Eastern nations at the present day, was not that of a free republic, nor of a limited monarchy; but it was an absolute despotism. The king, in the discharge of his high prerogatives, was amenable to no earthly tribunal, and had no other check on his authority than the law of God as given to Moses. And the course adopted by Solomon to insure the stability of his throne from internal faction, however different it may have been from that pursued by Western Christian nations in modern times, was precisely that which is customarily pursued in similar circumstances by all the monarchs of the East. And its necessity was no doubt believed to be correctly founded in the known temperament and character of eastern people. By exhibiting firmness of mind, decision of purpose and promptness of action, the severe punishment of a few individuals may have prevented, and doubtless did prevent, the sacrifice of many lives. The antecedents of all these men were such as to warrant the young king in regarding them as capable of devising any plot for their own aggrandisement, and their influence with all classes of citizens was, from their position, so great that a favorable opportunity alone was wanted to carry into execution any treasonable measures they might resolve upon. Adonijah, Solomon's half brother, had already, as we have seen, attempted to seize the reins of government, for which he had received only a conditional pardon. It was confidently believed that he still meditated the attainment of the object of his ambition, notwithstanding the ill-success which attended his former attempt. A secret conspiracy between him and Joab was still evidently in existence, though the extent of that conspiracy was unknown. It is not improbable that Abishag, the youngest and most beautiful of David's wives, was a party to that conspiracy, and designed by the bestowment of her hand upon Adonijah to strengthen his claims to the throne.

The whole Harem of an eastern monarch was a part of the regal succession, and when Adonijah solicited Abishag in marriage through Bathsheba, Solomon regarded the act as treasonable in itself, and only another scheme of his to accomplish his cherished design. The king viewed it as a matter of political expediency at least, to frustrate the supposed plot, by immediately removing the rebellious subject, and accordingly gave orders to Benaiah, who had been raised to

A*

the chief command of the army in the place of the dismissed Joab, to put him to death. Joab, apprehensive from the part he had taken on a former occasion, as well as perhaps from conscious guilt in reference to more recent transactions, fled to the altar on Mount Zion, as Adonijah had formerly done, for protection. This turbulent and factious, though qrave soldier, had long merited the severest penalty of the law; for there rested on his head the blood of two military commanders, Abner and Amasa, whom David had greatly delighted to honor; and he still remained disaffected toward the reigning prince. Solomon, therefore, in ordering the execution of so dangerous a foe, would seem to have consulted the peace and security of the state which had been entrusted to his keeping.

Abiathar, a descendant of Eli, and of the line of Ithamar, the younger son of Aaron, was one of Adonijah's most powerful adherents. He had deserved death for the part he took with the conspirators; but in consideration of the services which he had rendered to David in his affliction, his punishment was mitigated. He was deposed from the high priesthood, or rather suspended from the further exercise of the priestly functions and deprived of the emoluments of his office, and required to confine himself to his private estate at Anathoth, a few miles from Jerusalem, which belonged to him as a priest. Zadok, who was of the elder line of Eleazar, had been appointed high priest by Saul, and had acted jointly with Abiathar during the reign of David; he was now invested with the sole powers of the pontificate.

Shimei also was evidently a dangerous character, and deeply stained with that most detestible of all baseness, an insolent triumph over a fallen master. Him, therefore, Solomon charged to confine himself within the city, and not to go beyond it at the peril of his life. At the end of three years, however, Shimei was induced to violate his solemn engagement in order to recapture two fugitive slaves, who had escaped to Gaza. His life, taken by Benaiah, at once paid the forfeit of his perfidy. Solomon was now confirmed in the entire and undisputed possession of the regal power and authority. The hearts of the people became firmly attached to their new sovereign, and they paid him cheerful homage and obedience.

This monarch commenced his reign with such a serious attention to religion and the ordinances of public worship, as fully to justify the belief that he was truly and sincerely devoted to the service of Jehovah. He is declared by the sacred historian to have "loved the Lord, walking in the statutes of David his father." (1 Kg. 3: 3.) Soon after the death of David, he held a national religious festival of peculiar solemnity, before the Tabernacle of Moses at Gibeon. Here he worshipped Jehovah according to the regular and instituted mode, and fervently supplicated the divine blessing on himself and his people. In consequence of this public acknowledgment of his dependence upon God, and of the special providence of the Most High, he received a signal manifestation of the divine favor towards him. In the visions of the night Jehovah appeared to him, and gave him permission to ask for whatever he most desired, with the implied pledge that it should be granted. Most men in such a case would no doubt have requested an increase of wealth, of power, and of honor. But Solomon's heart was not set on any of these things. Passing these by, therefore, he simply expressed a desire for sound wisdom to enable him to discharge the arduous duties of his high and responsible station to the glory of God and the benefit of his subjects. This remarkable petition of Solomon is deserving of the highest encomium. "He rightly judged that in praying for such a degree of wisdom and knowledge as was necessary to the better government of his people, he was not only supplicating a blessing for himself but for them. The *nature* of that wisdom which he desired is also worthy our particular notice. It was not a depth of scientific knowledge, a minute acquaintance with the hidden powers of nature, a thorough understanding of all the properties of matter and of mind, or a profound skill in tongues, for which he prayed; but for that wisdom which would enable him to discharge the duties of his station for the glory of God and the general good. And this should be the aim of every man, let his rank in life, or his pursuits be what they may. All knowledge that is not calculated to promote the divine honor, and the benefit of our fellow-creatures, if not injurious, is at least useless. A man may possess a very accurate acquaintance with books, and with the sciences; he may have his head filled with the lumber of learning, and know all the events of history; yet with all this reputation of wisdom, he may be a fool, because what he possesses is not applied to a single useful purpose." (Watkins.) The request of Solomon was acceptable to Jehovah, who announced to him in reply, that his utmost desires should be satisfied, and that what he had not asked, additional wealth and dignity far beyond what were enjoyed by contemporary monarchs, should be bestowed on him. The promise of long life was also given him, on the condition that he persevered in obedience to the divine laws. From this solemnity he returned to Jerusalem, and there again with fervent gratitude offered many sacrifices and sealed his vows of fidelity to the Lord before the ark of the Covenant. Such a public and marked respect for the national religion could not fail to be productive of the most salutary effects throughout the land.

David had bequeathed to his son a prosperous and united kingdom, stretching from the frontiers of Egypt to the foot of Lebanon, and from the Euphrates to the Mediterranean Sea. Thus a wide field was opened to him to engage in commerce, to advance the peaceful arts of civilized life, to enrich his empire without extending it, and to employ all his resources in promoting the material comfort and prosperity of his people, instead of expending them in the maintenance of large standing armies, or in carrying on expensive wars. For such a condition of affairs and such measures and pursuits Solomon was exactly fitted. Nature had not formed him for the hardy and daring pursuits of military life, nor impressed him with the love of that distinction which is consequent on fearless courage, reckless enterprise, and successful warlike achievements. On the contrary, the original structure of his mind, and his taste, were adapted to reflection, science, literature and refinement, to the arts of peace and the elegancies of social life.

Only a short time elapsed before an opportunity occurred

for the display of Solomon's superior *judicial* wisdom. Two women who resided together had each been delivered of a son; but one of the infants soon after died, and its mother took the corpse and laid it beside the other woman, as she slept, taking away the living child in its stead. This occasioned a violent altercation between the women, each claiming the living child as her own. The case was referred to Solomon for his decision, in whose presence each maintained her right to the living child. Their pleas seemed equally valid, their claims equally strong, and no positive evidence, beyond their own contradictory assertions, could be adduced to determine the contest. The king, therefore, adopted an expedient which displayed his quick discernment and acute judgment in the strongest light. He ordered the child to be divided between them. This dreadful sentence so operated upon the maternal feelings of the real parent, that she at once relinquished her claims in favor of her rival, rather than witness the destruction of her child. By this artifice Solomon discovered that she was the real mother, and immediately caused the child to be delivered to her.*

The *political* wisdom with which Solomon was endowed was also soon evinced in his adopting that line of policy for which every thing had been prepared by his father, and for which he was eminently fitted. This policy was clearly and definitively marked by the alliance which he formed with the king of Egypt, and his marriage with a daughter of Pharaoh. Palestine at that time bordered on Egypt: for Idumea was a province of the kingdom; the Amalekites and other tribes of the Desert were subjugated to Israel, and the power of Philistia had been crushed. Egypt was then united and strong. A war with that country, on the one hand, could

---

* Expedients somewhat similar to this, for discovering truth, and administering justice, occur in heathen writers. Diodorus Siculus informs us, that Ario Pharnes, king of Thrace, when called on to arbitrate between three men, who affirmed that they were the sons of the king of Cimmerius, and claimed the succession, discovered the right heir by ordering each of them to shoot an arrow at the dead king's body. Two of them showed their readiness to obey; but his real son refused. Suetonius, also, says, that the Emperor Claudius discovered a woman to be the real mother of a young man, whom she would not own, by commanding her to marry him. The evidence, which was doubtful before, now became decisive; and, shocked at the idea of committing incest, she confessed the truth.

not fail to be extremely prejudicial to the integrity and prosperity of Solomon's kingdom; while, on the other, unrestricted commercial intercourse with it was sure to be highly advantageous to Israel. The matrimonial alliance with the princess of Egypt, therefore, was an act of sound political sagacity on the part of Solomon. By this means he converted a jealous rival into a puissant relative. He made her his favorite queen and assigned her separate apartments in the city of David till he should build her a stately and sumptuous palace suited to her rank, and ornamented with every costly material that art or luxury could devise—a purpose which he accomplished soon after he had completed the temple. It is supposed by many expositors that this marriage gave rise to the composition of that series of idyls known by the title of The Cantacles, or Song of Solomon, to which a place was assigned by the Jews in their Sacred Canon. From certain obscure intimations in 1 Kg. 11: 2, and Neh. 13: 14, this Egyptian princess is thought by some to have exerted an influence with Solomon in favor of the introduction of idolatrous worship at a later period; but the statements of Scripture in regard to this point are by no means sufficiently clear and satisfactory, to warrant such an opinion. Indeed it is far more probable that the Egyptian princess in consenting to become queen of Israel, consented at the same time to become a proselyte to the religion of her adopted country.

In consequence of this alliance with Pharaoh, a very extensive and advantageous commerce was carried on with Egypt, particularly in wine, olive oil, and honey,—staple products of Palestine—and in manufactured articles from the interior of Syria, for which there were obtained in exchange horses, flax, linen thread, fish, and other commodities which were consumed in Palestine and other neighboring countries. The grape did not grow in Egypt; and at a later period, the activity of the wine trade there, was such as to attract the attention of the observant Greeks. The hills of Palestine are well adapted to the culture of grapes; and the olive tree to this day grows and flourishes almost without care in any corner or nook around Jerusalem, where it seems to have no soil, and yields an abundance of fruit. Of the oil ex-

pressed from the fruit, great use is made for a variety of pur.
poses. With the addition of an alkali it is converted into
soap: it supplies at the table and for culinary purposes, the
place of butter; and the darkness of night is illumined by
its light. Hence the olive groves of Judea, with Egypt for a
market, must have been of the greatest importance and value
to that country. Honey, also, which abounds in Palestine,
was another article of export of the first importance, inasmuch as sugar at that early period was unknown.

But the alliance with Egypt was advantageous to Solomon
not merely in a commercial point of view. It must also
have had the effect of deterring the neighboring subjugated
powers from rising against his government, and of keeping
down any disaffection in his own land. Pharaoh at an early
period, we are informed, went up to Philistia at the head of
his army and captured the strong city of Gaza, which he
gave to his daughter as a marriage-dower.

Solomon also renewed the intimacy and friendship with
Hiram, king of Tyre, which had existed between that king
and David; and entered into a covenant with him which indicates even a closer alliance than had before obtained. Indeed, so strict was this confederacy that Tyre in the time of
Solomon may be regarded as a port of Palestine, and Palestine as the granary of Tyre. In this league was included the
maritime cities of Tyre, Aradus, Sidon, and perhaps Tripoli,
Byblus and Berytus. By means of the artistic skill of the
Phœnicians, and particularly of the Tyrians, Solomon was
not only assisted in hewing timber for elegant uses in the
mountains of Lebanon; but was enabled to carry on a very
extensive and lucrative maritime commerce. Tyre furnished
the ship-builders, and most of the mariners and pilots; while
the fruitful plains of Palestine victualled the fleets and supplied the manufacturers and merchants of the Phœnician
league with all the necessaries of life. One branch of commerce in which the Hebrews, in connexion with this enter-
prising people, engaged, was the traffic of the Mediterranean
Sea. This was carried on principally with Tarshish (*Tarsessus*),
a city in the south-west of Spain, not far from the Straits of
Gibraltar; and the trade to this place became so extensive

and celebrated that *Ships of Tarshish* seems to have been the common name for large merchant vessels generally.* Another branch of commerce was that which, with the assistance of the Tyrians, was carried on by the Red Sea. The conquests of David had made the Hebrews masters of the eastern arm of this sea (the gulph of Akaba or Eleanitic gulph), at the head of which Solomon built or improved the towns and ports of Elath and Ezion-Geber. From these ports Tyrian ships sailed to Sheba, at the southernmost angle of Arabia, and thence to Ophir, the most distant point of the commerce, which is supposed to have been in the province of Oman in Arabia, beyond the Straits of Babelmandel. The return merchandise procured at Ophir consisted of gold and silver, ivory, monkeys, peacocks, and spices in great abundance; almug or sandal and other scented woods and precious stones; which in part were re-shipped by the Phœnicians to the ports of the Mediterranean. With this branch of commerce was connected the inland trade of the Arabian peninsula, carried on by the caravans of the native tribes, who transported into the interior on the backs of camels a portion of the valuable commodities obtained from Ophir. From the character of the merchandise exported from Ophir, and the length of time (three years) often consumed in the voyage to and from that port, many critics have thought that Ophir must have been situated on the eastern coast of Africa (Zanguebar), or on the peninsula of Malaya, rather than on the southern confines of Arabia felix. With regard to the length of time consumed in the voyage, it may be remarked that the Phœnicians combined the two professions of seaman and merchant, and moving from one point to another bought and sold according to the nature of the cargo and the wants of the people with whom they traded. There were no factors to whom they could consign their goods, or who could provide them at short notice with such commodities as they might desire in return. The length of time occupied in making a voyage, therefore, furnishes no data by which to

---

* 1 Kg. 10: 22, "the navy, or fleet, of Tarshish," i. e , ships similar to those with which the Tyrians traded with Tarshish. This is a more probable interpretation of the phrase than that which would make another Tarshish on the Red Sea.

judge correctly of the distance passed over. And as to the first objection, it has been clearly ascertained that the merchants of Sheba (Sabæa) maintained a regular intercourse with India, and that at the very time when Egypt enjoyed the monopoly of Oriental spices in the European markets, the Sabæans possessed similar advantages with respect to Egypt. It is not necessary to suppose, therefore, that the merchandise, for the most part of Eastern origin, with which the Phœnician ships were freighted in the return voyages from Ophir, was the product of that country. It is quite probable that it was obtained by the Sabæan merchants in their own ships from beyond the Ganges.

Another line of commerce was that across the Syrian Desert to Babylonia and Assyria. In order to prosecute successfully this important branch of trade, Solomon brought some of the tribes of the Desert into subjection, took possession of the city of *Tiphsah* (*Thapsicus*) on the western bank of the Euphrates, and built *Tadmor*, called by the Greeks and Romans *Palmyra*, or the City of Palms. This celebrated city, destined to power and fame under another dynasty, was situated in the midst of the Desert at a convenient distance intermediate between the Euphrates and Hamath, on the Orontes. Josephus places it two days' journey from Upper Syria, one day's journey from the Euphrates, and six from Babylon. From these various sources of wealth it happened that the precious metals and other valuable commodities became so abundant in Palestine, that in the strong, hyperbolical language of the Sacred historian,—"Silver was as stones, and cedar-trees as sycamores." It should be remembered that in the case of Solomon, the commercial wealth of the community was concentrated in the hands of the government, and much of the vast trade carried on was a monopoly. We need not be surprised, therefore, at the immense riches of this eminent merchant-sovereign.

Solomon introduced important changes in the internal affairs of the country. He strongly fortified Jerusalem and its citadel Millo, Hazor, Megido, Gezer and several other cities, which he garrisoned with Israelites. He employed an additional standing force of 12,000 Cavalry and many war-

B

chariots, the horses for which were imported from Egypt.
This was an arm of military defence not in use in that country while its territory was confined to the promised land;
but it was now deemed necessary by Solomon in consequence of the extension of the kingdom and its exposed
condition.

It is evident, however, that the better portion of the nation did not concur in this opinion. It was manifestly the
design of divine providence in the establishment of the Hebrew commonwealth, that the Israelites should not be a
migratory or commercial people, but attached to the soil of
Palestine, and devoted chiefly to agricultural pursuits. In
accordance with this their peaceful occupation, the wars in
which they might engage were to be defensive rather than
offensive and aggressive. And such was wholly their character during the administration of the Judges; and even the
wars which David carried on were for the most part of this
nature, although they resulted in the conquest and accession
of a large area of territory to the empire, and its extension
from the Euphrates to the borders of Egypt. In pursuance
of the same general plan, the Hebrews were not to maintain
large standing armies for which they could have no use, and
which rank morally, politically and financially, among the
greatest evils of any nation, whether in ancient or in modern
times. And especially were they forbidden the use of cavalry and the importation of horses from Egypt for warlike
purposes, which would inevitably tend to promote a military
ambition and the lust of foreign conquest. When, therefore,
Solomon added a large body of cavalry to the effective military force of the country, it naturally gave great offence to
the more religious and upright portion of the nation, for the
innovation was justly regarded as a palpable violation of the
prohibitory statutes of Moses (Deut. 17: 16), which the king
was solemnly bound to respect and observe. It was displeasing to them also, as increasing the burden of taxation, already too onerous to be borne; and, further, as entirely
unnecessary as a means of national defence; for it was
remembered how gloriously David, without horses or chariots,
had vanquished the pride of Hadadezer's chivalry, and how

all the honor of victory had been ascribed to Jehovah, with whom the horse is but a vain thing.

The safe-guard of political liberty among the Hebrews, and the only check on the royal prerogative and the encroachments of the crown, were the divine sanctity of the Mosaic law and the rights reserved to the separate tribes. David had made attempts to centralize the nation, but Solomon proceeded much farther, and divided the land of Israel into twelve equal districts, without regard to the individual tribes or their separate territories. Over each of these districts he appointed a purveyor for the collection of the royal tribute, which was received in kind. This measure, though ostensibly intended for economical purposes, had unquestionably a political object, viz., to consolidate the kingdom and strengthen the regal power; and to destroy the individuality of the tribes, with all its old and cherished associations, by means of a central despotism. This innovation, involving as it did the usurpation of powers not hitherto exercised by the sovereign, though it led to no serious consequences during the reign of Solomon, no doubt had its influence, so distasteful must it have been to the people, in preparing the way for the great national schism which occurred in the reign of his successor.

The immense wealth accumulated by a prudent and economical use of the treasures inherited from his father, by an extensive and successful commerce; and by a careful and wise administration of the public revenue, soon enabled Solomon to carry out the cherished purpose of David; and erect a magnificent temple in the metropolis for the service of the only living and true God, which in beauty and splendor exceeded any former work of architecture. The co-operation and assistance of Hiram, under whose administration Tyre reached its highest prosperity, were of the greatest importance to Solomon in the construction of this great national work. The fir and cedar timber required for the building could be obtained only from the forests of Lebanon; and the Sidonian artizans were the most skillful workmen in every kind of manufacture, particularly in the precious metals. Accordingly Solomon applied to Hiram for architects and laborers to superintend and assist in the work. The application was favorably received, and it was arranged that Tyrian workmen should hew and prepare the timber for the sacred edifice, to be delivered at one of the ports of Israel, and paid for year by year with wheat, barley, oil, and wine. The timber was accordingly cut and worked on Mount Lebanon, transported on the backs of mules across the Phœnician territory to the sea, and then floated down along the coast on rafts to Joppa (Jaffa), the port nearest to Jerusalem, whence it was conveyed by the pass of Bethhoron to the Holy City. Solomon furnished many thousand men out of all Israel, chiefly aborigines of the country, who were in a state of bondage, to quarry the massive stones for the foundation and walls, and to aid in hewing and transporting the timber. The work, for which preparations had been made at an earlier period, was commenced at the beginning of the fourth year of Solomon's reign, and though prosecuted with the utmost vigor, occupied seven years and a half. The stones and timbers were so perfectly fitted one to the other, in the mountains, " that there was neither hammer nor axe nor any tool of iron heard in the house while it was building"; or as it has been expressed with much poetical beauty,

" Like some tall palm the noiseless fabric grew."

There was nothing but noise in Lebanon; nothing in Zion but silence and peace—typical of that quietness and peace which should ever characterize the Church of God. The erection of this sacred edifice was the great event of Solomon's reign. The descriptions which are given of the building in the books of Scripture and in Josephus, are not very exact or even perfectly intelligible. Indeed no one can have failed to observe, that owing to the imperfect form in which arithmetical calculations were made and preserved in that remote period, as well as to the liability of transcribers to commit mistakes in copying the sacred records, little certainty in such cases can be obtained as to the minuter details. In fact, for the main purpose which the sacred historians had in view, round numbers were quite sufficient, and their descriptions, as they were not designed to convey exact scientific information, or to furnish professional details, should not be read with too critical an eye, nor condemned as defective or erroneous, simply because not expressed with literal exactness nor in the present terms of the art.

The spot selected for the foundation of the Temple was that part of the consecrated hill denominated Mount Moriah, or the Mount of Vision, the place, it is believed, where the patriarch Abraham, one thousand years before, prepared at the command of God, to offer in sacrifice his beloved and only son Isaac. Prodigious labor was required to level the unequal surface of the rock for the foundation. The sides on the East and South, which were very steep, were faced with an immense wall built from the bottom of the valley, the huge stones of which were strongly mortised together and indented into the solid mass of the precipice. The space thus prepared presented the appearance of an irregular quadrangle, around which a wall of considerable height was reared. Within the wall was a court, subsequently appropriated to such Gentiles as manifested an inclination to witness or participate in the Hebrew rites: while an inner division, also separated by a wall, was allotted to the descendants of Jacob, whose birth-right entitled them to approach more nearly to the sacred shrine. Along this wall on the inside ran a portico, over which were chambers for different sacred purposes. The court of the Priests, which was again within that of the Israelites, supplied that of the temple itself. And as there was a regular ascent by means of a stair from each court to the next one above it, the level rose in every platform from the outer wall to the porch of the main edifice. The court of the priests contained the great altar of burnt-offering, and the spacious tank or molten sea for ablution. The dimensions of the Temple itself were inconsiderable when compared with the consecrated structures of other nations and of later times. It was in fact but an enlargement of the Mosaic tabernacle, constructed for the most part after the same model, but built of the most costly and durable materials. It consisted of a propylæon or tower, a temple and a sanctuary, called respectively the porch, the holy place, (ὁ ναος) and the most holy place. In the front facing the East, and looking towards the Mount of Olives

B*

stood the porch—a lofty tower rising to the height of 210 feet. Either within or directly before the porch stood two pillars of brass, including their capitals and bases above sixty feet high. These were named Jachin and Boaz—durability and strength—symbolical of the perpetuity of the Temple and of the religion and ritual institutions of which it was a part. The capitals of these pillars were of the richest workmanship, with net-work, chain-work and pomegranates. These pillars, as indeed all the ornamental work of the edifice, were made by Hiram Abif, the son of a widow woman of the tribe of Dan, who had been married to a Tyrian brass-founder. The porch was of the same width as the temple, viz. 35 feet; its depth 17½ feet. The length of the main building, including the holy place, 70 feet, and the holy of holies 35 feet, was in the whole 106 feet; the height 52½ feet. Along each side, and perhaps at the back of the main building, ran an aisle, divided into three stories of small chambers. These aisles, the chambers of which were appropriated as vestearies, treasuries, lodging rooms for the officiating priests, and other kindred purposes, seem to have reached about half way up the main wall of the building; the windows in the latter being above them. This would seem to be a very small and diminutive edifice for the worship of a great nation. It was, in fact, however, sufficiently spacious for all the purposes for which it was designed. The uses to which it was applied were very different from those of a Christian Church. The principal parts of the Jewish worship, all of which except the psalmody, consisted of symbolical rites and sacrifices, it must be remembered, were performed in the open air, in the court of the priests at the eastern end or in front of the temple. The interior of the edifice was reserved exclusively for those periodical and more special acts of devotion in which only the priests took a part; and as for the most holy place, it was entered only once in the year by the High Priest alone, the representative of Aaron, when he made the great atonement for the sins of the people. There was no occasion, therefore, for a large and spacious building. The name of *The Temple*, however, was very naturally extended to all its precincts,—to the several courts which sur-

rounded it, whether occupied by the priests or the people.
But, notwithstanding the building itself was of moderate
dimensions, the costliness of the materials and the richness
and variety of their details, amply compensated for this; and
its real magnificence—that which rendered it one of the
seven wonders of the world—consisted in its unequalled
metallic splendor, and its richness of decorations—in its
hewn stones, some of which were between 17 and 18 feet in
length, its noble cedar beams, and its rich and curious carv-
ings.

No sooner was the sacred edifice completed than its solemn dedication took place with a pomp worthy of so august
an occasion. All the chieftains of the different tribes, and
all of every order who could be brought together, were assembled. All the tribe of Levi, amounting in David's time
to 38,000 without regard to their courses, including the whole
priestly order, attended. The assembled nation also crowded
the spacious courts. The grand ceremony commenced with
the offering of innumerable burnt-sacrifices. Then followed
the removal of the ark—the symbol of the divine presence
—from Mt. Zion to the temple. The entire body of the
priests, accompanied by the vocal and instrumental per-
formers and guards of the Levites, opened the procession.
Then followed the ark, borne by the Levites to the open
portals of the Temple, with their voices and instruments
chanting such splendid odes as the 47th, the 96th and 132d
psalms. There can be no reasonable doubt also that the
24th psalm, composed by David and sung on the occasion of
the removal of the ark to Mount Zion, was adopted and used
at the dedication of the Temple. The ark having been
received and deposited by the priests in the most holy place,
and the symbolic cloud having filled the house, Solomon
himself ascended the brazen scaffold which had been erected
in front of the temple, knelt down, and spreading his hands
towards heaven, with the greatest solemnity, and most devout
and ardent piety, consecrated the Temple to God. The
prayer of dedication which he offered on this occasion is
inimitable as a composition for grandeur and sublimity, and
excites equally our astonishment and admiration, as an ex-

hibition of the spiritual conceptions of Deity and the elevated tone of religious sentiment, which prevailed in such an age among such a people. Then indeed Solomon shone in his highest lustre, and his behavior on this sacred occasion was so grand and majestic as to elicit universal admiration and unqualified praise. This magnificent spectacle took place at the usual time of the feast of Tabernacles, which, instead of occupying one week, on this occasion extended through two, during which 22,000 oxen and 120,000 sheep were offered in sacrifice, the people feasting on those parts of the animals which were not set apart for holy uses. This sacred edifice was designed henceforth to be the great centre of unity in religious worship, to the Hebrew nation,—the one most holy place, to which all eyes and hearts were to be directed—the sole depository of the sacred symbols:—where the public worship of Jehovah was to be conducted in a manner befitting the august and awful majesty of the King of kings and Lord of lords. And as it fulfilled a prophecy and was a symbol of Jehovah's dwelling with his chosen people, so it was itself likewise both a prophecy and a type,—a type of the Jewish people and Church, and a prophecy of God's continual presence with those who fear and worship him in spirit and in truth. Its history, therefore, is an index to the history of the Jews themselves. When it fell, they scattered; and as it rose from its ruins, they again gathered around it; and its final destruction was succeeded by their dispersion among all the civilized nations of the world. Its erection was the great event of Solomon's life.

This splendid Temple, erected according to the divinely ordered model (1 Chron. 28: 11, 12, 19) delivered to Solomon by his royal father, stood 425 years; when it was entirely destroyed by Nebuchadnezzar, King of Babylon. Its re-edification was commenced 69 years subsequently by Zerubbabel; but owing to numerous hindrances it was not completed till B. C. 611, when it was solemnly dedicated to the service of Jehovah, 73 years after its destruction by Nebuchadnezzar. The temple built by Zerubbabel is commonly designated *the second* temple, as Solomon's is *the first*. It has been frequently represented as much larger than that of Solomon; but if the dimensions given in Ezra 6: 3, (comp. Josephus' Antiq. xv. 11. 1,) relate to the main building, as they undoubtedly do, then it was even less in length, no greater in breadth, and only one half its height. And while it was inferior to the first in size, it was still more inferior in splendor, for the Jews were then too poor to erect a very magnificent structure; so that the old men who had seen the former, were moved to tears on beholding the latter, which appeared to them like nothing in comparison with it. (Ezra 3: 12. Hagg. 2: 3, seq.) The Temple of Zerubbabel, after it had stood about five centuries, required to be entirely reconstructed. The work of renovating and beautifying it was undertaken by Herod the Great about 16 years before his death, and was continued for some years after, so that the Jews remarked to our Saviour that it had been in the process of re-construction 46 years. This temple has been sometimes called the *third*, but not with strict propriety, for Zerubbabel's was not taken down at once, but only by degrees to make room for that of Herod, because the Jews were averse to its entire demolition, from the apprehension that the king would not be able to carry his intentions as to its rebuilding into effect. (Josephus' Antiq. xv. 11. 2.) The wishes of the Jews were respected by Herod, and hence they have never recognized but two temples, which coincides with the prophecy of Haggai (Hagg. 2: 9).

Herod's Temple was 10 cubits longer than Zerubbabel's, and exceeded both that and Solomon's in breath. In height it exceeded Zerubbabel's by 10 cubits, but was 20 less than Solomon's. It was also a far more splendid edifice than the one which it replaced, and continued till A. D. 70, when it was completely destroyed by the Romans under Titus. The Emperor Julian, through hatred of Christianity, undertook to rebuild the Temple, A. D. 363; but, after considerable preparation, and much expense, he was compelled to desist in consequence of subterranean fires which burst forth from the foundations, and the attempt was abandoned.

Soon after the conquest of Jerusalem by the Saracens, the Caliph Orman erected a magnificent mosque on the neglected spot, where the temple of Solomon once stood, and this edifice is not less venerated by the

Mohammedans, than the original structure was by the
Jews.

The description which is given of Solomon's temple and
of the palaces erected by him, as well as the many incidental
allusions which we meet with in the writings even of the
earlier prophets, to the splendor of the private structures of
Jerusalem,—to houses of hewn stone, houses ceiled with
costly wood, decorated with gold, and ivory, and fitted up
with every device which elaborate luxury might ask for,
prove beyond a doubt, that the Hebrews, isolated as they
were, had at that early period reached a state of advancement in the arts of life—substantial and decorative—which
places them at least on a level with, if not in advance of, any
people who were their neighbors and contemporaries, or of
any that are known to us by their records and their monu-
ments.

Having thus provided for the appropriate celebration of
the national worship according to the expressed wishes of
his father David, the command of Jehovah, and his own convictions of duty and obligation, the attention of Solomon
was next directed to the erection not far from the Temple of
a palace of suitable magnificence for himself, and another in
a retired part of the country for his Egyptian Queen. These
edifices, though far less celebrated than the Temple, were
even more extensive structures, and occupied more time in
building. His own palace was 180 feet long by 90 in breadth·
Thirteen years were consumed in building it; and from the
quantity of cedar used in its construction, it was called the
House of the forest of Lebanon.

In consideration of the services rendered by Hiram to
Solomon in furnishing materials for the building of the
Temple and the royal palace, and of a loan of 120 talents of
gold, the Hebrew king gave to him 20 cities and the surrounding territory in the land of Galilee, adjoining the
dominions of Hiram. These cities were inhabited not by
Israelites, but by the Aborigines of the country; they were
not included in the territory allotted to the twelve tribes, but
subsequently obtained by conquest. Solomon had the right,
therefore, to dispose of them in this way. But they were

not acceptable to Hiram, probably because the Tyrians were wholly addicted to commerce, and therefore were not disposed to remove from the seashore where they were so commodiously situated for that purpose, to a portion of the country where the soil required the diligent labors of agriculture, to which they were not accustomed. The harmonious relation, however, which subsisted between the two kings was not interrupted by the return of these cities to Solomon; and hence it is presumed that a satisfactory arrangement in some other way was made between the parties.

Peacefully, prosperously and happily, for the most part, did the years of Solomon's reign pass away. That reign has been rightly called the halcyon day of Israel, and second in importance only to that of his father David. The celebrity which this monarch acquired by his immense wealth and regal magnificence was great and wide-spread; but it scarcely excelled that which he obtained on account of his extraordinary wisdom and learning. Admiration of the latter, no less than of the former, attracted crowds of distinguished foreigners and literati to his capital. Among these the most renowned was the Queen of Sheba. The costly presents which she brought, after the oriental fashion, to the Hebrew monarch, evince the close intimacy which had arisen between the States of Sabæa and Israel, and the importance and extent of the commercial transactions which had been carried on between them. The Queen, in order to test the intellectual powers of Solomon, came prepared with many hard questions, i. e. with riddles or enigmas, agreeably to an oriental custom which can be traced back among the Hebrews to the time of the Judges, (Judg. 11: 12,) and which afterwards prevailed among the Greeks. These riddles were usually proposed at feasts and compotations that the time might not be spent merely in eating and drinking, but that there might be something to exercise the wit and ingenuity of the guests. The wisdom and magnificence of the king more than equalled the Queen's highly raised expectations. She expressed the highest degree of admiration and astonishment at what she saw and heard, and returned to her own country with devout thanksgivings to the Lord, who had so distinguished and honored his servant Solomon.

The very greatness and opulence of the Hebrew monarch, however, became the occasion in the latter part of his life, of his declension from that course of religious devotion and moral propriety which distinguished his earlier years. This departure from the path of duty not only tarnished his fair fame, but precipitated the rupture and final overthrow of the kingdom. While he greatly promoted the material interests of his people by commercial enterprise, and encouraged and advanced the useful arts and civilization by the lavish expenditure of money on stately edifices, and other public improvements, he set the example at the same time of pernicious and demoralizing luxury and effeminacy, and of a gradual relaxation of the Mosaic religion, which not only wrought a deplorable change in his own moral and religious character, but proved disastrous to the well-being of the nation. Religion cannot dwell with impurity; sensual indulgence will unavoidably eradicate the love of holiness from the heart, and the mind so contaminated can never entertain any becoming sentiments of God, or any love for the precepts and ordinances of his religion.

In countries where polygamy is not disreputable, an unlimited indulgence as to the number of wives, instead of being regarded as a reproach, is looked upon as the chief luxury of wealth, and the most appropriate appendage of royalty. The splendor of an eastern court is regarded as complete only when amidst wealth and luxury the greatest number of female beauties are found there. But Solomon not only went to the utmost extreme in this particular, but in direct violation of the laws of Moses, admitted numerous foreign women, who were probably captives taken in war from the neighboring countries, without any necessity or plausible pretext, into his harem; and was weak enough, towards the close of his life, to permit them the unrestricted exercise of their idolatrous heathen worship within his dominions; and even to appropriate to the obscene and barbarous deities of the contiguous nations a part of one of the hills which overlooks Jerusalem. By thus giving his countenance to, if he did not actually join in, an idolatrous worship, in the sight of the very temple, which he had consecrated to Jehovah, the God of all the earth, he set at naught the fundamental principles of the Mosaic constitution, which he was most solemnly bound to respect, and preserve with sacred inviolability. He virtually revolted against the established religion of his country, and brought upon himself the guilt of high treason. This crime appears the more enormous in him contemplated as the author of the earlier portion of the book of Proverbs, which is full of the most earnest dissuasives from sensuality and the illicit indulgence of passion. This manifestation of evil in one, the evening of whose days should have been pre-eminently distinguished by those virtues which he so earnestly and eloquently inculcated in earlier life, added to his oppressive exactions, greatly alienated the affections of his people, and especially of the more pious and virtuous among them. Solomon was undoubtedly guilty of a grievous sin in multiplying wives to such an extent, even where polygamy prevailed, and admitting heathen women into his seraglio. No doubt it was in part a fault which naturally grew out of the circumstances of the age, the habits of the people, the degraded condition of females, and his official position as the most wealthy and powerful monarch of his time, which was thought to require in him a corresponding display of pomp in the extent of his harem. These considerations may serve to mitigate the offence, but they cannot justify it in the sight of man, and most surely not in the sight of God. No wonder then that dark clouds began to gather on all sides about him. No wonder that Jehovah manifested his displeasure at the gross degeneracy and impiety of one whom he had so highly honored and blessed.*

---

* The b'ots and blemishes in the lives of such men as David and Solomon have ever been a frequent and favorite subject of unfair and malignant comment on the part of the adversaries of Scripture. The existence of such blots, some of them very dark ones, will not be denied. And as they were there, the Scripture is too faithful a mirror not to give them back. But whatever the extent of the sin of any, Scripture is in no wise compromised by it, nor yet the righteousness of God, whose word and utterance that Scripture is. The Bible has faithfully recorded these sinful actions of theirs, but does not praise or justify them; on the contrary, it most frequently expresses the strongest moral disapprobation of them. And where it is silent, this very silence furnishes an opportunity for the better exercise of the moral

C

Accordingly he announced to Solomon, probably through Abijah the prophet, that, because he had broken the Covenant by which he held his crown, the kingdom should be rent and divided, and a part of it given to one of his subjects. The tranquility which had hitherto distinguished Solomon's reign, now began to be disturbed by foreign enemies and by intestine feuds. Hadad, a prince of the royal family of Edom, who when a child had escaped from the bloody massacre of his race by Joab, and taken refuge in the court of the Egyptian king, now that he had reached maturity, took up arms, regained possession of his ancestral throne, and commenced a petty and harassing warfare against the Israelites, by which the commerce between the Red Sea and Palestine, which was carried on by caravans through the desert, was greatly impeded. But Solomon neither took effective measures to check the revolt, nor curtailed the insane luxury of his court. On the contrary, as his commerce fell off, and his revenue from that source became diminished, he resorted to heavier and more oppressive taxation of the people. In the north, Razon, a Syrian adventurer, who had been an officer in the army of Hadadezer, seized upon Damascus, established its independence, and made it the seat of the kingdom of Damascene Syria. The internal commerce of Solomon across the Syrian Desert, at least by its natural channels, was thus cut off. A domestic enemy still more dangerous, appeared in the person of Jeroboam, the son of Nebat, of the tribe of Ephraim. This man had distinguished himself in the service of the king, in consequence of which, he had been appointed superintendent of the laborers of his

---

sense of the reader, that applying the rules drawn from the Scriptures and from the immutable principles of morality graven in all hearts, he may pass his own independent judgment on the deed, either excusing or accusing, according to his convictions of right. Nor is the fact of these faults and failings, yea of these great and grievous sins, of men in the main good, though far from being perfect, inconsistent with their position as the bearers in their time of God's promises, and the witnesses for his truth. Such bearers of his word, such witnesses for his truth they were; and as such having indeed a treasure, but having it in earthen vessels, so that it is nothing strange if the earthen vessel should sometimes appear. The truth and transcendent importance of the moral principles and maxims contained in the books of Proverbs, are not in the least impaired or shaken by the errors and sins which sullied a portion of the writer's life.

own tribe and that of Manasseh on the public buildings at Jerusalem. A conference with the prophet Abijah, inspired him with more ambitious thoughts and aims. On a certain occasion, they met without the walls of the city, and Abijah tore in pieces a new garment with which one or the other was clothed, and giving ten pieces to Jeroboam, assured him by this symbolical act, that in consequence of the idolatrous conduct of the king and people, the government of ten tribes, after the death of Solomon, should be transferred to him, and be continued in his line, on the same conditions as those on which it had been assured to David. This is the first symbolical action which we meet with in any prophet of the Old Testament; but in after ages instances of the kind were not unfrequent. This significant act of Abijah was soon noised abroad, and the jealousy of Solomon was aroused, which rendered the life of Jeroboam no longer safe in Palestine. Hence he fled into Egypt, where he was hospitably entertained by Shishak, the first king of the Diospolitan dynasty who now occupied the throne. It was the same person who in the reign of Rehoboam invaded the kingdom of Judah, at the head of a large army, and enriched himself with the spoils of the Temple.

It is generally believed that these divine chastisements opened the eyes of Solomon to the enormity of his offences, and that in the evening of his days he truly repented and returned to a better course of life. The strongest proof we have of his repentance is found in the book of Ecclesiastes, which bears the clearest internal evidence of having been written by him in old age, after a long and varied experience. In this book he passes in review the stores of knowledge he had accumulated, the immense wealth which he had possessed, the magnificent works he had constructed, the homage he had received from his subjects, the toils and anxieties he had experienced, and the sins and follies of which he had been guilty, and comes to the wise and pious conclusion and to the humiliating confession that every thing belonging to this world is unsubstantial, unsatisfactory, illusive and vain; and that to fear God and keep his commandments is the whole of man—the sum of his duty and his happiness.

Solomon died B. C. 975, at the close of a peaceful and prosperous reign of 40 years. But the evils which he had brought upon the land by his misconduct in the latter part of his reign were irreparable, and with him expired the glory, power, and integrity of the Hebrew monarchy.

II.

THE WRITINGS OF SOLOMON.

King Solomon appears to have been not only the wisest, but the most learned man of his times. He far excelled all his contemporaries, as a poet, naturalist, philosopher, and ethical writer. He is related to have been the author of a thousand and five songs. Of these, however, none have been preserved except two Psalms and the Canticles, called in Hebrew "the Song of Songs," perhaps because it was regarded as the best of his compositions belonging to that class.*

---

* Two Psalms are ascribed to Solomon in the titles prefixed to them, viz., the *seventy-second* and the *one hundred and twenty-seventh*. With regard to the latter there appears to be but little difference of opinion among critics. Nearly all seem disposed to concede its authorship to the wise king. It is a short psalm belonging to the Psalms of Degrees, and was probably composed for the purpose of being sung at the dedication of the Temple. It may have been written by Solomon during the preparation for building that sacred edifice, or while its construction was in progress; and seems to have been intended as an expression of the well known maxim of Solomon, " A man's heart deviseth his way; but the Lord directeth his steps." Prov. 16: 9. Comp. also Prov. 10: 22. With regard to the authorship of the former Psalm there is far less unanimity of opinion than with respect to the latter. The preposition *lamed* ל is sometimes the sign of the genitive, indicating *possession, property*, and then is properly translated *of;* at other times it is the sign of the dative, and then denotes *to, for*, or *concerning*. Some critics maintain that the latter is the import of the preposition here, and that the Psalm was composed by David near the close of his life, concerning his son, on the delivery to him of his kingdom, in which he invokes the divine blessing upon him and predicts the prosperity and splendor of his reign. Others suppose that David, having written the psalm on his dying bed, committed it to Solomon to be inserted in the Collection of Psalms which he had prepared for the public services of the sanctuary. Against these opinions there lies this weighty objection. that the preparation *lamed* in every other place where it occurs in the titles prefixed to the Psalms without any thing to limit its application, *always* indicates the author. This is conceded by those who advocate the Davidic origin of the psalm. It would be contrary to all philological propriety to make this an exception to the general usage, unless the exigency of the place, arising from internal evidence, imperiously demands it. But this has never been satisfactorily shown; for, although the Psalm is of such a character, as that it might have been written by David re-

The united voice of antiquity and the concurrent testimony of all generations ascribe this poem or collective series of idyls to Solomon; and internal evidence strongly corroborates that testimony. "The whole hue of the book," says Pareau, "and its exquisite poetic elegance seem to us to point so strongly to the very splendid age of that king, and to his genius wholly disposed to florid diction, such as he has shown in the book of Proverbs, *e. g.*, in chap. vii. 10–15, that though his name were not inscribed in the commencement of the book, we should readily suspect that he was its author." The book has always been classed among the Canonical and inspired writings of the Old Testament, and, though not quoted in the New Testament, it unquestionably formed a part of the Jewish Scriptures, (Josephus' Antiq. viii. 2, 5, and Contr. Ap. 1, 8,) was translated by the authors of the Septuagint Version into the Greek language, is included in all the ancient catalogues of sacred books, and expressly attested by Melito in the second century, Origen in the third, Jerome near the close of the fourth, and in the fifth by the Jewish Sargum and Theodoret, bishop of Cyprus. With regard to its scope and design, a great variety of opinions have been entertained. The subject of the book is confessedly *Love;* but what kind of love, and between what parties, are questions which have greatly perplexed critics. Some

specting Solomon, yet there is nothing in it to preclude the idea that it was written by Solomon himself, and therefore rightly ascribed to him The circumstance that at the end of the psalm there is appendid the superscription, "the prayers of David are ended," does not in the least militate against this opinion; for this superscription announces nothing more than that David is to be regarded as the principal author of the first book or collection of Psalms of which this psalm forms the conclusion; because there are several psalms in this collection which were undoubtedly composed by others. The Messianic character of the 72d Psalm is admitted by all the best commentators, either in a primary or secondary sense. Those who adopt the latter view suppose that it was written primarily with a view to celebrate the splendid reign of Solomon, and that only in a secondary and remote sense is it descriptive of the Messiah and his kingdom. But even if we should admit the principle of a two-fold application and double sense in any case, we see no good reason why, according to some of the most judicious interpreters, this psalm should not be regarded as applicable immediately and exclusively to the Messiah, and as entirely prophetic of him. Interpreted as a prediction of his glorious and universal reign, it is clear and free from all exaggeration; applied to Solomon, it is replete with immeasurable hyperbole. The most ancient Jewish Rabbics interpreted it of the Messiah, and the greatest violence must be employed to adapt it to any other subject. The imagery of the psalm is undoubtedly borrowed from the peaceful and brilliant reign of Solomon, as is that of the second psalm from the martial and triumphant reign of David.

C*

maintain that the subject of the poem or poems is *physical love;* that the poem is a mere amatory song, descriptive of wedded love; an epithalamium or nuptial dialogue in praise of marriage, and especially of monogamy: that it was composed on the occasion of the marriage between Solomon and the princess of Egypt, and was designed to celebrate that event; that Solomon and the princess are the characters introduced into it, and that it has no religious element or object. Others suppose that the chaste mutual love of two young persons antecedent to marriage is here celebrated. But the great body of oriental scholars and Biblical critics, both those who have denied the inspiration of the poem, and those who have regarded it as an inspired composition, maintain that it is an *allegory.* The Jewish writers from the earliest times have always regarded it as such, and it is hardly probable that on any other supposition it would have been admitted into the sacred canon. Some commentators, however, hold that its primary and literal sense has reference to the event of Solomon's marriage, while in a deeper secondary and mystical sense it is allegorical. Others, however, maintain that it is simply and purely a sacred allegory, without any historical basis whatever, and without having been even suggested by any particular event in the life of Solomon; but that it is descriptive of the mutual love which subsists between Jehovah and his ancient people, or prophetically between Christ and his Church, or Christ and each individual Christian, clothed in figures borrowed from the ardor of human passions. There can be no reasonable doubt that it is a sacred allegory, having only a single sense, though the style, language and form of the poem may have been suggested to Solomon's mind by his own marriage with the Egyptian princess. It is intended, we think, to describe the covenant relation and attachment of Jehovah to his ancient people; but not in such a sense as to exclude Christ and the Christian church. The Jehovah, whose love to his people under the old covenant is depicted, is also no other than Christ, the divine logos, who, in all times has revealed to mankind the will and glory of God, and who offered himself in a human form a sacrifice to redeem and purchase to himself a glorious church, identical in substance, though differing in outward form and dispensation from the Jewish. Though not strictly prophetical of Christ and his Church, therefore, yet it includes the latter as a component part of the one Church of the living God, and the former as the great head of that church in all ages and under every dispensation.

As to the idea, entertained by some, that the descriptions in this book represent the relation of an individual soul to Christ, the vital union and mutual love subsisting between Christ and every true disciple of his, we think they can be thus applied only by way of accommodation, and that in making such an application of them the greatest caution is necessary, lest it should lead to mysticism and engender spiritual pride. The Song of Solomon has been objected to by some, as being indelicate in its expressions. But much of this apparent indelicacy is chargeable to the translation, and is not the fault of the original poem; some of it arises from mistaking descriptions of the dress for descriptions of the naked person; and some from a change of manners and customs.

It would appear from the statement in 1 Kg. 4: 33, that the natural history of plants and animals was a favorite study with Solomon, and occupied a large portion of his time and attention. His works, however, in that interesting department of knowledge, whatever they may have been, have suffered the same fate as the most of his poems: and had they been handed down to our times, they would doubtless have been valuable rather as a collection of facts than for the development of any important principle. They had no claims on the ground of inspiration or from their importance in a religious or ethical point of view, to be preserved with special care and scrupulous regard by the Jews, and hence, like all except the historical and religious literature of the Hebrews, has long since passed down the stream of time into the ocean of oblivion. But the books of Proverbs and Ecclesiastes from the pen of the royal scholar have been preserved in the Hebrew and Christian canons to our times, in the former of which is exhibited the ethical wisdom of Solomon, and in the latter his philosophical wisdom

The book of *Ecclesiastes*, (Heb. קֹהֶלֶת, *qocheleth*,) or *the Preacher*, is ascribed to Solomon in the work itself, and was regarded as his composition by the early Jewish interpreters, and the great body of ancient Christian divines. With this opinion the general scope and subject matter of the book well correspond, on the supposition that it was written in the latter part of his life, after he had been brought to true repentance for his sins. Peculiarly truthful, appropriate and impressive does the book become in regard to the emptiness and vanity of all earthly objects, possessions, pursuits and expectations, when viewed from the stand-point of the varied experience and extensive observation of such a king as Solomon, at the close of his mortal career. Doubts respecting the authorship of the book, however, have been entertained in recent times by critics of different schools of theology, chiefly in consequence of its phraseology and style, and from some expressions which incidentally occur in it. The first writer of note who called in question the commonly received opinion respecting the author of the book, was Grotius, who has since been followed by Stuart, Hengstenberg and some other orthodox commentators, to say nothing of those which belong to the rationalistic school. But, we remark, a sentiment so uniform and so long entertained both in the Jewish and Christian churches, is not to be set aside except by the most decisive evidence against it: and it may well be doubted whether much more weight has not been given to the objections urged against it, than a careful consideration of the facts will warrant. The canonical authority of the book is undeniable, whatever doubts or speculations may be thrown in the way of its authorship. Our Lord does not, indeed, quote directly from it in his discourses, but he makes frequent allusions to it. To enter further into the discussion respecting the authorship of Ecclesiastes or to analyze minutely its contents and argument would transcend the scope of the present introduction.

Two books classed by the Lutheran and Reformed churches among the Apocrypha, have been attributed to Solomon, viz: "The Wisdom of Solomon," and "The Wisdom of Jesus, the Son of Sirach." The first has been thought to bear a resemblance to the canonical book of Ecclesiastes. . But though it is ascribed to the same author, and contains many sublime ideas respecting the perfections of God, and many excellent moral precepts, it could not have proceeded from his pen, because it exhibits clear and indisputable marks of a later age. It contains, for instance, numerous citations from the prophetical writings of Isaiah and Jeremiah, who did not live till long after the reign of Solomon. The book, moreover, was never extant in the Hebrew language, but was evidently composed in Greek, as we now have it; it was never admitted into the Jewish canon, and appears to have been unknown to Philo and Josephus. It was apparently written by an Hellenistic Jew, residing in Egypt, probably at Alexandria, for the benefit of those of his nation who did not understand Hebrew. But who he was or where he lived, whether before or shortly after the Christian era, is uncertain. It has been admitted into the second canon (*Deutero canonical*) by the Roman Catholic Church, because found in the Septuagint version, translated from that into the Vulgate, and declared canonical by the third council of Carthage. But Jerome calls it pseudepigraphal and refrained from correcting the old Latin version of it, inserted in the Vulgate, because, as he says, he desired only to amend the Canonical books. The Book entitled "The Wisdom of Jesus, the Son of Sirach," or "Ecclesiasticus," has been attributed to Solomon from its marked resemblance to the Book of Proverbs, of which it is in part a designed imitation. It is cited as his by several of the fathers; the Councils of Hippo, (A. D. 393,) and Carthage, (A. D. 397,) pronounced it the work of Solomon, and their decision was adopted by the Council of Trent. It is accordingly placed by the Romish Church among the Deutero canonical books. It is unquestionably a work of great value, much admired for the excellence of its political, moral and religious precepts, and regarded as not inferior in many respects to the Proverbs. Still on critical grounds it has no claim to be regarded as the work of Solomon, or as an inspired production. It was indeed originally written in Hebrew, and Jerome says that he had met with it in that form; but the original has long since perished, except some forty passages preserved in the Jewish Rabbinical writings. It must have been composed long after the time of Solomon. For that monarch, together with the succeeding prophets that flourished before and after the Captivity, is here mentioned (ch. 27: 13, etc.). The High Priest Simon, who lived a little before the Maccabees, is spoken of (ch. 1: 1–21). The words of the Prophet Malachi are cited (ch. 48: 10, from Mal. 4: 6); and the author describes himself in circumstances that could not have occurred to Solomon. (vid. ch. 34: 10, 12. 51: 6.) And, finally, it virtually disclaims the idea of Solomon's being the author; for it professes to be the production of one Jesus, the Son of Sirach. (vid. Title and ch. 50: 27.) Of the real author we know nothing more than what he has himself disclosed. The present Greek translation was made by the grandson of the author, bearing the same name, who lived about B. C. 131.* It was probably written about B. C. 180. But there is no evidence that it ever formed a part of the Jewish canon, or was written by divine inspiration, and consequently is very properly placed with the "Book of Wisdom," by Protestant Christians, among the Apocryphal books, useful to be read for edification, but having no peculiar authority.

The pre-eminent wisdom of Solomon was promulgated to the world partly in brief aphorisms, sententious and prudential maxims and proverbial sayings, clad in the pleasing and attractive garb of poetry. And if David is the first and most successful writer of psalmodical poetry, Solomon is on the other hand, the first and most successful writer of proverbial poetry. Of proverbs he is said to have spoken three thousand. 1 Kg. 4: 32. A part of them (about 500) have been preserved and transmitted to our times in the Book which we have attempted to explain in the following pages. This species of ethical and didactic composition obtained among the Hebrews the general appellation of *Mashal*, (מְשָׁלִים, מָשָׁל.) for which the English language furnishes no term of exactly equivalent power. The Hebrew verb (מָשַׁל,) from which the

---

* According to Winer, the Greek translator belongs to the time of Evergetes the second, who reigned in the second half of the second century before Christ,

noun is derived, signifies 1. to *rule*, to *govern*, 2. to *compare*, to *liken*, to *assimilate*. From the latter of these two general significations are derived the collateral meanings to *speak a parable*, to *utter a proverb*, to *discourse in figurative language*. Hence the kindred noun *Mashal* came to signify a *similitude*, a *comparison*, a *parable*, a *proverb*, a *fable*, an *allegory*, a *pithy sentence* or *sententious saying*, an *apothegm*, the *gnome* (γνώμη) of the Greeks, a *parallelistic distich* or *poem*. The same latitude of signification is found in the corresponding Syriac and Chaldee terms. Thus we see that the Hebrew noun embraces within the comprehensive scope of its generic meaning the παραβολή and the παροιμία of the Greeks, and the English *parable* and *proverb*. Accordingly we find the Greek term παροιμία, the Latin *proverbia*, and the English *proverb* employed in the Scriptures in the wide Hebrew sense of *parable, moral similitude, sententious maxim, allegory* or figurative discourse, and *didactic instruction*. In the New Testament, παραβολή and παροιμία are used interchangeably. What the first three Evangelists call παραβολαί (*parables*), St. John calls παροιμίαι (*proverbs*). See John 16: 25. 10: 6. This book is denominated "the Proverbs (מִשְׁלֵי, παροιμία, *proverbiæ*,) of Solomon."

A *proverb* is a short pithy sentence, which embodies a well known and admitted truth, or common fact, ascertained by experience or observation, and which passes current among the masses of society. Being founded on a self-evident truth, or on a fact established by general experience and observation, the whole force and pungency of the Proverb lies in its application, and not in the depth and ingenuity of the original form. It has been briefly and pertinently defined as "one man's wit, and all men's wisdom." A *maxim* is a principle generally received or admitted as true. A *proverb* therefore is a maxim, but a maxim does not necessarily become a proverb. It must first pass the ordeal of universal suffrage, before it can obtain a place in the proverbial literature of a nation. And in order to this, it is requisite that it should meet a general want and accord with the popular taste and feeling. A maxim may be just and important; but if its circulation is

restricted by the nature of the subject to a single science
(e. g., philosophy, mathematics, hermeneutics, etc); if it relates to matters which do not occupy public attention, or
come within the ordinary scope and range of general thought,
its use will be too limited to justify us in placing it among
the Proverbs of a people. Though it may be "the wit" of
one, it is only the wisdom of a particular class, and its use
will be confined to that class. "Proverbs in conversation,"
says Matthew Henry, "are like axioms in philosophy, maxims in law, and postulates in mathematics, which nobody
disputes, but every one endeavors to expound so as to have
them on his side." Cervantes happily calls them "short sentences drawn from long experience." "Proverbs," says a late
writer, "come from the character, and are alive and vascular.
There is blood and marrow in them. They give us pocket-
editions of the most voluminous truths. There is no waste
material in a good proverb; it is clear meat, like an egg—a
happy result of logic with the logic left out; and the writer
who shall thus condense his wisdom, and as far as possible
give the two poles of thought in every expression, will most
thoroughly reach men's minds and hearts." A Proverb, like
a comparison, admits of an unlimited application to analogous
cases. Like the parables of our Lord, Proverbs may be divided into two distinct classes, viz., *literal* and *figurative* or
allegorical. The former class comprises those which admit
only of a literal interpretation, and are to be understood according to the plain, obvious, grammatical meaning of the
terms in which they are expressed. The latter comprises
those in which one thing is said and another meant. In the
former case the literal sense exhausts the meaning; in the
latter, it is of no further use than to suggest the applied
meaning. The following are examples of the first class:
"Honesty is the best policy," "Right wrongs no man," etc.
To the second class belong such proverbs as these: "Drink
water from your own cistern," "Every one draws the water
to his own mill." So the corresponding Italian proverb,
'Every one rakes the embers to his own cakes." "There is
many a slip between the cup and the lip." "Strike while
the iron is hot." "Physician, heal thyself." "Those who

live in glass houses should not throw stones." These and similar proverbs have a real sense quite distinct from their literal meaning, and this must be determined from the connection in which they are employed, and the particular application which is made of them. Among the Greeks proverbs were called παροιμίαι (from πάρα, *near*, and οἶμος, *way*) *wayside idioms*, because common, and adapted to meet daily wants; and also for the purpose of distinguishing them from the more logical and discriminating harangue of schools and philosophers. The Romans termed them *adagia*, because they were *ad agendum apta*, practical maxims fitted for quickly solving the problems of daily life. *Brevity* appears to be one of the constituent elements of a proverb. It is, indeed, more than this. It is a prime excellence, without which it can retain neither the name nor the nature of a proverb. This is indicated by the word itself—*proverbia*, (from *pro* and *verbum*), *for*, or *instead of words*, i. e. few words. As the pronoun is used in the place of a noun, to avoid its too frequent repetition, so the proverb is a representative phrase resorted to for the purpose of avoiding tedious explanations and arguments. Hence it is made as compact and portable as possible, and compressed within the compass of the fewest possible terms. And not only is it made as brief as possible, but in other respects it often assumes a shape most convenient for the memory to retain. A large number of proverbs, in every language, have taken the form of poetry; and particularly in European languages, they have availed themselves, to a considerable extent, of the mnemonic aid supplied by rhyme and alliteration. The Hebrew language, though not rhythmical, is much more favorable to conciseness of expression than the English. We are often compelled to employ many words to express an idea which, in the Hebrew, is enunciated in very few. Thus, in the Hebrew proverb, "A man's heart deviseth his way; but the Lord directeth his steps," *twelve* words are employed in our standard version; and it can not well be translated with less; while in the original there are only *seven*. So again in the proverb, "When a man's way pleases the Lord, he makes even his enemies to be at peace with him," there are *seven-*

D

teen words in the standard English version, and but *eight* in the original. Many English proverbs, however, are very brief: e. g., "Extremes meet;" "Right wrongs no man;" "Forewarned, forearmed;" "Man proposes, but God disposes;" "Light gains make heavy purses." Horace insists upon Brevity as one of the express rules of didactic poetry:

"Short be the precept, which with ease is gained
By docile minds, and faithfully retained."

The same sentiment is expressed by Solomon in the parabolic manner. (Eccl. xii. : 11.)

"The words of the wise are like goads,
And like nails that are firmly fixed."

"It is the property of a proverb," says Henly, "to prick sharply, and hold firmly;" and Herbert entitles his collection of proverbs "Jacula Prudentum,"—something hurled, and striking deep.

The Proverb has its origin in the nature of man, and is admirably adapted to the wants of social life, particularly in its earlier stages. By the concise and epigrammatic style which characterizes it, and by the exact correspondence between the different members which compose it, the attention of the hearer or reader is awakened, the ear is pleased, and the memory is aided. The assistance furnished to the memory by the peculiar structure of Proverbs will be apparent, when we consider that, in the earlier periods of the human race, and for a long series of years, the facilities for acquiring and diffusing knowledge were very limited. The art of printing, which, in modern times, has produced such a wonderful revolution in the world of letters, was then unknown. The labor and expense attending the copying of books, prevented their multiplication to any considerable extent; and the ability to read or write was confined to very few. Instruction, for the most part, was necessarily communicated orally, and the memory of the scholar was almost the only store-house in which the maxims of the teacher were deposited. Hence, we find that in the infancy of nations and of society, the usual mode of didactic instruction was by brief, detached, and easily-remembered aphorisms, proverbs, gnomes, comparisons, and enigmas. These were the result of much thought and careful observation; and they were clothed in the most pleasing and attractive garb which the language could furnish, the effect of which was usually hightened, especially in the case of the Hebrews, by the introduction of a judicious antithesis, both in the sentiment and the expression. They were kept in constant use and circulation, were committed to memory by all classes with little effort, and became to the masses the maxims by which the conduct of life was regulated. Compositions of this character may be viewed as a kind of picture—writing, which addresses itself with effect to the senses, particularly of a rude and uncultivated people, who can profit by the fruits of reasoning, without being able to attend to its forms. Hence, we find that the literature of all the nations of antiquity which occupy a conspicuous place in history, abounds in proverbs. The sayings ascribed to the wise men of Greece are of this character. The "Works and Days" of Hesiod, which furnishes the earliest specimens of Grecian didactic poetry, contains many precepts on the conduct of life, expressed in proverbial form. After Hesiod, the didactic productions of the Greeks consisted almost entirely of moral precepts or sentences, expressed with brevity, terseness and force, and denominated gnomes, γνῶμαι. From this circumstance, the writers have been called Gnomic poets. This method of imparting ethical instruction accorded, also, with the sedate and deliberate character of the Romans. But it was in the East, among the Hebrews, Syrians, Arabians, Egyptians, Persians and Scythians, that it most prevailed; and it is there that, from the fixed and unvarying character of the habits and literature of the people, the ancient reverence for proverbs and gnomes still exists.

But while it is true that proverbial sayings originated in the childhood of the human family, and are particularly adapted to a period of limited culture, their *utility* is by no means confined to such a state of society. Hence, we find that the literature of modern nations, both oriental and occidental, from China to Mexico, abounds in compositions of this kind. The place they occupy in the domain of literaturé becomes, it is true, less conspicuous and important, as civilization and intellectual culture, the arts and improvements of social life, and popular education advance; still, they will never be entirely banished from that domain. Embodying, as they do, in concise, attractive, and easily-remembered sentences, the results of extensive comparison, observation, and experience, they will always be classed among the most valuable guides of human conduct, in the various and complex relations and affairs of human life. Proverbs "give a deep insight into domestic life, and open for us the heart of man in all the various states which he may occupy. A frequent review of proverbs should enter into our readings; and although they are no longer the ornaments of conversation, they have not ceased to be the treasures of thought."

The Proverbs current among a people unquestionably have no small influence upon their character, as well as furnish a clue and index to that character. They are to the morals of a nation what gold coin is to its currency—portable, rich, and always passable; or, as Cicero says, "They are the salt-pits of a nation; treasured preservatives against corruption." They throw great light, therefore, on the domestic manners, temper, and character of a people, and furnish valuable materials for an accurate history of their modes of thought, their social habits, and private morals.

In the writings of Solomon the term *proverb* (מָשָׁל) is employed in its widest and most comprehensive sense. The book of Proverbs abounds in moral and religious sentences and precepts, which do not strictly come under the head of proverbs. It contains, also, several didactic and connected discourses of considerable length, in commendation of religion, virtue, and prudence, interspersed with salutary warnings against vice and folly. We find in it, also, several beautiful moral sketches, such as that of the inexperienced young man, in the 7th chapter; of the strange woman, in the 9th; of the drunkard and glutton, in the 23d; and of a virtuous woman, in the 31st. The last chapter, in particular, contains a lengthy and eulogistic description of a good wife, and the eighth chapter, a magnificent personification of the divine attribute of wisdom. The whole, however, is displayed in the peculiar form and style of Hebrew poetry; and, hence, the book is classed by Bishop Lowth among the *didactic poems* of the Bible. Ewald places it under the head of *Gnomic poetry*, the rise of which among the Hebrews he attributes to Solomon. It has not inappropriately been styled the *Gnomological Anthology* of the ancient Hebrews. The book is the most extensive and useful of Solomon's productions which have come down to our times, and is a striking monument of his intellectual power and practical wisdom. In an ethical point of view, it may be regarded as one of the most instructive and valuable portions of Holy Scripture; and it has been uniformly held in the highest estimation by the best and wisest men, both in the Jewish and Christian Church. By the early fathers it was called the παυάρετον σοφίαν, *wisdom embracing all virtues.* (Eusebius' Eccles. His. Lib. 14, c. 25.) Basil speaks of it as the ὅλως διδασχαλία βίου, a universal instruction for the government of life. Jerome's direction to one of his friends, for the education of his daughter, was—"Let her have, first of all, the Book of Psalms, for holiness of heart, and be instructed in Solomon's Proverbs, for her godly life." Luther pronounced this book to be the best book on Economics in the world. "No doubt," says Patterson, in his Commentary on the Epistle to the Hebrews, "many of the Proverbs are, so to speak, the very common-places of morality. But on these common-places the safety, health, and happiness of the moral world depend. Even in these common-places, the wise and inspired mind of Solomon rose superior to the discoveries and apprehensions of distinguished heathen sa:es. Interspersed are many germs and evolutions of profound and majestic moral principles. The whole sphere of duty and obligation is traversed and overtaken by the Book of Proverbs. And the pointed power of the style, and the divine authority of the rules, give the book a vast pre-eminence. The Queen of Sheba traveled from the ends of the earth to hear the wisdom of Solomon. Men possessing the Bible, need not, for that important end, to go to Palestine, or to traverse wide-spread

D*

continents or surging seas. The wisdom, the words of Solomon are very near them. In the Book of Proverbs they are
treasured up in store, and are accessible alike to prince and
peer, to man, woman, and child." "Solomon's Proverbs,"
remarks Dr. Gray, in his Introduction to the Old Testament,
"are so justly founded on the principles of human nature,
and so adapted to the permanent interests of man, that they
agree with the manners of every age, and may be assumed
as the rules for the direction of our conduct in every condition and rank of life." Coleridge says, "The Book of Proverbs is the best statesman's manual which was ever written.
An adherence to the political economy and spirit of that
collection of apothegms and essays would do more to eradicate from a people the causes of extravagance, debasement,
and ruin, than all the contributions to political economy of
Say, Smith, Malthus, and Chalmers together." "The cautions against suretiship," says Jasper Adams (Moral Philos.
p. 41) "will be most commended by those who have had
most experience in human affairs. No where do we find
stronger commendations of industry, frugality, chastity, temperance, and integrity; or more serious warnings against
idleness, strife, envy, drunkenness and rioting. No where
are pride, covetousness, selfishness, the indulgence of rash
anger, and the abuse of the tongue in the manifold ways of
falsehood, slander, secret calumny, false witness and blasphemy, more forcibly reproved. No where are the wiles, the
cunning and the hardened front of the woman 'who forsakes
the guide of her youth, and forgets the covenant of her God,'
and 'whose house is the way to hell, going down to the
chambers of death,' more vividly described. All authors,
ancient and modern, cannot furnish such a picture of the
virtuous woman (ch. 31: 10–31). Every duty in life is enjoined and skilfully commended to our notice, and not only
every vice, but every species of folly and even indiscretion,
is guarded against. But it is in his concern for the young,
and in his commendation of wisdom, that the wisest of men
has put forth all the strength of his persuasive power and
eloquence." "Some of the Proverbs," says Mountford, "are
of no use to us in our circumstances. But all of them are

interesting as spiritual remains. Vestiges they aie of an era in the human mind, long, long back; words of caution, spiritual armor, fashioned for the use of the young in the anxious minds of experienced sages; proved advice for behavior in the house, the city, and the field; and immortal truths, which wise men coined out of their mortal sufferings." "As some of the pioverbs of the other oriental nations, and particularly the Arabians, who are most celebrated in this way, are not of a moral nature, and have often no other merit than a certain degree of point and acuteness, so likewise," says Pareau, "in this book of Solomon there are maxims occasionally more remarkable for the acuteness of genius displayed in them, than for their moral utility. But by far the greater part of them are conducive to probity of conduct; and there is no collection of proverbs, which, particularly if respect be had to antiquity and usefulness, equals, much less surpasses that of Solomon."

This book has an historical value aside from the practical instruction conveyed in it. It presents us with a view of the Jewish religion and morals as pervading the common life and daily walk of the Hebrews, which is not so fully developed in the historical books, and which is more favorable than we might gather from the accounts of the numerous ceremonies and external ritual forms and observances elsewhere enjoined.

In order to appreciate properly the proverbs of Solomon we must look at them from a Jewish and not a Christian stand-point. Though the precepts which the book inculcates are of an exalted character, they are not based on the distinctive principles and highest motives of Christianity. The retributions of another life are not, it is true, entirely disregarded, and ignored; yet they are not brought as frequently and prominently into view, as we should expect to have found them, had the work proceeded from the pen of an Apostle of Christ. Its appeals are most commonly made to the human agent acting for the present time, rather than for an eternal future. At the same time, it frequently, and in the most impressive manner, presents the great idea of Jehovah's constant watchfulness and superintending Providence, and sets forth the safety of the good, as enjoying his blessing and protection; and the danger of disobedience, as provoking his displeasure. The moral precepts of Solomon, therefore, rest on the foundation of religion and true piety, and in this respect differ heaven-wide from the systems of the ancient heathen moralists. It is our privilege as Christians, favored with the clearer light of the New Dispensation, to occupy higher ground than did Solomon, in regard to the sanctions of duty and virtue; and though we may not attach a meaning to the language of the book different from what the writer intended, yet in applying its maxims to the practical purposes of life, we may add to the weighty temporal considerations therein presented the higher motives and sanctions of eternity derived from the Gospel of Christ.

In regard to the style in which this book is written, the remarks of Holden are equally true and beautiful. "Though in the charms of high-wrought poetry it must yield to several parts of the sacred volume; yet in judicious brevity, in elegant conciseness, in nice adjustment of expressions, and in that terseness of diction, which gives weight to precept and poignancy to aphoristic truth, it stands pre-eminent, and remains an illustrious monument to the glory of its author."

The Book of Proverbs is written in poetry. Hebrew poetry, like that of all other nations, is characterized by sublimity of thought and a highly ornate and figurative style of composition, dealing largely in the free and fervid language of imagination and passion. Like that of other nations, also, it has phraseology, distinguished in its whole complexion from what serves the plainer and humbler uses of prose; admitting bold ellipses and transpositions, unusual and artificial expressions, abrupt introductions and conclusions, brief unexplained allusions, and paradoxes. In this poetic phraseology of the Jews, certain idiomatic constructions frequently appear, unknown to Western nations, one of the most remarkable of which is the sudden and abrupt change of person and number, which we often meet with; such as the following examples:

" *They* are a perverse and crooked generation;
Do *ye* thus requite the Lord, O foolish people and unwise!"

Deut. 32: 5, 6.

"God be merciful unto us, and bless us;
And cause *his* face to shine upon us,
That *thy* way may be known upon earth,
Thy saving health among all nations."
                                        Ps. 67: 1, 2.

But unlike the poetry of Western nations, it has neither
rhyme nor rhythm; *i. e.*, the consecutive lines do not terminate in words or syllables of similar sound for the purpose
of pleasing the ear, nor are they regularly measured by met-
rical feet.   But it has one feature which is peculiar to it, by
which it is strongly marked, and which is worthy of special
attention.   I allude to what is termed *parallelism of sentiment*
or *thought-rhythm*.   This characteristic of Hebrew poetry is
very ancient, as appears from Gen. 4: 23, 24; it is both highly
simple and distinguished for no small power; adapted also as
it is to music, particularly when sung by two alternate choirs
(1 Sam. 18: 17. Ezra 3: 11. Neh. 12: 24.), it afforded great
delight to the Hebrews, and they constantly adhered to it,
as long as they cultivated poetry.   Indeed they seem to have
carried it in some degree into their prose compositions, though
not by any means to the extent contended for by such writers
as Bishop Jebb, Mr. Boys, Mr. Roe, and Dr. Forbes.   By Hebrew parallelism is meant that correspondence of relationship in respect to thought which is found to exist between
the several members of a sentence, or the parts of a more
extended composition.*   With regard to its external form,
or the distribution of its members, each of the verses of the
same poem are for the most part divided into two, sometimes
into three, and more rarely into four members.   As it regards
the sentiment itself, there are several varieties of parallelisms.

   1. The *Synonymous*, i. e., parallels so arranged, that the

---

* The Hebrew noun *mashal* appears to be employed with special allusion to the
parallelism in Num. 21: 27. 23:7. Job 27: 1.   In these cases the word is rendered
parable in our Standard Version; but is neither of them does either parable or proverb, in the modern and usual sense of the word, seem to be appropriate.   The corresponding word in the Sept. is παραβολὴ. which is from παρά and βάλλω, *I place
along side of*, viz. for the sake of comparison.   This may appropriately designate not
only a *parable* or an analogical comparison of two ideas, or a *proverb* or sententious
maxim, but a *parallelism*, or the placing together of two lines or sentences, according
to the usual structure of Hebrew poetry; in other words, a *parallelistic distich*, or
poem.

same sentiment is repeated, mostly in other words signifying the same thing. Thus,

> "The earth is the Lord's, and all that is therein;
> The world, and they who inhabit it.
> For he hath founded it upon the seas,
> And established it upon the floods." Ps. 24: 42.

There is frequently something wanting in the latter member which must be supplied from the former, in order to complete the sentence. Thus,

> "Kings shall see him, and rise up;
> Princes (*shall see him*), and they shall worship him."
>
> Isa. 49: 7.

This is, probably the most common species of the parallelism.

2. The *gradational.* In this kind of parallelism, the second, or responsive clause so diversifies the preceding one, as generally to rise above it, forming a sort of climax; and sometimes by a descending scale in the value of the related terms and periods, forming an anti-climax; but in all cases with a marked distinction of meaning. Thus,

> "Happy is the man,
> Who walketh not in the counsel of the ungodly,
> Nor standeth in the way of sinners,
> Nor sitteth in the seat of the scornful." Ps. 1: 1.

3. The *antitethic.* This is a parallelism in which the sentiments in the two connected members of any verse stand opposed to each other. This is not confined to any particular form; and hence the degrees of antitheses are various; from an exact contraposition of word to word, singulars to singulars, plurals to plurals, &c., through the entire sentence, down to a general disparity, with something of contrariety in the two propositions. This species of parallelism is admirably adapted to adages, aphorisms, acute sayings, and detached sentences, and it generally adds no little force and point to the sentiments themselves. It is of less frequent occurrence in the prophetical writings, but abounds in the Proverbs of Solomon, much of the elegance, acuteness, and force of which arises from the antithetic form, the opposition of diction and sentiment, as in the following examples:

" A wise son rejoiceth his father;
But a foolish son is the grief of his mother."
Prov. 10: 1.

Here every word has its opposite, the terms *father* and *mother* being relatively opposite.

" The memory of the just is blessed;
But the name of the wicked shall rot." Prov. 10: 7.

In this instance there are only two antithetic terms, for *memory* and *name* are synonymous.

" Faithful are the words of a friend;
But deceitful are the kisses of an enemy." • Prov. 27: 6.

Here again every word has its opposite; *faithful, deceitful; words, kisses; friend, enemy.*

4. The *constructive* or *synthetic.* This is a species of parallelism in which the different members answer to each other, only by a similar form of construction. Word does not answer to word, and sentiment to sentiment, as equivalent or opposite; but there is a correspondence and equality between different propositions, in respect to the shape and turn of the whole sentence, and of the constructive parts; such as noun answering to noun, verb to verb, member to member, negative to negative, interrogative to interrogative. Thus:

"The law of the Lord is perfect, converting the soul;
The testimony of the Lord is sure, making wise the simple;
The statutes of the Lord are right, rejoicing the heart;
The commandment of the Lord is pure, enlightening the eyes;
The fear of the Lord is clean, enduring forever;
The judgments of the Lord are true and righteous altogether."
Ps. 19: 7–9.

5. The *introverted.* This is that species of parallelism which is so constructed, that whatever be the number of its members, the first answers to the last, the second to the penultimate, or last but one, and so on throughout, in an order that looks inward, or, in military phrase, from flanks to centre. Thus,

" My son, if thy heart be wise;
My heart also shall rejoice;
Yea, my lips shall rejoice;
When thy lips speak right things." Prov. 23: 15, 16.

"And it shall come to pass in that day;
Jehovah shall make a gathering of his fruit
From the flood of the river;
To the stream of Egypt;
And ye shall be gleaned up, one by one,
O ye sons of Israel." Isa. 27: 12.

Such is the nature of this leading principle of Hebrew versification and such are the principal varieties of the parallelisms, which are distributed throughout the Old Testament, and are occasionally met with in the New Testament. The parallelisms which occur in this book chiefly belong to the first, the third, and the fourth classes. There are, however, a few examples of the second. The synonymous occurs most frequently in the first part, the synthetic in the last, and the antithetic in the middle. The form is chiefly that of the simple parallelism, consisting of two members or clauses in each verse. There are comparatively few triplets.

The Canonicity and Inspiration of the Book of Proverbs, are attested by its unquestioned reception among the sacred writings of the Jews which received the sanction of our Saviour, and by the numerous citations from it in the Christian Scriptures, as a part of the Oracles of God. Michaelis remarks that "the canonical authority of no part of the Old Testament is so ratified by the evidence of quotations, as that of the Proverbs.* The Apocryphal book called "The Wisdom of Jesus, the Son of Sirach," or "Ecclesiasticus," bears a very striking affinity to the book of Proverbs; and yet it is a remarkable fact that in not a single instance is it quoted by the Apostles and Evangelists. The difference between Canonical and Apocryphal is no where so strongly marked as in this example.' Ecclesiastical history has recorded only one dissentient from the judgment of the Universal Church with regard to the canonical and divine authority of the Proverbs, and that one condemned by her authoritative Council.†

---

* Compare ch. 3: 11, 12, with Heb. 12: 5, 6.=3: 34, with James 4: 6, and 1 Pet. 5: 5.=10: 12, with James 5: 20, and 1 Pet. 4: 8.=25: 6, 7. with Lu. 14: 9, 10,=25: 21, 22, with Rom. 12: 30.=27: 1, with James 4: 13, 14.

† Theodore Mopsuestia, condemned by the 5th General Council at Constantinople, A. D 553.

At what period of .Solomon's life, the canonical books ascribed to him were severally composed, is a question to which different answers have been given, but which in the absence of positive testimony can never, of course, be definitively settled. Some Roman Catholic writers, among whom is Cornelius a' Lapide, maintain that the book of Proverbs was written during the early part of the king's reign, while he was yet a young man; that the book of Ecclesiastes was composed subsequently, during the period of his middle life; and they assign the composition of the Canticles to his old age. The Jewish commentators, with more probability, place the composition of the Proverbs in the middle life of the king; while others maintain that it embodies the experience and observation of his whole life. It would seem quite probable, by comparing Prov. 4: 3–6, with 1 Kg. 2: 1–4, that the first part of this book was composed shortly after the death of David, and before Solomon had fallen into that oriental luxury and effeminacy which brought reproach and dishonor upon his later years. Living, as he did, about 260 years before the reign of Cyrus, under whom the seven wise men of Greece flourished; and 670 years before Alexander the Great, under whom lived Socrates, Plato, and Aristotle, it is evident that Solomon could have drawn no part of the materials for his collection of Proverbs from heathen moralists and philosophers, as Grotius and others have supposed, even had there been much intercourse between the Hebrews and Gentile nations, which was not the case. On the contrary, it seems more probable, as some of the Christian fathers assert, that they derived much valuable information from the writings of the renowned monarch of Israel.

This Book may be conveniently divided into six parts. The *first* part, comprising the first nine chapters, is an appropriate introduction to the sequel, and breathes throughout the polished and philosophical genius of Solomon. It consists of connected moral discourses in commendation of Heavenly Wisdom objectively as an attribute of the Deity, subjectively as the great inward principle of piety and morality. The practice of virtue, and especially the virtue of chastity, is also earnestly enjoined. "This portion of the

E

book," says Bishop Lowth, "is varièd, elegant, sublime, and truly poetical; the order of the subjects is in general excellently preserved, and the parts are very aptly connected. It is embellished with many beautiful descriptions and personifications; the diction is polished, and abounds with all the ornaments of poetry; so that it scarcely yields in elegance and splendor to any of the sacred writings." The *second* part begins at Chapter X. and extends to Chapter XXII. 17. This portion is entirely unlike the preceding, and consists of disconnected proverbs, each composed of a single distich framed according to the laws of Hebrew parallelism. "It is a proverbial philosophy without any endeavor at beauty or poetical charm. All the relations between man and man, the civil, political, commercial, and all religious relations, are not merely touched upon, but the soundest maxims, the best rules of conduct, are presented in such short terms, that it is easy to keep them in memory. Every verse is a prolific theme on which chapters might be written; yet few of the verses contain in the original more than six or seven words, scarcely any exceeding eight words. The second member of the verse contains almost always a contrast of sense to the first part, and enforces the maxim contained in the first clause, as the shade elevates the light of a picture. This method of arrangement is peculiar to this book. The parallelism of other Hebrew poems is so constructed, that the second line is a supplement to the sense of the first, so that it may properly be called a rhyme of sentiment instead of sound."* The *third* part extends from Chapter XXII. 17, to Chapter XXV. It is distinguished from the second part by a closer connexion between the verses, and a more negligent use of the parallelism. The *fourth* part begins at Chapter XXV. and extends to Chapter XXX. This comprises another collection of the maxims and proverbs of Solomon, formed at a later period under the direction of King Hezekiah. The *fifth* part commences at Chapter XXX. and extends to Chapter XXXI. This portion comprises some proverbial maxims ascribed to an unknown individual by the name of Agur.. The *sixth* part, which embraces the last

---

* Wise's History of the Israelitish nation, Vol. I. p. 411.

Chapter, consists, 1. of instructions given to one King Lemuel by his mother. This person is supposed by some to have been Solomon under a fictitious name; but by others, with more probability, an Arabian or Idumæan prince, of whom we have no further information. 2. An acrostic poem in commendation of a frugal, industrious, virtuous, housewife. The description has no equal in the whole range of literature. The poem, which is complete in itself, is composed with extraordinary artistic skill, and is one of the most simple and beautiful specimens of lyric eulogy to be found in the Hebrew Scriptures. It is alphabetically arranged in the original, the verses regularly commencing with the letters of the Hebrew alphabet in consecutive order. Acrostic or Alphabetical poems were not uncommon among the Hebrews and other nations of the East. A number of the Psalms and the book of Lamentations are alphabetical.

The following special rules and observations will assist the reader in the interpretation of this book.

1. It is manifestly not the design of the Book of Proverbs to furnish maxims which can have only an *individual* application. At the same time, it is equally true, that with few exceptions, these proverbs have not an unlimited and *universal* application, but only that which is *general*. *e. g.*, ch. 10: 17. 16: 7. 22: 6.

2. Nothing more is frequently intended than what usually occurs, and not what is good and proper in itself. Indeed a proverbial maxim may as a sentiment be false, while as a matter of fact it may be strictly true. *e. g.*, Might makes right; The end justifies the means. Upon such false principles as these men are continually acting, and to their own minds at least justify, on the ground of them, oppression, slavery, and an endless variety of wicked acts.

3. A thing is sometimes represented as really *done*, in order to indicate what *ought* to be done, although too often neglected. *e. g.*, ch. 16: 12, 13.

4. Some maxims, which, taken in their broadest and most unqualified sense, and without regard to the circumstances which gave rise to them, appear to be inconsistent with the law of fraternal kindness, (*e. g.*, the warnings against sureti-

ship,) are only salutary and impressive admonitions against indiscreet and imprudent actions.

5. Particular attention should be paid to the structure of Hebrew poetry, especially to the laws of Hebrew parallelism.

6. The force and significancy of the maxims contained in this book will be most clearly seen and felt, when they are studied in the light of Scripture examples. They are comprehensive principles of action best understood when examined in connexion with particular cases.

One word with respect to the execution of the present work. To give a faithful and accurate translation of an author is the most difficult part of an interpreter's work. When that is accomplished, more than half his task is performed. Such a translation of the Scriptures, or of any portion of them, is of the highest value to the reader, and quite supercedes the necessity of many explanatory remarks, which, otherwise, would be necessary to make the meaning of the author plain. In the translation which follows, it has been the aim of the writer to depart from our excellent standard version only so far as perspicuity, modern usage, and fidelity to the original text seemed to require. In the preparation of the notes he has endeavored to meet the wants both of the scholar and of the plain English reader. How far he has succeeded in this respect, he leaves it for the candid reader to determine.

THE PROVERBS OF SOLOMON.

PART I.
CHAPTER I.—IX.

[EXHORTATIONS TO THE PURSUIT AND ATTAINMENT OF HEAVENLY WISDOM.]

CHAP. I. 1—7.
[INTRODUCTION.—*Title, Design, and Scope of the Book.*]

1. The Proverbs of Solomon, the son of David, king of Israel.

2. That one may know wisdom and instruction;
That one may perceive the words of understanding;

1. We have in this opening verse a descriptive title to the book. The Proverbs are called Solomon's, for the same reason that the Psalms are called David's, because he was the author of the greater part of the book, and also because a considerable portion of it was arranged by him. The official title *king* refers here to Solomon, and not to David; for although David was likewise king of Israel, yet the word in this place, like the word *son* in the preceding phrase, is grammatically in apposition with Solomon. So Eccles. 1: 1, Comp. verse 12.

2. The Sacred writer in this and the two following verses, points out the design of this book. The literal rendering of the original

2. " From which men may learn wisdom and instruction."—NOTES

3. That one may receive the instruction of wisdom,
Righteousness, and justice, and uprightness:
4. Which will give prudence to the simple;
To the young (*man*) knowledge and discretion.

is, "for the knowing of wisdom," &c., and "for the perceiving of
the words of understanding,"—the import of which is the same as
in order that one may know and perceive," &c. The same remark is
applicable to the first words in verses 3 and 4. The term *wisdom* is
here employed in its widest sense, as denoting correct apprehensions
with regard to the whole circle of human duty, whether moral, religious, or prudential. The term *instruction* is usually applied to
the knowledge which is imparted by teachers to the young, particularly in relation to moral conduct. The precise shade of meaning,
however, can be best learned from the context, in the several passages where the word occurs. This remark applies also to the terms
understanding, knowledge, &c., which often occur in connexion with
wisdom and *instruction*, and are sometimes used interchangeably
with them. By *words of understanding*, are meant words uttered by
intelligent and virtuous persons, and adapted to make the reader or
hearer intelligent, wise and virtuous. *To perceive* the words of understanding, is to gain an accurate knowledge of the instructive
lessons taught. There is doubtless special allusion to the contents
of this book. (לָרַעַת, Kal infin. constr. of יָרַע, with the prefix prep.
indicating the end and purpose. הָבִין; Hiph. infin. of בִּין).

3. The nouns *Righteousness, Justice* and *Uprightness*, are here designed to cover the entire ground of moral action, and comprise
whatever is right and proper, conformable to law, both divine and
human, and accordant with strict probity of heart and life. (See
ch. 2: 9.) These nouns are not in regimen with the word *instruction*, for the verse consists of two parallel members; but they are
governed by the verb in the first clause, taken in the sense of *acquiring*, instead of *receiving*. "That one may *acquire* or *attain to*
righteousness," &c. (לָקַחַת, Kal infin. constr. of לָקַח, with the prefix prep.)

4. The word עָרְמָה, *arma*, rendered *prudence*, primarily signifies *cunning, guile, craftiness*, taken in a bad sense: (Ex. 21: 14, Josh.
9: 4); but in this book it is uniformly employed in a good sense,
and by interpreters is variously translated *caution, discernment, sagacity, prudence*. The last is here adopted as being more agreeable
to the phraseology of our common version than the others, and suffi-

5. A wise (*man*) will hear, and will increase (*in*) learning;
And a man of understanding will gain wise counsel;
6. So as to understand a proverb, and a deep maxim;
The words of the wise, and their dark sayings.
7. The fear of Jehovah is the beginning of knowledge;   .   .
(*But*) fools despise wisdom and instruction.

---

ciently expressive of its meaning. (See ch. 8: 5, 12. Comp. the root עָרַם, *aram*, ch. 15: 5. 19: 25.) By the *simple* is meant the young and inexperienced, who are peculiarly liable to be led astray by evil counsel and example. (לָתֵת, Kal inf. constr. of נָתַן, with prefix.)

5. By *wise counsel* is meant that sound judgment, skill and discretion in the management of one's affairs, which the pilot exhibits, who understands how to steer his vessel safely into port. By employing the word תַּחְבֻּלוֹת, *tachbuloth*, (from חָבַל, *chabal, to tighten a cord, to bind,* hence the nouns חֶבֶל, *chebel, a chord, a rope,* and חֹבֵל, *chobel, a sailor, a pilot.*) Solomon beautifully represents human life as a voyage, and Wisdom as the pilot directing its course. (יֹסֵף, Hiph. fut. of יָסַף. נָבוֹן, Niph. participial adjective from בִּין.)

6. These words indicate the consequence of pursuing the course pointed out in the preceding verse. The wise man who faithfully attends to the Proverbs and other instructive lessons contained in this book, will so enlarge his knowledge, and acquire such soundness of judgment and discrimination of mind, as will enable him easily to comprehend the obscure and enigmatical sayings of wise and learned men. מְלִיצָה, *melitza,* properly signifies *interpretation,* and is so rendered here in our common version; but it evidently denotes in this place by metonymy *that which needs interpretation, an obscure, intricate, profound maxim,* or *saying.* So Noyes and Stuart. The Septuagint Greek version has σκοτεινὸς λόγος, *dark speech.* The parallelism requires this rendering in preference to that given in the common version, which, however, is supported by the Latin Vulgate, and the Greek versions of Aquila and Theodotian. *Dark sayings—*i. e., *difficult sayings, enigmas, riddles.*

7. *The fear of Jehovah* denotes *reverential awe,* and not *servile*

. 7. " *The principal part,*" Holden—" *the sum,*" Boothroyd.

dread. It is the fear of a child towards its parent, and not that of a slave towards his master, or of an oppressed subject towards a tyrannical and despotic ruler. It springs from a loving heart; and while it restrains us from the commission of sin, it prompts to cheerful, filial obedience. (Comp. Ps. 4: 4.) It is indeed but another name for *true, inward, vital religion*—a prominent part being put for the whole; as in James 1: 27, where pure and undefiled religion is described as consisting in visiting the fatherless and widows in their affliction, and in keeping oneself unspotted from the world. This complex feeling—*reverential awe*—is represented as the *beginning of knowledge*. That religion which has its seat in the heart, is the foundation of all that is truly valuable in knowledge, of all that is virtuous and honorable in practice, and of all that adorns and dignifies human nature. The word יְהֹוָה, *Jehovah,* wherever it occurs in this book, we have uniformly transferred, instead of translating. It is the name which the Deity appropriates to himself, and by which he was known to the ancient church under the Jewish dispensation. It denotes *existence—self-existence—independent existence,* and implies *immutability* and *eternity;* hence it belongs to no other being, and can be appropriately applied to no other. It is equivalent to the august name (Ex. 3: 14) "I am that I am." The true import of the word is supposed to be paraphrastically expressed in Rev. 1: 8, "which is, and which was, and which is to come." Accordingly Rabbi Bechai, an ancient Jewish writer, says, "These three tenses, past, present, and to come, are comprehended in this proper name, as is known to all." But the Greek word κύριος, by which it is very inadequately represented in the Septuagint, and of which our English word *Lord* is an accurate translation, merely conveys the idea of *dominion, power, authority,* and designates the Deity as the Ruler and overseer of the world. The Jews attach so much sanctity to the name *Jehovah,* that in reading the Hebrew Scriptures, they never, with the single exception of the priestly benediction, (Num. 6: 24–26) pronounce it, but always substitute עֲדוֹנָי, *Adonai,* another title, which is frequently applied to the Deity, and which is also in our standard version rendered *Lord.* But the Scriptures afford no warrant for this extreme scrupulousness, and superstitious reverence for the term. If it was lawful for Moses to *write* the name, it certainly cannot be unlawful or improper for us to *read* and to *speak* it, in the absence of any express prohibition to the contrary.

The word translated here *beginning,* (רֵאשִׁית, *reshith*) commonly signifies the *first* in respect to *time*, and so may denote the *foundation, origin, source,* of any thing. Thus understood, inward piety is declared to be the commencement, the starting point, the basis of all true knowledge. .Without this we shall never know God, and never properly and truly know ourselves. "The root of wisdom is to know the Lord." (Ecclus. 1: 20, so also Ps. 111: 10.) But the word sometimes denotes the *first* in respect to *dignity* and *importance.* And this is evidently its meaning in ch. 4: 7. It is so understood in this place by some expositors, who accordingly render it *the chief,* or *principal part,* the *sum, perfection* of knowledge. (So marginal reading, Comp. Job, 28: 28.) The assertion of the Sacred writer, taken in this sense, is unquestionably true and important. But the passage in ch. 4: 7, is not parallel, and in ch. 9: 10, which is really so, a different word is employed, (הְּחִלָּה, *tehilla,*) which always denotes *priority of time.*

In the Sacred Scriptures, wickedness is denominated *folly* (Gen. 34: 7), and wicked men are called *fools* (1 Sam. 25: 25, Ps. 14: 1), the epithet being applied to them as expressive of the obliquity of the heart rather than of a weakness of the intellectual powers. Sept.—"The fear of the Lord is the beginning of wisdom; and there is a good understanding to all that practice it; and piety towards God is the beginning of discernment, but the ungodly will set at naught wisdom and instruction."

CHAPTER I. 8–19.

[*The Duty of Obedience to Parental Instruction enjoined, vs.* 8, 9. *Warnings against evil company, vs.* 10–19.]

8. Hear, my son, the instruction of thy father,
An I reject not the teaching of thy mother.

8. Solomon places reverence for parents next in order and importance to reverence for Jehovah. The expressions, *Hear—hearken to —give ear to*—imply attention, consideration and obedience. Comp. ch. 4: 10. The term *son,* in this place, and for the most part elsewhere in this book, is merely an expression of endearment used by

8. "*The precepts of thy mother,*" Holden, Noyes—"*the lessons,*" French—"*the admonition,*" Boothr.

1*

9. For they (*shall be*) a graceful wreath to thy head,
And chains around thy neck.

---

instructors when addressing their pupils, for the purpose of securing
their respectful attention. The word תּוֹרַה, *tora*, in the second
member of the verse, generally signifies *a law;* but here it corresponds with *instruction* in the parallel clause, and evidently imports
not a law, or authoritative statute, but *teaching, instruction, advice,
precept,* (see ch. 3: 1. 4: 2. 6: 20. 7: 2, &c., where the word occurs in
the same sense.) Indeed this is the primary and etymological signification of the word, the root of which is יָרָה, *yara*, הֹירָה, *hora, to
teach.* It is worthy of remark that no ancient system of religion or
morals, except that which is found in the Bible, recognizes the just
and equal claims of the mother with the father to filial regard and
obedience. (תֵּטֹּשׁ, Kal fut. 2d pers. from נָטַשׁ.)

9. The moral beauty and loveliness resulting from regard to the
instruction and teaching just mentioned, are here symbolized by
familiar objects of personal adornment. The instructions and ad
monitions of faithful parents and teachers, carried out in the life,
are compared to wreaths, tiaras, and necklaces, which were very
generally worn in the East by both sexes, but particularly by
females, as ornamental decorations of the head and neck. These
ornaments, by imparting elegance and gracefulness to the human
form, gave additional charm and attractiveness to those who wore
them. In like manner, those who exhibit in their disposition and
deportment the virtues which characterize the pious and good, are
thereby rendered morally beautiful and lovely, both in the sight of
God and man. To adorn the person with extrinsic ornaments, appears to be an instinct of humanity. Under various forms and
modifications, we find the tendency existing every where. (Comp.
Gen. 41: 42. Dan. 5: 7, 16, 29. Cant. 1: 10. 2 Sam. 1: 24.) Hesiod,
describing the dress of a virgin, in his "Works and Days," says,
"They put golden chains upon her person." In the order of *time,*
decoration in fact precedes dress; the ornamental is antecedent to
the useful. This regard for outward adornment cannot indeed be
said to rank very high among the exercises of the human faculties;
yet it is quite above the reach of inferior animals. The natural
fondness for personal ornaments and decorations, however, is often
indulged in to excess, and then becomes the occasion of folly and
sin, by pampering pride and vanity, and causing an extravagant
and wasteful expenditure of money, which should be applied to

10. My son, if sinners entice thee, consent thou not.
11. If they say, "Come with us;
"Let us lie in wait for blood;
"Let us lurk secretly for him who in vain is innocent;

---

some better use. Against this excessive and criminal indulgence
the instructions of the New Testament are frequently directed. Ornaments, however, are alluded to in this passage, neither for the
purpose of approving nor of condemning them; but merely to indicate that moral qualities are really and emphatically the true adornment of a rational and immortal being. (See 1 Tim. 2: 9, 10. 1 Pet.
3: 3, 4.) A "*graceful* wreath" is equivalent to a *beautiful* wreath;
for חֵן, *hen*, like the Greek χάρις, signifies *gracefulness, beauty, elegance*, as well as *grace, favor, kindness*. See ch. 31: 30. Sept., "a
crown (στέφανον) of graces." The second noun in the original
supplies the place of an adjective, and qualifies the first, according
to a common idiom of the Hebrew language. Thus, a *graceful roe*,
—lit. a roe of gracefulness, ch. 5: 19; *a precious stone*,—lit. a stone
of beauty, ch. 17: 8. One of the Rabbinical writers has an elegant
express on similar to that in the text. Vajiher Rabb. § 12. "The
words of the law are a coronet to the head, a chain to the neck,
tranquility to the heart, and a collyrium to the eyes." Sept. "A
chain of gold round the neck."

10. Temptation, in this world of trial, is no uncertain contin-
gency, but a fixed and inevitable fact, arising out of the infirmity
and depravity of human nature. Nor does the Christian life form
an exception to this remark. So far from being exempt from temptation, the pious man is peculiarly liable to it in some of its forms.
"If thou come," says the wise son of Sirach, "to serve the Lord,
prepare thy heart for temptation." (Ecclus. 2: 1.) There is then
no exemption in this moral warfare; and the rule applicable to all
sinful inticements is, "Consent thou not." (יִפְתּוּךָ, Piel Fut. of בָּהָה
with suffix. תֹּבֵא put for תֹּאבֵא, Kal fut. of אָבָה=אֹבֵא.)

11. The adverb חִנָּם, *chinnam*, may signify *without cause*, as it is
here rendered in our common version. In that case it would limit
the verb, and the sense of the line would be, 'Let us lurk secretly
and clandestinely in ambush to destroy the innocent man without
any provocation or justifiable cause, but simply from the desire of
plunder.' (See ch. 26: 2. Ps. 35: 7, 19.) So French and Noyes. Or

13. "Let us swallow them up alive, like sheol;
"And whole, as those that go down into the pit:

it may denote *in vain*, and qualify the noun נָקִי, *nâqi;* the meaning
would then be, 'Let us conceal ourselves in ambush for the purpose
of destroying him, who is indeed entirely innocent of wrong-doing,
but whose innocence shall afford him no protection.' (See v. 17.
Ezek. 6: 10.) The position of the adverb in the sentence would
seem to indicate that it was intended to modify the noun rather than
the verb. So Holden, Boothroyd and Stuart. The stealthy mode
of waylaying travellers here alluded to is still practiced by the no-
madic tribes of the East. (לְכָה=לְן with ה paragogic. Kal imperative of יָלַך.)

12. In the preceding verse the infamous conduct of highway
robbers in pursuit of plunder is portrayed in language properly applicable to the habits of wild beasts. The figure is continued in
this verse, and the same persons are described as proposing to spring
suddenly and unexpectedly upon their innocent victims and utterly
destroy them, so that no trace of them shall be left, just as the grave
swallows up, as it were, those who are deposited therein. The Hebrew word *sheol* (שְׁאוֹל) has no term of exactly equivalent power in
our language. It signifies generically the *lower* or *under-world*, the
invisible world, the *abode*, or *place of the dead.* It comprehends the
local habitation of the dead body, (the grave, or sepulchre,) and the
invisible abode of the soul, irrespective of its condition as happy or
miserable. It corresponds very nearly to the Greek *Hades* (ᾅδης.)
and the Latin *orcus* and *Infernus.* It is sometimes employed with
specific reference to the locality of the dead body, and accordingly
is frequently translated in our standard version *the grave,* as in the
present instance, or *the pit,* as synonymous with בּוֹר, *bor,* and קֶבֶר,
qeber. It is also frequently represented by the English word *Hell,*
which, at the time our standard version was made, (1611,) was employed in the same general and indefinite sense as the Hebrew
Sheol and the Greek *Hades.* But as that word has come to be employed exclusively in a limited sense to denote *the place of punishment*
in the invisible world, corresponding to the *Gehenna* (Γέεννα) of
the New Testament, it has ceased to be the appropriate representative of *sheol.* Most modern commentators, therefore, either transfer

13. "Like the grave," French—"like the under-world", Stuart—"as Hades does
the living," Holden—"as the under-world the living," Noyes.

13. "We shall find all (*kinds of*) precious treasure;
"We shall fill our houses with spoil;
14. "Thou shalt cast thy lot among us;
"We will all have one purse."

---

the Hebrew term, or adopt the Greek word *hades*, by which it is represented in the Septuagint version, leaving the precise sense in each place of its occurrence to be gathered from the context. Some, however, render it by the compound term *under-world*, in imitation of Gesenius and other German writers. We have transferred the original word, as being quite as intelligible to the English reader as the exotic Greek *Hades*. The term *pit*, in the parallel clause, shows that there is special allusion here to the *grave*, for in Hebrew parallelisms the specific term limits the signification of that which is more general. Comp. Ps. 16: 10, where the word *corruption*, in the second clause, can apply only to the body, and consequently limits the word *sheol* to the grave,—the receptacle of the body. Sheol is here, by personification, represented as a monster swallowing and utterly consuming the dead.

The adjective חַיִּים, *chayyim*, may be connected immediately with the verb נִבְלָעֵם, *niblaam*, and rendered as in our standard version; or it may be employed substantively as the object after the verb יִבְלַע, *yibla*, understood, and then it would denote *the living*, and the clause be rendered "Let us swallow them up, as sheol does the living." This last construction is adopted by Holden and Noyes, and is favored by the position of the word in the sentence— a circumstance, however, which is not conclusive. The first view is supported by Ps. 55: 15 (16.) and Ps. 124: 3, where the word occurs, and is rendered by *quick* in our standard version, and where there is probably an allusion to the sudden and entire destruction of Korah and his company. (Numb. 16: 30, 33.) "Usually, the grave devours or swallows up the dead; but the depredators, in this case, propose to do to the *living*, what the grave does to the dead, in consuming them, yet not literally, but figuratively. The idea is that of sudden and unexpected destruction in the midst of life, and in *the full state of health*." (Stuart.) For the phrase "go down to the pit," see Ps. 85: 4, Ezek. 26: 20. 31: 11.

13, 14. In these verses the plunderers are described as predicting with confidence the successful issue of their foray. Lit. *all pre-*

---

13. "*Valuable treasure*," Holden—"*precious wealth*," Stuart—"*precious substance*," S. V., French, Noyes.

15. My son, walk not thou in the way with them;
Refrain thy foot from their path;

16. For their feet run to evil;
And they make haste to shed blood.

17. Surely in vain the net is spread
In the sight of any bird!

18. But these (*men*) lie in wait for their own blood;
They lurk secretly for their own lives.

19. Such are the ways of every one that is greedy
of gain;
It taketh away the life of its possessors.

---

cious treasure, i. e., treasure of every kind. In the expression "to cast thy lot among us," there is allusion to the custom among freebooters of dividing their plunder by lot; and the sense is, 'Though thou art young and inexperienced in enterprises of this kind, thou shalt have an equal share in the booty with ourselves, who are veterans of the trade; and whenever we determine, by casting lots, to whom any portion of the plunder shall belong, thou shalt draw lots with us, and stand an equal chance of appropriating it to thyself.' See Ps. 22: 18. "We will all have one purse," is literally "one purse shall be to us all," *i. e.*, 'the money we obtain shall be placed in one common purse, of which all shall have right to an equal share. No discrimination will be used, and no preference shown to one above another.' (בְּתֵינוּ, Irreg. plur. of בַּיִת, with suffix, תָּפִיל, Hiph. fut. of רָפַל.)

15, 16. Solomon here warns his youthful reader against associating with persons like those described in the preceding verses; for the path they tread, though it may be strewed with flowers, is only a path of evil—perhaps of blood. Syriac: "*innocent* blood." "To run to evil," is an idiomatic expression denoting an eager desire to commit wickedness. See Isa. 59: 7, a parallel passage. (תֵּלֵךְ, Kal fut. 2d pers. of יָלַךְ.)

17-19. Solomon here tells us that even the birds, though by no means remarkable for caution and foresight, have discernment enough to perceive, and instinct sufficient to avoid, the destructive net when placed before their eyes. But the men whom he has just described, less wary than the birds, in their eager pursuit of unjust gain, rush on to their own destruction. Some commentators suppose the meaning of the sacred writer to be, that, as the bird does not take warning, even when it sees the net prepared for its capture, so the persons in question, while busily employed in plotting against the property and lives of others, are blind to the ruin which their misdeeds are sure ultimately to bring on themselves. Comp. ch. 7: 23. Gain greedily sought, and acquired by unlawful and unrighteous means, often proves the temporal as well as spiritual ruin of those who are led captive by it. "How great a cheat is wickedness. It consumeth the ensnarers, and murders the murderers; holds a dark lantern in one hand, while with the other it discharges silently a pistol into our bosoms." (Jermin.) *Any bird*—lit. *every possessor of a wing*—poetic for bird. *Greedy of gain*—lit. *plundering the plunder*—a usual Hebraism to express intensity. (מְזוֹרָה, Pual part. of זָרָה, with vav. fulcrum. יְקַח, Kal fut. of לָקַח.)

CHAPTER I. 20–23.

[Heavenly Wisdom personified and represented under the character of a Female Teacher, invites all men to attend to her Instructions and embrace her Precepts, and warns them of the consequences of neglecting God and Divine things.]

20. Wisdom crieth aloud without;
    In the wide streets she uttereth her voice;

---

20. Many expositors are of the opinion that our Saviour Jesus Christ, the second person in the adorable Trinity, is here characterized by the term Wisdom, and that this chapter is throughout prophetical of him and his ministry on earth, and of the calamities which should fall upon the Jews for their rejection of him. But it seems far more consonant with the character of this book to regard Wisdom here as True Religion, personified after the Oriental manner, and represented as a female teacher, who, having opened her school, and taken her station at the places of usual concourse, earnestly and affectionately invites all whom she sees to forsake the paths of ignorance, folly, and sin, and to attend upon her instruc-

21. At the head of the noisy streets she calleth;
At the entrance of the gates;
In the city she uttereth her words;
22. "How long, ye simple (*ones*), will ye love sim-
plicity?
"(*How long*) will scoffers delight in scoffing?
"And fools hate knowledge?

---

tions. (תָּדִנָה, Kal fut. 3d pers. fem. of רָנַן, the fem. ending וָה
being added to distinguish it from the 2d pers. masc. So ch. 8: 3.
חָכְמוֹת is plural in form, but sing. in meaning. תִּתֵּן, Kal fut. fem.
from נָתַן.)

21. The *gates* of the city were the places of general resort in
ancient times. There were the *market-places* and the forum, where
causes were judicially tried, and there the inhabitants' resorted
either for business or friendly conversation. What the *Bourse* is in
Paris and the Exchange in London, the open spaces about the gates
of the walled towns were to the Orientals, and still are in many
parts of the East. הוֹמִיּוֹת, *homiyyoth*, Kal Part. fem. plur., used
substantively from הָמָה *hama*, to *make a noise*. The Sept. Syr. Chald.
and Arab. versions, however, read "on the top of the *walls*," as if
from חוֹמוֹת, *chomoth*, i. e. the city-walls.

22. This triplet forms a gradational parallelism, in which one
term rises above another, and the thought expressed in the second
member is an advance on that which is expressed in the first, and
so of the third. The terms *simple, scoffers*, and *fools*, are descriptive
of three distinct classes of persons, one rising above another in guilt
and wickedness. The first appears to comprise those, who, from
inexperience, natural infirmity and credulousness, easily fall into
the snare laid for them by the crafty and designing, and thus at
length become similar in character to their treacherous corruptors
and deceivers. The second class embraces such as scoff at and
deride religion, even though they be found in the ranks of the out-
wardly moral and respectable. The third class is composed of those
who have become still more hardened, abandoned and vicious.
Comp. Ps. 1: 1, where a similar parallelism occurs. (יֶאֱהָבוּ, Piel
fut. of אָהַב. לֵצִים, Kal. part. plur. of לִיץ.)

---

22. "*And ye scoffers delight*."—Holden and Boothroyd.

23. "Turn ye at my reproof!
"Behold, I will pour out my spirit upon you;
"I will make known my words to you.

24. "Because I have called, and ye have refused;
"(*Because*) I have stretched out my hand, and no
one hath regarded;—

25. "But ye have rejected all my counsel,
"And have slighted my reproof;

26. "I myself will laugh at your calamity,
"I will deride when your fear cometh;

---

23. To the several classes of persons named in the preceding verse, Wisdom addresses herself, and exhorts them to forsake their dangerous paths and evil ways, to sit at her feet, to listen to her reproof, counsel and advice, and to follow implicitly her teachings. To such as listen to her voice and obey her instructions, she promises in abundant measure the communication of her own enlightening, hallowing, ennobling and purifying spirit. She declares that she will impart to them such instructions as will enable them to escape the snares of death, and make them wise unto salvation. The precepts and promises of True Religion go hand in hand. Obedience is sure to be followed by its appropriate reward. No one is asked to serve God in vain; for the ways of piety are invariably ways of pleasantness, and all her paths peace. (תָּשֻׁבוּ, Kal fut. put for the Imperative. אַבִּיעָה, Hiph. fut. of נָבַע. אוֹדִיעָה, Hiph. fut. of יָדַע.)

24, 25. *Ye have refused*, viz. to listen to my instructions. To *stretch out the hand*, is here to be regarded as a beckoning gesture, inviting the hearer to approach, and not as one designed to enforce the language of the speaker, or to offer assistance to one needing help. See Isai. 65: 2. *Have slighted my reproof*, is literally *have not been willing* viz. to profit by my reproof. (הְמִיאָנוּ, Piel fut. of מָאָן. מַקְשִׁיב, Hiph. part. of קָשַׁב.)

26. The speaker here takes his stand at the close of man's probationary period, or at least looks forward in anticipation to the time when the final trial and retribution shall take place, and intimates what treatment the incorrigible sinner may then expect to receive from her who would have guided him into the way of life. *I myself*, or *Even I*, is emphatic: 'I who have warned and entreated you so often and so earnestly, who have borne your rebuffs so long

27. " When your fear cometh like a tempest; .
" And your calamity approacheth as a whirlwind ;
" When distress and anguish come upon you.

28. " Then will they call upon me, but I will not
answer ;   .
" They will seek me diligently, but they shall not
find me.   .

---

and so patiently, and who sought only your true happiness,—even
I will in the hour of your utmost need regard you as my enemies
and leave you to reap the bitter fruits and suffer the just consequences
of your folly and perversity. *Laughing at* and *deriding* are figurative expressions denoting the highest and most contemptuous indignation. Comp. Ps. 2: 5. The English verb *to mock* is now commonly employed in the sense of *to mimic*, which is plainly not the
meaning of the writer. *Your fear* is here put by metonymy for the
object of fear, rather than the emotion. ' 'I will deride when that
which you fear—that calamity which causes terror and alarm to you,
—will suddenly and inevitably come upon you, and overwhelm you
like a tempest and a whirlwind.' So φοβος is used in 1 Pet. 3: 14.
(בְּבֹא, Kal Infin. constr. of בֹּוא with prefix prep.)

27. The imagery employed here is exceedingly vivid and awful.
(שָׁאֲוה. The consonants of the text require to be pointed and read
שַׁאֲוה. But the Masorites or Jewish punctists to whom we are indebted for the Hebrew text as it now stands, have pointed the word
in accordance with the Keri, or marginal reading, שׁוֹאָה=שׁוֹאֲה, for
which see Gesen. Lex.)   .

28. The sudden change of persons from the second to the third
is a circumstance of frequent occurrence in the Hebrew Scriptures.
It is well suited here to the dramatic character of the whole representation. Those to whom Wisdom had been calling and beckoning
—whom she had entreated to listen to her words of kindness and
to give heed to her counsels, are now supposed to have passed along
the high way regardless of her friendly and affectionate warnings,
and to be beyond the reach of her voice. Perceiving that her entreaties are of no avail, she turns away, not in anger, but in sorrow,
and, soliloquising, continues to speak of them in the third person,
and to paint in vivid colors the certain misery consequent on unre-

---

27. " *Advances as*," Stuart—"*overtaketh*," trench and Noyes.

29. " Because they have hated knowledge,
" And have not chosen the fear of Jehovah ;—

30. " (*Because*) they have slighted my counsel,
" And despised all my reproof ;—

31. " Therefore shall they eat of the fruit of their own way,
" And be filled with their own devices.

32. " For the turning away of the simple shall slay them,

---

pented and unforsaken sin. *Then*—when the day of reckoning shall come, the wicked who have transgressed God's law, who have persisted in their rebellion, and rejected with scorn the invitations and overtures of mercy, will call upon the Most High, but in vain. Prayer, once omnipotent, will then be powerless. The verb שָׁחַר, *shachar*, rendered in our standard version *to seek early*, properly signifies *to break, to break forth*, as the light or dawn of day. Hence the kindred noun שַׁחַר, *shachar*, denotes *the dawn, the morning*. It then acquires the secondary meaning of *to seek*, and intensively *to seek carefully, diligently, earnestly*, as those may be supposed to do who in pursuit of some desired object, rise early, and commencing their search on the first appearance of the light, pursue it with the utmost diligence till they discover it. The connexion shows that the allusion here is not so much to the *time* when the search commences, as to the *manner* in which it is prosecuted. See ch. 7: 15. 11: 27. All the diligence with which men may apply themselves to obtain renewing and sanctifying grace and pardoning mercy, after the period of their probation shall have terminated, will not avail to redeem the time past in forgetfulness of God, and secure the blessings promised only to the faithful.

31. As it is just that men should reap according to what they have sown, and eat such fruit as they have planted, so the ungodly shall suffer the punishment due to their transgressions, and *be filled, sated, glutted, surfeited* (for such is the intensive meaning of the original) with the inevitable results of their own plans, devices and crimes. The allotments of eternity will be according to the character formed and the course of conduct pursued in time. This is not only accordant with the principles of the strictest justice, but results as a necessary consequence from the very nature of things.

32. The *turning away* or defection of the obdurate transgressor

"And the security of fools shall destroy them ;

33. "But he that hearkeneth to me shall dwell safely,
"And shall be tranquil without fear of evil."

---

from proffered instruction and admonition will prove his ruin; and the careless *security*—that fancied security, which results from reck-lessness, unbelief, and disregard of divine things, and begets a fatal tranquility, ease and unconcern—will terminate in his utter destruc-tion. So Gesenius (Lex.), Boothr. and Stuart.

33. The preposition מֵ *me*, before פַּחַד *Phachar*, seems plainly to have here the signification of *without* rather than *from*, for the phrase *quiet* or *tranquil from fear*, would mean *quiet through* or *by reason of fear*, which is evidently very far from the true idea, which is that he shall be exempt from fear. So Stuart. "Shall not be disquieted by (or with) the fear of evil." French and Noyes. (שַׁאֲנַן, Pilel from שָׁאַן, not used in Kal.)

CHAPTER II.

[The benefits attending the pursuit of true wisdom, and the evils to be avoided by its possession.]

1. My son, if thou wilt receive my words,
And treasure up my commandments within thee :—

---

1. The earnest appeal of Wisdom personified terminates with the close of the preceding chapter; Solomon here resumes his ad-dress to his youthful readers, and points out the proper course to be pursued in order to the attainment of that knowledge which makes men wise unto salvation. There must be the disposition first to *receive* the precepts of divine truth, and then to *treasure them up* or carefully keep them in the memory or in the heart, not for conceal-ment, but for custody and use. (תִּקְח—Kal fut. of לָקַח.)

---

32. "*The carelessness of fools,*" Holden and Noyes—"*recklessness,*" French—"*tranquillity,*" Junius, Piscator.

2. If thou wilt apply thy ear to wisdom,
And incline thy heart to understanding;
3. Yea, if thou wilt call for knowledge,
And utter aloud thy voice for understanding;
4. If thou wilt seek her as silver,
And search for her as for hidden treasure;—

---

2. Respectful, earnest and serious attention to divine things, and the application of the whole mind and heart to them, are necessary to secure their possession and enjoyment. To *apply the ear*, signifies to place oneself in a listening attitude. Literally it is *to erect* or *prick up* the ear, a metaphor borrowed from those animals who point or prick up their ears in listening, in order to catch more easily any passing sound. (הַקְשִׁיב, Hiph. infin. from הִקְשִׁיב. תַּטֶּה, Hiph. fut. from נָטָה.)

3. The terms employed in this and the following verse are designed still further to indicate the earnestness with which we are to apply ourselves to the attainment of true religion. The word תִּתֵּן, *titten*, properly signifies *to give forth* the voice, and here, from the exigency of the passage, *to utter aloud*. Alas! how few manifest any considerable measure of this earnestness in their pursuit of heavenly wisdom.

4. *As silver—as for hidden treasure*, i. e., with that eagerness and earnestness which men display in their search for silver and hidden treasure. True religion is called in Isaiah 33: 6, *a treasure*, and by our Saviour it is compared to a treasure hidden in a field. It is indeed a treasure beyond all price; but though it be the free gift of God (ver. 6), it must be sought in the use of all appropriate and divinely appointed means. When these means are employed as God directs, with all faithfulness, sincerity and humility, a blessing will attend them, and the desired object will be obtained. Of special importance is prayer. "There may be attention, earnestness, sincerity; yet without one spiritual impression upon the conscience, without one ray of Divine light in the soul. Earthly wisdom is gained by study; heavenly wisdom by prayer. Study may form a Biblical scholar; prayer puts the heart under a heavenly pupilage, and therefore forms the wise and spiritual christian. The word first comes into the ears; then it enters into the heart; there it is safely hid; thence arises *the cry—the lifting up of the voice* in awakened prayer." (Bridges.) But prayer must not stand alone, or in the

5. Then shalt thou understand the fear of Jehovah,
And find the knowledge of God.

6. (For Jehovah giveth wisdom;
From his mouth (*proceed*) knowledge and understanding;

7. He layeth up safety for the righteous;
A shield is he to those that·walk uprightly.

---

stead of diligence. It should rather give life and energy to exertion
Ora et labora, "Pray and labor," is the old and true maxim. Comp.
Matt. 11: 12. "We are all," says the heavenly-minded Leighton,
"too little in the humble seeking and begging this divine knowledge; and that is the cause, why we are so shallow and small pro-
ficients. 'If thou cry and lift·up thy voice for understanding, and
search for it as for hid treasure,' get down upon thy knees, and dig
for it. That is the best posture to fall right upon the golden vein,
and go deepest to know the mind of God, in searching the Scriptures, to be directed and regulated in his ways: to be made skillful
in ways of honoring him and doing him service." (תַּחְפְּשֶׂנָּה, Kal
fut. of חָפַשׂ, with suff. of the 3d pers. fem.)

5. This verse and the 9th form the apodosis of the sentence, while
the four preceding verses make up the protasis.

6. Verses 6–8 are parenthetical, and thrown in for the purpose
of assigning the ground of the assurance contained in the preceding
verse. It is the immutable and omnipotent Jehovah, who imparts
true wisdom and the highest and best knowledge to those who earnestly and sincerely desire them. He is emphatically the author
of every good gift, and no good thing will be withheld from those
who are of an upright mind. (See Job 32: 8. Dan. 2:21. James 1:
5, 17.)

7. He *layeth up* as a treasure safety or help for the righteous, *i. e.,*
he is their ever ready helper and·protector. The word תּוּשִׁיָּה,
tushiyya, occurs in ch. 3: 21, 8: 14, and 18: 1., where it is translated
in our standard version *sound wisdom.* The *usus loquendi* of the
writer would therefore favor the same rendering here. But the ancient versions give it a different meaning, as synonymous with
תְּשׁוּעָה, *teshua.* Thus the Sept. σωτήριαν, *salvation;* the Vulg.
salutem, safety, which is clearly supported by the parallelism. A

---

7. "*Salvation,*" Boothr.—"*help,*" Stuart.

- 8. He keepeth the paths of justice,
  And preserveth the way of his saints.)

9. Then shalt thou understand righteousness and justice,
  And uprightness, yea, every good path.

---

similar example occurs in Job 6: 13, where the parallelism requires the rendering *help, safety, succor*. So Gesenius (Lex.) God is called *a shield* in ch. 30: 5. Deut. 33: 29. Ps. 3: 3. 18: 2. (The Hebrew word וְעֵינָם, in the text would be normally pointed יֵעֵנִם; but the marginal Keri bids us read יֵצֵנִם, which is the reading found in many manuscripts, and is probably the true one, as it is a continuation of יִתֵּן in ver. 6.)

8. The Hebrew in the first member of this verse reads, "*for keeping* the paths of justice." The subject, therefore, may be either *God*, or *the upright* spoken of in the preceding verse. If the former is the subject, then the sense is either that God protects and guards the just and upright—*justice* being the abstract used for the concrete, viz. those who walk in the paths of justice and equity; which is favored by the parallelism: or, that God always does what is right—or shows that he discriminates between the pious and the ungodly. If *the pious* spoken of in vs. 7, are the subject, then the clause may be explanatory of "those who walk uprightly," as Piscator and Boothr. suppose, or it may indicate the purpose and design of God in affording protection to the righteous, viz. in order that they may keep the precepts of justice and equity; form a right judgment in regard to all moral questions, accurately discriminate between good and evil, and discharge their sacred duties in a proper manner. There is no grammatical impediment in the way of joining this clause in construction with the preceding, and the sense thereby elicited is good. We prefer, however, in a doubtful case like this, to adhere to the rendering of the ancient versions and our standard translation, which is approved by the majority of interpreters.

9. This verse is immediately connected with vs. 5, and forms a part of the apodosis of the sentence, indicated by the correlative conjunction *then* (אז, *az*.) It contains a specification and comprehensive summary of the things which should be most desired by man, and which are assured to him, if he will attend to the teach-

---

8. "*To them that keep the paths of judgment*," Boothr.—"*his pious worshippers*," French—"*his servants*," Noyes.

10. When wisdom entereth into thy heart,
And knowledge is pleasant to thy soul;
11. Discretion shall preserve thee,.
Understanding shall keep thee;
12. To deliver thee from the way of the wicked—
From the men that speak perverse things;—
13. Who forsake the paths of uprightness,
To walk in the ways of darkness;—

ings of wisdom. The last expression, *every good path*, is generic, comprising every desirable good. *To understand*, here imports to know experimentally and practically.

10. The particle כִּי, *ki*, is here taken by Stuart and some other commentators in a causal sense, and rendered *for, because*. But the meaning is plainer if, with all the older interpreters, we take it in the conditional sense of *if* or *when*, and regard it as the protasis, or antecedent of the hypothetical proposition, and the next verse as the apodosis, or consequent of it. So Gen. 4: 12, and elsewhere.

11. Discretion and understanding are here personified, and represented as watching over the youthful aspirant after virtue, and protecting him from the allurements of vice. See ch. 6: 12. The image is taken from the custom of military guards keeping watch over the safety and tranquility of the city.

12. The phrase מִדֶּרֶךְ רָע, *midderek' ra*, may be rendered *from the way of evil*, i e., from the way which leads to evil or sin; or, *from the evil way*, i. e., from a vicious course of life,—the second noun limiting the first as an adjective. The latter is the rendering of the Sept. Vulg. and Chaldee. But the parallelism seems to require that רָע, *ra*, should be taken in a concrete sense, as a noun of multitude, denoting the wicked in general, corresponding with the second member of the verse, where they are particularly described as those who speak perverse things. So Boothr, Holden, French and Noyes. *From the men*—literally, *from the man*. But the word אִישׁ, *ish*, is here used in a collective sense, as is evident from the fact that the predicates which follow are plural. *Perverse things*, i. e., who speak falsely and deceitfully. (הַיְצֵל. Hiph. infin. of נָצַל.)

13. In the preceding verse, the writer alludes to the *speech* of the wicked; here, to their general conduct—*ways of darkness*, i. e., ways

12. " *The way of evil*," Junius, Piscat, Stuart—" *the evil way*," Geier, Dathe, Rosenmu.

14. Who rejoice in doing evil,
And delight in the perverseness of the wicked;—
15. Whose ways are crooked,
And who in their paths are perverse.
16. To deliver thee from the strange woman;
From the stranger who uttereth smooth words;
17. Who forsaketh the friend of her youth,

---

of sin. Sin is often represented in Scripture under the figurative term darkness. See Rom. 13: 12. Eph. 5: 11. *To walk*, i. e., in order that they may walk. "They choose darkness rather than light, because their deeds are evil." (לָלֶכֶת, Kal infin constr. of יָלַךְ.)

14. *The wicked*—Sept. "wicked perverseness,"—Stuart, "evil perversions." But as the idea of *evil* is implied in the terms *perverseness* and *perversions*, some suppose that the expression is intensive, and equivalent to *the most profligate deeds*. So Boothr. Vulgate —"in rebus pessimis." But we prefer to take the term in the concrete and collective sense, as in vs. 12,

16. The construction of this verse is similar to that of verse 12. Discretion and understanding (v. 11) will so guard thee as *to deliver thee*, &c. In the earlier periods of Jewish history, women of profligate habits and abandoned character among the Hebrews were for the most part *strangers* and *aliens*, belonging to some one of the neighboring heathen nations. The terms, however, which are here used, זָרָה, *zara*, (a participial noun from זוּר, *zur*, and denoting *one who turns aside*, viz. from the paths of rectitude,) and נָכְרִיָּה, *nakriyya*, came in process of time to be employed to designate persons of this class, irrespective of their origin, and hence were sometimes applied, as in the present instance, to Hebrew women, because their conduct resembled that of foreign or heathen women. That the woman here referred to was of Hebrew origin, is evident from v. 17, where she is represented as *forgetting the covenant of her God*. An *adulteress* is here particularly alluded to, and adultery is the crime specifically condemned. But what is here said applies equally, by sound principles of construction, to incontinence and unchastity generally. *Smooth words* here denote *flattering, enticing*, and *deceitful language*, employed for the purpose of alluring the unwary into the paths of sin.

17. *Friend.* See ch. 16: 28. 17: 9, where the same word is ren-

---

17. "*The guide of her youth*,"—S. V., Holden, Boothr.

And forgetteth the covenant of her God.
18. For her house sinketh down to death,
And her paths to the shades.

---

dered in our Standard Version *friend.* The word אַלּוּף, *alluph,* comes
from אָלַף, *alaph,* which from the Arabic sig. *to join together, to asso·
ciate.* Our Translators, following the Vulgate (dux) and other
Latin versions, have rendered it in this and several other places,
(Ps. 55: 13. Jere. 3: 4. Mich. 7: 5,) *guide.* But the meaning here
given to it is equally appropriate in all these places, and is better
supported by the context. It is accordingly adopted by most modern expositors. (See Gesen. Lex.) By *the friend of her youth,* some
suppose *Jehovah* to be intended (compare Jere. 3: 20. Isa. 54: 5);
others, a *father,* or *guardian,* who is the natural protector of youthful
beauty. (Holden.) But the majority of commentators, with much
more probability, understand by the expression the *husband,* to
whom the female in question had been married in early life. See
Joel 1: 8. So *vice versa* a married woman is called repeatedly *the
wife of youth,* i. e., married in youth. Prov. 5: 18. Mal. 2: 15. In
the expression *the covenant of her God,* there is allusion to the marriage covenant, in which appeal was made to God, who was invoked
to witness the mutual vows and promises made by the contracting
parties.

18. Some commentators regard the noun מוּת, *muth, death,* as the
abstract put for the concrete, *the dead,* and so translate it. But it is
more poetical as well as forcible to regard it as a personification of
the king of terrors, who exercises sway and dominion over the
lower world, (שְׁאוֹל, *shcol,* ᾅδης, *Hades,*) where he has his dwelling-
place. The sense, however, is the *region,* or *abode* of the dead. See
Job 28: 22. Ps. 9: 14. By the corresponding term רְפָאִים, *rephaim,*
(the *shades*) in the second member, (lit. *the weak*) is denoted the
spectres or *ghosts* of the departed dead, (the *manes* and *umbræ* of the
Latins,) which the Hebrews supposed to dwell in *sheol.* These appear to have been regarded as destitute of blood and animal life,
but yet as possessed of some faculties of mind. (See Gesenius'
Lex.) The terms employed serve to convey to our minds some idea
of the imperfect conceptions entertained by the early Hebrews regarding the separate existence and faculties of the soul. In the

---

18. " *Her paths unto the dead,*" S. V., French,; Holden—" *to the mansions of the
dead,*" Noyes.

19. None that go to her return,
Nor do they attain to the paths of life.

20. That thou mayest walk in the way of good (men),
And keep the paths of the righteous;

21. For the upright shall dwell in the land,
And the perfect shall remain in it.

22. But the wicked shall be cut off from the land,
And transgressors shall be rooted out of it.

---

expression found in the first clause of the verse there is an allusion
to the earth swallowing up Korah, his company, and their habita
tions. The sentiment inculcated is, that destruction and ruin are
sure to be the result of illicit and criminal indulgence of passion.
(שָׁעָ֫תָה, Kal preter 3d pers. fem. from שִׁ֫יַח.)

19. *Return*, viz. fr m the way which leads to destruction. *Paths
of life*, i. e. which lead to a tranquil and happy life. It is here intimated that it is as difficult for one who has become intimate with
an adulteress to recover from the temporal and moral ruin in which
such intimacy involves him,'as it would be for one who has departed
to the world of the dead to return to the abodes of the living. The
imagery is borrowed from travellers, who having once departed from
the right way, are unable afterwards to find it   (יְשׁוּ֫בוּן, Hiph. fut. of
שׁוּב, not used in Kal.)

20. This verse is logically connected with verse 11. Discretion
and understanding shall keep and preserve thee, *in order that* thou
mayest walk in the way of the good, &c.   לְמַ֫עַן, *lemaan*, corresponds
with לְ, *lamed*, at the beginning of vs. 12 and 16.   So Geier, Le Clerc,
Stuart, and others.   Some, however, as Holden, Bothr., French and
Noyes, render it *Therefore*, and regard the verse as constituting an
inference from the discourse immediately preceding.

21. By *the land*, is doubtless particularly intended the land of
Canaan, for the sacred writer is speaking of and to Hebrews; but
his remarks are equally applicable to all lands, and to every people.   Comp. Matt. 5: 6.   The expression *perfect* is not to be taken in
an absolute, unqualified sense, but relatively and comparatively.
The sentiment is, that the upright shall be spared from death and
enjoy long life in contradistinction to the wicked, who "shall be
cut off" in the midst of their days.

22. *To be cut off*, and *rooted out*, (lit. *plucked up by the roots*,) from

the land, denote the utter destruction by an untimely death of transgressors and of their offspring, who tread in their steps. The
imagery is taken from the cutting down and rooting up of trees.
Comp. Ps. 37: 34.

CHAPTER III. 1–10.

*[Exhortation to obedience, to reliance upon God, and to the payment
of the offerings prescribed by the Mosaic law.]*

1. My son, forget not my teaching,
But let thy heart keep my commandment,
2. For length of days, and years of life,
And peace shall they add to thee.

---

1. *Teaching.* See ch. 1: 8. The word *commandment* is here used
in a collective sense, and the precept applies to all the laws of God.

2. A long, happy, and prosperous life is frequently alluded to in
this book, as the natural consequence of obedience to the divine
commands, and a strict and faithful adherence to the principles of
integrity and uprightness (see ch. 9: 11. 10: 27); while, on the contrary, a short life, and premature, perhaps violent death, are described as the result and just punishment of disobedience and
iniquity. (see ch. 2: 21.) All such statements are of course to be
taken as *general*, and not *universal* propositions. The fifth commandment of the Decalogue is of the same tenor. Temperance,
chastity, probity and industry—virtues inseparable from true piety
—do in the natural course of things, and in accordance with the
laws which govern the physical and moral world, conduce to the
health of the body, to the tranquility of the mind, to prosperity
and longevity. The rendering *years of life* is more literal and less
prosaic than *long life*. So Marg. Reading. And *peace*, i. e., prosperity
or good of every kind. *Shall they add* is equivalent here to the passive
will be added or multiplied. (The Hiph. יוֹסִיפוּ, is employed as a
substitute for the future of Kal, which is not used.)

---

1. "*My admonitions,*" Boothr.—"*my doctrine,*" Holden—"*my instruction,*" Stuart.

3. Let not mercy and truth forsake thee:
Bind them around thy neck,
Inscribe them on the tablet of thy heart.
4. So shalt thou find favor and good success,
In the sight of God and man.

---

3. By *mercy and truth* may here be intended objectively the kindness or mercy and faithfulness of God towards us; (Comp. ch. 14: 22), and then the words contain an exhortation to conduct in such a manner as not to provoke Jehovah to withdraw the manifestation of his regard from us, and to withhold the fulfilment of his promises. Or, the expression may refer subjectively to the reciprocal duties of humanity, mercy, sincerity, kindness and truthfulness on the part of man towards his fellow-man. (Comp. ch. 20: 28.) The context favors the latter interpretation. Act not in such a manner as to indicate that you are destitute of benignity, truthfulness and fidelity, but on the contrary let these virtues be conspicuously and habitually displayed in your conduct, and be the objects of your pride and regard. Neck jewels were among the ornaments most commonly worn by Eastern females. The imagery here employed is supposed by some to be drawn in part from Deut. 6: 8, to which there is evidently an allusion. It was a custom prevailing among the ancient Hebrews, founded on a literal interpretation of that passage, to wear on their foreheads and wrists precepts of the law written on slips of parchment. The figurative expression, *tablet of the heart*, occurs in ch. 7: 3. Jere. 17: 1. 2 Cor. 3: 3, and contains an allusion to the two tables or slabs of stone on which the Decalogue was engraved by the finger of God. Some Commentators regard the first clause as · containing a *promise* rather than a *precept*, and translate it, "Loving kindness and truth shall not forsake thee." But this mode of construction disturbs the contiguity of thought between this clause and the two following members of the verse, and requires an unnecessary departure from the ordinary import of the particle אַל *al.* (יִצֹּר, Kal fut. of יָצַר.)

4. *Thou shalt find*—Lit. *and find*, the imperative form of the verb being carried forward from the preceding verse in the sense of the future. The reward or fruit of adopting the course recommended, and exhibiting the virtues spoken of in the preceding verse, is here subjoined. This is two-fold; as it regards others, both God and ·

· 3. " *Kindness and faithfulness*," Stuart. 4. " *Favor and kindness*," Holden— " *and great esteem*," Boothr.

5. Trust in Jehovah with all thy heart,
And lean not on thy own understanding.
6. In all thy ways acknowledge him,
And he will make thy paths plain.

---

man, *favor*: as it regards the possessor, *good success, prosperity*. The marginal reading of שֵׂכֶל, *Sekel*, is *good success*, which is preferable to *good understanding*. It denotes a good not yet in possession of the person addressed, whereas the very fact of obedience to the foregoing precepts, shows the previous possession of a good understanding. The root in Hiph. הִשְׂכִּיל, *hiskil*, frequently sig. *to be successful*, to *prosper* (see Deut. 29: 9. Josh. 1: 7, 8. Prov. 17: 1); and this signification of the derived noun is quite suitable to the context. So Junius,-Noyes, Stuart, and Marg. Reading. The sentiment of the couplet is, that favor with God and man, and real prosperity shall attend him, who treasures up in his memory and heart, and exemplifies in his daily conduct, the precepts here inculcated. (Comp. ch. 13: 15.)

5. Here follow several excellent precepts concerning the sincere worship of God, the first of which relates to entire trust and confidence in him, as opposed to self-confidence. Trust is natural to a dependent creature, although trust in Jehovah is abhorrent to the feelings and inclinations of wicked men. As the most sceptical in regard to revealed religion are often the most credulous in respect to other things, so those who are the most unwilling to trust in God, are ever ready to put implicit confidence in their fellow-men or their own judgment and sagacity. . But although we are thus reluctant to cast ourselves on the protecting arm of the Almighty, and to repose our confidence in him, the only firm and reliable support at all times and under all circumstances for the soul of man, is the Lord our Righteousness, He will never deceive, never disappoint us. *With all the heart*, is with the undivided and undissembled sincerity of our souls, devoid of all hypocrisy and deceit. The phrase is used in opposition to *a double heart*. Ps. 12: 2. *Lean not* for support, as one leans upon a staff, *i. e.*, rely not with confidence. (Comp. 2 Kgs. 18: 21. 5: 18. Isa. 10: 20.) (תִּשָּׁעֵן. Niph fut. of שָׁעַן, not used in Kal.)

6. The next precept enjoined is the devout acknowledgment and recognition of God in all our ways, which is the inseparable com-

---

6. "*Make straight thy paths*," Stuart—"*direct thy paths*," S. V., Holden, Boothr.

7. Be not wise in thy own eyes;
Fear Jehovah, and depart from evil.
8. It shall be a healing medicine.to thy body,
And moisture to thy bones.

---

panion of faith and confidence. In the whole curiculum of life, in private as well as public business, in secular as well as sacred things, in prosperity as well as adversity, the good man recognizes God as his guide and counsellor, habitually acknowledges his superintending care and providence, and labors in every way and in all situations to promote his glory. To the precept in the first clause of the verse is subjoined the appropriate promise in the second. He will make plain paths for your feet. He will conduct you in the paths of duty, of virtue, and of happiness. (Comp. ch. 11: 5.) (רְעֵהוּ, Kal imperative of יָרַע, with pronominal suffix. יְשַׁר, Piel fut. of יָּשַׁר.)

7. The admonition in the first clause of this verse respecting modesty or humility flows naturally from the preceding precepts respecting sincere trust in God and a right acknowledgment of him. Be not puffed up with a vain conceit of thy own importance, thy knowledge, and superior wisdom. Self-confidence is often but another name for self-deception. Even the heathen moralist Seneca has said: "I suppose that many might have attained to wisdom, had they not thought that they had already attained to it." (Comp. Rom. 12: 16. 1 Cor. 8: 2. Gal. 6: 3.) *In thy own eyes,* i. e., in thy own opinion or conceit. *Fear Jehovah, &c.* This clause does not properly contain two distinct precepts, but one precept followed by a promise made on the condition implied in the promise; or a consequence naturally following the observance of the precept. 'Fear Jehovah, and then you will depart from evil.' The clause corresponds in form and import to Ps. 4: 4. "Stand in awe, and sin not,"—i. e., "Stand in awe, and then you will not sin.' So Gen. 42: 18. "*This do and* (you shall) *live.*" Ps. 37: 27. Prov. 7: 2. 9: 6. 20: 13, etc. (For this peculiar use of two imperatives joined by *and,* see Rodiger's Gesenius' Gram., sec. 127. 2, also sec. 152. 1. d.) The sentiment inculcated is, that the fear of Jehovah, or true religion, is the only sure safeguard and preservative against sin.

8 True religion is not only the best and only sure preservative against sin for the future, but an infallible remedy and antidote for the wounds which past sins have inflicted on the soul, It is here

· 9. Honor Jehovah with thy substance,
And with the first fruits of all thy produce.

---

compared to a healing medicine, the effect of which, applied to the disordered body, is to eradicate the disease and restore the part affected to its normal state. "Though thou art distempered with sin, · spiritually sick and diseased, so that from the sole of the foot to the crown of the head there is no soundness in thee, but wounds, and bruises, and putrifying sores, yet they will be bound up by the fear of Jehovah; they will be molified with the ointment of piety, and religion, and thou wilt be restored to pristine health and vigor." (Holden.) The noun רִפְאוּת, riphuth, the root of which is רָפָא, rapha, to *heal*, to *cure*, is not found elsewhere. It is rendered *health* by Sept., Boothr., Noyes,—*soundness* by French, and *healing* by Stuart. It seems rather to indicate the *instrument* by which health is restored to the diseased body, than the state of health, and then with Holden should be rendered *medicine*, or *healing medicine*. So Marg. reading. The word translated *body*, properly signifies *the navel*, as in the Standard Version. But it may be here put by synecdoche for the whole body. So Sept. Instead of *body*, however, the Syriac and Arabic versions read *flesh*, and this reading is favored by other passages where the bones and flesh are employed as corresponding terms in parallel distichs. See ch. 4: 22. 14: 30. Ps. 38: 3. In Eastern countries, great use is made of external applications to the stomach and bowels, as remedial agents in most of the maladies to which the people are subject. Thus Sir John Chardin remarks on this passage,—"It is a comparison drawn from the plasters, ointments, oils and frictions, which are made use of in the East in most maladies; they being ignorant in the villages of the art of making decoctions and potions, and the proper doses of such things, generally make use of external medicines." The word שִׁקּוּי, shiqqu, signifies *moisture*, or a *moistening* of the bones, the latter of which is the marginal reading. See Job 21: 24, where the root שָׁרָה, shaqa, occurs in Pual. Comp. also Prov. 15: 30. 17: 22. There is probably allusion to the *marrow*, which was supposed to keep the bones in a soft and healthy state. This was thought to be dried up by means of sickness and sorrow. Holden: *a lotion*.

9. The word הוֹן, *hun*, which is translated indiscriminately *riches*, *wealth*, *substance*, in our Standard Version, is here rendered in the Sept. *just labor*, i. e., with those things which thou hast acquired by just labor. We have in this precept the rule of sacri-

10. So shall thy barns be filled with plenty,
And thy vats shall overflow with new wine.

---

fice. It is a costly precept to the selfish and worldly man, but a
privilege as well as a duty to the real Christian. There is allusion
here to the statutes of the Mosaic laws which enjoined the presenta-
tion to Jehovah of the first fruits of the ground. Most of these
fruits were required to be offered at the Sanctuary, or given to the
priests for their use: but some were directed to be consumed in social festivity with the Levites and strangers, the widow and fatherless. And with regard to many of them, the proportion to be consecrated to Jehovah was left to the discretion of the offerers. (See
Ex. 23: 19. Deut. 26. Mal. 3: 10. Ecclus. 7: 29, 32.) The presenta-
tion of these offerings to God was regarded as a suitable expression
of gratitude to him for the blessings of his providence, and hence it
was viewed as an honor shown to Jehovah, and as such he was
pleased to accept them. No man is impoverished by contributing
of the abundance with which God has blessed him, to the support
and upholding of his kingdom and cause in the world, to the maintenance of public worship, the ministry of the Word, and the spread
of the Gospel. Indeed it is the way not to diminish but to increase
his worldly possessions, for God has promised to bestow in more
abundant measure his blessing upon the liberal giver, and to crown
with success his laudable undertakings. Deut. 28: 4, 5. 2 Chron.
31: 10.

10. The promise follows the precept. *Be filled with plenty*, i. e.,
plentifully, abundantly filled. *Thy vats*—the word יֶקֶב, *yeqeb*, some-
times denotes the *wine-press*, ($\lambda\eta\nu\acute{o}\varsigma$), i. e., the trough, or receptacle
in which the grapes were trodden with the feet, and from which the
expressed juice flowed into a lower vat placed near. But properly
it sig *the wine vat* ($\dot{v}\pi o\lambda\acute{\eta}\nu\iota o\nu$) into which the new wine or must
flowed. And such appears to be its meaning here. (See Joel 2: 24.
4: 13, [3: 13]. Hagg. 2: 16. Jere. 48: 33.) *Shall overflow.*—So the
verb פָּרַץ, *para'z*, here sig.. Neither the *wine-press* nor the *wine-vat*
can be said, as in our Standard Version, to burst from the quantity
of wine made; the term applying only to a wine-cask, or wine-skin.
New wine.—By *new* wine (תִּירוֹשׁ, *tirosh*,) here, is intended *must*, or
the new unfermented juice of the grape. Some, however, regard it
as denoting the *vintage fruit* before it is pressed, and not the liquid
wine.

3*

CHAPTER III. 11-20.

[*Exhortations to patience under the Divine chastisement, vs. 11, 12.
The inestimable value of true wisdom set forth, vs. 13–18. The
wisdom of God displayed in the creation of the heavens and the
earth.*]

**11. My son, despise not the chastening of Jehovah,
Nor be impatient under his correction.**

- 11. Up to this point the instructions of Solomon have respect to
what should be *done;* but now, to what should be *endured.* And
as the two preceding verses chiefly concern the prosperous and the
wealthy, so this verse and that which follows it, refer to the afflicted
and depressed. Prosperity and adversity, success and disappointment, are commingled in the present allotment of man. For one is
set over against the other, and serves to check and counteract the
evils which arise from the excess of either. Each is equally fruitful
in opportunity for honoring God, and each is equally necessary to
our moral and spiritual discipline and improvement. (Compare
Deut. 8: 5. Job 5: 17. Ps. 118: 12. Prov. 13: 24. Heb. 12: 5, 6. James
1: 6. Rev. 3: 19.) The Hebrew word מוּסָר, *musar,* signifies primarily, *instruction, teaching,* and then secondarily *restraint, correction,
chastisement,* as constituting a necessary part of that moral education
by which character is formed. (See ch. 22: 15. 23: 13.) Parental
correction wisely administered in a proper form and at the proper
time, for the purpose of salutary moral discipline, is no proof of
aversion or malevolence, but, on the contrary, an evidence of kindness and a suitable regard for the future well-being of the child.
Now Jehovah deals with us as with children. "The gem cannot
be polished without friction, nor man perfected without adversity."
Hence it is the duty of the Christian to bow meekly to the rod which
the all-wise disposer of events may see fit to apply, and seek to appropriate the lessons it may be designed to impress upon him.
"Non sentiri mala tua, non est hominis; et non ferre, non est viri."
"It is inhuman not to feel your afflictions ; and unmanly not to bear
them." (Seneca.) *To despise* a thing is to make light of it, to cast
it aside as of no value, meaning, or power. Afflictions which do
not happen by chance, but proceed from God, and which, apparently,
are not the immediate consequence of our own folly and wicked-

12. For whom Jehovah loveth he chasteneth,
Even as a father, the son in whom he delighteth.
13. Happy is the man that findeth wisdom;
And the man that getteth understanding.

---

ness, are worthy of special attention and prayerful consideration, just because they come from One who is as good as he is wise, and therefore must have some benevolent design in view, though that design may not be obvious to the unreflecting mind. Men *despise* such afflictions, when they treat them with affected or real unconcern; when they fail to receive them as Divine admonitions, having an intelligent purpose and design; or when perceiving the practical lessons which they are adapted to suggest, they fail to apply those lessons to the emendation of their errors and the due regulation of their lives. The second member of the verse is thus rendered in the Septuagint,—"Nor faint when thou art rebuked by him," and this rendering is followed by the author of the Epistle to the Hebrews. (See Heb. 12: 5.) The verb קוּץ, *quts*, however, never has any such meaning. The primary signification of the word is *to loathe, to feel disgust, to abhor;* and it is rendered by *loathe* or *abhor* in Num. 21: 5. 1 Kings 11: 25. Isa. 7: 16. The feeling indicated by it is not expressed with sufficient force by the word *weary*, in our Standard Version. I have rendered it *to be impatient*, after Boothr., French, and Noyes.

12. Solomon here assigns the reason why afflictions should be borne with fortitude and submission by the good man, viz., because they do not happen by chance, but are sent by God, not in anger, but in love, and from a regard to his salvation. The Hebrew manuscripts from which the Septuagint version was made, had no vowel points. Hence the translator mistook the noun אָב, *ab, father*, with the particle of comparison prefixed for a verb in the participial form, as though it were וְכָאָב, *vekaab*, instead of וּכְאָב, *ukeab*, and rendered it "and *scourgeth* every son." This version is followed in the Epistle to the Hebrews, ch. 12. 6. The rendering thus given suits the parallelism, but is not sustained by the Chaldee and Syriac, which support the Masoretic reading. (וְכִיחַ, Hiph. fut. of יָכַח.)

13. The Heavenly wisdom of which Solomon here speaks does not spring up spontaneously in the mind. It is something extrinsic—something *to be found* by diligent search—something *to be obtained*

---

13. "*Draweth forth understanding*," Stuart.

14. For the gain of her is better than the gain of silver,
    And her revenue than (*that of*) fine gold.

15. She is more precious than pearls:
    And all thy desirable things cannot be compared with her.

---

by faithful labor and application: by fervent, persevering prayer, and the study of God's Word. It has not an earthly origin, but descends from above, and is bestowed upon us and wrought in us by the Holy Spirit. The word rendered *getteth*, properly signifies *to draw out* from another, *to draw forth* something for one's own use, and here to draw forth or obtain from God, the source of all good. (Comp. ch. 8: 35. 18: 22. Ps. 144: 13. Isa. 55: 10.) To possess this wisdom is to enjoy the highest felicity which man is capable of enjoying in this life and the life to come. The word rendered *happy*, is plural in form. אַשְׁרֵי, *ashre*, literally, *Oh the happinesses* of the man —a strong and emphatic expression to indicate enjoyment of every kind and in the highest degree. So Ps. 1: 1. 32: 1. מָצָא, *matza*, Perfect, *has found and still finds*. (יָפִיק, Hiph. fut. of פּוּק.)

14. The gain or acquisition of true wisdom is here declared to be better or of more value to the possessor than the gain or acquisition of silver; and the benefit to be derived from it far superior to that which is obtained from the possession of the purest gold. The word סָחַר, *sachar*, properly sig. *gain* resulting from traffic in *merchandize*. (Comp. 31: 18. Isa. 23: 18.) The metaphor is therefore taken from mercantile pursuits and occupations. Sept. "It is better to traffic for her, than for treasures of gold and silver." (See ch. 8: 10, 18, 19. 16: 16.) The word חָרוּץ, *charutz*, (R. חָרַץ, *charatz*, *to dig*,) probably signifies *gold*, as *dug out of the earth*, in its native state, pure and unalloyed with base metals. All the ancient versions interpret it of the better sort of gold.

15. Verses 14 and 15 are climactic: the writer ascends from silver to gold, from gold to pearls, and from these to every desirable

---

14. " *The merchandize of it*," S. V , Holden—" *her merchandize* " Boothr.—" *For she can purchase better things than silver purchases*," French.=" *the produce of it*," Holden, Stuart—" *her increase*," Boothr.—" *And she produceth better things than doth fine gold*," French.

15. " *All thy jewels*," Stuart—" *all the objects of desire* " Boothr.—" *And none of thy precious things is to be compared*," French.

16. Length of days is in her right hand,
And in her left are riches and honor.
17. Her ways are ways of pleasantness,
And all her paths are peace.

---

thing. Sept. "And she is more valuable than precious stones; nothing evil shall resist her; she is well known to all who approach her, and no precious thing is equal to her in value."

16. Hitherto the dignity of wisdom is shown by comparison; now the rewards of wisdom follow. By an elegant personification, wisdom is represented as a queen dispensing her blessings and benefits to her followers *with both hands*—a form of expression designed to indicate the *abundance* of her gifts. It is highly probable that Solomon alludes here to the promise of God to him contained in 1 Kings 3: 11–14. 2 Chron. 1: 11, 12. Intelligent piety is eminently conducive, from its salutary influence on the mind and on the habits of life, to prolong human existence, and favor the acquisition of a worldly competency. The declaration of the Sacred writer, however, must not be regarded as of *universal*, but only of *general* application. "It is certainly not a uniform experience, that a man lives long in proportion as he lives well. Such a rule would obviously not be suitable to the present dispensation. It is true, that all wickedness acts as a shortener of life, and all goodness as its lengthener: but other elements enter into and complicate the result, and slightly veil the interior law. If the law were according to a simple calculation in arithmetic, 'the holiest liver, the longest liver,' and conversely, 'the more wicked the life, the earlier its close,' the moral government of God would be greatly impeded, if not altogether subverted." (Arnott.) For similar descriptions of the value of Heavenly Wisdom, See ch. 8: 11,18,19. Job 28: 12–28. The Sept. adds to this verse, "Out of her mouth proceeds righteousness; and she carries law and mercy upon her tongue."

17. The ways here mentioned are the ways which wisdom points out to those who choose her for a leader. *Pleasant ways*—comp. ch. 15: 26, (pleasant words). *Peace*—prosperity. Some ways are pleasant, but not free from danger; others are safe, but not pleasant. The ways of true wisdom, however, are all not only pleasant, but prosperous and safe and tranquil. They lead to solid and permanent happiness.

18. She is a tree of life to those that lay hold of her;
And happy is he who retaineth her.
19. Jehovah by wisdom hath founded the earth;
By understanding he hath established the heavens:
20. By his knowledge the depths were cleft asunder,
And the clouds distil the dew.

---

18. *A tree of life* denotes here not a *living tree* as opposed to one which is dead, but a tree whose fruit imparts or preserves life. There is allusion in the figure to the tree of life in the garden of Eden. (Gen. 2: 9. 3: 22.) As the tree of life in Paradise was a preserver of corporal life to those who partook of its fruit, so True Wisdom brings spiritual health and life to those who seek and follow her instruction. And not only so, but she is the means also of prolonging temporal life and of multiplying all its enjoyments. (מְאֻשָּׁר, Pual part. of אָשַׁר.)

19. After giving a description of the benefits which heavenly wisdom confers upon her votaries, the Sacred writer shows still further its dignity and worth, by adverting briefly to the important influence it exerted at the creation of the physical world. In what precedes, wisdom is spoken of as something acquired and possessed by man—a moral quality—a spiritual principle, not innate, but derived from above. Here the writer alludes to it as an inherent and essential attribute of Divinity, which was specially displayed in the work of creation. (See Jere. 10: 12. 51: 15.) "Who can contemplate the wonderful works of Omniscient Power; their variety and beauty, their magnitude and grandeur; their nice adjustment and adaptation to each other, so that nothing is wanting, nothing redundant, nothing superfluous, and not exclaim, in the words of the Psalmist, "O Lord, how manifold are thy works! in Wisdom hast thou made them all!" (Ps. 104: 24) The eloquence of Cicero is unequal to do justice to this ennobling subject" (Holden.) The terms *Wisdom, Knowledge*, and *Understanding*, are so often used interchangeably in this book, that they may be regarded as entirely equivalent expressions, and employed one for the other merely to give variety to the diction.

20. Allusion is here made to the original formation of the aerial expanse, in which a portion of the aqueous fluid is held suspended

---

20. '*Are broken up*," S. V., Holden—"*burst forth.*" Boothr. Noyes—"*were cleft,*" Stuart ="*drop down the dew,*" S. V., Holden, Noyes—"*drop dew,*" French.

in the form of clouds, (Gen. 1: 6, 7,) so that the waters with which
the earth was covered, and with which the air was filled, appeared
to be separated, and a part congregated above the firmament and a
part below. By this wise arrangement and gracious provision of
the Almighty Creator, the earth is constantly supplied with fertilizing showers. The signal beneficence of God is displayed in the
dew, especially in warm regions, where copious showers of rain are
of rare occurrence, and consequently there is the greatest necessity
for the nocturnal dew to invigorate and refresh the plants. In the
dry regions of Palestine, the dew gathering upon the tents wets
them as if it had rained all the night. The verb רָעַף, raaph, signifies to distil, i. e., gently drop or let fall, viz. the dew. See Job 36:
28. The word טַל, tal, dew, is here either employed in the sense of
שְׂעִירִם, seirim, gentle showers, (Deut. 32: 3,) or else the statement
must be regarded as made in accordance with the popular belief in
the time of Solomon, which ascribed the dew to the clouds, as the
source from which it proceeded. Hence the expressions which so
frequently occur in the Old Testament, the dew of heaven, and the
heavens drop down the dew. (Gen. 27: 28, 39. Deut 33: 28. Zech. 8:
12. Hag. 1: 10.) Modern experiments and observations, however,
have shown that the clouds, so far from being the origin of dew,
are unfavorable to its formation. For after a cloudy night, little or
no dew is seen in the morning: while after a cloudless one, particularly succeeding a very warm day, dew appears in profusion. Dew
is the moisture or vapor in the air near the surface of the earth,
which condenses in the form of drops in consequence of coming in
contact with cooler bodies, upon the surface of which it is deposited.
The atmosphere always contains within it more or less aqueous
vapor in an invisible form, which may be made to separate from the
apparently dry air of a warm room, by placing in it a pitcher of
cold water. The air in contact with the pitcher sheds its moisture,
which collects on the outer surface of the pitcher in minute drops.
The quantity of dew deposited is proportionate to the amount of
moisture which the atmosphere happens to contain.

CHAPTER III. 21–35.

[*The benefits resulting from the constant observance of the precepts of wisdom described, vs. 21–26. Exhortations to the observance of various precepts, vs. 27–35.*]

` 21. My son, let not (*my instructions*) depart from thy sight :
Keep sound wisdom and discretion.
22. For they shall be life to thy soul,
And grace to thy neck.

---

21. The Sacred writer here returns to the exhortation to the pursuit and study of wisdom, with which the chapter begins. It is sufficient to remark, once for all, that frequent repetitions of the same sentiments are found in this book, sometimes in the same words, and at others in words slightly changed. This is done for the purpose of impressing more firmly on the mind of the reader the magnitude, the certainty, the necessity, or the utility, of the precepts enjoined. The subject of the plural verb *depart* is not expressed in the original. Some regard the two nouns *wisdom* and *discretion* in the succeeding clause of the verse as the subject by anticipation. This mode of construction is not without precedent, and may possibly be the correct one; but it is liable to the objection that both the nouns referred to are feminine, while the verb is masculine. If we fall back on v. 1, of the chapter, then there is the same difficulty. It is better to avoid this anomaly by regarding the things previously mentioned as the subject—the instructions pertaining to wisdom contained in the preceding part of the chapter. The image here, as in ch. 4: 21, where nearly the same words are found, is drawn from one to whom something is committed for safe keeping, and who is enjoined to keep it continually before his eyes, that it may not escape him. If we would profit by the precepts of wisdom, we must retain them in the memory—we must hold them firmly, and guard them with assiduity.

22. *To thy soul,* i. e., to thee. *Grace* (חֵן *chen,*) here either de-

---

21. " *Let not these things,*" Holden—"*let them not,*" S. V., Boothr., French, Noyes, Stuart.
22. " *Ornament to thy neck,*" Holden—"*graceful ornament,*" Boothr.—"*grace,*" S. V., French, Noyes, Stuart.

23. Then shalt thou go on thy way safely,
And thy foot shall not stumble.

24. When thou liest down, thou shalt not be afraid;
Yea, thou shalt lie down, and thy sleep shall be
sweet.

25. Be not afraid of sudden terror,
Nor of the desolation of the wicked, when it cometh.

notes *beauty, gracefulness, ornament,* or it is put for לִוְיַת חֵן, *livyath chen, graceful ornament,* (see chap. 1: 9. 4: 9.) The word גַּרְגְּרֹת, *gargeroth,* properly signifies *the throat, the gullet;* but is used every where of the *external throat, the neck.* The Sept. reads the verse thus: "that thy soul may live, and that there may be grace round thy neck; and it shall be health to thy flesh, and safety to thy bones."

23. The image here employed is drawn from a traveller who prosecutes his journey in safety and without meeting with accidents on the way. The sense is: Wisdom being our leader, we shall prosperously succeed in whatever we attempt to do. "Guided by wisdom, thou shalt pass thy days in security and comfort; and in all thy intercourse with the world, thou wilt be safe from falling into sin; even as the traveller who journeys by the light of the sun proceeds on his way securely." (Holden) (תֵּלֵךְ, Kal fut. of נָגַף.)

24. The good man, when he lies down to sleep, has no cause for fear, his mind is not disturbed with the consciousness of wickedness, nor his breast agitated by disquieting and restless cares. Under the apprehension of danger, sleep is apt to be disturbed, dreamy, and unrefreshing. *Sweet sleep* accompanies and is the evidence of a tranquil mind, and a sense of security. Tranquil sleep is placed among those good things which the pious enjoy, in Lev. 26: 6. Job 11: 19. Ps. 3: 6. 4: 8.

25. The word שׁוֹאָה, *shoa,* primarily signifies *tempest, storm,* see chap. 1: 27. Ezek. 38: 9; then *desolation, destruction, ruin,* see Ps. 35: 8. Isa. 10: 3. 47: 11. The phrase *desolation,* or *destruction, of the wicked,* is ambiguous. It may be understood actively of the destruction which the wicked threaten to bring on the pious, as in Ps. 35: 17, the Psalmist prays that he may be delivered from *their destruction.* So the Sept., "neither of approaching attacks of ungodly

25. "*Distructive tempest,*" Stuart.　26. "*From the snare,*" Stuart.

26. For Jehovah shall be thy confidence;
And he will keep thy foot from capture.

27. Withhold not good from those who need it,
When it is in the power of thy hand to do (*it*).

---

men," Vulg., Castellio; or it may be taken passively, and denote the
desolation or destruction which is approaching the wicked—the
tempest of divine displeasure which will sweep them away, as in
Ps. 35: 8. The sense according to the latter is more elegant and
more consonant with the analogy of Scripture. So most commentators.

26. Solomon here adds the reason why he who is imbued with
true wisdom should not fear any terror or alarm, let it come ever so
suddenly and unexpectedly. The figure in the second clause is
borrowed from snares or traps in which the feet of wild animals are
caught. A firm and abiding confidence in God will alone afford us
effectual security against the snares which temptation spreads in
our path.

27. Among the precepts which Solomon here introduces which
relate to our duties towards others, the first place is given in this
and the following verse, to beneficence and liberality. *Those who
need it,*—literally *its lords, owners, possessors.* By this is meant, as the
context shows, the *needy* and *indigent*, who are proper objects of be-
nevolence, and to whom, on the ground of humanity, it is due. In
ch. 17: 8, the *recipient* and not the bestower of a gift is called *its
lord* or *possessor*, (בְּעָלָיו, *bealav*.) So the Sept., "Forbear not to do
good to the poor." The precept has respect not so much to the law
of justice, as of charity, and inculcates a duty which we owe not so
much to those who have a legal claim upon us, as to those whose
character and circumstances are such as to render them the proper
objects of our kindness and beneficence, and give them a sort of
claim upon our aid and succor. Those who receive wealth from
God should not regard themselves as its absolute lords or owners,
but only as dispensers of God's bounty (1 Peter 4: 10) to the poor.
Every possessor of the good things, whether of this life or the life
to come, is bound by the command of the Supreme Giver, as well as
by the common ties of humanity and universal brotherhood, to contribute a portion to those who are in want. The possessors of this
world's goods are not at liberty to withhold the portion which be-

---

27. "*A favor*," Boothr.=" *From the indigent,*" Holden—"*from those to whom it
belongs,*" Stuart.

28. Say not to thy neighbor, "Go, and come again;
" And to-morrow I will give:" when thou hast it
by thee.

29. Devise not evil against thy neighbor,
When he dwelleth securely with thee.

---

longs to the poor. It is not left to their mere option whether they
will give according to their ability or refuse. This is a matter
which has been settled by the law of a higher power. But, notwithstanding, the poor have not a right which they can plead and
enforce before a human tribunal. The acknowledgment of such a
right to the possessions of another, would lead to anarchy and
every evil thing. It appears to be the purpose of God in the present
world to do good to his creatures by the inequality of their condition. The design of this providential arrangement is to produce
gentle, humble, contented thankfulness on the one side, and open-
hearted, open-handed liberality on the other. In *the power of thy
hand* is an idiomatic expression equivalent to *in thy power.*

28. Not only are we required to help the unfortunate and give
to the poor, according to our pecuniary ability, respect being had to
the just claims which our relatives and creditors may have upon us;
but we are enjoined to give promptly and cheerfully, without unnecessary postponement and delay. To give quickly is to give
twice. Delay is often dangerous, both to the giver and receiver. It
may prevent that seasonable communication of a favor which makes
it doubly valuable; and it most commonly proceeds from an indolence and languor of mind which ought to be corrected. (לְרֵעֶיךָ
with vowels for the singular=לְרֵעֲךָ. So the Keri, which reading
many manuscripts have in the text, and with which the Vulgate,
Chald. and Syr. coincide. So the verbs in the singular number
which follow, require. אֱהֹב, Kal fut of נָתַן.)

29. Another duty towards those with whom we live, is here inculcated; viz. ever to act towards them in entire good faith. It is
supposed by some that the precept has respect to the rights of hospitality, and that the expression *dwelleth securely with thee,* refers
particularly to the traveller who seeks temporarily a friendly lodge,
and who feels secure in it, relying on laws of hospitality, which are
nearly universal in hither Asia. " The host is not to lay a plan for
robbing his guest, who has entrusted himself to his care and pro-

---

29. " *Near thee,*" French.

30. Contend not with a man without cause,
When he hath done thee no harm.

31. Envy thou not the man of violence,
And choose none of his ways.

32. For the perverse (*man*) is an abomination to
Jehovah;
But he hath communion with the upright.

33. The curse of Jehovah is upon the house of the
wicked;
But he blesseth the habitation of the righteous.

---

teetion." An act of this kind was regarded not simply as a breach
of hospitality, but a crime of a very grave character. · It is better,
however, to take the precept in a wider sense, as applicable to neigh-
borly intercourse generally. So Sept. "Devise not evil against thy
friend, living near thee and trusting in thee." Syr. "Devise not
evil against thy neighbor, dwelling with thee in peace."

30. Solomon here admonishes us to abstain from all unjust and
causeless strife and contention with others. Where no wrong has
been done or intended, there is no justifiable cause for quarrelling
or litigation. The Sept. reads the second clause thus: "lest he do
thee some harm." (תַּרוֹב.=Keri, תָּרִיב, or else should be pointed
תָּרוֹב.)

31. By *the man of violence* is intended one who oppresses others
by his power, and acquires wealth by open violence. The sentiment
of the verse is, 'Do not be offended by the success and prosperity of
wicked men, so as, because you see them flourishing in glory and
ill-gotten riches, to imitate their violent, rapacious, and wicked
deeds.' See Ps. 37: 1 seq.

32. Reasons are assigned in this and the following verse why
we should not envy the successes of wicked men. The first is, because the deeds of the wicked are held in abhorrence by God, while
he takes the righteous into favor. By *communion* is meant familiar
intercourse and fellowship, such as exist between intimate and con-
fidential friends. See Job 19: 19. Ps. 25: 14.

33. Another comparison is here drawn between the pious and
the wicked, in order to dissuade us from envying the temporary success of the latter. In the preceding verse the two are compared
with reference to the divine approbation or disapprobation; here

34. Surely he scorneth the scorners;
But showeth favor to the humble.

35. The wise shall inherit glory;
But fools shall bear off shame.

---

they are compared with reference to the prosperous or infelicitous issue of their affairs.

34. Stuart renders אִם, *im*, by *when*, and makes the verse the protasis and the following verse the apodosis. Others render it *if*, and render: 'if he scorneth the scorners, he also showeth,' &c. While the ancient versions generally pass it by without notice. The Æthiopic, however, renders it *surely*, as in our standard version. The Sept. reads the verse: "The Lord resisteth the proud; but giveth grace to the humble." The passage is quoted from this version by St. James (ch. 4: 6), and by St. Peter (1 Epl. 5: 5), with the single difference, that the word *God* is substituted by them for *Lord*. The Septuagint version, though not a literal translation, gives substantially the sense. Scoffers at religion are as a class actuated in their hostility to divine truth by pride and self-conceit; and pride in a depraved and dependent creature, God abhors. On the contrary, he regards with special approbation the humble, and bestows upon them favors both temporal and spiritual.

35. The final consequence of pursuing the path of wisdom on the one hand, and the path of folly and wickedness on the other, is here described in strong and emphatic terms. The wise shall finally obtain glory, honor and exaltation, as their lawful inheritance; while shame, disgrace and infamy shall be the portion of fools. Commentators differ in respect to the subject and predicate of the second clause: some regarding *fools* (כְּסִילִים, *kesilim*,) as the subject; others, *shame* (קָלוֹן, *qalon*). They also differ with regard to the exact subject of the participal מֵרִים, *merim*, (Hiph. part. of רוּם) as the verb from which it comes signifies both to *lift up, raise, exalt, elevate*, and to *lift up*, or *take up*, for the purpose of *bearing away*, and hence to *bear off*, to *take away*. Some accordingly translate the clause, 'But shame shall exalt fools,' i. e., it shall bring them into the most conspicuous disgrace, spoken ironically. Not materially different from this is the rendering of the Vulgate, "the exaltation of fools is ignominy," and our Standard Version, "shame shall be

---

35. "*Ignominy*," French—"*shame shall exalt fools*," Holden—"*disgrace raiseth fools to notice*," Boothr.—"*shame shall sweep them away*," Stuart.

4*

the promotion of fools." "Shame," says Muntinghe, "is the no-
bility conferred on fools." Stuart, taking the verb in the second
sense, renders, "Shame shall sweep away fools." Others, however,
as Piscat, Rosenm., French, Noyes, &c., make *fools* the subject, and,
taking the verb in the second sense, translate, as above, "Fools bear
off shame," or "ignominy" This corresponds best with the parallel clause, and avoids the necessity of supposing irony to have
been employed—a figure of rare occurrence in the Scriptures, and
not to be admitted, except in cases of obvious necessity. The word
fools is to be taken in a distributive sense=each one of them.)

CHAPTER IV.

[*Exhortations to the attainment of Wisdom, the study of which is
earnestly commended, vs. 1–13. Warnings against the example
of evil men, vs. 14–19. The observance of the precepts of Wisdom urged on the ground of its promised rewards, vs. 20–27.*]

1. Hear, ye children, the instructions of a father;
And attend, that you may learn understanding.
2. For I give you good instructions;
Forsake ye not my teaching.

1. The youthful readers of the Proverbs are here addressed under the tender appellation of children, whom an affectionate father,
deeply solicitous for their welfare, invites to attend to the instructive precepts which he communicates, in order that they may acquire a right understanding in respect to the great duties of life.
Comp. ch. 1: 8. (לָרַעַת, Kal infin. of יָרַע, with prefix prep)

2. Solomon here alludes to the excellence of the precepts he inculcates, and assigns this as a reason why they should be attended
to and not forsaken.

3. When I was the (*favorite*) son of my father;
A tender and only child in the sight of my mother;
4. He taught me, and said to me.
" Let thy heart retain my precepts ;
" Keep my commandments and live.

---

3. The particle בִּי, *ki*, may here be taken either in a *causal* or a temporal sense.   Taken as a *causal* particle (*for*), the verse would be continuative of the preceding and contain another reason drawn from the example of the writer, in favor of obeying the precepts of wisdom.   As if he had said: ' I was formerly young like yourselves, and stood in the relation of a favorite son to my father, who instructed me, as I now teach you; and as I obeyed him, and it was well for me, so do you the same.'   So Sept., Vulg.   By others, however, it is regarded as an adverb of *time* (*when*), logically connected with the following verse.   Thus taken, the sense would be: ' When I was young like you, my parents, with whom I was a great favorite, taught me the precepts of wisdom, as I am endeavoring to teach you, and as I listened and profited by *their* instructions, so do you listen to and profit by *my* instructions.'   Solomon speaks of himself as having been the son of his father in an emphatic sense, *i. e.*, favorite son—one specially beloved.   Some commentators connect the adjective *tender* (רַךְ, *dak*), in the second member of the verse, with *son* in the first, and so the ancient versions appear to have done.   This construction, if adopted, would of course supercede the necessity of introducing the word *favorite* in the version to express the emphasis.   The reading adopted above, however, is in accordance with the Masoretic accents, and followed in our Standard Version.   See 1 Chron. 22: 5. 29: 1.   The word יָחִיד, *yachid*, (*only*) is here used in a figurative and emphatic sense.   Solomon was regarded by his mother with that strong and peculiar affection, with which an *only* child is usually regarded.   He was not really the only child of Bathsheba, but her favorite son.

4. The instructive lessons which David is here said to have given to Solomon, extend to the close of the 9th verse; and in the 10th Solomon resumes his discourse.   Some, however, think that they reach to ch. 5: 16.   The expression *let thy heart retain*, signifies something more than simply to *remember*; it imports an *affectionate remembrance*;—such a regard for the precepts in question as leads to

---

3. " *For I was*," Holden, Noyes, Stuart.

5. "Get wisdom, get understanding;
"Forget not; and depart not from the words of my mouth.

6. "Forsake her not, and she will keep thee;
"Love her, and she will preserve thee.

7. "Wisdom is the principal thing: (*therefore*) get wisdom;
"With all thy possessions, get understanding.

---

an exemplification of them in the life. Words may often be lost to the memory, and yet retained in the heart, inwrought into our moral constitution, and held firm by a permanent and sanctifying affection. He taught, *i. e.*, the *father*, who occupies the first place in the instruction of children. But the Sept. has the plural form, referring to both parents: "Who spoke and instructed me, (*saying*) let our speech," &c. The Chaldee has: "and Jehovah taught me and said to me." *And live.*——This is an emphatic expression, for "thou shalt live long and happily." So ch 7: 2. 9: 6. This verse is the only one in the chapter which has three parallel members or clauses. The Syriac version contains an additional member not found in the present Hebrew text, which reads as follows: "Let my law be as the apple of the eye." If this were admitted as a part of the original text, uniformity would be restored to the poetic structure of the chapter. (יֹרֵנִי, Hiph. fut. of יָרָה.)

5. Solomon exhorts his readers, that like merchants they should spare no labors, by which they may make some accessions to the treasures of wisdom. The object after the verb *forget* is not expressed. We may supply *my words* from the latter part of the clause.

7. Heavenly wisdom is the most important, the most valuable and the most desirable possession; therefore, among all his other acquisitions, whatever they may be, man should not fail to obtain this; he should moreover esteem it *above* all other things, and procure it, if necessary, at the sacrifice of everything else. Comp. Matt. 13: 45. It is evident that רֵאשִׁית, *rasheth*, here means the *chief*, the *principal*, or *most excellent* thing, and not *beginning*, as it does in several other places in this book. Some critics, however, following the Vulgate, render the clause: "the beginning of wis-

---

7. "*Above all*," French.

8. "Exalt her, and she will promote thee;
"She will bring thee to honor, when thou dost embrace her.

9. "She will give to thy head a graceful wreath,
"A glorious crown will she deliver to thee."

10. Hearken, my son, and receive my words,
And the years of thy life shall be many.

11. I will instruct thee in the way of wisdom;
I will conduct thee in the paths of rectitude.

12. When thou goest, thy step shall not be confined;
And when thou runnest, thou shalt not stumble.

---

dom (is this); get wisdom," *i. e.*, he at length begins to be wise,
who is solicitous for acquiring wisdom. The beginning of wisdom
is, to know its value, and to apply the mind to its attainment. This
interpretation, however, is manifestly forced, and borders on the
absurd: for the acquisition of wisdom cannot with propriety be
called the beginning of it.

8. The verb to *embrace* is employed figuratively to indicate an
affectionate attachment—by metonymy of the sign for the thing sig-
nified. Religion does not demand our homage and service for
nought. Whatever honor and devotion we render to her, she will
abundantly repay, even in this world; while in the world to come,
-the promised reward is life everlasting. (כַּלְסְלֶהָ, Pilpel Impera.
with suffix of כָלַל.)

9. *Graceful wreath*—see ch. 1: 9. *a glorious crown*, lit. *a crown of
glory*, which is equivalent to a glorious—splendid—brilliant crown.
The language is figurative, and designed to convey the idea of the
richest reward. (תְּכַנְגֶךָ, Piel fut. of כָנַן, found only in Piel. put for
תְּכַנְגָן לָךְ, as in Jos. 15: 19. נְתַתָּנִי is put for נָתַתִּי לִי.)

10. See 1 Kings 3: 14. (קַח Kal. impera. of לָקַח.)

11. *In the way of wisdom*, i. e., in the way which leads to wisdom, or in the mode and method of obtaining wisdom. A similar
phrase occurs in Ps. 25: 9, 13. 32: 5. 1 Sam. 12: 23. The second
member is an exegetical illustration of the first, by the continuation
of the metaphor derived from *the way*. (הוֹרֵתִי=הֹרֵתִי, Hiph. pract.
of יָרָה.)

12. The thought here is climactic, and the parallelism grada-

13. Take fast hold of instruction: let (*her*) not go;
Keep her, for she is thy life.

14. Enter not into the paths of the wicked;
And go not in the way of evil (*men*);

15. Avoid it; pass not by it;
Turn from it, and pass away,

16. For they sleep not, unless they have done mis-
chief;
Yea, their sleep is taken away,
Unless they have caused (*some one*) to fall.

---

tional. *Running* indicates more rapid motion than merely *going*.
To *be confined* or *straitened* as to one's step, is to be beset and impeded in one's course by difficulties and obstacles. Comp. Ps. 119:
45. The path of rectitude is not only a straight, safe, and plain
path, but it is a smooth and unobstructed path, and he who walks
in it steadily and perseveringly, will be able without difficulty to
pursue the even tenor of his way. (יֵצֶר, Kal fut. of יָצַר.)

13. The expression *take fast hold of*, implies determination of purpose and intensity of interest. And the phrase *she is thy life*, indicates that heavenly wisdom or divine instruction is the chief source
and spring of happiness. Solomon here compares divine teaching
to a precious treasure, which is not only seized with avidity when
offered; but most carefully and diligently guarded lest it should
escape us. *Thy life*, i. e., the source of safety, prosperity and happiness. (הֶרֶף, Hiph. fut. apoc. 2d pers. of רָפָה, instead of the normal apoc. הֶרֶף.)

14. This verse contains a dissuasion from consorting with wicked
men, as in ch. 1: 15. This counsel is frequently repeated, because
such association is most perilous and pernicious, inasmuch as a
great part of mankind are influenced by example, and induced by
the apparent happiness and prosperity of the wicked, to follow
their steps.

16. The latter member of this verse is explanatory of the former.
Unless they have done mischief by causing some one to fall, *i. e.*, by
bringing ruin upon some one. (יָרֵעַ, Hiph. fut. of רָע. יַכְשׁוֹלוּ.
If this be intended for Kal fut. it should be pointed יְכָשׁוֹלוּ; but this
would give an irrelevant sense. The Keri has יַכְשִׁילוּ, Hiph. fut. of
כָּשַׁל.)

17. For they eat the bread of wickedness ;
And drink the wine of violence.

18. But the path of the righteous is like the light
of dawn,
Which shineth more and more unto the perfect day.

17. This verse is connected with the preceding by the causal
particle *for* (כִּי) because it assigns a reason why the men of whom
the writer is speaking enjoy no pleasant sleep, unless they have done
some mischief, viz. they spend their whole lives in rapine and violence. By *bread of wickedness* and *wine of violence*, we are to understand food procured by iniquity, violence and rapine. These men
subsist on the spoils of plunder and robbing. Some commentators,
with less probability, understand the passage as expressing figuratively the great delight which the wicked experience in their base
deeds. "They cannot sleep unless they have done mischief; for
if they have committed no trespass, if they have done no deed of
violence, they are deprived of their highest gratification, and sleep
is banished from their eyes." Holden.

18. The comparison here drawn between the habitual course of
the righteous and the advancing light of day, is very beautiful and
instructive. The path of the righteous is not here compared, as
some suppose, to the apparent diurnal course of the sun from the
time of its first appearance to the period of its meridian height; but
to the morning light which precedes the rising of the orb of day.
This is scarcely perceptible at first, but gradually increases, becoming brighter and brighter, till it reaches its culminating point
at the appearance of the sun, and terminates in the full blaze of
day. The truly good man—the pious and upright Christian—in
his habitual walk and character—is as the light. He possesses an
illuminating power, *i. e.*, an instructive power: for light is an emblem of knowledge. He teaches by his principles and by his example. Hence our Saviour said to his disciples, "Ye are the light
of the world." And St. Paul, writing to Christians, said, "Ye
were sometime (*i. e.*, formerly) darkness: (*i. e.*, in an ignorant and
unconverted state); but now are ye light in the Lord." The way
of the wicked, on the contrary, is as *darkness*. It possesses no such
instructive power. Its influence is all on the side of error and of
vice. The pious and virtuous example of good men is, moreover, as
a *shining* light, *i. e.*, it is not a concealed and hidden light, which
does no one any good; but conspicuous and entirely exposed to ob-

19. The way of the wicked is as thick darkness;
They know not on what they stumble.

20. My son, attend to my words,
Incline thy ear to my sayings.

21. Let them not depart from thy sight;
Keep them within thy heart.

---

servation, so that all within the sphere of its influence and operation, may enjoy and be benefitted by it. It shines to its possessors
in the joy and comfort of it, and to others, in the luster and honor
of it. The Christian also is an advancing and increasing light—
shining more and more. This epithet indicates the progressive nature, the ascending progress, the increasing strength and usefulness
of true religion, as reigning in the heart and ruling in the life.
Sept. "The ways of the righteous shine like light; they go on and
shine, until the day is fully come." The Christian grows in grace.
At first the religion of the new born soul is like the morning spread
upon the mountains and not yet reaching the valleys. Though it
be light, and a shining light, it is not in its commencement the light
of the sun in his rising or his noon-day splendor: but the feeble,
glimmering light of the early dawn. Yet it is not stationary, but
continually advancing in clearness and power, until it reaches the
highest state of perfection of which it is capable in this world.

19. How striking the contrast between the course of the righteous
and that of the wicked. The way of the wicked, instead of being
one of constantly increasing brightness, and consequently of safety,
tranquility, joy and usefulness, is ever like thick, impenetrable
darkness,—a compound of ignorance, error, sin, and misery, which
continually increases, till at length it terminates in the blackness
of darkness and despair forever. While pursuing this sinful and
destructive course, like travellers in a dark and dangerous road,
they perceive not the pitfalls which lie in their way, but are in constant danger of plunging headlong into ruin. Comp. Jere. 23: 12.

20. (הֵט, Hiph. fut. apoc. of נָטָה, instead of the normal form,
הַטֵּה.)

21. To *keep* the precepts of wisdom *within the heart,* is to esteem
them most highly and guard them most carefully, as a precious
treasure, which is kept not in an outer apartment, exposed to observation and to the grasp of the plunderer, but in the most retired

---

13. "*In the midst of thy heart,*" Holden, Stuart.

22. For they are life to those that find them ;
And a healing medicine to all their flesh.
23. Keep thy heart with all diligence ;
For out of it are the issues of life.

and secret place, where it will not be likely to be discovered.
(יָלִיזוּ‎. Hiph. fut. of לִיז‎, inflected after the Chaldaic form with Dag-
hesh in the ל‎, instead of יָלִיזוּ‎.   So we have יָלִינוּ‎ from לוּן‎.)

22. The precepts of wisdom afford security, prosperity and happiness to those who hear and lay them up in their hearts. Comp.
ch. 3: 22. 4: 13. *A healing medicine.* See ch. 3: 8. 12: 18. 13: 17.
16: 24. " To those who receive the words of wisdom, inwardly
digest them, and model their conduct by them, they are the cause
of a long and prosperous life, and are as salutary as healing medicines to a disordered body." (Holden.)

23. The *heart* here denotes the inner man, including the thoughts,
disposition, affections, passions, desires, and motives of action.
This is man's citadel, and here lies his most valuable treasure. To
keep the heart is to guard it, to watch over it, to protect and fortify
it against the ingress of evil and the assaults of temptation. There
is implied in thus keeping the heart the use of all appropriate
means for that purpose, especially of prayer. *With all diligence,* i. e.,
with the utmost care and assiduity. Or the phrase may be translated, *above all watching;* or as in the margin of our Bibles, *above all
keeping,* i. e., above every object of thy watchful care, keep thy
heart. Let this occupy your chief and unremitted attention. The
heart is here represented as a fountain—the fountain of moral and
spiritual life; and guarding it with the utmost diligence, alludes,
perhaps, to the vigilance exercised over fountains, springs and
wells in the East, where their value, from the scarcity of water at
particular seasons, is greater than we can well estimate. The *issues
of life.*—In the human body the heart is the fountain or source
whence issues all the streams of blood which flow through every
part of the bodily frame: and so essential is this to the existence
and health of the body, that the blood is called *the life.* Comp.
Gen. 9: 4, 6. So the mind is the fountain of moral action—the cen-
ter and source of holiness and of sin. The right conduct and happiness of life depend on the healthy condition of the inner man—
the due regulation of the various powers and voluntary exercises of

22. " *Health,*" Boothr.—" *healing,*" Stuart—" *soundness,*" French, Noyes.
5

24. Put away from thee perverseness of mouth,
And remove far from thee frowardness of lips.
. 25. Let thy eyes look straight forward,
And let thy eye-lids direct (*their way*) before thee.

---

the soul. As is the fountain so will be the streams which issue
from it. As the streams which flow from a natural fountain are
limpid or turbid, according to the condition of the fountain or source
from which they spring, so will the conduct of human life, the deportment of the outer man be virtuous or vicious, according as the
inner man is pure or corrupt. See Matt 15: 19.

24. The first of the streams which flow from a depraved, ill-
regulated and ill-guarded heart, is a *perverse mouth*, i. e., speech corrupt, tortuous, contrary to the divine command—profanity, ob-
scenity, mendacity, slander, calumny, &c. The power of speech is
one of the grand peculiarities and blessings which distinguish the
human race from, and elevate it far above all other terrestrial animals. It is indeed a most wonderful and inestimable gift. But it
is liable to great abuse, and while using it, we should never forget
that God is one of the listening, and that we are as accountable to
him for what we *say* as for what we *do*. Both the words rendered
perverseness or *perversity*, and *frowardness* or *deceitfulness*, are abstract
nouns, the strong significancy of which is better indicated here by
translating them as such, rather than as qualifying adjectives. So
Marg. Reading, and the best commentators. See ch. 6: 12. (הָקֵר,
Hiph. impera. of כּוּר.)

25. The next outlet from the hidden fountain within to the external world, is through the eyes. The imagery is drawn from the
conduct of travellers, who keep their eyes fixed in the direction of
the road along which they are passing, and do not permit them to
wander to one side or the other, lest some accident should befall
them, or they should miss their way. The precept inculcates the
importance of keeping steadily in view, under all circumstances,
the great end and duties of life, and of being constantly on one's
guard against the enticements of outward things. Let the heart's
aim be always simple and upright. No secret longings and side-
glances after forbidden things; no mental reservations, crooked by-
ways and hypocritical pretences. But let your path, both in appearance and reality be a straight-forward one, and keep your eye.

---

25. "*Be directed*," Boothr. French, Noyes—"*keep a direct course*," Stuart.

26. Ponder the path of thy feet;
And let all thy ways be established.
27. Turn not to the right hand nor to the left:
Remove thy foot from evil.

---

steadily fixed upon the object towards which you are directing your steps. (Comp. Philip. 3: 14.) The term *eye-lids* is only another designation of the eyes, by synecdoche of a part for the whole. The verb יַיְשִׁירוּ, *yayshiru*, is the Hiph. of יָשַׁר, *yashar*, and properly signifies transitively to *make straight* or *direct* one's way. The expression in this sense is of frequent occurrence. See ch. 3: 6. 9: 15. 11: 5. The object is sometimes inserted after the verb, and in other cases, as in this, omitted, and should be supplied, or the rendering varied, so as to express the same idea. (See Robinson's Gesenius' Lex.) Some Commentators render it intransitively *be directed*. The sense is the same. (יַבִּיטוּ, Hiph. fut. of נָבַט. יַיְשִׁירוּ. Hiph. fut. instead of the usual form יַיְשִׁירוּ.)

26. Another and the third outlet of the issues of life is *by the feet*. The precept enjoins due consideration as to the course of life we pursue. The admonition applies to every step we take, whether in itself apparently important or unimportant. One false step may have an influence upon, and give a determinate character to all our future life and prospects. *Ponder*—פַּלֵּס, *palles*, lit. *weigh in a balance.* Comp. Ps. 119: 6.

27. The sacred writer in this verse inculcates a strict observance of the divine commands, from which we are not to deviate either on the one side or the other. To this distich the Sept., Vulg., and Arab. add the following: "For God knows the ways on the right hand, but those on the left are crooked. And he will make thy ways straight, and will guide thy steps in peace." (תֵּט, Kal fut. apoc. 2d pers. of נָטָה, instead of the normal form הַטֶּה.)

CHAPTER V.

[*Warnings against the seductive influence and ruinous consequences
of vice and profligacy, vs. 1–14.   Exhortations to lead a chaste and
virtuous life, and to maintain inviolate the purity and sanctity of the
marriage bed, vs. 15–23.*]

1. My Son, attend to my wisdom ;
Incline thy ear to my understanding,
2. That thou mayest preserve discretion,
And that thy lips may keep knowledge.
3. For the lips of a strange woman distil honey ;
And her mouth is smoother than oil.

1. By *my wisdom*, is meant the wise and wholesome counsel and
instruction which Solomon gave—the advice dictated by his wisdom, knowledge, and experience.   (הַט, Hiph. fut. apoc. of נָטָה, instead of the normal form הִטָּה.)

2. In ch. 3: 1, the writer speaks of *the heart* as keeping knowledge: but here he mentions *the lips*, and not without emphasis. For
his purpose is to say, that 'by attending diligently to my precepts
of wisdom, you will enjoy this fruit, viz. that you will be wise in
heart and lips, *i. e.*, that you will not only think wisely, but also
speak wisely,—not only will you be wise for yourself, but also be
qualified to instruct others in wisdom.'   Comp. ch. 10: 13, 21, 32.
15: 7. 16: 21.   The Sept. and Vulg. add the following clause at the
end of this verse: "Attend not to a deceitful woman;" which some
commentators think is required by the context as a suitable introduction to what follows.   There is not sufficient authority, however,
for inserting it in the text.

3. The Hebrew word נֹפֶת, *nopheth*, properly signifies a *sprinkling,*
dropping; whence the phrase נֹפֶת צוּפִים, *nopheth tzuphim, the dropping
of the honey comb,* i. e., pure virgin honey; the same as יַעַר, *yaar,* in
Ps. 19: 11.   It cannot mean the *honey-comb* (צוּף, *tzuph*), as our
Standard Version has it; for that is not eaten. See ch. 24: 13.   The
same expression occurs in Canticles 4: 11, and it is equally common
to the Greeks and Eastern nations.   Thus Homer, Iliad, A. 249.

"Words sweet as honey from his lips distilled."

4. But in the end she is bitter as wormwood ;
Sharp as a two-edged sword.

5. Her feet go down to death ;
Her steps take hold on Sheol.

6. The way of life she doth not ponder ;
Her paths are devious, while she regardeth it not.

In like manner Moschus in his description of Cupid. Idyl, A. 8.
"A wretch unfeeling, yet his tale is sweet,
His tongue is honey, but his heart deceit."
Theocritus, Idyl K. 26.
"More sweet her lips than milk in luscious rills,
Lips whence *pure honey*, as she speaks, distills."
Her mouth is literally *her palate*, considered as the organ of speech,
which is only another term for *lips* or *tongue*. Comp. ch. 8: 7, where
it is represented as *uttering* truth. Both *lips* and *mouth* (or palate),
have here a tropical meaning, and denote the *words spoken*—the language which proceeds out of the mouth and from the lips. Thus
honeyed words, and *words smoother than oil*, are figurative expressions,
highly descriptive of the insinuating, enticing, persuasive language
of a lewd woman, who artfully employs every blandishment to se-
duce unsuspecting youth into the vortex of ruin. (נָפַת comes from
נ.ף. הַמַּפְנָה, Kal fut. 3d pers. fem. of יָמִיף.)

4. The pernicious consequences of licentiousness form a frequent
topic of remark and warning in this book; and urgent and manifold
are the cautions and admonitions which the author suggests against
the fascinations of this most deceptive and ruinous vice. *In the end*,
is literally, *her end is*, by which is intended not the end to which
she herself comes, but the end to which she leads her votaries—the
consequences of yielding to her seductive enticements. The pleasure she promises her victims terminates in bitterness and woe.

5. *To go down to death*, is to descend to the abode or place of the
dead—the dwelling-place and kingdom of the king of terrors, as
the parallelism shows. Comp. ch. 2: 18.

6. She gives no heed to the course of her life, or to that course
of conduct which leads to life, but plunges reckless and headlong
into a whirlpool of dissipation and crime, the inevitable result of
which is destruction. The context requires us to take תִּלְּפֵס, *teph-*

---

5. " *The grave*," French—" *hades*," Holden, Boothr.—" *the under-world*," Noyes
" *the world beneath*," Stuart. 6. " *Lest she should ponder the way of life*," Holden.

5*

7. And now, ye children, hearken unto me,
And depart not from the words of my mouth.
8. Remove thy way far from her;
And approach not the door of her house.
9. Lest thou give thy bloom to others,
And thy years to the cruel;—
10. Lest strangers be filled with thy wealth,
And thy earnings be in the house of a stranger.

---

alles and יַרְדֵּ, *teda,* as in the 3d pers. fem., and not the 2d pers.
masc., as in our Standard Version. So the Sept. Vulg. Chal. Syr.,
and the best ancient and modern commentators. The conjunction
פֶּן, *pen,* which commonly signifies *lest,* appears to have in this place
the power of a negative adverb. (See Gesenius' Lex.) So Sept. and
Vulg. *Her paths are devious,* i. e., crooked, tortuous. She is perpetually vascillating; and yet she does not regard it, but rushes on
fearlessly to that destruction which is the sure consequence as well
as just punishment of her iniquity. Noyes renders the second
member of the verse—"Her paths sink, when she thinks not of it,"
i. e., suddenly, unexpectedly, before she is aware of her danger.
See Job 9: 25.

7. The Sept. and Vulg. read the verbs and address here in the
singular number, instead of the plural. Solomon here uses the
plural, as in ch. 4: 1, but in the next verse returns to the singular.

9. In this and the following verse, Solomon depicts the consequences of intercourse with lewd women. By *thy bloom* is here
meant thy *youthful bloom*—the beauty, vigor, and strength of thy
body: and by *thy years,* thy *life.* The phrase *others,* may refer not
only to the *harlot,* but also to her associates, attendants and children. By *the cruel* may be intended the harlot herself, who may be
so denominated, because she treacherously and cruelly allures unguarded youth to destruction. Accordingly Holden renders, "to
the *cruel harlot.*" Others think that the *husband* of the adulteress is
intended, to whom this epithet is applied, because, if he pleased,
he could demand the death of the adulterer; and others still, *a master* to whom the adulterer might be sold into bondage, as the punishment of his crime by the injured husband. So Stuart, "to a
cruel *master.*"

10. *Wealth*—properly *strength,* and so marginal reading: but here
put by metonymy for *wealth, riches,* regarded as the fruit and result

11. And lest thou-mourn in thy latter end,
When thy flesh and thy body are consumed.

12. Then wilt thou say, " How have I hated instruction !   .

"And (*how*) hath my heart despised reproof!

13. "I have not hearkened to the voice of my teachers,
" Nor inclined my ears to my instructors !

14. "I have been well nigh in all evil ;
" In the midst of the congregation and of the assembly."

15. Drink water out of thy own cistern,
And running water from thy own well.

---

of exertion. See Hos. 7: 9. So *earnings*, properly *labor, toil:* but here, by the same figure, *earnings, gains*, the product of labor.

11. The verb נָהַם, *naham*, rendered *to mourn*, is applied to indicate the roaring of lions, ch. 19: 12. 20: 2. 28: 15. and in Isai. 5: 30, to the roaring of the sea when agitated by a tempest. It is a strong expression, denoting the groaning and lamentation of him, who by a course of dissipation and licentiousness, has not only consumed his property, but reduced himself to a state of disease and wretchedness. The Sept. and Syr. render *and it repent th r.* By *thy flesh and body*, is intended thy whole body. Synonymes are joined to express universality. Instead of "thy flesh and thy body," the Sept. and Syr. read by hendiadys, *the flesh of thy body.*

13. *My heart* is equivalent to the personal pronoun *I* in the first clause. (מוֹרָי, participial noun from the Hiph. of יָרָה. הִפֵּיחִי, Hiph. praeter of יָטַה.)

14. *All evil* denotes evil of every kind. *In the midst of the congregation*, &c., i. e., in the most public manner, so as to be a shameful spectacle to all men. Some commentators suppose that the clause has reference to the trial, condemnation and punishment of one accused of the crime of adultery, in a court of justice.

15. This is an allegorical proverb, the general import of which is, 'meddle not with that which belongs to another.' Some think that it denotes here, that every one should take care of his own possessions, and live on the fruits of his own labor, without invading

. 16. So shall thy fountains overflow in the streets,
In the wide streets, as streams of water.

17. They shall belong to thee alone,
And not to strangers with thee.   .

---

the possessions of others. But the subsequent context shows that
it is here applied to the marriage relation, and is designed to inculcate the duty of maintaining inviolate the marriage covenant He
who desires to live chastely, innocently, and happily, must confine
himself to his own lawful sources of enjoyment, and not go abroad
in quest of forbidden pleasures. He who pursues the latter course,
violates his most solemn vows and obligations, disobeys the express
command of God, hardens his own conscience, and brings dishonor
and disgrace upon himself and others. In the East, in addition to
public reservoirs, private dwellings are generally provided with
cisterns and wells, and it is to such that the allusion is here made.

16. The allegory introduced at vs. 15, is kept up till the second
member of v. 18, which furnishes the key to its interpretation.
While the preceding verse declares the duty of sacredly respecting
the conjugal relation on the part of the husband, this verse describes
its *advantage* in respect to society at large, and the public good.
Not only is a numerous offspring assured as the reward of conjugal
fidelity, but the children born in lawful wedlock will occupy important and influential positions in society. Comp. Hos. 13: 15.
Ps. 68: 26. Isa. 48: 1. In Canticles (4: 12) the spouse is called "a
spring shut up," and "sealed." The Sept (Vatican codex), and
Aquila, insert the negative particle אל, *al*, before יפצו, *yaphulzu*,
(e. q. μὴ ὑπερεχείσθω,) and this reading appears to have
been adopted by Origen and Clement of Alexandria. Stuart pre-
fers this reading, and translates the verse, "Let (not) thy fountains
issue forth abroad, thy water-brooks in the street," *i. e.*, guard well
thy house against the approach of seductive persons. But the
negative is wanting, not only in the Alexandrine codex of the Sept.
and in the Arabic version. but also in many MSS. which Parsons,
the continuator of the critical edition of the Greek Version commenced by Holmes, consulted, and also in those MSS. from which
the Complutensian editors prepared their Greek translation.

17. Where the marriage covenant is sacredly and inviolably regarded, the faithful husband has the gratifying assurance that the

---

17. "*Let them be for thee alone, and not for strangers with thee,*" Stuart, Eothr.

18. Thy fountain shall be blessed,
And thou shalt rejoice in the wife of thy youth.

19. A lovely hind—a graceful ibex,—
Her breasts shall satisfy thee at all times;
And thou shalt be always ravished with her love.

20. Why, then, my son, wilt thou be ravished with
a strange woman;
And embrace the bosom of a stranger?

21. For the ways of a man are before the eyes of
Jehovah,
And he pondereth all his steps.

22. His own iniquities shall take captive the wicked
(man);
And by the cords of his own sins he shall be bound.

---

numerous offspring composing his household is really and entirely
his own, and no part of it another's.

18. In this verse the honor and respect in which the virtuous
and lawful wife of a faithful husband is held among all persons,
and the enjoyment and satisfaction experienced in consequence of
it, are depicted. Some interpret the *blessing* here spoken of as consisting in a numerous offspring. But this would be a mere repetition
of what is said in v. 16.

19. The *Hind* is the female deer, and the animal called the *roe*
(יַעֲלָה, *yaala*,) in our Standard Version, is the wild, or mountain
she goat—the ibex, according to Gesenius and the best Commentators.
The animals here mentioned are very elegant in form and gentle in
their disposition and habits; hence they are highly esteemed and
much caressed by their owners. The hind is celebrated for affection
to her mate; hence in the East, according to Roberts, a man, in
speaking of his wife, often calls her by the name of that animal.
(See Cant. 2: 9,) The Arabs also have a common expression.
"More beautiful than the ibex." *Shall satisfy*—shall satiate, every
conjugal desire. The verb שָׁגָה, *shaga*, translated *ravished* here and
in v. 20, properly signifies *to err, to wander*; then to *wander* in mind
from wine; hence *to reel, to stagger, to be intoxicated*. Here used figuratively of one *led away*, or *ravished* with love.

21–23. Solomon in these verses warns his reader against illicit
intercourse—1. on the ground that even the most secret sins com-

23. He shall die from neglect of instruction;
And through the greatness of his folly, he shall
stagger (*into the grave*).

---

mitted by man are known to God, who will sooner or later punish
the guilty—2. from the fact that he may not hope to escape even the
natural consequences of his iniquities in this world, like the wild
beast caught in the toils of the hunter. (Comp. ch. 7: 22, 23.) He
will inevitably become the captive slave of his own vile passions
and habits, and lose all power of self-control—3. on the ground,
that at last a miserable death will overtake him, and, like a drunkard, he will stagger and tumble into a premature and dishonored
grave.

CHAPTER VI. 1–5.

*[Admonition not rashly and unadvisedly to incur pecuniary liability
for other persons.]*

1. My son, if thou hast become surety for another—
(*If*) thou hast stricken hands with a stranger—

---

1. The design of the sacred writer in this and the following
verses, is to administer salutary caution against suretyship entered
into rashly, inconsiderately, without regard to circumstances, and
to an extent beyond what the individual can afford to risk. It is
not against suretyship for a friend at all times and under all circumstances that Solomon here protests, for that would not only be
unkind, but inconsistent with the spirit of the Mosaic law, (Lev.
19: 18,) and with the advice which he himself has given in other
passages of this book. (ch. 14: 21. 17: 17. 18: 24. 27: 10.)   The
term יֵעַ, *rea*, is quite indefinite, and is translated in our Standard
Version *friend, neighbor, fellow, companion*, and *another*.   The corresponding term *stranger* in the parallel clause, would seem to indicate

23. " *Shall he reel*," Stuart—" *he shall go astray*," Holden—" *But—went astray*,"
Boothr.—" *wherein he goeth astray*," French.
1. " *Thou art pledged*," Stuart.="*thy friend*," Sept , Vulg., Boothr., Stuart—
" *thy neighbor*," Holden.

2. (*If*) thou art ensnared by the words of thy mouth,—

(*If*) thou art caught by the words of thy mouth,—

3. Do this, then, my son, and free thyself;

For thou hast fallen into the hands of thy neighbor.

Go, prostrate thyself, and be urgent with thy neighbor.

---

that the person here intended is not a particular friend, to whom we may be under special obligations, or who for any cause may have special claims upon us, but one who on the contrary does not sustain any such relation to us, as renders it a duty as well as an act of kindness to assist him in the way here alluded to, as far as prudence will allow. Comp. ch. 11: 15. The conjunction אִם, *im*, *if*, the sign of conditionality, which is expressed in the first clause of this verse, is to be mentally carried forward to the second clause, and also to the two clauses of the following verse. To *strike hands*, i. e., to bring them together with force, in reference to a contract or covenant entered into between two parties, was an outward symbolical gesture among the Hebrews, confirmatory of such agreement, equivalent to the signing and sealing of an instrument—the customary mode of plighting faith; just as *joining* or *shaking hands* is not an uncommon gesture in the ratification of unwritten, verbal contracts among Western nations at the present day. Nestor complained that the Trojans had violated the engagement which they had sanctioned by libations of wine, and giving *their right hands*. The sense then is, 'If by giving thy hand to a creditor in presence of the debtor, thou hast become responsible for the payment of another's debt.'

2. 'If thou hast committed thyself by a rash promise made for the benefit of another in haste and without due consideration.' Many commentators think that in this verse the consequence of the act mentioned in the preceding verse, or the apodosis of the sentence, is contained; and so the authors of our Standard Version appear to have regarded it. But I prefer, with Rosenmueller, French, Noyes, Stuart, and others, to regard the verse as belonging to the protasis.

3. Here follows the apodosis of the sentence, in which the surety is advised what to do. The Sept. and Vulg. read the first clause, "My son, do what I command thee, and deliver thyself." There is no doubt that *neighbor* in the second clause refers to the same person as it does in the third. But whether the debtor or the creditor is

4. Give not sleep to thy eyes,
Nor slumber to thy eyelids.
5. Free thyself as a gazelle from the hand (*of the hunter*);
And as a bird from the hand of the fowler.

---

intended by it, is a matter of dispute. The meaning may be, that
the surety has placed himself at the mercy of the debtor, for whom
he has become responsible, and who by neglect, misfortune or fraud,
may subject him to the necessity of paying the debt. He is therefore advised to go to the debtor, to prostrate himself to the earth in
token of profound respect, and in the way of supplication, after the
oriental manner, and urge him to pay the debt as soon as possible,
and thus release him from the liability which he had incurred. So
it was understood by the authors of the Septuagint Version, who
have translated the 2d and 3d clauses thus: "for on thy friend's
account thou art come into the power of evil men; faint not, but stir
up even thy friend for whom thou art become surety." Or the meaning may be that the surety has placed himself in the power and at
the mercy of the creditor, (*i. e.*, has given him a right to enforce
payment of the debt ensured,) and he is advised to go to him to
whom the pledge has been given, and obtain, if possible, a release
from the liability, which he had unadvisedly incurred. The former
construction seems more probably the right one. *Go*—to your debt-
or. (הִנָּצֵל, Niph. reflexive of נָצַל. לֵךְ, Kal impera. of יָלַךְ.)

5. In this and the preceding verse, the surety is advised to lose
no time by delay, but hasten to free himself from his liability; and
in this respect to resemble the fleetness of the gazelle when pursued
by the hunter, and the swift flight of the bird escaping from the
power of the fowler. The gazelle is the most graceful and beautiful of all the varieties of the antelope. It inhabits Egypt, the Bar-
bary States, Asia Minor and Syria: and its remarkable fleetness is
proverbial in the countries where it is found. The first member of
the verse is elliptical; the ellipsis is supplied in the version, as in
the Standard version, according to the obvious sense. (So Junius
and Piscator.) Instead of מִיָּד, *miyyad, from the hand*, in the first
clause, the Sept. Syr. and Chald. appear to have read מֵחֲבָלִים, *ma-
chabalayim, from the toils*: and for the same word in the second clause,
מִפַּח, *mippach, from the net*, or *snare*, and so several Hebrew MSS.
have it. Comp. Sirac. 27: 22. Psal. 124: 7.

---

5 "*As a roe from the toils*," Holden, Boothr.—"*from the snare*," French.= "*a
bird from the snare of the fowler*," Boothr., French.

CHAPTER VI. 6–11.

[Exhortation to imitate the persevering and provident industry of the ant.]

6. Go to the ant, thou sluggard;
Consider her ways, and be wise.
7. She has no leader, overseer, or ruler;

---

6. In the preceding verses the Sacred writer advises haste with particular reference to one who has become surety for another. But now from a special precept he passes to a general, in which he dissuades from sloth generally, and urges diligence and activity in all our pursuits and engagements, from the example of the industrious ant, whose persevering and provident habits are held up for imitation. "It is a shame," says the heathen moralist Seneca, "not to learn morals from the small animals." The ant has been famous from remote antiquity for industry, ingenuity, and economy; and for an instructive comprehension of the advantage to be derived from division and combination of labor. Frequent allusions have been made by poets and moralists of all ages to this animal, as an example of the qualities and habits to which we have alluded. Horace thus speaks of them. (Satyrs I. 1. 33. seqq.)

Parvula (nam exemplo est) magni formica laboris
Ore trahit quodconque potest, atque addit acervo,
Quem struxit, haud ignara ac non incauta futuri.

"Thus the little ant (for she may serve for an example,) of great industry, carries with her mouth whatever she is able, and adds to her heap, which she piles up, by no means ignorant of, and not improvident for the future."

Virgil, Aen. 4. 402, seqq.

Ac veluti ingentim formicas farris acervum
Cum populant, hyemis memores. tectoque reponant,
It nigrum campis agmen prædamque per herbas
Convectant calle angusto; parts grandia trudunt
Obnixas frumenti humeris; pars agmina cogunt,
Castigantque moras; opere omnis semita fervet.

"As when a swarm of ants, mindful of approaching winter, plunder a large granary of corn, and hoard it up in their cells " etc.

7. The ant has no leader to guide her in her work, nor is she compelled to labor by a superior: but she engages in her daily toil

6

8. Yet she prepareth in summer her food,
And gathereth her provision in harvest.

---

from the instinctive love of employment; hence her diligence is the
more remarkable. "It is worth mentioning that Aristotle, having
spoken of cranes, bees, and ants, as living in a political state, says
that the two former lived under a ruler, the latter not." (Noyes.)
In mentioning this circumstance, Solomon may have been influenced
by the habits of the people among whom he dwelt. Rev. Mr.
Thompson remarks on this passage as follows: "Laziness seems to
have been a very prevalent vice in this country (Palestine) from
days of old, giving rise to a multitude of popular proverbs. When
I began to employ workmen in this country, nothing annoyed me
more than the necessity to hire also an *overseer*, or to fulfil this office
myself. But I soon found that this was universal and strictly
necessary. Without an overseer, very little work would be done,
and nothing as it should be. The workmen, every way unlike the
ant, will not work at all unless kept to it and directed in it by an
overseer, who is himself a perfect specimen of laziness. He does
absolutely nothing but smoke his pipe, order this, scold that one,
and discuss the how and the why with the men themselves, or with
idle passers by, who are strangely prone to enter earnestly into
every body's business but their own. Thus overseeing often costs
more than the work overseen."

8. Comp. ch. 30: 25. 10: 5. The illustration of the sacred writer
is here drawn from the popular belief in respect to the habits of the
ant. It has been ascertained by naturalists that at least in cold climates, (for their observations have hitherto not extended beyond
Northern climates,) do not hoard up for the supply of their wants
during the winter season, but consume together in the evening what
has been collected during the day: and for the obvious reason, that
they do not require food during that season, because it is passed by
them in a torpid state. This fact, however, if it be universally
true furnishes no argument against the inspiration of the sacred
writer; for revelation was not designed to teach natural science,
history, or philosophy, but simply religious and moral truth. It
was no part of the Holy Spirit's work to correct popular errors in
respect to matters which lie beyond the scope of his particular design. In the illustration of divine truth, therefore, the sacred writers do not hesitate to employ the popular ideas and language of the
times in reference to natural phenomena, whether these ideas were

9. How long, O sluggard, wilt thou repose?
When wilt thou rise from thy sleep?
10. "A little sleep"—"a little slumber"—
"A little folding of the hands to rest."
11. So shall thy poverty come upon thee like a robber,
And thy want, as an armed man.

accordant or not with strict philo-ophical or scientific truth. In the
Septuagint version there is found the following addition to this verse,
in which an illustration is drawn from the habits of the bee,—"Or,
go to the bee, and learn how diligent she is, and how earnestly she
is engaged in her work; whose labors kings and private men use
for health; and she is desired and respected by all; although weak
in body she is advanced by honoring wisdom."

10. This verse contains the reply which the sluggard by his
conduct virtually, if not in words, actually makes to the inquiry
put to him in the preceding verse—his earnest expostulation when
called upon to leave his bed and engage in the active duties and
appropriate pursuits of life. He insists on more self indulgence,
let the consequences be what they may. He cannot bear to be
roused from his indolent repose, and to shake off dull sloth, which
rests like an incubus upon him. How often alas! do we witness
similar inactivity, stupidity, and recklessness among men in regard
to their spiritual interests and duties!

11. Man was created for activity; all his powers and faculties
were given him to be diligently employed for some good end. And
when this law of his nature is violated, then we may ordinarily
expect that a just retribution in some form will follow. The usual
punishment of sloth and indolence is poverty. Those who do not
sow, must not expect to reap. The Hebrew Piel participle מְהַלֵּךְ,
mehallek, denotes not simply one who walks, a *traveller*, but a *robber-
traveller*, a *highway-man*, as is evident from the parallelism. So
Marginal reading, Sept. "*an evil traveller.*" It is here intimated
that destitution shall come upon the idle and lazy man suddenly,
unexpectedly and irresistably, as the robber attacking his victim.
Armed man, is literally a *man of the shield*, i. e., one who is armed
with a shield, and hence a soldier or invading enemy. The Septuagint adds the following antithetical clause,—"But if thou be diligent, thy harvest shall arrive as a fountain, and poverty shall flee
away as a bad courser."

11. "*Like a traveller,*" Holden, Boothr., Stuart—"*invader,*" French,

CHAPTER VI. 12-15.

[The designing and crafty behavior of the wicked man described.]

12. An ungodly man—a man of wickedness—
Walketh with a perverse mouth.
13. He winketh with his eyes,
He talketh with his feet,
He maketh signs with his fingers.

---

12. In this and the three following verses the base and perfidious man is described, and his lot and end. *An ungodly man—literally, a man of Belial,* i. e., a wicked, base, abandoned wretch. (Comp. Deut. 15: 9. 2 Sam. 22: 5. Ps. 15: 4. Prov. 16: 27. 19: 28. Nah. 1: 11, 15.) *Walketh with,* &c., i. e., speaks constantly perverse things. The term *walk* is here used in a moral sense for *conducts, behaves,* as in numerous instances.

13. Solomon here represents the person he describes as intimating to his associates, by significant signs with his eyes, hands and feet, the base and mischievous designs which he is plotting, but wishes to conceal from those who may be present. " The Orientals are wonderfully proficient in making communications to each other by means of signs and gestures with the eyes, the hands and the feet. The number of signs of this sort which have a wide and most extensively understood signification, and which are in fact in current use among the people, is very large." (Kitto.) The people of the East are not accustomed to wear either shoes or sandels in their houses, so that their feet and toes are exposed. "When guests," says Roberts, "wish to speak with each other, so as not to be observed by the host, they convey their meaning by the feet and toes. Does a person wish to leave a room with another, he lifts up one of his feet, and should the other refuse he also lifts up a foot, and then suddenly puts it down on the ground. When merchants wish to bargain in presence of others without making known their terms, they sit on the ground, have a piece of cloth thrown over the lap, and then put each a hand under, and thus speak with their fingers. When the Brahmins convey religious mysteries to their disciples, they teach with their fingers, having their hands concealed in the folds of their robes." (In the text the *yodh* (י) of plurality before the suffix *vau* (ו) is left out in עֵינָיו and רַגְלָיו, but cor-

14. Perverseness is in his heart;
He deviseth evil continually;
15. Therefore shall his calamity come suddenly,
In a moment shall he be destroyed without remedy.

rected in the marginal Keri. This peculiarity is of frequent occurrence in this book. מֹרֶה, Hiph. part. of יָרָה.)

14. (The pointing of כִּדְנִים belongs to the Keri מִדְיָנִים. The
text should be pointed מְדָנִים.)

15. Sudden destruction is here predicted as the reward of the
base man's malignity. The Septuagint adds the following to this
verse: "For he rejoices in all things which God hates, and is ruined
by reason of impurity of soul."

CHAPTER VI. 16–19.

[Various offences enumerated which are highly displeasing to God.]

16. These six things Jehovah hateth,
Yea, seven are an abomination to him:
17. Lofty eyes, a false tongue,
And hands that shed innocent blood:—

16. The sacred writer here subjoins several acts of wickedness,
which are specially displeasing to God, not that every species of
wickedness is not displeasing to him, but that these acts are distinguished among the number, as being highly pernicious to human
society. A similar form of expression to that found here, occurs in
four other places in this book, (ch. 30: 15, 18, 21, 29,) and this mode
of enunciation appears to have been common among the Hebrews,
and also among the Arabians and Persians. (See Job 5: 19. Eccles.
11: 2. Amos 1: 3.) (The pointing of the word הוֹעֲבוֹת belongs to
the Keri הוֹעֲבַת, the singular instead of the plural. But the plural
is perhaps preferable as being more intensive. In that case the
word should be pointed הוֹעֲבוֹת.)

17. *Lofty eyes* are significant of *pride* and *haughtiness.* Marg.
reading, *haughty eyes.* Comp. Ps. 18: 27. 101: 5. Prov. 30: 13. The

6*

18. A heart that contriveth wicked devices,—
Feet that are swift in running to evil,—
19. A lying witness, who breathes forth falsehood,—
And (*a man*) that soweth discord among brethren.

---

phrase is opposed in sense to the *meek-eyed*. Job 22: 29. Pride,
falsehood and murder, are the three offences enumerated in this
verse.

19. The four remaining offences are a continual plotting of evil—
the eager pursuit of mischief—perjury, and the sowing of discord
among friends. *Who breathes forth*, i. e., who utters falsehood with
every breath—one who has a fixed habit of lying—who makes no
effort to tell the truth. (יָפִיחַ, Hiph. fut. of פּוּחַ.)

CHAPTER VI. 20—35.

[*Attention to parental instruction enforced, vs. 20-23.   Its tendency
to guard youth against the seductive arts of profligate women pointed out, v. 24.   The great danger of associating with persons of that
description indicated and illustrated, vs. 25-35.*]

20. Keep, my son, the commandment of thy father,
And reject not the teaching of thy mother;
21. Bind them continually to thy heart,
Tie them around thy neck.

---

20. See ch. 1: 8, where the same formula is found. Instruction
is valuable, let it come from whom it may. But from parents it is
authoritative—the ordinance of heaven. As it is the imperative
duty of parents to impart the best instruction to their children, so
it is the imperative duty of children constantly to regard that instruction. (תִּטֹּשׁ, Kal. fut. of נָטַשׁ.)

21. Comp. ch. 1: 9. 3: 3. It is probable that from a literal construction of such passages of Scripture as this, the practice arose
among Eastern nations of having mottoes or proverbial sayings in-
terwoven into the most ornamental and conspicuous parts of their
dress, in the same manner as we now find similar mottoes interwo-

22. When thou goest out, they shall guide thee;
When thou liest down, they shall watch over thee;
And when thou wakest, they shall commune with
thee.

23. For (*his*) commandment is a lamp, and (*her*)
teaching a light;
Yea, the reproofs of instruction are the way of life.

24. They shall keep thee from the evil woman;
From the stranger with a smooth tongue.

25. Desire not her beauty in thy heart,
Nor let her captivate thee with her eye-lids.

---

ven into the insignia of. the various orders of Knighthood in the
different courts of Europe.

22. The plural pronouns *they* in this verse refer to the commandments and teaching in v. 20. In the original the singular number
is plainly used for the plural, as is shown by the connexion. The
wise and wholesome instructions of parents if, instead of being disregarded and rejected, are treasured up in the memory, and held in
high estimation, will be a constant and faithful companion and
monitor, guiding, guarding, and advising on all occasions.

23. In reference to the beautiful metaphor here employed, see
Ps. 119: 105. "As in the darkness, a light or torch shows us the
way we should go, so in the darkness of human ignorance, which
surrounds us through our whole life, divine revelation teaches us
what we should do, and what we should avoid." (LeClerc.) *Reproofs of instruction*, i. e., instructive reproofs and admonitions.
Some render the phrase the *rebukes of correction*. These instructive
admonitions are called the *way of life*, because they point out the
way and means of life. They tend to prolong life, as well as to
render it prosperous and happy.

24. In the preceding verses, Solomon describes the fruit of instruction and moral discipline generally, as teaching the prudent
governance of the whole life: now he descends specifically to their
utility, as affording protection from the evil of carnal lust. By *evil
woman* is here meant a woman addicted to evil, doing or thinking
nothing but evil; just as "a man of tongue," "a man of fraud," "a
man of blood," are Hebrew phrases expressive of the highest degree
of *evil-speaking, fraud*, and *bloodthirstiness*. Comp. ch. 2: 16.

25. The Hebrew women were in the habit, (and the custom still

26. For by a harlot (*a man is brought*) to a piece of bread ;

And the adulteress layeth snares for the precious life.

27. Can a man take fire into his bosom,
And his clothes not be burned ?

28. Can a man walk on burning coals,
And his feet not be scorched ?

29. So is it with him, who goeth in to his neighbor's wife ;

Whoever toucheth her, shall not go unpunished.

---

prevails among the women of the East generally,) of coloring their eye-lids, or rather their *eye-lashes* and *eye-brows*, with a black powder or paint made, as is supposed, of a preparation of antimony (*stibi-cum*). By this they were rendered more dark and strikingly de-fined, which was regarded as a very great ornament. Comp. 2 Kg. 9: 30. Jere. 4: 30. Ezek. 23: 40. Sept. "Let not the desire of beauty overcome thee, neither be thou caught by thy eyes, neither be cap-tivated with her eye-lids." (יְפִי makes with a suff. יְפִיהָ.)

26. Degradation, disgrace, and poverty, are among the conse-quences which result from frequenting the houses of lewd women (see ch. 5: 10. 29: 3); while the crime of adultery among the He-brews was punished by the death of both the guilty parties. (See Lev. 20: 10. Deut. 22: 22. Comp. Ezek. 16: 40.) The distich is quite elliptical. In the first member both the subject and predicate verb require to be supplied.

27. The writer here shows the impossibility of the adulterer's escaping the fearful consequences of his crime. In the phrase " to take into the bosom," there is allusion to the custom of folding to-gether the loose outer garment and supporting it by a girdle around the waist, so that various articles could be carried in the bosom. Comp. Luke 6: 38.

28. (תִּכָּוֶינָה, Niph. fut. 3d pers. plur. of כָּוָה).

29. The Hebrew verb נָקָה, *niqqa*, in Niph. conj., signifies *to be clean* in a moral sense, *to be innocent, free from blame, to be free from punishment,* i. e., to go unpunished. It is rendered in the Standard

---

29. " *Shall not be innocent,*" St. Ver , Geier. Shultens, Stuart—" *shall not be (held) guiltless,*" Boothr., French.

30. (*Men*) do not despise a thief,
When he steals to satisfy his appetite, because he is
hungry;

Version in this place and in ch. 28: 20, in connexion with the negative particle לֹא, *lo, shall not be innocent*. But in ch. 11: 21. 16: 5.
17: 5. 19: 5, 9. it is rendered *shall not be unpunished*. (See also Jere.
49: 12.) We have observed uniformity, and translated the phrase
throughout *shall not go unpunished*. This is also the more fertile
sense, as it presupposes conviction and condemnation. A man can
no more have criminal intercourse with another's wife and escape
punishment either in this world or the next, than he can walk on
burning coals without suffering injury.

30. The Hebrew verb בּוּז, signifies to *despise*, to *spurn*, to *contemn*,
or hold in contempt, in which sense it occurs in seven places in this
book, besides the present passage. (ch. 1: 7. 11: 12. 13: 13. 14: 21.
23: 9, 22. 30: 17.) If such be the meaning here, then the sense of
the passage, taken in connexion with the following verse, is this:
'Men do not spurn and despise a man for taking what does not belong to him merely to satisfy the cravings of appetite when hungry;
but on the contrary look upon his fault with the feeling of pity.
Nevertheless, should he be detected in the act, such is the rigor of
the law, that even for this comparatively venial offence, he must
suffer the punishment which that law imposes.' This appears to
have been the sense in which it was understood by the translators
of our Standard Version, and so Stuart and others. But some, influenced by the context, render the verb in this place, *to disregard*,
to overlook, and interpret the passage as meaning that 'men do not
overlook or treat with indifference as guilty of no crime and unde-
serving of punishment a thief who steals, even though it be to
satisfy his present hunger; and when caught he must suffer the
penalty of the law.' Gesenius, while he retains the meaning *to
despise*, yet interprets the word in this instance in the sense of "do
not overlook his crime, and let him go unpunished,"—a sense, however, which the word no where else bears. French endeavors to
obviate the difficulty by translating the verse interrogatively; "Do
not men hold in contempt the thief, though he steal to satisfy his
appetite, because he is hungry?" But for this rendering there is
no authority. It seems to be preferable to adhere to the customary
meaning of the word, and interpret the passage as above. Sept.

---

30. "*Do not disregard*," Holden—"*do not overlook*," Noyes.

31. But (*if*) caught, he must repay seven-fold ;
All the wealth of his house must he give up.

32. He that committeth adultery with a woman, is
void of understanding ;
He that doeth this, destroyeth his own life.

"It is not to be wondered at if one should be taken stealing, for he
steals that when hungry he may satisfy his soul; but if he should
be taken," &c.

31. If the thief who steals merely to satisfy the demands of appetite is liable, when caught, to severe punishment, how much more
deserving of the severest punishment is he who is guilty of the
crime of adultery. His sin claims no sympathy whatever. "His
plea is not the cry of hunger, but of lust; not of want but of wan-
tonness; not the lack of bread, but of understanding." Theft by
the Jewish law, was punished by making ample restitution, and if
the offender was unable to make such restitution, he was ordered to
be sold into involuntary servitude until the demands of the law
were satisfied. The term *seven-fold* is, as usual, a certain and definite put for an uncertain and indefinitely large sum, and is employed to denote a full and complete satisfaction and restitution.
Comp. Ex. 22: 1–4. Lev. 25: 39. Four or five fold was the extent of
the divine requirement. Comp. Luke 19: 8. The plea of necessity
or urgent want, it would seem was not a valid one in justification
of theft under the Mosaic dispensation. It was indeed permitted
to pluck ears of grain in the field sufficient to appease the present
hunger of the individual; but the use of the reaping-hook for the
purpose of carrying off a portion for future use was prohibited.
(See Deut. 23: 25. Comp. Matt. 12: 1, 2. Lu. 6: 1.) A careful consideration of the law as contained in Deut. 24: 19–22. 14: 28, 29.
15: 7. Lev. 25: 35. Deut. 15: 11. will show that it was scarcely possible under that dispensation to be reduced to such a state of indi-
gence and destitution, as to be compelled to steal in order to support
life. Should such an instance occur, it might be presumed to be
attributable entirely to the fault of the individual. Moses, therefore, made no provision for such a case, and hence, thefts committed
under such circumstances of palliation, was not exempt from punishment.

32. The commission of the crime against society here spoken

---

32. "*Destroys himself,*" Noyes—"*he who would destroy his own life—let him do
this,*" French.

33. Stripes and dishonor shall he receive,
And his reproach shall not be wiped away.

34. For jealousy (*maketh*) a man furious;
And he will not spare in the day of vengeance.

35. He will accept of no ransom;
He will not be content, though thou offer many gifts.

---

of is a proof that the guilty man is destitute of understanding—void of reason: for no man in the possession of a right mind would so yield himself up to the dominion of passion as to commit such a suicidal act. Adultery was a crime punishable with death by the Levitical law. (Lev. 20: 10.)

33. Should the guilty party escape with his life, yet the least punishment which he might expect would be corporeal chastisement and dishonor.

34. The first clause of the verse is literally, "For jealousy is the rage (or fury) of a man": the import of which evidently is that jealousy creates in the breast of man a feeling of the most violent and lasting resentment. This is the case among the people of the East, with whom it is very common and powerful, and frequently carried to an extent of which we have no example among Western nations.

35. The first clause of the verse is literally, "he will not lift up the face to any ransom." "To lift up the face," is a phrase figuratively employed to denote *acquiescence, consent, approval*. The injured man will not be satisfied, or consent to remit the penalty of the law on the adulterer, though many valuable gifts be offered him to appease his anger. (אָשָׂא, Kal fut. of נָשָׂא.)

---

33. "Be blotted out," French, Stuart.
34. "For jealousy is the fury of a man," French, Noyes.
35. "He will not pay regard to any ransom," French, Noyes.

CHAPTER VII.

[*A further exhortation to attend to instruction in religion and morality, vs.* 1–4. *The arts of the adulteress described, and their destructive effects upon those who become ensnared by them pointed out, vs.* 5–27.]

1. My son, keep my words,
And treasure up my commandments within thee.
2. Keep my commandments, and live;
And let my teaching be as the pupil of thy eye.
3. Bind them upon thy fingers;
Inscribe them on the tablet of thy heart.
4. Say to wisdom, "Thou art my Sister";
And call understanding, "Kinswoman."

---

2. The imperative *live*, is here equivalent to the future, *thou shalt live*. The *pupil or apple of the eye*, is literally the *little man of the eye*; a form of expression in which there is allusion to the reflected image of a man seen in the pupil of the visual organ. The Greeks call it *χορη*, and *χοράσιον*, *damsel*, and *little damsel;* the Latins *pupa* and *pupella*, words of the same import as the Greek. From the Latin *pupella* comes our English word *pupil*. The precept suggests the extreme care and vigilance requisite for the preservation of so delicate an organ as the eye. Such should be the care with which parental instruction should be preserved. See Deut. 32: 10. Ps. 17: 8. The Sept. introduces this verse with the following precept not found in the present Hebrew text—"My son, honor the Lord, and thou shalt be strong and fear none but him."

3. See ch: 3: 3. 6: 21. 'Bind these precepts as you would a string around your fingers, that as often as you observe them, you may recollect monitions so necessary for you.' Stuart thinks the allusion is to finger rings with large signets, on which were inscribed some weighty sentence or maxim. The language is to be understood figurative.

4. "*Thou art my sister*," i. e., Love wisdom as you would a sister, and cultivate with her habits of the most endearing intimacy and friendship. Comp. Job 17: 14. The Sept. renders the second member: "and gain prudence as an acquaintance for thyself."

5. That they may keep thee from the strange wo-
man;
From the stranger who uttereth smooth words,
6. For through the window of my house—
Through the lattice I looked out;
7. And I saw among the simple ones—
I observed among the youth,
A young man void of understanding.
8. He was passing through the street near her corner,
Yea, he was going the way to her house.
9. At twilight, in the evening,
At midnight, yea, in the thick darkness.

---

5. See ch. 2: 16.

6. By *the lattice* is meant a latticed window, made like our Venetian blinds, for the purpose of shutting out the sun's rays and
the rain, and admitting the cool breezes. (See Judg. 5: 28.) Sept.
"For she looks from a window out of her house into the streets, at
one whom she may see of the senseless ones," &c.

7. (אֵרֶא, Kal. fut. 1st pers. apoc. of רָאָה.)

8. *Her corner*, i. e., the corner of the street where the adulteress
mentioned in v. 10 was in the habit of stationing herself for the
purpose of meeting and decoying her paramours. (Comp. v. 12.)
The expression, however, may denote the house of the harlot, as the
parallel line would suggest.

9. *At twilight*—lit. in the breeze of the day, *i. e.*, at the time
when the cool wind begins to blow—at the close of the day. (Comp.
Gen. 3: 8.) *In the evening*—Heb. *in the evening of the day*. *At midnight*—lit. *in the pupil* (of the eye) *of night*. As the pupil is in the
centre of the eye, so it is here put figuratively for the middle of the
night, when the darkness is the greatest. "The sacred writer represents this young man as wandering about from the first shades
of evening until the night is far advanced, in the hope that the
darkness would screen him from observation." (French.) "A young
man that breaketh wedlock, saying thus in his heart, 'Who seeth
me? I am compassed about with darkness, the walls cover me, and
nobody seeth me; what need I fear? the Most High will not remember my sins,'—such a man only feareth the eyes of men, and know-

---

7. "*That I might see,*" Stuart.

10. And behold! a woman met him,
In the attire of a harlot, and subtle of heart.
11. (Noisy is she, and refractory;
Her feet abide not in her house.
12. Now she is abroad, then in the wide streets;
And near to every corner she lieth in wait.)
13. She caught hold of him, and kissed him;
And with an impudent face, she said to him;

---

eth not that the eyes of the Lord are ten thousand times brighter
than the sun, beholding all the ways of men, and considering the
most secret parts." Ecclus. 23: 18, 19.

10. *A woman.* The Heb. noun is anarthrous: but it is probable
that the woman referred to is the one spoken of in the preceding
verse. Sept. "*the* woman." *Attire of a harlot.* It seems highly probable from this expression that harlots were distinguished among
the Hebrews by some peculiarity of dress, though the Scriptures
furnish no information as to what it consisted in. Among the Athe-
nians, the courtesans wore flowered garments; and at Rome they
were permitted to wear the *stola;* but were distinguished by a peculiar head-dress, called *mitra* or *mitella.* Dr. Richardson mentions
seeing the wretched women of that class in a large commercial town
in Egypt in the harlot's attire, sitting at the doors of their houses,
and calling on the passengers as they went by, in the same manner
as we read of here. *Subtle of heart,* is literally *guarded* or *reserved
of heart,* i. e., disguising her real designs, and artfully prepared to
make such false and deceptive representations to the young man, as
might induce him to listen to her solicitations, and at the same time
conceal her guilt from the absent husband whom she wronged.
Vulg. "prepared to captive hearts." Sept. "having the appearance
of a harlot, that causes the hearts of young men to flutter."

11. This verse and the one following, are parenthetical, and descriptive of the habitual disposition and conduct of the harlot,
while she is hunting for her prey, which not finding in one place,
she seeks for in another. (חֹמִיָּה, Part. pres. form of חָמָה.)

13. After the parenthetical description in the two preceding
verses, the narrative is here resumed. *With an impudent face,* lit.
she strengthened her face, i. e., assuming a bold, impudent and shame-
less countenance. (Sept. ἀναιδεῖ προδώπω, Vulg. procaci vultu.)
21: 29. Deut. 28: 50.

14. " Peace offerings (*were due*) from me ;
" This day I have performed my vows.

15. "Therefore came I forth to meet thee ;
" Diligently to seek thy face ; and I have found thee!

16. " I have spread my couch with coverlets ;
" With embroidered tapestry of Egyptian thread :

---

14. The adulteress or harlot is here described as enticing youth under the garb of religion. She pretends to have that day performed some vow which she had made (Lev. 27: 2) by presenting peace or thank-offerings to Jehovah in grateful acknowledgment of certain benefits received, and now she had prepared the customary feast on the sacrifice for the entertainment of her friends. This class of offerings consisted of oxen, sheep, or goats. A part only of the animal required by the law, was retained by the priests, (Lev. 7: 29–36); the remainder was returned to the offerer, with which a sacrificial feast was prepared, to which the friends of the offerer were invited. (Lev. 7: 13. Deut. 12: 6.) It is to such a feast that the adulteress is here described as urging the unwary youth. *Were due from me*—lit. were *upon me* (Ps. 56: 12), *i. e.*, they were upon me as a duty to be performed; or, the obligation lay on me to make the offering.

15. The adulteress pretends to have a great regard for her victim, and a great desire to see him and extend the hospitalities of her table to him.

16. Solomon here alludes to a kind of coverlets, made of the richest materials—the finest thread or yarn, either of cotton or flax, termed Egyptian thread, because probably, the best article of the kind was manufactured in Egypt. They were also embroidered and richly ornamented with figures and devices. Such embroidered carpets and coverlets are in use at the present time. " The Arabs," says D'Arvieux, " have coverlets of all sorts; some are very beautiful, stitched with gold and silk, with flowers of gold and silver." " When it was dark," says Dr. Chandler, " three coverlets, richly embroidered, were taken from a press in the room which we occupied, and delivered, one to each of us; the carpet or sofa and a cushion serving with the addition, instead of a bed."

---

16. " *With embroidered fine linen of Egypt*," French—"*with coverlets of the fine linen of Egypt*," Boothr.—"*with tapestry of the thread of Egypt*," Noyes—"*with embroideries of Egyptian linen*;" Holden.

17. "I have sprinkled my bed
"With myrrh, aloes, and cinnamon;

18. "Come, let us take our fill of love till the morning;
"Let us enjoy ourselves with caresses.

19. "For the man is not at home;
"He hath gone a distant journey.

---

17. Perfumes were an article of luxury in great repute among the people of the East, and also among the more sensuous and luxurious Greeks and Romans. They are still in the highest request among Eastern nations. The spices named in the text were costly and favorite ones, imported from Africa and India. (Comp. Ps. 45: 8. Cant. 4: 14.) *Myrrh* (Heb. *mor*,) is a gum exuded by a tree (*Balsamodendron Myrrha*) or shrub found in Arabia and Eastern Africa. It is highly aromatic and medicinal and moderately stimulating, and was celebrated in very ancient times as a perfumer and fumigator, as well as for its uses in medicine. *Aloes* (Heb. *Ahalim*) properly lign-aloes, (Num. 24: 6,) is a tree still known in India by the name of Aghil, and in Europe as the Eagle-tree (*Aquilaria Agallochum*). It should be carefully distinguished from that species of the plant from the juice of which the resonous substance or drug used in medicine is formed; for that is bitter and nauseous and emits no agreeable odor. The wood of the tree in question is highly odoriferous, and was used to impart fragrance to linen in which dead bodies were wrapped. (John 19: 40.) *Cinnamon* is the well known bark of the *laurus kinnamomum*, a plant found in India and China; but the best kind is imported from Malabar and Ceylon. Of these a liquid extract is probably here intended; for the Heb. word נוּף *nuph*, properly signifies *to wave up and down*, and hence specifically *to sprinkle*,—an act which is performed by such a motion. The rendering *to perfume* in our Standard and other versions, is according to the sense, but not the letter, and fails to convey the exact shape in which the thought is presented in the original. So Sept.

18. The verb רָוָה, *rava*, properly sig. *to drink to the full, to be sated with drink;* here figuratively *to be sated with forbidden pleasures.* So ch. 5: 19. (לְכָה, from לָךְ, Kal impera. of יָלַךְ. נִתְעַלְּכָה, Hithp. fut. of יָעֲלֹס, with ה paragogic.)

19. הָאִישׁ, *haish, the man,* is ambiguous, and may denote either

---

17. "*I have perfumed my bed,*" Holden, Boothr., French, Noyes.

19. "*My husband,*" Boothr., French—"*the master,*"—Holden—"*the good-man,*" Noyes.

20. " He hath taken a purse of money with him ;
" At the time of the full moon he will return home."

the *Husband* of the woman, or the *Master*, or *Keeper of the house.*
Some critics think that the woman spoken of was a slave, and that
the man here alluded to was her Master, on the ground of the im-
probability that a harlot, who is described as lying in wait at every
corner, should have a husband. The translators of the Septuagint,
however, understood the word as referring to her husband; for they
have rendered it *my husband*, as though they read אִישִׁי, *ishi.* So the
authors of our Standard Version; for among the earlier English
writers the term *goodman* was a common appellation for the head of
a family, or husband. If this be the meaning, as it most probably
is, the Hebrew article is to be understood in an emphatic sense. *At
home*—בְּבֵיתוֹ, *bebetho*, lit. *in his house*, which was the Hebrew mode
of expressing *at home.*

20. The *purse of money* which the husband or master is here said
to have taken with him, is introduced in order to show that, antici-
pating a long and expensive journey, he had made ample provision
for it, and that consequently his return need not be expected before
the time appointed. A sudden, surprise, therefore, was not to be
apprehended. *With him*—lit. *in his hand.* " From ch. 1: 14, and
Isa. 46: 6, it may be collected that the ancient Hebrews had bags or
purses for the reception of money, which might, therefore, be carried in the hand, or tied to some part of the dress. Nevertheless,
it is correctly rendered by our English translators " with him;" for
it is probable, that the ancients did not *usually* carry their purses in
their hands, but in their girdles, or rather they were a part of the
girdle itself. בְּיָד, *beyad*, means *with, apud*, Gen. 44: 16, 17. Ex. 21:
16, though the two latter texts are mistranslated in E. V. "in his
hand "; so likewise, 1 Sam. 9: 8, it should have been *with, apud.*"
(Holden.) *At the time of the full moon.* The Heb. word כֶּסֶא, *kese*, is
found only in this place and Ps. 18: 4, where it is written כֶּסֶה.
Some understand by it the *new moon.* (So Aben-Ezra and Piscator.)
Others take it for *scenopegia,* the feast of Tabernacles or Booths. (So
Chald.) The best expositors, however, agree in rendering it *full
moon.* So Aquila and Vulg. "After many days," Sept. and Syr.

20. " *At the new-moon,*" Boothr.—" *at the time appointed,*" Holden—" *at the
stated day,*" French.

21. By her many persuasive words she enticed him;
By the smoothness of her lips she seduced him.
22. He goeth after her straightway,
As an ox goeth to the slaughter,
Or, as one in fetters (*goeth*) to the punishment of the
fool.
23. Until an arrow pierceth his liver;
Even as a bird hasteneth into the snare,
And knoweth not that it (*is set*) for its life.

21. לֶקַח, *leqach*, commonly sig. *doctrine, teaching, instruction;* but
here it denotes *persuasion, persuasive* and *captivating language. She
enticed him*—lit. *she made him turn away,* &c., from the right path.
Sept. "She prevailed on him to go astray." The word *lips* must be
taken figuratively for what the lips utter, as the parallelism shows.
(הִפַּתְהוּ=הִטַּתּוֹ, Hiph perf. fem. of נָטָה, with suffix.)

22. By "one in fetters," is meant a *prisoner*, or person convicted
of some crime, and about to suffer the penalty of the law—*the fool*,
i. e., of folly, or crime, by metonymy of the concrete for the abstract.
The word אֱוִיל, *avil, fool*, is in regimen with מוּסָר, *musar*, and not
the subject of the proposition. So the English expression, "a criminal goes to the punishment of his folly." Some render the last
clause, "As a hart boundeth into the toils." But this version, although it makes good sense, and suits the connexion, not only requires a change of reading אַיָּל, *ayyal,* for אֱוִיל, *evil,* but puts a
meaning on עֶכֶס, *akas,* and מוּסָר, *musar*, not authorized by usage.
Sept. "as a dog to bonds, or as a hart shot in the liver with an arrow." "The ox, like all the lower animals, is neither tormented
by reflecting on the past, nor guessing at the future; he grazes without a doubt, amidst the green pastures, and fattens for the knife,
unconscious of the doom that awaits him; and when his owner
comes and leads him away to the slaughter, his brute imagination
only figures a richer meadow, or a more agreeable companion.
Equally unconscious and cheerful is the miserable youth, whom an
abandoned woman has entangled in her toils, and leads away to
forbidden pleasures. He is not aware of his danger, and his misery;
he goes with blind infatuation, and pitiable mirth, to his destruction." (Paxton.)

23. This verse has three clauses, the first of which seems to be-

21. "*By her much fair speech,*" Boothr., Noyes—"*with the flattery of her lips,*"
—Holden, Boothr.—"*with her smooth talk,*" Stuart. 23. "*Its liver,*" Boothr , French.

24. Now, therefore, ye children, hearken to me;
And attend to the words of my mouth.

25. Let not thy heart incline to her ways;
Go not astray in her paths.

26. For many are the wounded, whom she hath cast
down;
Yea, countless are those whom she hath slain.

27. Her house is the way to Sheol,
Leading down to the chambers of death.

---

long either to the last clause of the preceding verse, or to something
which has dropped from the text. The unwary youth who allows
himself to be caught in the coils of a libidinous woman is compared
1. to an ox going to the slaughter-bench—unconscious of his fate,
and perhaps dreaming of rich pastures, 2. to a criminal in chains
to prevent his escape, on his way to execution, yet unfeeling and
careless of his impending fate till the fatal arrow penetrates his
heart, 3. to a bird hastening into a snare, thinking only of the
tempting bait, and not knowing that its life is in danger.

25. The first member contains an exhortation not to enter upon
the dangerous paths of the evil doer; the second not to continue in
them, but at once to abandon them. (יֵשְׁטְ, Kal fut. apoc. of שָׁטָה.
תֵּרַע, same form of הָעָה.)

26. "The most valiant heroes, the most puissant soldiers, that
never have yielded, but stood undaunted against all other assaults,
have generally been vanquished and frequently destroyed, by the
allurements of women." (Hammond.) The fate of Hannibal's army
in Italy, is an example in point. The adjective עֲצֻמִים, alzumim,
may signify either strong, mighty, powerful, viz. in mind or body, or
numerous—numerically strong. Accordingly some interpreters (Luther among others) render it mighty. But the latter sense, in which
the word occurs in Num. 32: 1. Ps. 35: 18. Amos 5: 12. is required
by the parallelism, as it corresponds with רַבִּים, rabbim, in the first
clause. The Sept. Symm. and Theod. render it αναρίθμητοι,
innumerable, countless, and they are followed by the majority of modern translators.

27. In the expression chambers of death, or of the dead, (see ch. 2:

---

27. " To the under-world," Noyes, Stuart—"to Hades," Holden, Boothr.—"the
grave," French.

18. 5: 5.) there is allusion to the form of the sepulchres in which the Hebrews commonly deposited their dead. These were spacious vaults beneath the ground, around which were cut out small recesses, each designed to hold a body, and hence called chambers. The ultimate consequences of yielding to seduction, and becoming victims to the alluring, but deceptive wiles of unprincipled women, are here portrayed in graphic terms. The house of the adulteress is the way which leads to death, and they who frequent it rush on to their own destruction. (הִפִּילָה, Hiph. of נָפַל.)

CHAPTER VIII. 1–21.

[*Heavenly Wisdom personified and represented as inviting the children of men to receive her instructions, vs. 1–5. The inestimable value of these instructions described, vs. 6–11. The inseparable connexion of wisdom with all which conduces to the enjoyment and well-being of life, vs. 12–21.*]

1. Doth not wisdom call aloud?
And understanding utter her voice?
2. On the top of the high places, by the way-side;
In the midst of the high-ways, she taketh her station;—

---

1. In other parts of this instructive book (ch. 1: 20. 3: 13, 20. 9: 1–6.) and elsewhere in the Old Testament and apocryphal writings (Ecclus. 14: 1, etc.) abstract wisdom is personified and represented under the form of a female. But no where else is the prosopopœa carried on to so great a length and with such variety of illustration, as in this sublime chapter. The interrogatory form is here adopted in order to express an affirmation the more emphatically.

2. It was usual for persons desirous of communicating intelligence, or proclaiming good news of general interest, to occupy conspicuous places, where they could be most widely and distinctly

3. By the gates,—at the entrance of the side of the city,—
In the avenues of approach she crieth aloud.

4. "To you, O men, do I call,
" And my voice is to the sons of men,

5. " Ye simple (*ones*), understand prudence,
" And, ye fools, be of an understanding heart.

6. " Hear, for I will speak excellent things ;
" And the opening of my lips (*shall be*) uprightness.

7. " For my mouth shall speak truth ;
" And falsehood is the abomination of my lips.

---

heard. (Isa. 40: 9. 52: 7, 8. Ps. 72: 3. Lu. 12: 3.) A variety of expressions is employed in this verse and the one following, in order to indicate the intense anxiety and profound solicitude of Heavenly Wisdom to benefit mankind. She occupies every place where she may hope to reach the human ear and instruct the human heart. (נִצָּבָה, Niph. reflexive of נָצַב, to *station*, or *place oneself*, *to take one's stand*.)

3. The gates here spoken of are not the gates leading to private dwellings or to the palaces of kings and princes, as the Sept. has it, but those which were placed at the various entrances of the city. (תָּרֹנָּה, Kal fut. of רָנַן, see ch. 1: 20.)

5. The word עָרְמָה, *arma*, is a middle term (*vox media*), being sometimes used in a bad sense (*craftiness, guile, artful, cunning*); at others, in a good one, (*prudence, sagacity*,) as it always is in this book. See note ch. 1: 4.

6. *The opening of the lips* is put by metonymy for the *words uttered by the lips.*—*Uprightness*, i. e., without any duplicity—in honest sincerity.

7. *My mouth shall speak*, is lit. *my palate shall meditate*, and so Sept. Syr. Chald. and Vulg. But the *palate* is manifestly put by synecdoche for the *mouth. Falsehood.*—The word רֶשַׁע, *resha*, commonly means *wickedness*, but here specifically *falsehood*, because it stands opposed to אֱמֶת, *emeth, truth.* So Sept. Syr. and Arab. versions.

---

6. " *Shall be right things,*" Holden—" *My lips shall utter things that are right,*" Boothr, Noyes.
7. " *Wickedness is the abomination,*" etc. Holden, Boothr., French, Noyes.

8. " All the words of my mouth are righteous,
" There is in them nothing deceitful or perverse.

9. " They are all plain to the intelligent,
" And right to those that find knowledge.

10. " Receive my instruction, and not silver ;.
" And knowledge, rather than fine gold.

11. " For wisdom is better than pearls,
" And all desirable things are not to be compared
with her.

12. I, wisdom, dwell (*with*) prudence,
" And find out the knowledge of sagacious plans.

---

8. The substantive *righteousness*, with the preposition בְּ, *beth, in,*
is put for the adjective.

10. *And not silver*, i. e., rather than silver. The import of the
apparent prohibition is *comparative*, and not *absolute*, as the corresponding word in the second clause plainly shows. By an Hebraism, when two things are compared, the one is often enjoined to the
exclusion or rejection of the other. So Hosea 6: 6. " I will have
mercy, and *not* sacrifice," *i. e.*, 'I require the exercise of mercy
rather than, or in preference to, sacrifice.' It is a forcible mode of
indicating the superior importance of one thing to another. Comp.
ch. 3: 14, 15.

11. *Desirable things*, i. e., *precious;* the most valuable earthly possessions. Sept. " No valuable substance is of equal worth with it."
(יִשְׁווּ, Kal fut of שָׁוָה.)

12. The phrase *dwell with prudence*, is lit. *inhabit prudence*, a form
of expression intended to convey by a strong metaphor the idea of
an intimate and inseparable connexion between the two, so that
they who possess the one will certainly exhibit the other in the conduct of life. The phrase receives light from Isai. 57: 15, where Jehovah speaks of himself as " inhabiting eternity;" and from 1 Tim.
6: 16, where God is said " to inhabit light inaccessible," φῶς
οἰκῶν ἀπρόσιτον. The Hebrew word מְזִמּוֹת, *mezimmoth*, rendered *sagacious things*, is a middle term, being sometimes used in a
good, and at other times, in a bad sense. (See ch. 12: 2. 14: 17. 24:
8.) Here it is evidently employed in a *good* sense.

11. " *All the objects of desire,*" Boothr.—" *all precious things,*" Stuart—" *no precious things are to be compared,*" Noyes—" *no objects of delight,*" French.

12. " *Skillful plans,*" Stuart—" *artful devices,*" Boothr.—" *discreet things,*" Holden.

13. "The fear of Jehovah is hatred of evil.
" Pride and arrogance, and the evil way,
" And the perverse mouth do I hate.
14. " Counsel and sound wisdom are mine ;
" I (*have*) understanding ; to me (*belongeth*) might.
15. " By me kings reign,
" And princes decree justice.

---

13. The Infinitive construct. שְׂנֹאת, *shenoth*, is here used as a verbal noun=*hatred*. The sentiment is, that he who truly reverences Jehovah will by no means take pleasure in depraved thoughts, designs or deeds, but on the contrary will abhor and renounce all sin both of word and deed. Comp. Job 28: 28. Isa. 1: 16, 17. Ps. 97: 10. 1 John 4: 20. Instead of יִרְאַת, *yirath*, *the fear*, and שְׂנֹאות, *shenoth*, *hatred* or *to hate*, Doederlein, Dathe, Boothroyd, and some others read יָרֵאתִי, *yarethi*, and שָׂנֵאתִי, *shanethi*, "I *fear* Jehovah; I hate evil." But the alteration is entirely unwarrantable, since it is contrary to all the MSS. and Vers., and is not required by the exigency of the place. *A perverse mouth*, is a mouth that speaks perverse things. (See ch. 2: 12.)

14. The same properties are predicated of God in nearly the same words in Job 12: 13. By *counsel* is probably meant the faculty of managing difficult affairs skilfully, and bringing them to a successful result. *I have understanding*—By the majority of commentators the substantive verb in the present tense is supplied—"I *am* understanding." But this interrupts the logical sequence of thought, and destroys the evident parallelism between this verse and Job 12: 13. (see also Job 12: 3.) As the possession of counsel and sound wisdom and might is ascribed to Heavenly Wisdom here, so it would be far more natural to suppose that the possession of understanding is also attributed to her, than that she is declared to be understanding itself, or the source and origin of it. The Sept. and Vulg. read " Prudence is mine,"—reading perhaps in their Heb. MSS. לִי, *li*, instead of אֲנִי, *ani*, or else translating according to the sense. Heavenly Wisdom is here described as having in her possession and at her disposal the invaluable qualities and properties here enumerated, and as ready to bestow them upon her votaries.

15. The principles of true religion enable kings and magistrates

14. "*I am understanding*," Holden, French, Noyes—"*with me is prudence*," Boothr.

16. "By me princes govern, and nobles,—
"Yea, all the judges of the earth.
17. "I love them that love me,
"And those that seek me early shall find me.
18. "Riches and honor are with me;
"Yea, durable riches and righteousness.

of all degrees to govern wisely, prudently, justly and happily. The thrones of kings and the authority of rulers can be permanently established only on the principles of true religion and of moral rectitude. *By me*, i. e., by my aid.

16. Sept. "and monarchs by me rule over the earth." Instead of אֶרֶץ, *eretz*, *earth*, in the end of the verse a large number of MSS. enumerated by Kennicott and De Rossi, read צֶדֶק, *tzedeq, justice,* which is also expressed in the Syr. Chald. Vulg. and Venetian Greek. If this word is intended to limit שֹׁפְטֵי, *shophete, judges,* then the proper rendering would be, "yea, all just judges." But the Vulg. supplies a verb, and renders as in v. 15, "and monarchs decree justice."

17. The Heb. verb שָׁחַר, *shachar*, properly sig. 1. *to seek*, then *to seek early.* Hence the derivative שַׁחַר, *shachar, the dawn of day, the morning.* 2. Intensively *to seek diligently*, or *earnestly.* It occurs in this book five times. In ch. 1: 24, the accessory idea of *early, seasonably*, seems plainly intended to be conveyed. In three instances of its occurrence (ch. 1: 28. 7: 15. 11: 27.) the *manner* of seeking appears to be indicated, viz. *diligently, carefully, earnestly.* In this place, Commentators are divided between *early* and *diligently.* Either rendering conveys a sentiment equally true and important, and although we cannot suppose that both are here particularly intended, yet both are ordinarily necessary to success. I prefer, however, the rendering in the version, because the young are particularly addressed in this part of the book. So Vulg. (The word אֹהֲבֶיהָ, in the text should be pointed אֹהֲבֶיהָ, i. e. those who love *her.* But the Marginal Keri reads אֹהֲבַי, those who love *me*, which is undoubtedly the preferable reading. So Sept. and Vulg. אֹהֵב is the contract form of אֶאֱהַב, 1st pers. fut. מְשַׁחֲרַי, Part. plur. of Piel with suffix.)

18. Riches and honor are *with* wisdom, i. e. not only in her pos-

17. "*Who earnestly seek me*," Stuart—"*that seek me*
18. "*And prosperity*," Noyes, Stuart.

19. "My fruit is better than gold, yea, than pure
gold;
"And my revenue, than choice silver.

20. "I walk in the way of righteousness;
"In the midst of the paths of equity.

21. "That I may cause those that love me to possess
wealth;
"Yea, I will fill their treasuries.

---

session, but at her disposal, to be bestowed upon such as seek and
find her. (Comp. ch. 3: 16.) Rank and wealth "are the two strong
cords by which the ambitious are led,—the two reciprocally supporting rails, on which the train of ambition runs." But Heavenly
Wisdom enters into competition with the world's most powerful attractions, and offers us not only riches, but *enduring* riches, so called
in specific contrast with those earth-born, sublunary riches that
make for themselves wings and fly away. *Righteousness.*—The
word צְדָקָה, *tredaqa*, may here signify the *fruits of righteousness—
prosperity*, by metonymy, of cause for effect, as it frequently does,
particularly in Isaiah.

20. Some interpreters give the Hiph. causative sense to the Piel
verb אֲהַלֵּךְ, *ahallek*, and render it *to lead, to conduct*. According to
this rendering, the meaning of the distich is, that Heavenly Wisdom conducts her votaries in the way of righteousness and in the
paths of equity. But there is no other example of the verb in Piel
being used in a transitive and causative sense. It is rendered intransitively both in the Sept. and Vulg. It no doubt here imports
habitual walking.

21. The object for which Wisdom proceeds in the way of righteousness and equity is here assigned, viz. for the purpose of making
her votaries acquire not frail, perishable wealth, but true, spiritual, substantial riches.

---

20. "*I lead*," Boothr.

CHAPTER VIII. 22–36.

[Wisdom as an attribute of the Deity poetically personified and represented as efficiently present with the Almighty at the creation of the world, and as a favorite counsellor and instrumental assistant in that mighty work, vs. 22–31. The chapter closes with an exhortation to attend to the precepts of Wisdom, vs. 32–36.]

22. "Jehovah possessed me (*in*) the beginning of his way,
    "Before his works of old.

---

22. From Wisdom in general personified, the sacred writer proceeds to speak of the *Wisdom of God*, also personified. The attribute of Wisdom exists in Jehovah in infinite perfection, and by him it was most wonderfully displayed in the work of creation. The ancient versions are divided in their mode of rendering the verb קָנָה, *qana*. The Sept. Syr. Chald. and Arab. translate it *created, formed;* while the Vulg. Aqui. Sym. and Theod. have *possessed.* The generic signification of the word would seem to be *to possess,* while the particular mode of possessing or acquiring, whether by creation, purchase, or otherwise, must be gathered, if at all, from the context and nature of the subject. The generic meaning is quite suitable here, whether we regard the sacred writer as speaking of the hypostatic word—the Divine Logos of John—the second person in the adorable Trinity, as many suppose; or of a personal attribute of Jehovah. The phrase רֵאשִׁית דַּרְכּוֹ; *reshith darko*, may be taken as an adverbial clause of time, the preposition בְּ *beth*, being omitted by ellipsis. "*In,* or *at* the beginning of his way." See Gen. 14: 4. 2 Sam. 21: 9, where there is a similar omission of the preposition. So the Syr. Chald. Vulg. Aquila. According to this rendering the meaning is, that Jehovah possessed wisdom at the time when he put forth his creative energy, and prior to the formation of material things. Or, the words may be construed as in apposition with the pronominal suffix in קָנָנִי, *qauani,* and translated "*as the beginning of his way,*"—"the *first,* or *firstling* of his way." The sense, according to this rendering would be, that wisdom was the first product of God's creative power. The former interpretation is prefera-

---

22. "*Created me,*" Stuart—"*formed me,*" Noyes—"*the beginning of his way,*" Holden—"*the firstling of his way,*" Stuart—"*the first of his creation,*" Noyes.

23. "I was anointed from eternity:—
"From the beginning, before the world was made.

24. "When there were no. deeps, I was brought forth;
"When there were no springs abounding with water;

---

ble because it accords best with the parallel member, which seems to be exegetical of it. Some commentators understand by רֵאשִׁית reshith, *the beginning*, not the *primal*, but the *chief* production of creative power:—God's most wonderful work. And if there be no ellipsis of the preposition, then this is the preferable rendering, as being more forcible and better suited to the context. But the expression "before his works of old," in the parallel member, indicates quite clearly that wisdom as a divine attribute is not included among the works of God any more than is the power of the Deity, but existed before them all, being an essential and inseparable part of himself.

23. The figurative import of *to anoint* is *to invest with sovereignty*,—anointing with consecrated oil being the outward symbol of such investiture. Wisdom is here represented as the first Queen of the world, constituted such by Jehovah himself, before the creation of the material universe. Compare Ps. 2: 6, where the verb נָסַךְ, *nasak*, which properly signifies *to pour out*, is used in the same sense. The representation here corresponds with that in ch. 3: 16, where Wisdom is described as a *Queen*, dispensing riches and honors with one hand, and a long and prosperous life with the other. Three adverbial phrases are employed in this verse, conveying essentially the same idea, viz. that divine wisdom existed and was invested with authority anterior to the original creation of the material world.

24. This verse and the two following verses contain a poetic amplification of the idea conveyed in the two preceding verses, that wisdom existed *before* all created things. The expression *I was brought forth*, is figurative, and adapted to the prosopopœia. Wisdom is represented as a person, and the commencement of her active operations is described as the beginning of her existence. (חוֹלָלְתִּי Pulal of חוּל.)

---

23. "*I was anointed to reign*," Boothr.   24. "*I was born*," Holden, Stuart.

25. "Before the mountains were settled,
" Yea, before the hills I was brought forth.
26. "When he had not yet formed the earth, nor
the fields,
" Nor the first of the clods of the world.
27. "When he framed the heavens I was there;
" When he drew a circle on the face of the deep:
28. "When he established the clouds above;
" When the fountains of the deep were made strong;
29. "When he appointed the sea its bounds,
" That the water should not pass its border;
"· When he marked out the foundations of the earth:

---

26. *The fields*, i. e., the cultivated parts of the earth.

27. This verse and the two following, announce the fact that
Wisdom was present at the formation of all things, as an actor and
a counsellor of Jehovah. When Jehovah conceived the idea of
creating the world, infinite Wisdom drew the wondrous plan, and
superintended the work, while infinite power executed it. *When he
drew a circle*, i. e. "by establishing the present frame of the universe, caused the apparently concave surface of the heavens to form,
so far as our senses can discern it, a curved boundary to the waters
of the ocean." (French.) חוג, *chug*, is the *circle* or concave of the
arched heavens. (חקו, Kal Inf. constr. of חקק, with suffix.)

28. *The clouds above.* There is allusion here to the clouds not
individually and separately, but as an order or system. The establishment of the clouds is substantially equivalent to the establishment of the expanse in which they move. *Were made strong.*
The verb עזז, *azaz*, in Kal is intransitive. The *fountains* here
spoken of are those of the abyss, (Gen. 7: 11,) from which, according to the idea of the Hebrews, the ocean is supplied with water,
and not the reservoirs of water above the firmament, or in the skies.

29. *Its bounds.*—Comp. Job 38: 11. Ps. 104: 9. *Its border.*—Literally *its mouth*, or rather *its lip*, which is here put tropically for border, *edge, margin, shore, limit.* Ps. 133: 2. Some commentators refer
the suffix in פיו, *Phiv*, not to ים, *yam, sea*, but to יהוה, *Jehovah*, and

---

25. " *I was born,*" Holden, Stuart. 26 " *The first atom of the dust of the world,*"
French. 27. " *Established the heavens,*" Boothr., Stuart. 28. " *The abyss,*" Stuart
—" *rushed forth,*" Noyes. 29. " *And to the waters, which transgress not his command.*" French.

30. " Then I was at his side (*as*) an artificer;
" I was daily his delight :
" Rejoicing always in his presence ;—
31. " Rejoicing in the habitable part of his earth,
" And my delight was with the sons of men.

---

render the clause, " that the waters should not transgress his command."   Comp. Ex. 17: 1. Josh. 9: 14. Eccles. 8: 2. חֻקּוֹ, from the noun חֹק—root חָקַק. בְּחֻקוֹ=בְּחֻקּוֹ, Kal Inf. of חָקַק.)

30. *As an artificer*—architect, *builder*. In favor of this rendering of the Hebrew word אָמוֹן, *amon*, we have the noun אָמָן, *aman, workman*, Cant. 7:2, the Chal. אֻמָּן, *uman*, and the Syr. אוֹמָן, *omon*, all which are derived most clearly from the same root. Luther: *work-meister—master-workman*. Sept. αρμοζουσα, *arranging* every thing. Vulg. *cuncta componens, collecting all things.* The sentiment, according to this rendering is, that Divine Wisdom was the counseller and co-worker of Jehovah in the formation of the material world. Many expositors, however, take the Hebrew word in the sense of *alumna, nursling, foster-child*, or, as in authorized version, *one brought up by him*. In favor of this view, there is the repeated occurrence of the active participle אֹמֵן, *omen, one who carries a child, attends it and brings it up; a nursing*, or *foster father*. Num. 11: 12. Isa. 49: 23. Esth. 2: 7, etc. Either of these renderings is in harmony with the context, but the first is best supported on philological grounds, and by the ancient versions.

31. *And my delight.*—" This final clause of the description gives us the crowning idea of the whole. Wisdom, that dwelt from eternity, in the presence of God before the foundation of the earth, and that was present at its formation, as the counsellor, and co worker of Jehovah, now makes it a favorite abode, because there man, the object of her deepest love, is found. The interest that she feels in God's world, all centres in the *sons of men*. To their good she has from the beginning devoted herself. And her labors to recall them to the paths of truth and blessedness have been unwearied. This her delight in the children of men she makes the ground of a new appeal to them."   (Burrows.)

30. " *As a master builder*," Noyes—' *as a workman*,' Boothr.—" *the Fabricator*." Holden—" *as a nursing*,' French—" *as a confidant*," Stuart—" *a favorite*," Goode.

8*

32. "Now, therefore, ye children, hearken to me;
"For happy are they that keep my ways.

33. "Hear my instruction, and be wise;
"And reject it not.

34. "Happy is the man that hearkeneth to me,
"Watching daily at my gates—
"Waiting at the posts of my doors.

35. "For he that findeth me, findeth life,
"And obtaineth favor from Jehovah.

36. "But he that misseth me, wrongeth his own soul;
"All those that hate me love death."

---

32. There is here a return to abstract wisdom personified.

33. *Be wise,* i. e., ye shall be wise.

34. *Watching*—i. e., seeking admission with earnestness and perseverance, from an anxious desire to profit by the instructions of wisdom.

35. (מְצֹאִי. The pointing of this word is that of the Keri, which drops the final letter, while the consonants in the text indicate the plural number. If the word be the participle plur. instead of the Kal perf. in the sing. then it should be pointed מֹצְאַי, and the preceding word should be pointed מֹצְאֵי, *the finders of me.* יָפֵק, Hiph. fut. of פּוּק.)

36. *Misseth me.*—The word חֹטְאִי *chotei,* is here employed in its primary sense, viz. that of *missing a mark,* and stands opposed to מֹצְאִי *motzei, finding,* in v. 35. *Wrongeth his own soul*—doth injury to himself. *To love death,* here means to behave in such a manner as to show that they court their own destruction.

Many of the early Christian writers, and not a few modern expositors, understand by Wisdom, throughout this chapter, the Lord Jesus Christ in his pre-existent state—the Divine Logos or Word, of St. John—the second person in the Godhead, and neither wisdom in the abstract, nor the Infinite wisdom of God personified. Others regard the first part of the chapter (vs. 1–11) as containing an elegant personification of abstract wisdom, but conceive that in the remainder of the chapter the inspired writer passes to the con-

---

36. " *That wanders from me, injures his own soul,*" Holden.

templation of the hypostatic word, described under the name of wisdom. The advocates of this opinion admit that the New Testament writers have in no instance, by express reference, applied this chapter of Proverbs, or any part of it, to our blessed Lord. All that is claimed is, that in the title "Wisdom of God," by which our Saviour styles himself, (Lu. 11: 49. Comp. Matt. 23: 34,) and which St. Paul ascribes to him, (1 Cor. 1: 24,) there is supposed to be allusion to this portion of Scripture. It is further alleged that there is a striking resemblance between the description of the Logos by St. John and of Wisdom by Solomon, and hence it is inferred that they refer to the same concrete person, and that even the term Logos was suggested to the mind of John by that of Wisdom in the Proverbs. But it is certainly not self-evident that the mere fact of our Saviour's being called in the New Testament "the Wisdom of God," proves that the second person in the Godhead is intended in this chapter. What the author of this book apparently professes to describe is *Wisdom itself*, and the obvious design of the chapter is to exhibit the claims of Wisdom to be heard and respected, on the ground of her antiquity, her superior excellence, and her sympathy with the human race. If any thing more than this, or if something different from this is intended, might we not have expected some positive assertion or clear and unequivocal intimation of it? It can hardly be maintained that the mere naked title of "the Wisdom of God," given to Christ, is such proof as the case seems to require. And as to the description of the Logos in John's Gospel, though in some respects it is similar, yet in others it is widely different from that to be found in this chapter. The Logos is said to be not only in the beginning *with* God, but to be *God himself*; the work of creation is ascribed to him not as a mere instrumental agent, but in his proper character as God, and as performed by virtue of the power inherent in him as a divine being. He became incarnate, also, and sojourned among men. He lived, and acted, and suffered and died for the redemption of mankind. He was, therefore, a proper person, and not a mere attribute of the Deity. Nothing of this kind is affirmed of Wisdom in this book. She is indeed personified in this chapter, as in other parts of the Proverbs: she is described as present at the creation, but in the capacity of counsellor, planner, an instrumental assistant, and nothing more. What is here said of her in this respect is merely equivalent to the declaration of the Psalmist, (Ps. 104: 24,) that "in wisdom God made all his works." As to the authority of the early fathers upon which the chief reliance is placed in attempting to establish the

identity of the Wisdom of Solomon and the Logos of John, it is by
no means conclusive. Their testimony in regard to matters of fact
which came under their cognizance—as, for example, the doctrines
held by the Church—its government, rites, and usages,—is certainly
entitled to great respect. They were competent witnesses with
regard to whatever came under their own observation; but their
mere individual opinions in respect to the interpretation of particular
passages of Scripture, are not entitled to the same consideration.
They had the same and only the same Scriptures which we have.
They were not infallible any more than we are. They were liable
to mistake in the meaning which they attached to the language of
Scripture, from lack of judgment, from insufficient knowledge, from
the influence of erroneous principles of interpretation, and other
causes. Besides, the general consent of the Church fathers, who
flourished in the latter half of the *second* and in the *third* century,
(for in any authentic writings previous to the middle of the second
century, there is no allusion to this chapter of Proverbs,) cannot
establish the alleged fact of a well-authenticated tradition as to the
teaching of the inspired apostles in reference to this passage. In
view of these considerations, it seems to be the safer course to adhere to the literal and unprophetical interpretation of this portion
of Sacred Writ.

CHAPTER IX.

[*Heavenly Wisdom still personified and described as having prepared
a sumptuous entertainment, to which she invites all who stand in
need of her bounty, vs. 1–6. The different reception given to admonition and instruction respectively by the wise man and the scoffer,
vs. 7–9. The foundation of true wisdom, and the happy consequences of following her precepts stated, vs. 10–12. Warnings
against the delusions of folly, vs. 13–18.*

1. Wisdom hath builded her house;
She hath hewn out her seven pillars.

---

1. The personification of abstract wisdom which we find in the
preceding chapter is continued in this, and she is allegorically
represented as a glorious queen graciously inviting all the needy

2. She hath killed her fatlings;
She hath mingled her wine;
She hath furnished her table:
3. She hath sent forth her maidens;
She calleth aloud in the highest places of the city,

---

and misguided to her palace, where she has provided a splendid banquet, of which they may freely partake, if they will forsake the ways of error and sin. Comp. Matt. 22: 1–4. Lu. 14: 16–18. The plural form חַכְמוֹת, *chakmoth*, (*wisdoms*,) is used instead of the singular merely for emphasis and distinction, as in ch. 1: 20. The number *seven* was regarded by the Hebrews, Arabians and Persians, as a full, perfect, and sacred number. It is therefore often employed as a definite for an indefinite number to denote *completeness*. Comp. Ps. 12: 6. Lev. 26: 24. It here stands for that num———whatever it may have been, which was required for the firmness, stability, and ornament of wisdom's palace.

2. By *mingling her wine*, is supposed by some commentators to mean here *preparing it with spices, honey*, or *drugs*, in order to render it more intoxicating, as in ch. 23: 30. But the temperate nations of antiquity were not in the habit of drinking wine drugged or even undiluted, except at feasts of drunkenness and debauchery in which they sometimes indulged, when it was mixed with potent ingredients to increase its strength. The Hebrews were essentially a temperate people, and can hardly be supposed to have practised less restraint on their appetites than the Greeks and Romans. The interpretation alluded to is also unsuitable and incongruous here, as it does not comport with the character of wisdom. It is much more probable that the *mingling* here spoken of was mixing the wine with water, or perhaps with milk, as was sometimes done, to make it more refreshing and nutritious. Comp. Isa. 1: 22. 55: 1. Thus understood, the phrase imports that Wisdom had prepared and poured out into cups her wine ready to be drunk; just as in the following clause it is implied that the food was placed upon the table in a state of readiness to be eaten.

3. It was customary among the Hebrews for *females* to be employed as heralds of good tidings: see Ps. 68: 19. Isa. 40: 9. Hence Wisdom is here appropriately described as sending forth her female servants to give the invitations to the feast. Hasselquist remarks that at Alexandria, (Egypt) he saw on one occasion ten or twelve
g about the city, and inviting people to a banquet by a

4. " Whoever is simple, let him turn aside hither !"
To him who is void of understanding she saith,

5. " Come, eat of my bread,
" And drink of the wine which I have mingled.

6. " Forsake folly and live ;
" And go in the way of understanding !

7. " He that reproveth a scoffer, bringeth upon
himself shame ;
" And he that rebuketh a wicked (man, bringeth)
upon himself a stain.

---

peculiar cry or noise. *She calleth,* i. e., by the instrumentality of her
female messengers. Thus "Pharaoh sent and called Joseph";
which signifies that Pharaoh sent a messenger who called him, &c.
Gen. 41: 14.   was common among the Jews, and also not unfrequent among the Greeks and Romans, to represent what was done
by any one for another, as done by himself. See Matt. 8: 7. comp.
Lu. 7: 6. Mar. 10: 35. comp. Matt. 20: 20. This custom gave rise
to the legal maxim—*Qui facit per alium facit per se*—"He who does
a thing by means of another, does it himself," i. e., he is considered
in law as doing it himself. Chald. Syr. and Vulg. "that they
might call."

4. *Turn aside hither,*—lit. *depart hither,* i. e., turn aside from the
path of the simple, in which he is walking, and enter the palace of
Wisdom. (סָר, Kal fut. of סוּר, put for the usual form יָסוּר.)

5. *My bread,* i. e., the feast which I have prepared. לֶחֶם, *lechem,*
sig. first, *food* in general, and a *feast;* then, secondly and specifically
bread.

6. *And live,* i. e., ' that you may live,' or ' so shall you live.' The
Vatican Sept. "that you may reign forever." But the Alexandrine
Sept. "that you may live."

7. The phrase *bringeth upon himself shame,* here imports that he
receives in return for his friendly reproof shameful treatment. He
is vilified and abused by him whose good he sought.—The word
מוּם, *mum,* in the second member of the verse, sig. *a spot, blemish.*
It is sometimes used in a physical sense of a corporeal blemish;
and at other times, as here, of a moral spot, or stain. Literally, *it*

---

4. " *Turn hither,*" Boothr.—"*turn and come hither,*" French.
7. " *It is a blot,*" Stuart, Boothr.="*bringeth upon himself reproach,*" French.

8. "Reprove not a scoffer, lest he hate thee;
"Rebuke a wise (*man*), and he will love thee.

9. "Give (*instruction*) to a wise (*man*) and he will become still wiser;
"Teach a righteous (*man*), and he will increase (*in*) learning.

10. "The fear of Jehovah is the beginning of wisdom;
"And the knowledge of the Most Holy is understanding.

---

is his stain or blot, i. e., it is a reproach to him. Sept. "shall disgrace himself."

8. *Reprove not a scoffer*—"The sacred writer is very far from meaning to assert, that it is a matter of little consequence whether scoffers be reclaimed from their evil course, or that no hazard is to be run in endeavoring to effect this most desirable end. He merely states the result of his experience to be, that these wicked persons, while they continue in such a frame of mind, will not only refuse to listen to the voice of admonition, but probably heap upon such as presume to offer it, reproach and contumely." French. The text contains simply a salutary caution founded on experience and observation, against indiscriminate reproof. "Kindle not the coals of a sinner, lest thou be burnt with the flame of his fire?" Ecclus. 8: 10. Comp. Matt. 7: 6. *Rebuke a wise man.*—It is as great a proof of wisdom to take a reproof well, as to give it well. See Ps. 141: 5.

9. *Give to a wise man*, scil. *instruction*, or admonition, counsel, לֶקַח, *leqach*, which is to be supplied from the end of the verse. Comp. ch. 4: 2. Chald. "Teach a wise man." Sept. Syr. and Vulg. "Give an opportunity."

10. See ch. 1: 7. The repetition of the sentiment here, shows the importance which the writer attached to it. By the *Most Holy* is meant *God*, synonymous with Jehovah in the parallel clause. The plural קְדוֹשִׁים, *qedoshim*, like אֱלֹהִים, *elohim*, is used for the singular by way of eminence, and to give intensity to the meaning. See chap. 30: 3. Sept. and Vulg. "the knowledge of saints," or

---

9. "Give reproof," Holden—"give to a wise man," Stuart—"instruct the wise," Boothr.=" in true knowledge," Holden—"increase his learning," French, Noyes—"add to his learning," Stuart.

10. "Holy one," Holden—"of holy things," Booth.

11. "For by me thy days shall be multiplied;
"And years of life shall be added to thee.

12. "If thou art wise, thou wilt be wise for thyself;
"But if thou scornest, thou alone shalt bear (*it*)."

---

holy persons, *i. e.*, of pious persons generally, and especially of
those who instruct others in the fear of God. So Junius, Geier,
Castellio, Piscat. Others, "of holy things," *i. e.*, whatever relates
to the service of God. Both these interpretations, however, are opposed to the parallelism.

11. *And years of life,* &c.—Lit. "And years of life shall they add
to thee."—the third person plural of the active verb being used *impersonally*, as in ch. 3: 2.

12. He who becomes wise, and profits by the reproof and instruction of Heavenly Wisdom, will be wise to his own unspeaka-
ble advantage, both as it respects this world and the world to come.
But he who, on the contrary, scorns and scoffs at religion and sacred
things, shall alone endure the punishment due to his folly and wickedness. There is an ellipsis of the object after the verb *to bear*, indicating the *consequence* or *punishment* of such derision and neglect.
Hence some supply instead of the neuter pronoun, the word "punishment." "Every instance of truly wise acting is an accumula-
tion made sure for the benefit of the doer. It cannot be lost. It is
like water to the earth. The drop of water that trembled on the
green leaf, and glittered in the morning sun, seems to be lost, when
it exhales in the air unseen; but it is all in safe-keeping. It is held
in trust by the faithful atmosphere, and will distil as dew upon the
ground again when and where it is needed most. Thus will every
exercise of wisdom, although fools may think it thrown away, return into your own bosom, when the day of need comes round.
Equally sure is the law that the evil which you do, survives and
comes back upon yourself. The profane word, the impure thought,
the unjust transaction—they are gone like the wind that whistled
past, and you seem to have nothing more to do with them. Nay,
but they have more to do with you. Nothing is lost out of God's
world, physical or moral. Sins, like water, are not annihilated,
although they go out of sight. They fall at last with all their
weight on the sin-doer." Arnott. Sept. "Son, if thou art wise, thou
wilt be wise for thyself and for thy neighbor; and if thou shouldst

---

12. "*Bear the punishment.*" Holden, French.

13. The foolish woman is noisy:
She is simple.and knoweth nothing.

14. She sitteth at the door of her house—
On a seat in the highest places of the city—

15. To call to those who pass on the way,—
Who are going straight forward in their paths.

·16. "Whoever is simple, let him turn in hither:"
And to him who is void of understanding, she saith,

---

prove wicked, thou alone wilt bear the evil." The version then adds the following: "He that stays.himself upon falsehoods, attempts to rule the winds, and the same will pursue birds in their flight; for he has forsaken the ways of his own vineyard, and he has caused the axles of his own husbandry to go astray; and he goes through a dry desert, and (a land) appointed to drought, and he gathers barrenness with his hands." This addition is contained also in the Arabic and Syriac; but from whence the Greek interpreters drew it is not known. (לָעָךְ, Kal perf. 2d pers. sing. of עָל. תֵּעָא, Kal fut. of עָשָׂא.)

13. The foolish woman is literally the woman of folly. Some Commentators suppose the phrase to indicate folly itself, and take the passage to be an' allegorical description of folly personified and represented as a female, so as to form a contrast with the preceding personification of wisdom. But "as the term woman is expressly mentioned, and as the description, especially in vs. 17, 18, compared with ch. 2: 18. 5: 5. is that of a harlot, and as in this book the transition is frequent from discoursing of wisdom to warning against harlots, (see ch. 2: 16. 5: 3. 7: 5) it is more probable that a literal harlot is here intended." (Noyes.) Noisy,—see ch. 1: 22. 7: 11. Simple, or silly,—literally a woman (אֵשֶׁת, esheth, understood) of simplicities. The abstract for the concrete, and the plur. may be used to give emphasis and intensity to the meaning, in which case the import would be very simple. Knoweth nothing, i. e , which is proper and salutary. Sept. and Arab. "Knoweth no shame."

15. Travellers inform us, that it is still the practice in the East for prostitutes to sit at the door of their houses, dressed in the most alluring garb which they can display. Who are going, &c., i. e., who are attending to their own proper business, lit. who make straight their ways.

---

13. "Folly," Boothr. French.

17. "Stolen waters are sweet,
"And bread (*eaten*) in secret is pleasant."
18. But he knoweth not that the shades are there;
That her guests (*are*) in the depths of sheol.

---

17. *Stolen waters are sweet* is an allegorical proverb applied here to the crime of illicit intercourse with abandoned women. *Bread in secret* is lit. *bread of secret places*, i. e. bread (food) eaten clandestinely. The abandoned woman addresses only the depraved passions of men, and allures by proposing the pleasure of enjoying what is forbidden. "The power of sin lies in its pleasure; if stolen waters were not sweet, none would steal the waters. This is part of the mystery in which our being is involved by the fall. It is one of the most painful features of our case. Our appetite is disordered. Sin, which is death to a man's soul, is yet sweet to the man's taste. They who give the rein to carnal appetite are daily brought more under its power. It grows by what it feeds on. If sin had no sweetness, it might be easier to keep from sinning. Satan might fish in vain, even in this sea of time, if he had no bait on his hook, that is pleasant to nature. Beware of the bait, for the barb is beneath it. But it is only in the mouth that stolen water is sweet; afterwards it is bitter. Sin has pleasures, but they last only for a season, and that a short one." (Arnott.)

"Nitimur in vetitum semper, cupimusque negata;
  Sic interdictis imminet æger aquis."

"We always strive for what is forbidden, and desire that which is denied; just as a sick man thirsts for interdicted waters."

18. *The shades*, see ch. 2: 18. The Sept. adds the following: "But hasten away; delay not in the place, neither fix thy eye upon her; for thus shalt thou go through strange water; and do thou abstain from strange water, and drink not of a strange fountain, that thou mayest live long, and years of life may be added to thee."

---

18. "*The dead*," Holden, French, Noyes—"*miserable ghosts*." Boothr ="*Hades*,' Boothr. Holden—"*the under-world*," Noyes. Stuart—"*the grave*," French.

PART II.
CHAPTER X.—XXII. 16.

[VARIOUS CONNECTED PROVERBS.]

CHAPTER X.

1. The Proverbs of Solomon.
A wise son maketh a glad father;
But a foolish son is the grief of his mother.

---

1. With this chapter commences the second part of this instructive book. It is entirely unlike the first in its form and structure, as well as subject-matter. Instead of a continued discourse on the nature and excellence of Heavenly Wisdom, the advantages of virtue and the pernicious and destructive effects of vice, this part is composed of moral aphorisms and prudential maxims detached and following each other without any perceptible connexion. Hence the new title in the first verse, which more appropriately belongs to this portion of the book, since the preceding part is rather a suitable introduction to the proverbs properly so called. The Proverbs are here arranged with care and skill, for the most part in couplets, of which the sentiment expressed in the first member is in contrast with that in the second; thus forming a series of antithetical parallelisms. It is frequently the case in these proverbs, that a person or thing is expressed in the first line of the verse, and implied in the second, and vice versa. Thus in this verse *both* parents are to be understood as referred to in both clauses, although the father only is named in the one, and the mother in the other. See ch. 17: 25. 19: 23. Wisdom and folly, in the writings of Solomon, have reference, as has been before remarked, to moral conduct. A wise son is one who studies to become virtuous and pious; a foolish son is one who does just the opposite. He cares nothing for the wisdom which comes from above, and hence his course is perpetually downward.

2. The treasures of wickedness do not profit;
But righteousness delivereth from death.

3. Jehovah will not suffer the righteous (*man*) to famish.
But he repelleth the covetous desire of the wicked.

4. He that worketh with a slack hand becometh poor;
But the hand of the diligent maketh rich.

---

2. *The treasures of wickedness* are treasures acquired by wicked means, as in Micah 6: 12. Wealth obtained by unlawful and dishonest means, such as gambling, cheating, fraud, theft, oppression and extortion, or by pandering to the vices of mankind, instead of really and permanently profiting, is attended by a secret curse, which soon wastes it. It cannot protect the possessor from retributive justice in this world, much less from the penalty of God's violated law in the world to come. Matt. 16: 28. By *death* in this place, is probably not intended corporeal death in the ordinary course of nature, for from this neither wealth, however acquired, nor righteousness, however eminent, can ultimately protect us. It refers rather to death caused by sinful acts or sinful indulgences—premature or violent death. Righteousness, on the contrary, brings with it the blessing of a long and happy life. Such at least is its manifest tendency, and such is often its actual effect. The proverb, however, in both its parts, holds true, and even with greater certainty, in respect to the second death—the retributions of eternity. See ch. 11: 4. Some give to צְדָקָה, *tzedaqa*, here the specific signification of *beneficence*—liberality towards the poor. So Tobit 12: 8, 9. " It is better to give alms than to lay up gold; for alms deliver from death." But the restrictive meaning is quite unnecessary here, and not as suitable as the more general and ordinary signification. Sept. " Treasures shall not profit the lawless."

3. *The righteous*,—lit. *the soul of the righteous*,—an idiomatic expression for the righteous soul, or person. Comp. Ps. 37: 5. הַוָּה, *hava*, *a desire*, *cupidity*, from הָיָה, *haya*, *to be*, *to breathe after*, *to desire*. It is intensive, and denotes *eager*, or *covetous desires*. (יַרְעִיב, Hiph. used in a permissive sense.)

4. In this proverb, and also in the one which follows, indolence is contrasted with diligence. Industry was the law of paradise, and though now it bears the stamp of the fall, it is still overruled

---

5. He that gathereth in summer is a wise son ;
But he that sleepeth in harvest is a son causing
shame.

6. Blessings are upon the head of the righteous
(*man*) ;
But violence shall cover the mouth of the wicked.

as a present blessing. For in the ordinary course of Divine Providence the hand (*i. e.* the labor) of the diligent maketh rich; while
it is equally true, that poverty is very frequently the natural consequence of indolence. The maxim here laid down in reference to
the business and gains of this life, is equally applicable in a somewhat different sense to the concerns of eternity. Diligence is alike
necessary to the acquisition of treasures within or beyond the reach
of rust and decay. "Debts will rise above the gains; corruptions
will gain ground on the graces, unless there be a watchful heart and
a diligent hand." The Sept. adds to this verse: "A son who is instructed shall be wise, and shall use the fool for a servant." The
Vulg. subjoins to this verse: "He who contends with lies, feeds on
the winds; he also follows flying birds." (רָאשׁ, more commonly
written רָשׁ, Kal part of רוּשׁ, the aleph epenthetic.)

5. Not only is diligence necessary, but diligence at the proper
time. Forethought is here opposed to improvidence. A wise man
will have an eye on the future, and faithfully employ the summer
of life in making suitable provision for old age. So also will the
Christian improve the present opportunity to work out his salvation,
knowing that the night of death will soon overtake him. *A son
causing shame* is a base and degenerate son, who by his indolence
and folly brings poverty and disgrace on himself, and on the family
of which he is a member. Sept. "A wise son is saved from heat;
but a lawless son is blighted by the winds in harvest." (נִרְדָּם, Niph.
part. employed in the intransitive sense of Kal, which is not used.
מֵבִישׁ, Hiph. part. of בּוּשׁ, ch. 17: 2. 19: 26. 29: 15.)

6. Blessings from God are invoked on the righteous man for his
pious and virtuous example, his wise and friendly counsels, and his
beneficent deeds, by those who have profited by his example, or
have been benefitted by his deeds. The antithetical clause of the
verse may be rendered, *But the mouth of the wicked concealeth violence.*
Between these two renderings commentators are divided. The first

6. "*But the mouth of the wicked concealeth violence,*" French, Stuart.

7. The memory of the just (*man*) is blessed ;
But the name of the wicked shall rot.

is supported by the Sept. Vulg. and Chald. and is adopted by Junius, Piscator, Geier, Schultens, Dathe, Rosen., Holden, Boothr, and Noyes ; while the second is supported by the ancient Greek translations of Aquila, Symm, and Theodot., and adopted by A. Moret, Munster, Pagnini, Castel., French and Stuart. According to the former the sense would be, the wicked man will be struck dumb by the woes and disgrace brought upon him by his deeds of violence and baseness. Comp. Mic. 7: 10. Ps. 44: 16. Jere. 51: 51. The righteous man's good deeds shall return in showers of blessings on his head; while the violent wrong doing of the wicked man shall in its consequences and punishment cover his mouth—put him to shame and confusion of face—overwhelm him with infamy, disgrace, and mortification. According to the latter, the sense would be, the wicked endeavor by studied and deceptive silence or evasive language, to conceal the maliciousness of their hearts, and the injury which they meditate against others, that they may strike the surer blow. . In such cases, the injured party can hardly be expected to bestow a benediction, or invoke a blessing on the aggressor. This last thought, which is supposed to form the real antithesis, is here, as often elsewhere, implied but not expressed. The collocation of the words in the original would favor the opinion that *mouth* is the subject, and that *violence* belongs to the predicate. But in a case so doubtful, I prefer to adhere to our Standard Version.

7. The memory of the just and upright man shall be held in honor and esteem (lit. *for a blessing.* Sept. and Vulg. *with praises.*) Every one who recalls the remembrance of such a man, will do so with praising his virtues and invoking a blessing on him, as is still the custom in the East. On the contrary, the name of the wicked will be loathsome and disgusting while remembered, and soon will sink into oblivion. It seems to be an instinct of humanity to desire posthumous reputation. All men, in whom virtuous and generous feelings and sentiments have not been extinguished by the power of vice, desire to be kindly and affectionately remembered after their decease. This desire gives rise to many a noble and beneficent deed, and prevents the commission of many a wrong act. It is a feeling which is set in the machinery of God's moral government, as a valuable power impelling to righteous acts. It forms a link in that chain of motives for good, which God in his Word is pleased to sanction and approve.

8. The wise in heart will receive precepts;
But a foolish talker shall fall headlong.

9. He that walketh uprightly, walketh securely;
But he that perverteth his ways, shall be made known.

---

8. The heart is the seat of true wisdom, and a teachable spirit is the best proof of its existence and influence. The truly wise man will open his ear to all good advice and instruction, and especially to the precepts of God's holy word, and will escape the many evils to which the ignorant and foolish are exposed. On the contrary, the foolish talker—the man who shows that he is destitute of true wisdom by talking foolishly, inconsiderately and wickedly, will involve himself by his loquacity in trouble and danger. *Foolish talker,*—lit. *a fool of lips.* Sept. "But he that is unguarded in his lips, shall he overthrow in his perverseness." (יִלָּבֵט, Niph. as Kal intransitive, because Kal is not used.)

9. He who uniformly conducts himself with uprightness and integrity, acts safely. He treads on firm and solid ground, which will not give way under his feet, and precipitate him to the earth. But he that turns aside from the path of integrity, into crooked and dangerous by-paths, practising deceit, fraud, and dishonesty, *shall be made known,* i. e., shall be detected, exposed, and at length made to suffer the punishment due to his duplicity. "The term upright as applied to character, seems eminently direct and simple; yet in its origin, it is as thoroughly figurative as any word can be. It is a physical law declared applicable to a moral subject. When a man's position is physically upright, he can stand easily, or bear much. He is not soon wearied: he is not soon broken down. But if his limbs are uneven, or his posture bent, he is readily crushed by the weight of another; he is soon exhausted even by his own. There is a similar law in the moral department. There is an attitude of the soul which corresponds to the erect position of the body, and is called uprightness. The least deviation from the line of uprightness will take your strength away, and leave you at the mercy of the meanest foe. How many difficulties a man will go through, whose spirit stands erect on earth, and points straight up to heaven!" (Arnott.)

---

8. "*A prating fool,*" Holden, Boothr.=="*shall fall,*" Holden—"*shall rush headlong,*" Stuart—"*will be offended,*" Boothr.

9. "*Shall be detected,*" Hodgson, Durell—"*shall be discovered,*" Stuart—"*shall be punished,*" Noyes.

10. He that winketh with the eye causeth sorrow;
And a foolish talker shall fall headlong.

11. The mouth of the righteous (*man*) is a fountain
of life;
But violence shall cover the mouth of the wicked.

12. Hatred stirreth up strife;
But love covereth all offences.

---

10. *Winketh*, &c.—See ch. 6: 13. The second clause of this verse may have been inadvertently transferred by some copyist from verse 8. In the Sept. Syr. and Arab. the clause reads thus: "But he that reproves boldly is a peace-maker." The parallelism as it stands in the text is not antithetical but constructive.

11. Words of kindness, charity and wisdom, proceed from the mouth of the righteous man, as fertilizing streams proceed from the pure fountain. But the wicked utters the language of violence and injustice, which at last recoils upon himself, and brings merited disgrace upon him. See v. 6.

12. Hatred breeds contention; provokes, magnifies, and multiplies offences. But Love, full of candor and inventiveness, forgives, overlooks and palliates offences, conceals from observation and apologizes for the errors of others, removes aggravations, puts the most favorable construction on the motives and actions of offenders; and pours water instead of oil upon the flame. While it is ever ready to pardon and excuse the injury which another may have done, whenever a suitable apology is made, it does not rigidly scrutinize or wantonly expose his faults; nor will it uncover them to the public gaze, except so far as may be needful for the ultimate good of the individual, or for the benefit of the community. Some commentators render כָּסָה, *kissa, to pardon, to forgive,*—a sense which tropically the word sometimes has. (Ps. 85: 2. 32: 1. Neh. 4: 5.) But this signification more properly belongs to כָּפַר, *kaphar;* and though it is implied here, it does not exhaust the meaning. The term is complex. "Where hatred reigns every trifle excites contentions; the least slip is resented or aggravated; the best meant words or actions are misrepresented or misunderstood, and nothing is passed over. But where love prevails, mistakes or offences will be either overlooked, or speedily forgiven; so that notwithstanding the imperfections of those who live together, they bear with, and

---

12. *Pardoneth all offences,*" Boothr.—" *concealeth many offences,*" French.

13. On the lips of the intelligent (*man*) wisdom is found ;

But a rod is for the back of him who is void of understanding.

14. Wise (*men*) treasure up knowledge ;

But the mouth of a fool is near destruction.

15. The rich man's wealth is his strong city ;

The destruction of the poor is their poverty.

---

make the best of each other." (Scott.)   The latter clause of the verse is quoted by St. Peter (1 Pet. 4: 8), and alluded to by St. James (Ep. 5: 20).   Sept. "affection covers all that do not love strife."   (תְּעֹרֵר, Polel fut. of עוּר.)

13. The language of the intelligent man, being regulated by wisdom and prudence, procures respect and excites admiration.   On the contrary, that of the fool is such as to provoke contempt, indignation and punishment.   The usual corporeal punishment of the Mosaic law was stripes.   Solomon and his son Rehoboam admirably illustrate the contrast presented in this verse..   Sept. "He that brings forth wisdom from his lips smites the fool with a rod."

14. Wise men treasure up in their memory useful knowledge, and hold it ready for use at the proper time and place, when it will most conduce to their own benefit and that of others.   Comp. ch. 12: 23.   But fools are more forward to lay *out* than to lay *up*.   They may acquire knowledge, but they let it go as fast as they get it. They put their winnowing into a bag with holes, and soon exhaust their scanty stock.   Hence, though ever learning, they are never wiser, and often utter not only what is useless, but what is pernicious and productive of positive mischief to themselves and others. Comp. ch. 18: 7.

15. In this aphorism Solomon describes rather what *is*, than prescribes what *ought to be ;* and it is to be regarded as a general, not a universal truth.   " The verse acknowledges and proclaims a prominent feature in the condition of the world.   In all ages and in all lands, money has been a mighty power ; and its relative importance increases with the advance of civilization.   Money is one of the prin-

---

13. " *Of a man of discernment,*" French—" *of the prudent,*" Boothr.

14. " *But destruction is near the mouth of the foolish,*" Holden—" *causeth speedy destruction,*" French.

15. " *Their poverty is dismay to the poor,*" French, Noyes.

16. The gain of the righteous (*man tendeth*) to life :
The revenue of the wicked, to sin.

---

cipal instruments by which the affairs of this world are turned, and
the man who holds that instrument in his grasp, can make himself
felt in his age and neighborhood.   It does not reach the divine purposes, but it controls human action.   Over against this formidable
power stands the counterpart weakness." (Arnott.)   Poverty unhap-
pily too often proves an insuperable barrier to the successful and
beneficial employment of men's native talents and acquired abilities.   It greatly circumscribes their influence and usefulness.   It
compels them to give way to those who possess neither their intel-
ectual power nor their moral worth, and exposes them to severe privation, gross neglect, unjust reproach and calumny, and sometimes
o suffering and ruin.

> "Haud facile emergunt, quorum virtutibus obstat
>   Res angusta domi."   *Juvenal.*
> "This mournful truth is every where confessed,
>   Slow rises worth by poverty oppressed."   *Johnson.*

On the other hand, the rich man's wealth protects him from many
vituperations, procures for him influence, deference and respect far
beyond what his abilities or virtues entitle him to, and serves as a
talisman against many of the greatest vexations and sorrows of life.
See ch. 18: 11. where the same words are employed, but in a different relation, and in a somewhat different sense.   The Hebrew word
מְחִתָּה, *mechitta*, sig. not only *destruction, ruin,* but also *consternation,
terror, dismay, dread;* and the second clause may be translated,
"The poverty of the poor is their dread."   If this be the more accurate rendering, then the meaning would be that in consequence of
the numerous evils which poverty brings with it, it is the dread
of the poor.   It depresses their spirits and paralyzes their energies.
The former interpretation is supported by the Sept., which is followed by Holden, Boothr. and Stuart.   The latter by the Vulg. and
one of the Hexapla Versions, and is preferred by Geier, Gesenius,
Rosenm. French and Noyes.

16. The Hebrew word פְּעֻלָּה, *peulla,* properly sig. *work, labor, occupation.*   But here and in ch. 11: 18, it is put by metonymy for
gain, earnings, reward—the fruits of labor, as the parallelism shows.
The righteous man makes a proper use of the gain which he ac-

---

16. "*The work of the righteous,*" Stuart—"*the earnings,*" French, Noyes=="*ministers to life,*" French, Noyes=="*to ruin,*" Noyes—"*to destruction,*" Boothr. Holden.

17. He who keepeth instruction is (*in*) the way of life;
But he who refuseth reproof, goeth astray.

18. He who concealeth hatred (*hath*) lying lips;
And he who uttereth slander is a fool.

19. In the multitude of words there wanteth not offence;
But he who restraineth his lips, is wise.

---

quires in the honest pursuit of his vocation; therefore it conduces to his own support and enjoyment, as well as to the good of others. The wicked man, on the contrary, makes his acquisitions subservient only to selfish gratification and sensual enjoyment; hence to him they often prove a source of dangerous temptation and an occasion of sin, instead of a blessing. Some render חַטָּאת, *chattath, ruin, destruction*, by metonymy, instead of *sin*, from the parallelism.

17. The word מַתְעֶה, *mathe,* (Hiph. part. of תָּעָה, *thaa,*) is rendered by some *causeth to wander, leadeth astray,* i. e., he leads others astray by precept and example. But the intransitive meaning is preferable, on account of the parallelism, and is generally adopted by interpreters, both ancient and modern.

18. He who conceals his hatred under the semblance of friendly deportment, and disguises his enmity under false pretences, is a dissembler, and possesses lying lips. Disguised hatred and open slander, are both condemned in this couplet. Some commentators render "*with* lying lips" as in our standard version. According to this rendering the meaning is, that both he who conceals hatred, and he who utters slander are alike fools. The Sept. Vulg. and Syr. translate the first clause, "Lying lips conceal hatred," thus making "lips" the subject of the proposition in manifest violation of grammar, both as it regards gender and number. (מוֹצִיא, Hiph. part. of יָצָא.)

19. There is probably allusion in this apothegm to that much and idle talking (πολυλογία) which proceeds from vanity, self-conceit and folly, and is indulged in without regard to the feelings or character of others. Such loquacity or vain babbling is seldom harmless. It often leads to unwarranted interference with other

---

17. "*Leadeth astray,*" Stuart.   18. "*With lying lips,*" French.
19. "*In much speaking.*" French—"brimstones." Boothr. Stuart—"*sin.*" Hol.

20. The tongue of the righteous (*man*) is (*as*) choice silver;

. The heart of the wicked is of little worth.

21. The lips of the righteous (*man*) feed many;

But fools die for the want of understanding.

---

people's business, to detraction, falsehood, misrepresentation, inexcusable exaggeration, and the encouragement of low, impure and vulgar ideas. Indeed there are so many ways of offending God and man by the abuse of the gift of speech, that there cannot be a more necessary part of self-discipline and self-restraint, or one in which the exercise of true piety is more concerned, than the government of the tongue. (Comp. Eccles. 5: 1–7. Matt. 12: 36. Eph. 4: 29.) The government of the tongue, therefore, is a searching test of the sincerity of our religion. Consequently it is a part of wisdom in us to restrain our lips not in silence but in caution; and especially is it so, when smarting under unjust accusation and vituperation. "No useful speech is, of course, here condemned, nor that flow of decent language which takes place in the hilarity of social intercourse." The wise of all nations and times have taught that the prudent man should be sparing of words. "I have often repented," says Xenocrites, "that I have spoken, but never that I have kept silent." (רֹב, Kal inf. constr. of רָבַב.)

20. "The *tongue* utters words, the *heart* conceives them: so that *tongue* and *heart* have in this passage substantially the same thing in view." (Stuart.) Both are used metonymically for the words expressed. The words of the righteous man are choice silver, or *like* choice silver, the note of comparison being understood, *i. e.*, they are highly esteemed for the instruction they communicate: while those of the wicked are worthless. (Comp. Matt. 12: 34. Ecclus 21: 29.)

21. The usefulness of instructive discourse is here again commended under a new metaphor. It is said to *feed* many, since it expels ignorance and furnishes salutary nutriment to faith and virtue. To *feed* is figuratively to *instruct*. Teaching is frequently represented in Scripture under the image of *feeding*. (Comp. Jere. 3: 15. 23: 4. Ezek. 34: 6, 14, 23. John 21: 15. Acts 20: 28. Eph. 4: 11. 1 Pet. 5: 2, 3.) An Instructor was called by the Hebrews רֹעֶה, *roe*, *a feeder*, and so in the New Test. ποιμήν. The *lips*, i. e., by meto-

---

21. "*Fools die through the man, void of understanding*," French.

22. The blessing of Jehovah maketh rich,
And He addeth no sorrow with it.

---

nymy, *the words* of the righteous man supply many with spiritual food and intellectual nourishment. But fools, who will not receive instruction, perish for lack of knowledge. Some regard חָסַר, *chasar*, as a proper adjective, instead of being used substantively. If this be admitted, then the second member would read, "But fools die through the man void of understanding," *i. e.*, in consequence of listening to his wicked suggestions and precepts.

22. The leading thought implied in the divine *blessing* is an abundant increase or multiplication of favors, both temporal and spiritual. The *curse* of God, on the contrary, is a privation or loss of good, and the infliction of numerous positive evils upon those who are the objects of it. The blessing of Jehovah makes man rich in the best sense of the word; rich in comfort and in the possession of rational and spiritual delight, if not of material wealth. Some people grow rich without God's blessing; and some, with it. The difference between these lie here, that wealth acquired *with* God's blessing, in the way of his appointment, agreeably to his will, in obedience to his laws, and in humble dependence on his aid, brings no additional sorrow with it. It is obtained honestly and righteously, and it is enjoyed thankfully and with no reproaches of an accusing conscience. (See Eccles. 2: 21-23. 5: 10, 11. 6: 1, 2.) The meaning is not that the rich man, though he may have become such by the special blessing of God, will be exempt from sorrow; but that his sorrow will not in such a case be necessarily increased. Such is not the case generally with riches procured by unlawful means, or without regard to the will and approbation of the Most High. It is a very common disadvantage of riches, that first in acquiring them, and then in preserving and increasing them, as well as in their loss, much sorrow as well as care and anxiety, is brought on their possessors; but we may believe that, if God bestow the blessing, he will also grant with it a mind serene and free from anxious cares, so that the possessor will be enabled to enjoy his wealth. (יֹסִף, Hiph. fut. of יָסַף, with the yodh formative omitted.)

---

22. "*He addeth not sorrows to them,*" French—"*and with it, he giveth no sorrow,*" Boothr.—"*nor will he increase sorrow therewith,*" Stuart.

10*

23. As it is a pleasure to a fool to do mischief,
So is wisdom (*a pleasure*) to the man of understanding.

24. The fear of the wicked (*man*) shall come upon him;
But the desire of the righteous shall be granted.

---

23. The fool takes delight in doing mischief; but the man of understanding, on the contrary, takes delight in acting wisely. The particle וֹ *vav*, in the second clause, is used as a correlative term, answering to כ *ki*, *as*, in the first clause.

24. *The fear*—the *dread*, the *terror* of the wicked man:—put metonymically for the object of fear—that which the wicked fears and dreads as the consequence and punishment of his sins (as in Ps. 34: 4. Isa. 66: 4); on the contrary, the desire of the righteous man shall be granted by Jehovah. The verb יִתֵּן, *yitten*, is here used impersonally, or *Jehovah* may be understood as the implied nominative. "We are not to understand from this verse, that the wicked only fear, and the righteous have only desire or hope. The wicked have hope as well as fear; the righteous have fear as well as hope. Both characters experience both emotions. The difference between them lies not in the existence of these emotions in them now, but in their issue at last. In each character there are the same two emotions now; in each, at the final reckoning, one of these emotions will be realized, and the other disappointed. The wicked, in life, both hoped and feared; at the issue of all things, his fear will be embodied in fact, and his hope will go out as a lamp, when its oil is done. The righteous, in life, both hoped and feared; at the issue of all things, his hope will be satisfied, and his fear will vanish. Fear and hope are common to the two in time; at the border of eternity, the one will be relieved from all his fear; the other will be deprived of all his hope. The wicked will get what he feared, and miss what he hoped; the righteous will get what he hoped, and miss what he feared." (Arnott.) (תְּבוֹאֶנּוּ, Kal. fut. 3d pers. fem. of בּוֹא, with suffix.)

---

23. "*But wisdom is the delight of the man,*" &c. French—"*but wisdom belongeth to the man,*" &c. Stuart.
24. "*He will grant,*" Stuart.

25. When the whirlwind passeth over, the wicked
(*man*) is no more;
But the righteous (*hath*) an everlasting foundation.
26. As vinegar to the teeth, and as smoke to the eyes,
So is a sluggard to those who send him.
- 27. The fear of Jehovah prolongeth life;
But the years of the wicked shall be shortened.

---

25. In the day of calamity, when the storm of divine displeasure
is raging, the wicked are overwhelmed in the tempest. Their house
is built on the sand, and consequently tumbles down and falls to-
pieces. The righteous, on the contrary, have in the divine favor
and protection, an everlasting foundation, sure and stable; their
hope, faith and confidence, are built on the rock of ages, and they
remain firm and unmoved amid the most violent storms of trouble
and affliction. See Ps. 37: 36. Calamity is frequently represented
in Scripture under the image of a whirlwind or tempest. The particle בְּ *koph*, before the Infin. עֲבוֹר, *ebor*, is here indicative of *time*
when. The *wicked—is no more*, lit. *then is not the wicked*. Sept. "vanishes away."

> "As some tall cliff, that lifts its awful form,
> Swells from the vale, and midway leaves the storm;
> Though round its breast the rolling clouds are spread,
> Eternal sunshine settles on its head."

26. This proverb contains a lively figure of the vexations caused
by the sluggard to his employers. As vinegar and smoke produce
disagreeable and injurious effects, the one by setting the teeth on
edge, the other by irritating and inflaming the eyes; so an idle,
loitering messenger, by his remissness and want of punctuality, occasions disappointment, vexation and injury to those who place
confidence in him.

27. *The fear of*, or *reverance for* Jehovah, is not a single grace,
but includes the entire circle of graces. It differs essentially from
the subjective fear of the wicked in this respect, that they fear those
whom they hate; but the child of God fears him whom he loves.
The sentiment here expressed is one which is often repeated, and
on which much stress is laid by Solomon. *Prolongeth life*, is lit.
addeth days. See ch. 3: 2. comp. Ps. 55: 23.

---

25. "*As the whirlwind passes by, so is the wicked no more*," Noyes. "*the right-
ous is an everlasting foundation*," Noyes.
27. "*Shall be curtailed*," French, Stuart.

28. The hope of the righteous is joyful;
But the expectation of the wicked shall perish.
29. The way of Jehovah is a fortress to the upright;
But it is destruction to the workers of iniquity.
30. The righteous (*man*) shall never be moved ;
But the wicked shall not dwell in the land.

28. *Joyful*—lit. *joy*. The hopes of the righteous, both with regard to this life and the life to come, are in their very nature pleasurable, joy-inspiring and comforting, because they are founded on
a steadfast reliance upon the promises of God. But the expectations of the wicked, on the contrary, have no such promises to rest
upon, and consequently they are productive of no real satisfaction,
and are sure to end in disappointment. There is happiness in the
patient hope and enduring resignation of the pious; there is destruction to the brightest expectations and most ardent and passionate desires of the wicked. As to these last, Hope's fair torch will
at length expire, never to be relighted. (See ch. 1: 7. Ps. 112: 20.
Job 8: 19. 12: 20. 18: 14.)

29. *The way* of Jehovah denotes here his providential arrange-
ments and dealings with men. While these conduce to the well-
being, safety, and happiness of the righteous, who discern the wisdom and goodness of God in all his dispensations towards them,
they are productive of misery to the ungodly. What proves a savor
of life to one, to the other becomes a savor of death. (Ps. 18: 30.
Deut. 32: 4.) Some expositors interpret the phrase "way of Jehovah" in an objective sense, as denoting that course of life which
Jehovah prescribes and approves, as in Ps. 5: 9. 25: 4. 27: 11.
Others connect *way* with *upright*, instead of with Jehovah, as in ch.
13: 6, and render the clause thus, "Jehovah is strength to him that
is upright in his way." But the antithesis favors the common rendering, which is also more accordant with the analogy of Scripture.

30. *Never be moved*—i. e., shall never fall into overwhelming difficulty and irremediable ruin, but shall enjoy a permanent state of
security and prosperity. By *the land* is most probably intended the
promised land, i. e., Palestine. But under that promise a more general truth unquestionably lies. See ch. 2: 21, 22. The Heb. verb
מוֹט *mot*, in Niph. conj. is here and in Ps. 104: 5. 125: 1, translated

28. "*Endeth in joy*," French.
29. "*Him that is upright in his way*," French, Noyes—"*in the way*," Boothr.—
"*but is destruction*," French, Noyes—"*destruction shall be*," Boothr.

31. The mouth of the righteous (*man*) bringeth forth wisdom ;

But the perverse tongue shall be cut off.

32. The lips of the righteous (*man*) know what is acceptable;

But the mouth of the wicked is perverse.

---

in our English Version "removed," and the parallelism favors that rendering. But nearly all modern commentators agree in uniformly rendering the verb "to be moved," and this appears to be its only proper signification.

31. The metaphor in this aphorism is taken from a tree. The mouth of the righteous man utters wisdom and communicates knowledge, as a sound and healthy tree produces good fruit. But the tongue which utters perverse and pernicious opinions, is like a diseased and rotten branch, which we cut off as not only useless but injurious to the tree.

32. This aphorism, like the preceeding, relates to our conversation in the ordinary intercourse of life. The pious and instructive discourse of the righteous man is well pleasing and beneficial to his fellow men, and acceptable to God.

CHAPTER XI.

1. Deceitful balances are an abomination to Jehovah;
But a perfect weight is his delight.

---

1. *Deceitful balances,* or *scales.*—Literally, *balances of deceit,* so Marg. Reading. (See Hos. 12: 7 (8). Amos 8: 5. Mic. 6: 11.) By these are meant scales which are provided with false weights, i. e., weights either too heavy or too light.—*Perfect weight* is literally a *stone of completeness.* Stones were universally employed in ancient times for weights, and even now they are said to be the only weights used in many parts of Palestine. They were called *just, perfect,* or *complete,* when exactly of the heft required. Deut. 25: 13, 15. Marg.

---

1. "*A false balance,*" S. V., Holden, Boothr.—"*deceitful scales,*" French—"*false scales,*" Noyes—"*balances of deceit,*" Stuart="*just weight,*" S. V., Holden, Boothr. —"*complete weight,*" Stuart.

2. (*When*) pride cometh, then cometh shame ;
But with the lowly is wisdom.

3. The integrity of the upright shall guide them ;
But the perverseness of transgressors shall destroy
them.

4. Riches profit not in the day of wrath ;
But righteousness delivereth from death.

5. The righteousness of the perfect (*man*) maketh
his way plain ;
But the wicked (*man*) falleth by his own wickedness.

Reading, *a perfect stone.* One of the modes by which dishonest selfishness seeks to attain its ends is the use of false or inaccurate
weights and measures. This was doubtless in ancient times a very
common practice. But with the advance of civilization the oppor-
tunities of accomplishing the fraudulent trick become less frequent.
The dishonest dealer in modern times finds it easier to impose upon
his customers in the *quality* than in the *quantity* of his merchandise.
Hence the extent to which the shameful practice of adulteration is
carried. But the principle involved in this apothegm applies to
every kind of unfair and fraudulent dealing.

2. Shame, mortification and disgrace, are the frequent attendants
and consequents on pride. But true wisdom is the companion of
humility.

4. *The day of wrath* is the day of God's displeasure, when he
brings evil upon men as the just punishment of their sins. The
final judgment is emphatically such a day to the wicked. Compare
our Saviour's declaration, Matt. 16: 26, "What shall it profit a man
if he gain the whole world and lose his own soul"—his eternal *life?*
See Prov. 10: 2, where the same thought is enounced by a varied
expression. (יוֹעִיל, Hiph. fut. of יָעַל. הַצִּיל, Hiph. fut. of נָצַל.)

5. The literal meaning of the phrase *a plain way* is a smooth,
even, level, and straight road, in which one may walk without
stumbling, or losing his way. Righteousness is a most valuable
guide in all perplexities, and enables the good man to pass through
life in safety, comfort and prosperity. The wicked man, on the
contrary, by his base conduct, throws stumbling-blocks in his own
way, over which he falls and comes to ruin.

---

5. "*Good man,*" French, Noyes—"*the upright,*" Boothr. Stuart.="*will direct
his way,*" S. V., Holden, Boothr.

6. The righteousness of the upright will deliver them ;

But transgressors shall be taken in (*their own*) mischief.

7. When the wicked man dieth, his expectation perisheth ;

Yea, the hope of unjust (*men*) perisheth.

8. The righteous (*man*) is delivered from trouble ;

And the wicked cometh into it in his stead.

9. The impure (*man*) with his mouth destroyeth his neighbor ;

But by the knowledge of the righteous are (*men*) delivered.

---

6. Retributive justice not unfrequently takes place in this world, and unprincipled men reap in kind the just recompense of the injuries they have inflicted, or designed to inflict on others. This was particularly the case under the Mosaic law. (Comp. Ps. 7: 15, 16. 9: 15.)

7. The hopes of the righteous extend into eternity: but those of the wicked are bounded by time. Terminating in some earthly good,—riches, honors, or pleasures,—they are dissipated by death. (See ch. 10: 28. 14: 32.) The Septuagint rendering of the first clause of the verse is, "At the death of a righteous man his hope does not perish." This reading is preferred by Boothroyd, on account of its bringing out more fully the antithesis, which so frequently occurs in this part of the book. The authority, however, for this reading, is evidently insufficient; and yet the contrasted thought is doubtless implied. The apothegm clearly appears to be grounded on the belief in a future state of existence, because as it regards this world's prosperity, the hopes of the righteous at death come to an end as well as those of the wicked.

9. The Hebrew word חָרֵף, *chareph*, is commonly rendered *hypocrit*, after the Vulgate *hypocrita*, a meaning drawn from the Talmudic and Rabbinic usage, but apparently without foundation in the Hebrew, or any of its kindred dialects. It denotes a *profane, impure, godless* person,—one who is morally polluted, and uninfluenced by regard either to God or man. (See Job 8: 13. 13: 16. 17: 24.) Im-

---

9. "*The hypocrite*," S. V., Holden—"*the impious*," Boothr.—"*the profane person*," French, Noyes—"*a vile person*," Stuart.

10. When the righteous prosper, the city rejoiceth;
And when the wicked perish, there is shouting.

11. By the blessing of the upright the city is exalted;
But it is overthrown by the mouth of the wicked.

---

pure and unprincipled men often corrupt and destroy others by their unchaste conversation, by plausible professions and insinuations, by gross misrepresentations as to the nature of religion, its evidences, and its moral power, by slandering pious men and faithful ministers, and by prejudicing others against the humbling doctrines and holy precepts of God's word. The word rendered *knowledge* (הַעַת *daath*) may be used independently, and not in regimen with *the righteous*. In that case the clause should be rendered as in the Standard Version, and Vulgate, "By knowledge the righteous are delivered." The meaning would then be, that the righteous are preserved from fatal snares by means of their superior knowledge and virtue. Or, it may be limited by "the righteous," and the plural verb may have the indefinite nominative *men* understood as its subject. This construction is preferable as being more accordant with the context. While the impure and unprincipled corrupt and destroy many by their profane and ungodly discourse, the righteous, on the contrary, by their wise and instructive conversation, accompanied by a pious deportment, are instrumental in saving many from impending ruin. (יֵחָלֵצוּ, Niph. fut. plur. of חָלַץ.)

• 10. The real and permanent welfare and prosperity of a city depend on the intelligence, virtue, and integrity of its inhabitants. The presence and success of such persons in a community is, therefore, a proper subject of general rejoicing. And the removal of the wicked, whose presence and influence are productive only of evil and mischief, is a matter of gratulation, rather than of regret, to all who desire the best good of mankind.

11. By *the blessing of the upright*, is meant the various benefits which the upright are instrumental in conferring upon a city by means of their active exertions, their wise and prudent counsels, their virtuous example, their fervent prayers, and their constant regard for the public good. By these benefits the city *is exalted*, i. e., placed in a condition of security from outward invasion, as though protected by an impregnable wall of defence, and also rendered safe from internal dissension and anarchy. On the contrary, by the

12. He, who despiseth his neighbor, is void of understanding;
But a man of discernment holdeth his peace.
13. He, who goeth about, as a tale-bearer, revealeth secrets;
But he, who is of a faithful spirit, concealeth a matter.

treachery, falsehood, irreligion, pernicious counsel and vicious conduct of the wicked, it is weakened and at length overthrown.

12. The man who continually thinks and speaks contemptuously and disparagingly of others, shows not only that he is destitute of amiable feelings, but deficient in understanding, and puffed up with vanity and self-esteem. But the man of discernment, knowing the infirmity and imperfection of human nature, will avoid exposing unnecessarily the infirmities and faults of others, and refrain from speaking of them in disparaging, disrespectful and contemptuous terms. We have followed the Vulgate, Shultens, Piscat., Rosenm., Noyes and Stuart, in transposing the subject and predicate of the first member of this couplet. Not every man who is void of understanding despises his fellow-men. But every man who treats them with supercilious contempt shows thereby that he is deficient in good common sense and ordinary intelligence, as well as devoid of a right state of heart. (בָּז, Kal part. of בּוּז.)

13. The tale-bearer is one who goes about, like a travelling pedlar, trafficing in his neighbor's reputation and honor, and retailing the scandal and tittle-tattle, which he may pick up on his way. Such a person never hesitates to betray the confidence of friendship, in order to gratify his propensity for prating. This was expressly forbidden by the Mosaic law. See Lev. 19: 16. The word *tale-bearer* is not the grammatical subject of the proposition, but in apposition with the pronoun understood before הוֹלֵךְ, *holek*. So Marg. reading: "He that walketh, being a tale-bearer." "A tale-bearer is an odious character. He takes in all your story, if you are weak enough to give it to him, and then runs off to the next house and pours it into the greedy ear of jealous neighbors. His character is a compound of weakness and wickedness. He is feared less than bolder animals, and despised more. If he were not weak, he would

12. " *He that is devoid of wisdom despiseth,*" S. V., Holden—"*of understanding, despiseth,*" Boothr., French.

14. Where there is no wise counsel, the people fall;
But in the multitude of counsellors there is safety.

15. He shall suffer severely, who becometh surety
for a stranger;
But he, who hateth the striking of hands, is sure.

---

not act so wickedly; but if he were not wicked, he would not act
so weakly. He breeds hatred and spreads it. He carries the infec-
tion from house to house, like a traveller from city to city, bringing
the plague in his garments." (Arnott.) The opposite of such an
one is *the faithful spirit*—the man of true fidelity. He conscientiously
and studiously conceals the secrets with which he is entrusted, and
will not disclose what has been confided to him, by any means,
when he knows that such disclosure will injure another's peace or
credit, unless the honor of God and the good of society evidently
require it. Of inestimable value is the friend " who instead of the
weakness and wickedness of a tale-bearer, possesses the opposite
qualities of strength and goodness,—who is soft enough to take in
your sorrows, and firm enough to keep them." Horace has given us
a similar warning to that contained in the text.

" Per contatorem fugito; nam garrulus idem est;
Nec retinent patulæ commissa fideleter aures."

" Avoid the tale-bearer, for he is garrulous: his open ears retain
not faithfully the things committed to them."

A matter—i. e., any matter confided to him by his friend.

14. *Wise counsel.* Comp. ch. 1: 5, where the same word occurs,
and is translated in our Standard Version as here. For the sake of
uniformity, I have rendered the word in the same way, whenever it
occurs in a good sense. When the ship of state is without a skillful
pilot to direct its course, it is exposed to imminent peril. And when
God designs to punish any people, he places over them incompetent
and wicked rulers. See Isa. 3: 4. In the Sept. the second member
is translated, " But safety is found in much counsel,"—thus making
the safety of a nation to depend on the *abundance* of good counsel,
rather than on the *number* of counsellors. (רֹב, Kal Imp. of רָבַב.)

15. Rash suretiship (i. e. becoming responsible, by giving bonds
or other security for the pecuniary obligations of another), and the

---

14. " *No counsel,*" S. V., Holden, Boothr., French, Noyes—" *no guidance,*" Stuart—" *through much counsel,*" Boothr.—" *by an increase of,*" Stuart.

15. " *Shall smart for it,*" S. V., Boothr., Noyes—" *shall suffer,*" Holden—" *suffer
severely,*" French.

unhappy consequences which not unfrequently result from it, seem
to have been common in the days of Solomon, as well as in our own,
although the traffic of ancient times was small, compared with the
vast system of exchange now in operation among Christian nations.
The design of the warning here given, and of similar warnings in
this book, is not to condemn or discourage considerate kindness in
assisting a meritorious individual to rise above a temporary pressure,
or enable him to prosecute a lawful occupation in a safe and prudent
manner.   But the intention is to administer salutary caution against
the practice of becoming rashly and without due consideration,
bound for the faithful discharge of the pecuniary liabilities of others,
and especially of strangers, with whose character and circumstances
we are imperfectly acquainted, or who have no particular claims on
our aid; or to an *extent* which may not only involve ourselves and
those dependant upon us in embarrassment and distress, but deprive
those of their just dues to whom we may be indebted.   In the phrase
רַע יֵרוֹעַ, *ra yeroa*, which we have translated *he shall suffer severely*,
the word רַע *ra*, is regarded by many as the Kal Inf. abs. either of
the verb רִגְעַ, *rua*, or of רָעַע, *raa*.   But in this case it would be
either רוֹעַ, *roa*, or רֹי, *roa*.   Some, after the Sept. and Syr., make
it an adjective limiting the noun אִישׁ, *ish*, *man*, understood as the
subject of the proposition, and render the phrase, "An evil man
shall suffer," i. e., God punishes a wicked man for his wickedness
by permitting him to become surety for others, in order that he may
rush on to his own ruin.   But to suffer in consequence of becoming
surety for others is by no means confined to bad men: the good suffer quite as often and as severely from this cause.   Gesenius, with
more probability, regards it as a noun (*evil*) used intensively with
the verb in the manner of an infinitive.   In accordance with this
opinion, we have rendered it adverbially, "he shall suffer *severely*,"
after French: and this is probably the view taken of it by the translators of our Standard Version, in which it is rendered, "shall smart
for it."   Prof. Stuart gives to the verb a reflexive sense, and translates the clause, "An evil man showeth himself as evil, when he
giveth pledge for a stranger."   "This he does," says the Prof., "by
hastily pledging himself, and then not redeeming his pledge as promised."   But this appears to be a forced interpretation.   There is
nothing said about not redeeming the pledge given, nor is any thing
of the kind implied.   Nor is the reflexive sense of Niphal here war-
ranted by usage (comp. ch. 13: 20), or supported by the parrallel-
ism.

16. A gracious woman retaineth honor,
As strong (*men*) retain riches.
17. The merciful man doeth good to himself;
But a cruel (*man*) tormenteth his own flesh.

---

16. In the phrase *a gracious woman*, (lit. *a woman of grace*) there is reference rather to moral qualities than to personal attractions. It is equivalent to *virtuous* woman. The Heb. verb תָּמַך, *tamak*, signifies 1. *to acquire, to obtain;* and then 2. *to hold fast, to retain.* It is employed in the former sense in ch. 29: 23, where the same phrase occurs that is found here. In the latter sense it is found in ch. 3: 18. According to the first meaning the sentiment of the aphorism would be, ' A woman adorned with the purity and virtue of her sex, and with the graces of religion, obtains, acquires, secures for herself honor, respect and esteem from others; just as a strong man acquires riches.' According to the second meaning, the sense would be, ' The honor of a virtuous woman is her wealth, her most valuable treasure, in losing which she may be said to lose herself. Hence she clings to it with as much tenacity, as strong men hold fast their riches.' Either sentiment is true and important. But the epithet *strong* would seem more appropriately to apply to the act of *retaining* than to that of *acquiring* property. At least there seems to be no sufficient reason for departing from our Standard Version in respect to this word. Lewis translates the verse thus: "A virtuous woman is tenacious of her honor, even as the strong hold fast to their wealth." Sept. "A gracious woman brings honor to her husband; but a woman hating righteousness is a theme of dishonor. The slothful come to want; but the diligent support themselves with wealth."

17. All the good which a kind, humane, benevolent and merciful man does to others, returns with interest into his own bosom, as well in the inward satisfaction which he derives from the performance of duty, and the bestowment of benefits, as in the favor which his generous conduct secures for him both from God and man. Whereas cruelty to others, in its very nature, as well as consequences, renders a man wretched, a torment to himself, as well as to his family and

---

16. " *A graceful woman*," French, Noyes—"*a beautiful woman*," Stuart— '*a benevolent woman*," Holden="*obtaineth honor*," "*obtain riches*," Holden, Noyes—" *secureth honor*," "*secure riches*," Boothr.—" *taketh fast hold*," "*grasp at riches*," Stuart.

17. " *A benevolent man*," French—"*a man of kindness*," Stuart—"*rewardeth himself*," French.

18. The wicked (*man*) toileth for a deceitful recompense;

But he who soweth righteousness (*will have*) a sure reward.

---

friends. Some commentators reverse the subject in both members of the couplet, and translate thus: "He who doeth good to himself, is a kind man; but he who troubleth his own flesh is cruel," i. e., he who takes proper care of his temporal interests and bodily comfort, and cheerfully, freely and thankfully enjoys the bounties with which Providence has blessed him, is likely to be generous and kind to others, who are in less favorable and comfortable circumstances; while he who avariciously and penuriously denies himself the common enjoyments and even necessaries of life, is likely to be uncharitable and unkind towards others." Thus Ecclus. 14: 5, 6. "He that doeth evil to himself, to whom will he do good? he shall not take pleasure in his goods. There is none worse than he that envieth himself, and this is a recompense of his wickedness." So far as the grammatical construction is concerned, either rendering is admissible. But the sentiment conveyed by that in the text is more beautiful and more consonant with the analogy of Scripture than the other, and is in the main supported by the Sept. and other ancient versions.

18. The riches for which the wicked man toils and labors, and which he acquires, perhaps, by dishonest means, are fallacious, unstable and perishable. Hence the recompense which he receives from them disappoints his expectations; it does not compensate for the toil expended in the acquisition; and perhaps brings pain instead of pleasure· "Ye have ploughed wickedness, ye have reaped iniquity, ye have eaten the fruit of lies." Hos. 10: 13. The noun פְּעֻלָּה, *Peulla*, which commonly signifies *labor, business, work*, here corresponds with שֶׂכָר, *seker*, in the second line, and therefore means the *wages* of labor, *recompense*. On the other hand, he who sows righteousness, (i. e., whose conduct is upright, just and virtuous,) shall have a sure, satisfying, abundant, and enduring reward. It is sure because it comes in the way of natural law, as well as by the special promise of the divine blessing. It follows righteousness both in this world and through the merits of Christ in the world to come, as fruit follows the seed. It is satisfying, because

---

18. "*Fallacious earnings*," French—"*deceitful wages*," Noyes—"*deceitful gain*," Stuart.

11*

19. As righteousness (*tendeth*) to life,
So he, who pursueth evil, (*pursueth it*) to his death.

20. The perverse in heart are the abomination of Jehovah ;
But the upright in (*their*) way are his delight.

21. (*Though*) hand (*be joined*) to hand, the wicked shall not go unpunished ;
But the posterity of the righteous shall be delivered.

---

it will be just what the soul needs and *desires*. It is abundant; for every pious and upright man will receive just as much as his soul is capable of enjoying. It is enduring; because the true riches are imperishable and eternal as the soul itself. (Comp. Hos. 10: 12.) In the Sept. the second clause of the verse reads thus: "But the seed of the righteous is a reward of truth." But the second clause of v. 21 corresponds exactly with the original here. The two clauses have evidently by some means become transposed.

19. The righteous and the wicked are here contrasted in respect to their end. As a pious and upright course of conduct leads to present and future felicity, and consequently he who follows holiness (see ch. 15: 6) will attain to this felicity; so, on the other hand, he who practices evil, who follows a vicious and ungodly course of life, will do so to his own destruction. Life is the promised reward of the one; death the certain consequence of the other. (Comp. ch. 10: 16. 19: 23.) Sept. "A righteous son is born for life; but the persecution of the ungodly *ends* in death." So Syr. and Arab.

21. It was the custom in ancient times for persons to ratify public treaties and private contracts, and also to become sureties for one another by the striking together of their hands. See ch. 6: 1. It is still the custom of the Hindoos to ratify an engagement by one party laying his right hand on the hand of the other party. The earliest traces of written instruments sealed and delivered for ratifying the transfer of property, occurs in Jere. 32: 10-12. Conspirators are said to have taken a solemn oath of fidelity to each other by joining hand to hand in a circle. And hence the principal person in a combination for illegal and criminal purposes is called the *ringleader*. The ceremony in the East of friendly greeting, or of

---

21. "*Hand to hand,*" Rosenm., Stuart—"*though hand join in hand,*" S. V., Holden—"*with hand,*" Boothr.—"*through all generations,*" Gesen., Noyes - "*shall not be held guiltless,*" French—"*shall not go free,*" Stuart.

22. (*As*) a jewel of gold in a swine's mouth,
(*So*) is a fair woman, who is without discretion.
23. The desire of the righteous is only good ;
(*But*) the expectation of the wicked is wrath.

---

expressing regard for one another, is to touch their right hands respectively and then raise them to their lips and forehead. Our
Standard Version, "hand join *in* hand," conveys the idea of hand
clasped in hand, which is a European rather than an Oriental custom.   The proverbial expression, "hand to hand," is elliptical, and
equivalent to ' though hand meet hand,' and the sentiment expressed
in the verse is, ' though the ungodly combine together and heart
and will assent to heart and will in the perpetration of wickedness
and in affording mutual protection from danger, yet they shall not
escape detection, conviction and condign punishment.   On the contrary, the arm of the righteous man, strengthened by the invisible
protection and succor of Jehovah, will deliver him from all danger,
and not only himself, but his posterity also shall enjoy the benefit
resulting from his pious and upright conduct in a like deliverance.

22. The Hebrew women wore rings suspended from the nostril
by means of a hole bored through it.   (Isa. 3: 21. Ezek 16: 12.)
To this custom, which is not yet entirely extinct in the East, Solomon here appears to allude.   The import of the comparison is, As
a gold ring would be entirely out of place, unbecoming, thrown
away and dishonored, by being suspended from the snout of a filthy
swine; so female beauty is entirely misplaced and dishonored, when
unaccompanied with modesty, discretion, and propriety of conduct.
" The most beautiful ornament of a woman," says the Tamul proverb, "is virtue."   (כָרַת, Kal part. fem. of סְוּר, lit. *departing from*,
receding from.   See Marg. Reading.)

23. " Pure in character, and upward in direction is the current
of a righteous man's desires."   The wishes and aspirations of the
good are for things right and proper in themselves, and productive
of benefit to man, and these are bounded by moderation and due
submission to the divine will.   They are consequently approved of
God, and may be expected to be granted by him. (ch. 10: 24.)   But
the desires and expectations of the wicked, being formed without
regard to the will of God, or even in direct opposition to that will,
and having no solid basis to rest upon, however confidently cherished, will surely incur the righteous indignation of God, and result

24. There is (*one*), who scattereth, and yet increaseth ;
And (*another*), who withholdeth more than is meet,
yet he (*cometh*) to want.

25. The liberal soul shall be made fat ;
And he, who watereth, shall himself also be watered.

---

not only in disappointment, but in merited punishment. Sept.
"But the hope of the ungodly shall perish." (Comp. ch. 24: 28.)

24. Liberality, exercised with proper discretion, and from right
motives, does not impoverish the giver; but by the blessing of God
enriches him; while sordid and niggardly parsimony tends only to
poverty. It invariably impoverishes the soul, and not unfrequently
the purse. "God has put a mark of distinguishing favor upon the
exercise of that mercy which is his own attribute. He scatters his
blessings nobly around; and those that partake of his spirit do the
same." Comp. Ps. 112: 9. Those who distribute of their abundance to feed the poor, clothe the naked and supply the destitute with
the word of God and the means of grace, will reap a rich reward of
inward satisfaction, and will generally find that they have been
benefitted in their temporal condition, instead of being impoverished by their liberality. Seldom, however, does the covetous
worldling prosper in the long run even in this world. For God
often meets out to men according to their own measure; and bad
crops, bad debts, expensive sickness, and a variety of similar de-
ductions, soon amount to far more than liberal alms and benevolent
contributions would have done. No man, in fine, is so poor as he
who does no good with what he has. Sept. "There are those who,
sowing their own, make it more; and those who gather and are impoverished." (נוֹסָף, Niph. part. of יָסַף.)

25. This verse is explanatory of the preceding so far as the benevolent man is concerned. *The liberal soul*, (lit. *the soul of blessing*)
refers to the benevolent person described in v. 24, as "one who scattereth." *Soul* is put by synecdoche for *person*. *Shall be made fat*,
i. e., shall be enriched; a metaphorical expression—*watereth*—i e.,
is liberal to others. "An image taken from the refreshing and fer-

---

24. "*There is, who distributeth freely*," French="*and yet are his means increased*," French—"*and yet addition is made*," Stuart.
25. "*The beneficent man*," Piscat.—"*the bountiful man*," French, Noyes="*shall
be enriched*," French, Noyes.

26. Him, who keepeth back grain, the people will curse ; .
But blessing (*shall be*) on the head of him, who selleth it.

27. He, who earnestly seeketh good, seeketh favor ;
But he, who seeketh mischief, it shall come upon
him.

---

tilizing effect of copious showers upon the parched earth." (French.)
Com. Matt. 7: 2.   (תִּרְשָׁן. Pual fut. of דָּשֵׁן. מַרְוֶה, Hiph. part. of
רָוָה. יוֹרֶא, Hiph. fut. of יָרָה, the final א being exchanged for ה, or
perhaps the Hoph. fut. for יוּרֶה.)

26. He who hoards up grain in time of scarcity, for the purpose
of speculation, and of enhancing the price of breadstuff in the market, to the serious detriment of the poor, and refuses to sell except
at exhorbitant rates, must expect to incur, as he deserves, the displeasure and hatred of an indignant and injured people. On the
contrary, he who at such a time, instead of taking advantage of the
necessities of the community, sells his grain at a fair price and reasonable profit, exhibits a noble and generous spirit, and displays
true Christian philanthropy, for which he is sure to obtain the approbation and blessing of his fellow men. The word בַּר, *bar*, denotes *grain* in general, including such cereals (wheat, barley, rye,)
as were raised in Palestine and used for food by the Hebrews. Maize
or Indian Corn, was not known there. The word *corn* was used in
England at the time our Standard Version was made, and is still
used for *grain* generally. The principle involved in the passage
applies to every species of food necessary for the sustenance of man.
The expression, *blessing on the head*, is founded on the act of blessing, in which the hands of him who invoked the blessing were laid
on the head of the person blessed. (מַשְׁבִּיר, Hiph. part. of the de-
nominative verb שָׁבַר, from שֶׁבֶר, *grain*.)

27. He who seeks to promote the good of others, really seeks for
himself the highest and greatest good, viz., the approbation and
favor of God; and this he will most certainly obtain. On the contrary, he who seeks to do injury and mischief to others, will find
that the mischief he has meditated will recoil upon his own head.

---

27. " *Seeketh what is acceptable*," French—" *will seek for* (*God's*) *good pleasure*,"
Stuart.

28. He, who trusteth in his riches, shall fall;
But the righteous shall flourish as a leaf.

29. He, who troubleth his own household, shall inherit the wind; •
And the fool (*shall be*) a servant to the wise in heart.

30. The fruit of the righteous (*man*) is a tree of life;
And he, who winneth souls, is wise.

The verb בָּקַשׁ, *baqash*, never sig. *to procure*, as it is here rendered in our Standard Version.

28. The ungodly and worldly rich man, who puts his confidence in his wealth, and relies upon it for all his earthly happiness, shall ultimately fall, and it may be prematurely, as a withered and worthless leaf. But the righteous, who put their trust in God, shall flourish and prosper, like a verdant leaf. The verdant leaf, which receives its appropriate nourishment from the tree, is a frequent emblem of prosperity in the Scriptures. See Ps. 1: 3. Jere. 17: 8, et cet. The Heb. word עָלֶה, *ale*, uniformly sig. *a leaf;* the proper word for *branch* being קָעִיף, *seiph.* So Vulg.

29. A man may harass, vex, mortify and distress his family, by exacting of them unreasonable and oppressive labor, by harsh and unkind treatment, or by impoverishing them through gross mismanagement of his affairs, or the want of proper industry and economy, or indulgence in intemperance or other vicious practices. He who conducts in this manner, shall eventually experience only vanity and disappointment, ignominy, disgrace and ruin. He acts the part of a fool, and by his wicked folly he may so degrade and impoverish himself, as to be compelled to become the servant or slave of him who is wise enough to be virtuous, active, industrious and economical. *Household*—lit. *house*, but put by synecdoche for *household.*

30. *The fruit* of the *righteous man* is subjectively his words and actions; objectively the good effect of his example and conversation on others. "The good example, pious discourse, wise instructions, fervent prayers, and zealous good works of the righteous become exceedingly beneficial to those around them. They are as fruit from the tree of life; they promote the salvation of sinful man. As

---

28. " *As a branch,*" S. V., Junius, Shultens, Boothr., Holden.
29. " *House,*" S. V., Holden, Stuart.
30. " *And the wise man winneth* [*gaineth*] *souls,*" French, Noyes.

31. Behold! the righteous (*man*) is requited on the
earth :
Much more the wicked (*man*) and the sinner.

---

immortal souls are valuable beyond all estimation, he who thus
wins and allures them into the way of eternal life, is emphatically
the *wise man;* he proposes to himself the noblest end, he uses the
only proper means, he perseveres, and is prospered by God himself." (Scott.)

31. This apothegm is capable of two different interpretations,
according as we take the verb in the first clause of the verse either
in a good or a bad sense. In the former case the meaning would be,
'If God rewards the righteous man even in this life for his virtuous
and pious conduct, much more (not in degree, but in respect to certainty,) will he punish the wicked man also in this life.' This interpretation is favored by the Chaldee and adopted by Stuart, who
remarks that "the question is not, whether *all* the reward of the
righteous, or of the wicked, shall be dispensed in the present
world; but the text says, first, that here the righteous shall receive
blessings; and then, secondly, that the wicked shall surely have
some retribution, viz., by sudden and premature death, and by the
various evils which they must here suffer. If God's *mercy* bestows
the one, his *justice* will inflict the other." In the latter case the
meaning would be, 'Even the righteous man is punished in this
world for those occasional sins, which not with premeditated design, but through infirmity and the power of sudden temptation, he
commits; much more shall the habitually wicked man be punished
for the sins which he commits, not through infirmity, but deliber-
ately and with a high hand.' The argument in this case would be
from the less to the greater. This interpretation is favored by the
Vulgate, and nearly coincides in spirit, though not in the letter,
with the Septuagint version: "if the righteous scarcely are saved,
where shall the ungodly and the sinner appear?" to which the Syr.
and Arab. are similar. It is generally supposed that St. Peter (1
Epl. 4: 18.) quotes this verse from the Sept., though it is not introduced with the usual formula, "as the Scripture saith," "as it is
written," etc. The interpretation last given is most generally
adopted by commentators, and is on the whole to be preferred.
Thus explained a unity of sense will be given to the verb as expressed in the first clause, and implied in the second.

---

31. "*Recompensed,*" Holden, Stuart—"*rewarded,*" Boothr.

CHAPTER XII.

1. He, who loveth correction, loveth knowledge ;
But he, who hateth reproof, is stupid.

2. A good (*man*) obtaineth favor from Jehovah ;
But a man of wicked devices, He will condemn.

3. A man shall not be established by wickedness ;
But the root of the righteous shall not be moved.

4. A virtuous wife is the crown of her husband ;
But she, who causeth shame, is as rottenness in his bones.

1. By *correction* is here intended admonition, advice, rebuke, warning, as appears from the corresponding term *reproof* in the parallel line. He who is unwilling to be corrected for his errors, mistakes, faults and delinquencies, cannot be truly desirous of acquiring practical knowledge; for this correction is an important element in that moral discipline, which is indispensable to the acquisition of real knowledge. To hate reproof, then, administered in kindness and for our good, is a mark of stupidity justifiable only in the dumb cattle of the field.

2. A good man, who is actuated by the pure and upright motives of religion, is at all times the object of the divine favor and approbation But the man, who is constantly engaged in contriving mischief and plotting wicked schemes and devices, will ever be the object of divine abhorrence and condemnation.

3. Men are very apt to imagine that they may employ wicked means for the attainment of a laudable end—that the end in such cases justifies the means, and that consequently the desired end may be relied on with as much certainty as though proper and unexceptionable means were employed in securing it. But though success may for a time attend them, they will at last fail of their object. No man must expect to be firmly established by wicked means. But the righteous, whose foundation, like the roots of the stately oak, is embedded deep in the soil, shall stand firm to the last.

4. A *virtuous wife*—literally, *a woman of strength*, (Sept. γύνη

1. "*Instruction*," Sept., E. V., Junius, Holden, Boothr., Stuart="*remaineth (abideth) ignorant*," Boothr., French—"*remains stupid*," Noyes—"*is brutish*," E. V., Stuart.

5. The purposes of the righteous are just;
But the counsels of the wicked are deceitful.

6. The words of the wicked are to lie in weight for
blood ;   .
But the mouth of the upright shall deliver them.

αυδρεία,) by which is meant *moral strength,* virtue—all those moral
qualities indeed which go to make up a *good* wife,   (See Ruth 3: 11.
Prov. 31: 10.)   Such a wife is the ornament, pride and glory of her
husband.   In the metaphor here employed there may be allusion to
the ancient custom of adorning new married persons with a *crown.*
(Cant. 3: 11.)   The crown used at weddings was sometimes made
of leaves and flowers, and sometimes of more costly materials, according to the wealth and rank of the parties.   The ceremony of
crowning the contracting parties at nuptials, is still observed in the
Greek Church, and in some parts of the East.   The antithetical
clause teaches that the wife, who, by a disregard of her solemn obligations and appropriate duties, and by a course of conduct disreputable and unprincipled, brings shame, mortification and disgrace
upon her husband, is to him like an internal and incurable disease,
which is gradually but surely destroying him.

5. *Purposes*—not simply the *thoughts* which spring up in the
mind, as in E. V., but the purposes, plans, designs, which the mind
forms as the result of thought and reflection.   The word *counsels* is
here used in a bad sense, and denotes *evil counsels,* cunning, *crafty
designs.*   The purposes and designs of the righteous are just and
equitable towards men, as well as upright towards God; while those
of the wicked are charactized by deceit and duplicity.   (Comp. ch.
14: 22.)

6. Wicked men take counsel together how they may best gratify
their avarice, ambition, revenge, or lust; nor do they hesitate to plot
the destruction of their victims, if that destruction appears necessary to the accomplishment of their nefarious purposes.   But those,
who, by the base schemes of such, become exposed to imminent
peril, are not unfrequently rescued from danger by the timely inter-
position and friendly counsel of the upright.   Comp. ch. 11: 9.
(אֶרֹב, is the infin. put for a noun. יַצִּילֵם, Hiph. fut. of נָצַל, not
used in Kal.)

---

5. " *The thoughts,*" Sept., Vulg., E. V., Holden—" *the devices,*" French.

7. The wicked are overthrown, and are no more;
But the house of the righteous shall stand.

8. A man will be commended according to his wisdom;
But he, who is of a perverse heart, will be despised.

9. Better is he, who is despised, and is a servant to
himself,
Than he, who honoreth himself, and lacketh bread.

10. A righteous (*man*) regardeth the life of his beast;
But the tender-mercies of the wicked are cruel.

---

7. When the wicked are overthrown, then there is an end of them;
final destruction succeeds their overthrow. On the contrary, not
only are the righteous preserved, but their households or families
are blessed and established. Sept. "When the ungodly is overthrown, he vanishes away."

8. True wisdom—the wisdom of the heart, will always command
respect and consideration even from the most profligate; while the
man of a stubborn will and corrupt heart will be despised.

9. A man endowed with genuine humility and good common
sense, who adapts himself to his circumstances in life, and is ready
to do what is necessary for his own support and that of those who
may be dependent upon him,—to become his own servant, instead
of employing others whose services he can ill afford to requite,—
though he may be held in low esteem by others, and perhaps despised
by them for this very thing—is far happier, better off, and much
more deserving of respect, than one, who, reduced to poverty, regards it as derogatory to his dignity to labor for a maintenance, and
proudly boasts of his ancestors, his relations, and his social position, while he ignominiously casts himself upon his friends for support. So Sept., Vulg., Syr. and Ar. Others interpret the verse
thus: Better and happier is the condition of one, who, in moderate
circumstances, is enabled by prudent management to avail himself
of the assistance of others in conducting his affairs, than is that of
one, who, too proud to work, assumes the appearance of pomp and
splendor abroad, while his household is suffering from want.

10. *The tender mercies*—lit. *the bowels.* The Hebrews placed the

---

9. " *He who demeaneth himself,*" French="*hath a servant,*" E. V., Stuart="*than
he who affecteth grandeur,*" French.

11. He, who tilleth his (*own*) land, shall be satisfied
with bread ;
But he, who followeth vain persons, is void of understanding.

12. The wicked (*man*) desireth the net of the evil ;
But the root of the righteous yieldeth (*fruit*).

---

kindly affections in the bowels. (See 2 Cor. 6: 12.) The righteous
man is humane in his feelings, and treats with tender care even the
brute animals, who contribute to his wants and conveniences. On
the contrary, the wicked man shuts out from his breast the feelings
of compassion, and treats with cruel severity those, who may be
subjected to his power, and who should be the objects of his attention and solicitude. " They who delight in the sufferings and destruction of inferior creatures, will not be apt to be very compas-
sionate and benignant to those of their own kind." (Locke.)

11. He who diligently cultivates his own land, may expect an
ample supply of the necessaries of life as the reward of his industry.
But he who associates and spends his time with idle and worthless
persons, and who is too indolent to resort to honest industry for the support of himself and family, clearly manifests by such conduct a want
of understanding. (See ch. 28: 19.) Industry in any honest pursuit
is worthy of commendation, and occupation is the source of much
internal happiness, while at the same time it contributes to our
bodily comfort. Agricultural pursuits were those in which the mass
of the Hebrew people were engaged, and hence are here particularly
alluded to. The Sept. adds: " He that enjoys himself in banquets
of wine, shall leave dishonor in his own strongholds."

12. The antithesis in this couplet is obscure, as it is in many
other proverbs in this book. The word מָצוֹד, *matzod*, may signify
either *net, prey*, or *fortress*. According to the first, the meaning of
the first member would be: The wicked man desires the instruments
by which evil doers seek to accomplish their unrighteous purposes.
See Ps. 10: 8–10. According to the second, the sense would be: The
wicked man desires such prey, booty, or unlawful gain, as is obtained by evil doers in the execution of their unlawful deeds. According to the third, the sense is: The wicked man desires *protection*,
(*fortress* being used by metonymy for *protection, security*) from impending evils, but in vain. The last is the reading of the Vulgate

---

12. "*Longs after the prey of evil doers*," Noyes.

13. In the transgression of the lips there is an evil snare;
But the righteous shall escape from trouble.

14. A man shall be satisfied with good by the fruit of his mouth;
And the recompense of a man's hands shall be rendered to him.

15. The way of a fool is right in his own eyes;
But the wise (*man*) hearkeneth to counsel.

16. A fool's wrath is quickly known;
But a prudent (*man*) hideth an insult.

---

and the Margin of E. V. The first is that of our authorized version, and this appears to be the most probable. The parallel clause declares that the righteous produce good works, as a good tree produces good fruit.

13. False, calumnious and malicious charges and remarks in relation to others, while they may tend to excite prejudice against those to whom they relate, are sure also to recoil in the end upon the individual who utters them, and involve him in difficulty and disgrace, from which the man of veracity escapes. (Comp. ch. 18: 7.) The Sept. adds to this verse the following: "He whose looks are gentle, shall be pitied; but he who contends in the gate, will afflict souls."

14. Virtue, both in word and deed, will always meet with an adequate reward in the inward happiness which the consciousness of right-doing always affords. *The fruit of his mouth*—figuratively *his discourse.*

15. The *way* of a fool denotes his course of action and conduct. The proposition in the second clause is reciprocal, and may be rendered as in our standard version. "But he who hearkeneth to counsel (is) wise." But the version here adopted preserves the antithesis more exactly, and is supported by the Sept. and Vulg. A fool is so self-conceited, that he thinks he needs no counsel or advice from others, and therefore asks for none; a wise man, on the contrary, will not rely upon his own judgment alone in matters of great importance, but with a prudent self-distrust, will solicit the sound advice of others.

16. *Quickly*—lit. *on the day*, i. e., as soon as it arises, on the com-

---

16. "*What is shame!*   ," Boothr.

17. He, who speaketh the truth, testifieth what is right;
But a false witness—deceit.

18. There are (*those*), who speak rashly, like the piercings of a sword;
But the tongue of the wise is a healing medicine.

---

mission of an offence. A fool discloses his anger instantly, without reflection or regard to consequences. But a prudent man, with commendable self-control, conceals his displeasure and mortification at receiving an insult, and suppresses the desire of retaliation and revenge.

17. *Who speaketh*—lit. *who breathes forth,*—a form of expression denoting figuratively habitual action. He who is uniformly accustomed to speak the truth in the ordinary transactions of life, (i. e., a man of veracity) may be relied upon when under oath in a court of justice. But one who has no regard for his word on ordinary occasions, may be expected to testify in such a manner as to deceive. Some commentators reverse the terms of the proposition in the first clause, and translate, "A righteous witness speaketh the truth." *Deceit*, abs. for concrete, what is deceitful, i. e., calculated to deceive.

18. The participle בּוֹטֶה, *bote*, is in the singular number, but is evidently *generic* here. I have, therefore, with Stuart, rendered it as though it were plural, which also agrees with the Septuagint, and accords with the English idiom in such a case. The verb בָּטָה, *bata*, (=בְּטָא) properly signifies *to babble, to talk foolishly, idly, rashly* and *inconsiderately*, and such is evidently its meaning here. (Comp. Lev. 5: 4 Psalm 106: 33.) He who foolishly indulges a love for talking, without regard to the feelings or reputation of others, often inflicts the deepest wounds upon them. The wise man, on the contrary, is tender of the feelings and good name of his fellow men, and so speaks to and of them as to sooth and allay irritation, instead of producing it. There is probably no one, who has not felt keenly the unkind, unfeeling, mischievous remarks of idle, and reckless talkers. "Many will *speak* daggers without compunction, who would be *afraid* to *use* them." Yet this little member—the tongue—is no less powerful to heal than to wound: "It gives in-

---

18. "*A babler is like,*" &c., Gesenius, Boothr.—"*there are those who prate,*" Stuart="*healeth,*" Sept., French—"*is health,*" Vulg., Noyes—"*is healing,*" Stuart—"*is medicine,*" Boothr.

19. The lips of truth shall be established forever;
But a lying tongue is only for a moment.

20. Deceit is in the heart of those, who devise evil;
But to the counsellors of peace there is joy.

21. No calamity shall befall the righteous (*man*);
But the wicked shall be filled with evil.

22. Lying lips are an abomination to Jehovah;
But those, who deal truly, are his delight.

23. A prudent man concealeth (*his*) knowledge;
But the heart of fools proclaimeth (*their*) foolishness.

---

stant healing to the piercings of the sword, even to the very wound which it may have been constrained to inflict. But it is the tongue of the wise that is *a healing*. Wisdom is the guiding principle,— not a loose loquacity; but a delicate discriminating tact, directing us how, when, what, to whom to speak; sometimes repressing; sometimes quickening." (Bridges.)

19. He who customarily speaks the truth shall be established in peace and happiness; while the habitual liar will soon be brought to disgrace. Falsehood may succeed for a short period: but detection and disgrace will soon follow. *For a moment*—lit. *while I wink*.

20. Duplicity and deceit are characteristic of those who plot evil for the injury of others. But those who with singleness of heart and purpose, endeavor to promote concord and harmony among men, will not fail to experience inward satisfaction: and often a high degree of joy at the success of their endeavors.

21. Rectitude of conduct is to the upright man an effectual security against many of the calamities of life, which fall heavily upon those who habitually transgress God's laws. (יְאֻבֶּה, Hoph. fut. of אָבָה, not used in Kal.)

23. A wise and prudent man is modest, unassuming and unostentatious, and forbears to obtrude his knowledge upon others. But the fool has so much vanity and self-conceit that he cannot refrain from exposing his folly and ignorance, and acts as if he was anxious that every one should know how great a fool he is. "The heart of fools is in their mouth: but the mouth of the wise is in their heart." Ecclus. 21: 26.

---

19. "*Only for the twinkling of an eye*," Stuart.

24. The hand of the diligent shall bear rule;
But the slothful shall be under tribute.

25. Heaviness in the heart of man maketh it bow down;
But a kind word maketh it glad.

26. The righteous (*man*) showeth his friend (*the way*);
But the way of the wicked causeth them to err.

27. The slothful (*man*) roasteth not his game;
But the wealth of the diligent man is precious.

---

24. Diligence is ordinarily the path to advancement; and if it should fail of this result, it will always command respect and exert a good influence in its appropriate sphere. *Under tribute*—i. e., in a state of dependence and subjection to others.

25. This maxim points out a very easy and cheap way of being useful to others, and shows the cheering efficacy of a kind word seasonably spoken to a stricken and disconsolate heart. (יַשְׂחֶנָּה, Hiph. fut. of שָׂחָה.)

26. The righteous man not only finds out the right and safe way in which to walk, for himself, but points it out to his friends, and acts as their guide in conducting them into it. But the way in which the wicked walk, is the downward road to destruction, and is sure to mislead them and cause them to err. The Heb. verb יָתֵר, *Yather*, is the Hiphel of תּוּר, *thur*, which sig. 1. *to spy out, to explore*, and 2. *to show the way, to guide*. The latter meaning is appropriate here, because it gives an important significance to the proposition, and preserves the antithetical connexion between the two members of the verse. Some, however, and among them the translators of our Standard Version, derive the word from יָתַר, *yathar*, which in Niphal sig. *to excel, to be superior to*, and render, "The righteous is more excellent than his neighbor." In that case, by "neighbor" must be intended a *wicked* neighbor; and even then, the aphorism, though true, would be unimportant, and the antithesis is lost.

27. The indolent man, who lives from hand to mouth, improvident as to the future, loses, for want of proper care and exertion, even the fruits of his own labor. But the diligent, industrious and provident man, places a just estimate on the products of his indus-

28. In the way of righteous is life;
And in her pathway there is no death.

---

try, and converts them to their appropriate use. The Heb. verb
חָרַךְ, *charak*, occurs only in this place. The corresponding Chaldee
verb חֲרַךְ, *cherak*, is found in Dan. 3: 17, where it is translated *to
singe*, viz. the hair. There may possibly be an allusion here, therefore, to the custom which prevails in some countries of drying and
partially roasting the game taken in hunting, which is not wanted
for immdiate use, in order to preserve it for future consumption.
" In Calabar (W. Africa), and perhaps also in other countries," says
Rev. H. M. Waddell, " small animals used for food—sheep, goats,
deer, pigs, &c., are not skinned; the hair is burned off, and the
creature is cut up and dried undressed in the skin; and almost all
fish or flesh meat that comes to market is partially roasted and
smoke-dried. A diligent man going into the wilds to hunt, if he
snares or spears a deer or wild pig, perfectly dries over the fire of
his hut, what he does not immediately require for his own use, proceeding on his hunting operations, curing as fast as he takes, till
he has obtained as much as he can carry home. Not so the indolent man; as long as his first beast lasts him, he idles his time, eating, sleeping, and lounging about his hut, and probably losing half
the animal by not quickly or perfectly smoke-drying it. At last
he returns with little to show for the time he has been away; and
the little that he has brought, being only half dried, is half rotten "
Sept. " shall catch no game."

CHAPTER XIII.

1. A wise son (*hearkeneth to*) the instruction of (*his*)
father;
But a scoffer heareth not rebuke.

---

1. It is doubtful whether מוּסַר, *musar*. is a noun or the Hoph.
participle of the verb יָסַר, *yasar*. If the former, then it signifies
instruction, and a verb must be supplied from the parallel clause, as
above. So E. V. But if the latter, then the first clause should be
translated, "A wise son is instructed by (his) father." So Stuart.

2. A man shall eat good by the fruit of his mouth;
But the soul of transgressors (*shall eat*) violence.

3. He, who keepeth his mouth, keepeth his life;
But destruction will be to him, who openeth wide his lips.

4. The soul of the sluggard longeth, and (*hath*) nothing;
But the soul of the diligent shall be made fat.

The former is preferable, because, while the sense is equally good, it corresponds better with the parallelism, and is favored by the ancient versions. The interpunction, moreover, is that of the noun in the construct state. A wise and docile son will listen respectfully to the faithful instruction of his parents, even when that instruction is mingled with reproof. The scoffer, on the contrary, being impatient of parental control, and determined to be guided by his own wayward judgment, disregards the wise and wholesome counsel of age, experience and affection. Sept. "A wise son is obedient to his father; but a disobedient son will be destroyed."

2. A wise and upright man will enjoy as well as communicate much good by the discreet use of his speech; but those who abuse that noble faculty and prostitute it to vile and wicked purposes will experience trouble, self-reproach, violence and disgrace. (See ch. 12: 14. 18: 20, 21.) *To eat*, is here used in a tropical sense for to *enjoy*, to *experience*. Some MSS. instead of אָכַל, *yokal, to eat*, in the first clause, read יִשְׂבַּע, *yisba*, to be *satisfied, satiated, filled;* and this reading is followed by the Syriac, Chald. and Vulg. versions. This reading is adopted by French and Noyes, who translate the second line, " But the appetite of offenders shall be sated with violence." Sept. " A good (man) shall eat of the fruits of righteousness; but the lives of transgressors shall perish before their time."

3. To keep the *heart* is to guard the citadel of the inner man; to keep the *mouth* is to set a watch at the gates. If they be well guarded, the city is safe. Leave them unprotected, and destruction is inevitable.

4. *To be made fat*, is a metaphorical expression signifying to *possess an abundance*, to be *fully satisfied;* and the aphorism is applicable both to temporal and spiritual prosperity. God gives every

---

4. " *The appetite of the sluggard longeth*," French, Noyes.

5. The righteous (*man*) hateth a false word ;
But the wicked. (*man*) is loathsome, and cometh to shame.

6. Righteousness keepeth (*him, who*) is upright in (*his*) way ;
But wickedness overthroweth the sinner.

7. There is (*one*), who feigneth himself rich, yet (*hath*) nothing.;
There is (*another*), who feigneth himself poor, yet (*hath*) great riches.

---

thing, but in the way of diligence. In the order of his providence he has connected by the law of sequence, industry and prosperity, idleness and poverty. "The soul of the sluggard," is literally "as to his soul, the sluggard." Sept. "Every slothful man desires, but the hands of the active are diligent."

5. A righteous man loves the truth and detests falsehood; both in himself and others. But a wicked man, on the contrary, delights in lying, and by his numerous and barefaced misrepresentations, becomes loathsome, odious and hateful to others, and thus brings shame and disgrace upon himself.

6. *In his way*, i. e., in his virtuous and upright conduct and course of life. Righteousness is a defence and protection to the upright man; but wickedness is the destruction of the sinner. *Sinner* —lit. *sin*, abstract for concrete.

7. One man makes a show and pretence of wealth, which he does not possess, in order that he may gain credit, position and influence among men, and the more easily impose upon them. Another, on the contrary, feigns himself poor—conceals under the garb and semblance of poverty the wealth which he really possesses, that he may keep it the more securely. And under the despotic governments of the East, where personal property is extremely insecure, there exist strong inducements for its concealment. Holden interprets the proverb in a spiritual sense: "Some," says he, "are sedulous to amass wealth, and yet are destitute of the true riches, religion and the favor of God; others voluntarily continue poor in the eyes of the world, and yet abound in true spiritual riches." (מִתְרוֹשֵׁשׁ, Hiphpal of רוּשׁ.)

8. The ransom for a man's life is his wealth;
But the poor (*man*) heareth not rebuke;
9. The light of the righteous shall rejoice;
But the lamp of the wicked shall be put out.

---

8. The value of riches is well understood. Not only do they place a man above want and exempt him from the many inconveniences and privations attendant on poverty; but they may shield him from the punishment of the law, or rescue him from imminent peril. They may give him the power to purchase a ransom for himself from the hands of lawless banditti, or redeem himself from slavery, or save himself from the grasp of cruel persecutors. The early Christians, when suffering persecution, are said to have quoted the first member of this proverb by way of justifying themselves for appeasing the wrath of their persecutors with presents. The meaning of the second clause is not so clear. The phrase *heareth not rebuke*, may be taken in this connexion as in v. 1, to signify, that the poor man (poor by his own fault), will not listen to those who reprove and censure him for the indolence and wastefulness which have made and keep him poor. The couplet, however, may be intended to exhibit a contrast of reciprocal advantages; in which case the latter clause would furnish an offset to the former, and should be interpreted accordingly. The sense of the proverb would then be: The rich man's wealth buys him off from condemnation, punishment or danger; but the poor man's insignificance is his protection against false accusation, unjust aggression, the cupidity of the avaricious and the taunts and upbraidings of envy. The antithesis, brought out quite prominently by this interpretation, is greatly in its favor.

9. The lamp of the righteous shall shine with a bright, cheerful, and constant light, like that of the sun (Ps. 19: 5), as if rejoicing in the consciousness of inward satisfaction, and in the benefits it confers upon others. But the lamp of the wicked shall be quickly extinguished. *Light* is a common emblem of prosperity. The prosperity of the righteous will be a constant source of joy and gladness; but that of the wicked will be brief and transcient. Sept. "The righteous always have light." Syr. and Chald. "The light of the righteous bringeth joy." The Sept. adds, "Crafty souls go astray in sins; but just men pity and are merciful."

---

8. "*The protection*," Holden="*no upbraidings*," French—"*no threatenings*," Sept., Noyes.

10. By pride cometh only contention;
But with the well-advised is wisdom.

11. Wealth (*obtained*) without effort, will be diminished;
But he, who gathereth by labor, will increase it.

---

10. The adverb *only* (רַק, *raq*) evidently qualifies *contention* (מַצָּה,
matztza) and not *pride*, as in E. V.   The writer does not mean to
say that contention is occasioned only and in every case by pride;
but that pride causes nothing but strife and contention: in other
words, that pride is the fruitful source of strife.   See ch. 28: 25.
This is seen in communities, states, churches, societies, families,
and often among intimate friends.   "Some point of honor must be
maintained; some affront must be resented; some rival must be
crushed or eclipsed; some renowned character emulated; or some
superior equalled and surpassed." (Scott.)   "Even in trifling disputes between relatives or neighbors—perhaps between Christians—
each party contends vehemently for his rights, instead of satisfying
himself with the testimony of his conscience, and submitting rather
to be misunderstood and misjudged, than to break the bond of the
divine brotherhood." (Bridges.)   Some commentators take רַק, *raq*,
for a noun signifying *emptiness, vacuity*, (=רִיק, *riq*,) and here denoting emptiness in respect to wisdom, i. e ignorance, and translate
the clause, "Ignorance (joined) with pride produces contention."
Holden.   Others regard it as an adjective signifying *vain, empty*, and
render: "A vain (man) by pride causeth contention." (נֹעָצִים, Niph.
part. of יָעַץ.)

11. The word הֶבֶל, *hebel*, signifies *a breath*, then *vanity*.   Wealth
obtained by a breath, or by vanity, may denote wealth procured
without personal effort, or with little exertion.   This would seem
to be the meaning required here by the antithesis.   The sentiment
would then be, 'Wealth acquired without personal exertion and
labor, but by inheritance, or dishonest and disreputable practices,
such as gambling, cheating, theft, oppression; or by pandering to
the vices and follies of men, is generally soon diminished, squan-
dered or lost.   But that which is obtained by personal effort, honest

---

11. "*Wealth through vanity is diminished*," Holden—"*The wealth of one given to
vanity*," Boothr.—"*substance dwindleth away sooner than a vapor, (or breath),*"
French, Noyes="*gathereth cautiously*," Holden—"*gathereth into his hands*," Noyes.

12. Hope deferred maketh the heart sick;
But desire accomplished is a tree of life.

13. He, who despiseth the word, shall be destroyed;
But he, who feareth the commandment, shall be recompensed.

---

industry and skillful management, is attended with a blessing, is more highly valued by the possessor, and more likely to endure and increase.' "Riches wear as they are worn and woven." "Lightly come, lightly go." "What is ill-gotten is commonly ill-spent." (Comp. ch. 10: 2. 20: 21.) Sept. "Wealth gotten hastily with iniquity is diminished; but he that gathers for himself with godliness shall be increased." *By labor*—literally, *into the hand*, i. e., into his own hand—the hand of him who is active and industrious in gathering it. Some, omitting the ellipsis in the first clause, render, "Wealth is lessened by vanity." Gesenius: "Wealth vanisheth more swiftly than a breath."

12. *Hope* is here put by metonymy for the *thing hoped for*. "We live by hope." The first springing of hope in the breast is a pleasurable emotion, not, however, wholly unmixed with pain. It is the sensation of hunger, which makes our food acceptable and pleasurable. But prolonged beyond a certain limit, and that sensation causes pain and distress. So is it with hope. When the realization of that for which we hope is long postponed, the heart becomes grieved and afflicted, and sinks into discouragement and despondency. But the attainment of the desired object is reviving, invigorating, and salutary; it imparts an animating power, and is the source of permanent delight. See v. 19. ch. 3: 18. "The rule expressed in the first clause of this verse is universal. 'Hope deferred maketh the heart sick,' whether the person hoping and the thing hoped for be good or evil. Thus far one thing happens to all. But the second member is a dividing word. The accomplishment of the desire is *a tree of life*. This belongs to the hope of the holy." (Arnott.) בָּאָה, Kal. Part. of בּוֹא.)

13. By the *word*, &c., of God, is here intended the Holy Scriptures, and particularly the preceptive part. He who treats with neglect or contempt the precepts and commands of God, contained in his most holy word, will bring ruin on himself as the just punishment

13. "*Shall bring destruction on himself,*" Stuart—"*shall be punished,*" Holden= "*he who reverenceth,*" French, Noyes="*shall be safe,*" French—"*shall be at peace,*" Stuart—"*shall be rewarded,*" Boothr.

14. The teaching of the wise (*man*) is a fountain of life,

To turn away (*men*) from the snares of death.

15. A good understanding procureth favor;

But the way of transgressors is hard.

16. Every prudent (*man*) dealeth with knowledge;

But a fool spreadeth abroad (*his*) folly.

17. A wicked messenger falleth into trouble;

But a faithful ambassador is a healing medicine.

---

of his misconduct. On the contrary, he who reverences and obeys the divine precepts, shall receive a just recompense of reward for his obedience. See ch. 11: 31. Jere. 18: 20. The phrase יֵחָבֶל לוֹ *Yechabel-lo*, literally signifies *shall be bound to it*, viz. the word, i. e., shall suffer the penalty it denounces.

14. The teaching or instruction of a wise man (Syr. of wisdom), is a fountain yielding moral and spiritual life and happiness, by means of which men are rescued from the snares of death.

15. Sound common sense, in connexion with upright conduct, secures the favor, approbation and confidence of men. In consequence of this, the way or course of life of such a one is rendered doubly easy and pleasant. But the way in which transgressors go —the broad road which leads to death—is *rough*, (Deut. 21: 4) *stony*, and consequently hard and laborious to travel. French, in order to make the parallelism more perfect, renders אֵיתָן, *ethan, harsh* instead of *hard*. The conduct of transgressors is such as, so far from conciliating the good opinion of others, creates dislike and disgust.

16. Every prudent man employs his knowledge in such a way as to render it most useful to himself and others. But an ignorant and foolish man is continually exposing his ignorance to his own prejudice.

17. By a *wicked messenger* is meant one who is negligent and unfaithful in executing the commissions entrusted to him Such a man gets into trouble and renders himself obnoxious to punishment for his want of fidelity. See ch. 10: 26. But the *faithful*, reliable, trust-worthy messenger, by the promptness, alacrity and fidelity with which he discharges his duty, affords relief from all anxiety, and soothes the mind of his employer, as a healing medicine soothes and alleviates the diseased body. See ch. 25: 13.

18. Poverty and shame are for him, who refuseth
instruction ;
But he, who regardeth reproof, shall be honored.

19. Desire accomplished is sweet to the soul ;
But it is an abomination to fools to depart from evil.

20. He, who walketh with wise (*men*), shall become
wise ;
But the companion of fools shall be destroyed.

---

18. The Septuagint renders the first clause thus: "Instruction ·
removes poverty and disgrace." One of the most important and
effectual preventatives of poverty, crime and disgrace, is a good
education. Comp. ch. 15: 32. By *instruction* may here be meant
simply wise counsel and good advice, given to another by a friend ·
for his temporal and spiritual benefit.

19. The thought expressed in the first member of this verse is
substantially the same as that in the second clause of v. 12. The
pleasure and satisfaction, which a wise and good man derives from
the attainment of a good object, which he has been long and earnestly desiring, abundantly compensate for the trouble, anxiety and
self-denial exercised in its pursuit. But fools, or ungodly men, are
so wedded to evil and so averse from every thing good, that they
cannot be induced to desire that which would be really beneficial
to them, or to take any steps for its attainment. They refuse to depart from their evil course, and to restrain their base desires and
lawless passions, although the sure result of their wicked course is
disappointment and failure.

20. "Every one desires to engrave his own image upon his com-
panions. We naturally, therefore, take our mould from their society.
It is not left to us to determine whether there shall be any influence
—only what that influence shall be. Walking with the wise—under
their instruction, encouragement and example, we shall be wise."
(Bridges.) "The principle of reciprocal attraction and repulsion,
pervades all nature, both in its material and spiritual departments.
Your character goes far to determine the company that you will
will keep; the company that you keep goes far to mould your character." (Keri, הוֹלֵךְ Part. instead of הָלוּךְ, Infin. and יֶחְכַּם, Future, instead of וְחָכַם, Imp. no doubt rightly. יֵרוֹעַ, Niph. Fut. of
רָעַ. There is a paranomasia between רֹעָה and יֵרוֹעַ.)

---

20. "*Walk with wise men, and thou shalt be wise,*" French.

21. Evil pursueth sinners :
But the righteous shall be recompensed with good.

22. A good man leaveth an inheritance to his children's children ;
But the wealth of the sinner is laid up for the just.

23. The tilled land of the poor (*yieldeth*) much food ;
But there are (*those, who*) are ruined for want of judgment.

24. He, who spareth the rod, hateth his son ;
But he, who loveth him, correcteth him early.

---

22. The posterity of a good and upright man inherit the property which he, by his industry and integrity, accumulated. But the wealth, which the sinner may have possessed, is often dissipated by his folly, extravagance, or profligacy: or else, it passes into the hands of strangers at his death, and becomes the property of the industrious and upright. Comp. ch. 28: 8. Job 27: 16, 17. Even the ancient heathen had a maxim like this, viz. "the third generation shall not possess ill-gotten wealth."

23. Land cultivated with skill, industry, strict attention and good management, by the virtuous poor, yields abundant food for their support and maintenance. While, on the other hand, there are those in easy circumstances, who, from want of industry and of ability to conduct their affairs with skill, prudence, and discretion, are brought to ruin.

24. The rod is the symbol of authority and power, as well as a common instrument of punishment: it is here put for correction administered in any form, whether by the infliction of corporeal punishment, when necessary, or in any other manner. He who, from want of energy, or from a mistaken regard for his children, withholds proper and effectual correction, when by their misconduct they deserve it, and when it is necessary for their future good, really treats them as though he hated them. But the parent who truly loves his offspring, and is solicitous for their welfare, will correct them in a proper manner and at the proper time, before they have acquired vicious habits which it may be difficult, perhaps impossible to eradicate. *Correcteth* him, is literally *seeketh* for him correc-

---

23. " *Much food is produced by the tillage of rulers; but it happeneth that it is destroyed for want of judgment,*" Holden—" *And there are, who are taken away, by reason of injustice,*" Stuart.

25. The righteous (*man*) eateth to the satisfying of
his desires ;
But the stomach of the wicked shall suffer want.

---

tion, i. e., prepares it for him and does not let him escape without
administering it

"Principiis obsta; sero medicina paratur,
  Cum mala per longas convaluere moras."—*Ovid.*

"Resist the beginnings: too láte is the remedy prepared,
  When evils have grown old by long delay."

25. "A righteous man never wants a sufficiency, because his
desires are moderate, and he makes a temperate use of God's blessings; whereas wicked men bring themselves to poverty by riot and
dissipation." (Bp. Patrick.)   *Desires*—literally *soul.*

CHAPTER XIV.

1. The wise woman buildeth up her house;
But the foolish teareth (*hers*) down with her hands.
2. He, who walketh in uprightness, feareth Jehovah;
But (*he, who*) is perverse in his ways, despiseth him.

---

1. The *wise woman*—lit. *the wisdom of women.*   *Wisdom* and *folly*
in the parallel members are abstracts put for concretes.   The plural
women is either used in the sense of ' the wise among women'; or in
a distributive sense—'every wise woman.'   A *married* woman is of
course intended, *house* being put by metonymy for *household,* and the
verb *to build* employed in a figurative sense.   A wise, prudent and
discreet wife, by her industry, economy, good management and
pious and virtuous conduct, promotes the comfort, happiness, and
prosperity of her family.   The foolish wife, on the contrary, by her
indolence, extravagance, wastefulness, and general mismanagement,
brings poverty, disgrace and ruin upon hers.   "A fortune *in* a wife
is better than a fortune *with* a wife."

2. *Uprightness*—lit. *his uprightness,* i. e. the upright course which
he prescribes to himself.   Real uprightness is an index of the true
fear of God in the heart, while perversity and disregard of the divine

13*

3. In the mouth of a fool there is a rod of pride ;
But the lips of the wise shall preserve them.

4. Where no oxen are, the stall is empty ;
But there is great increase by the strength of the ox.

---

law and authority, are sure indications that the transgressor despises
and contemns God. Integrity of life is an essential element and
evidence of a pious character:٭ while corrupt and unprincipled
conduct is the certain mark of a heart at enmity with God. See Ps.
11: 23. (נָלוֹז, Niph. part. of לוּז. בּוֹזֵהוּ, Kal part. of בָּזָה.)

3. *A rod of pride.* The unbridled tongue of the fool is a rod or
scourge for his own chastisement and the humbling of his pride.
He employs it for the injury of others; but it will at last recoil on
himself. The prudent lips of wise men are a safe-guard to them.
(תִּשְׁמוּרֵם, Kal fut. 3d pers. plur. fem. with the singular affix instead
of the plur. ם, probably by an error of the copyists.)

4. The Heb. word אֵבוּס, *cbvs*, signifies either the *stall* or *crib*
where cattle are fed; or else the *stable* or *barn* in which provender is
kept for their use. The word בַּר, *bar*, properly sig. *clean*. So here,
clean of provender, i. e., empty;—a satirical way of saying, that
there is a scarcity of provisions. So *cleanness of teeth* denotes *scarcity*
in Amos 4: 6. Good husbandry is indispensible to an abundant
harvest. If the fields are neglected, and permitted to lie fallow, no
crop will be raised, the barn and stall will be empty, and destitution and want will follow. But good husbandry is succeeded by a
plentiful supply of the necessaries and even the luxuries of life.
Oxen or bullocks were the animals principally employed in husbandry in the East, and especially in Palestine, where the multiplying of horses was prohibited by the Mosaic law to the Hebrews
(Deut. 17: 16). Men of every age and country have been greatly
indebted to the labor of the ox; for he was the first animal that re-
signed his neck to the yoke of the plough, which has so greatly
multiplied the comforts of men. As early as the days of Job, who
is supposed to have been contemporary with Isaac or Abraham,
"the oxen were ploughing," we are told, "in the fields, and the
asses feeding beside them," when the Sabeans attack the sons and

---

3. " *A sharp spear,*" Boothr.—"*an insolent scourge,*" French—"*a scourge of his
pride,*" Noyes—"*haughtiness is a rod,*" Stuart.
4. " *The crib is clean,*" Sept., E. V., Holden—"*the stall is clean,*" Boothr., French
—"*the fodder loft is clean,*" Noyes.

5. A faithful witness will not lie;
But a false witness uttereth falsehoods.

6. The scoffer seeketh wisdom, and (*findeth it*) not;
But knowledge is easy to the (*man of*) understanding.

---

servants of the patriarch. In times long posterior, when Elijah was commissioned to anoint Elisha as his successor in the prophetical office, he found him employed in plowing with twelve yoke of oxen. For many ages the expectations of oriental husbandmen depended on the labors of this useful animal. The ass indeed in the course of time was compelled to bend his stubborn neck to the yoke, and share in the labors of his companion; but the preparation of the ground in the time of spring, chiefly depended on the more powerful exertions of the ox. This may fairly be inferred from the proverb before us, in which no notice is taken of the ass, although it is more than probable that he had been yoked to the plough long before the time of Solomon. Oxen were used in Palestine not only in plowing the land and preparing it for the seed, and removing the crop from the field, but also for treading out the grain. Deut. 22: 10. 25: 4.

5. *Uttereth.* The figure here employed is taken from the act of *breathing*, and indicates the habit of lying. It is as natural and easy for a faithless witness to lie, as it is for him to breathe. See ch. 12: 17.

6. *The scoffer* here denotes the frivolous, superficial, irreverent and prejudiced sceptic, who pretends to be a candid inquirer on the subject of divine revelation, but who really has no desire to be convinced of the truth, and only seeks to find more ground for cavil and unbelief. The *man of understanding*, on the contrary, is one, who is possessed of reverential feelings towards divine truth, and actuated by proper motives in his search after it. The opposite results to which the two come in their religious inquiries correspond to the opposite states of their minds and hearts. "He that comes to seek after knowledge with a mind disposed to scorn and censure, shall be sure to find matter enough for his humor, but none for his instruction." (Lord Bacon.) Comp Ps. 25: 9.

"Hear the first law, the judgment of the skies;
He that hates truth shall be the dupe of lies."—*Cowper.*

(נָקֵל, Niph. part. of קָלַל.)

---

7. Go from the presence of a foolish man,
(*In whom*) thou perceivest not the lips of knowledge.

8. The wisdom of the prudent (*man*) is to understand his ways ;
But the folly of fools is deceit.

9. Fools mock at sin ;
But with the upright there is favor.

10. The heart knoweth its own bitterness :
And a stranger doth not intermeddle with its joy.

7. It is a waste of breath and often of temper to argue with a
man, who, for want of capacity or of information, cannot, or from
the influence of prejudice, will not reason.

9. To *mock at sin* is to deride it, to treat it as a light and trifling
thing, whether committed by ourselves or others. Fools affect to
deride the idea of the intrinsic evil of sin, or of its criminality as
opposed to the law of God. But the upright endeavor to cherish a
proper abhorrence of it as highly offensive to God and injurious to
man, and labor to maintain a conscience void of offence both towards
the one and the other. And hence they enjoy the favor and approbation of the Most High. Some commentators understand by
אָשָׁם, *asham*, here, not *sin* in general, but *a misdeed*; i. e., a failure in
duty, and by רָצוֹן, *ratzon, charity*, viz. towards those who come
short   They do not deride them as fools do.

10. We have in this aphorism a graphical illustration of man's
proper individuality. The inward consciousness of a human being
can alone be privy to his personal joys and sorrows, anxieties and
troubles. Men learn by experience the bitterness of suffering, both
corporeal and mental, far better than any one can tell them; and it
is impossible for another to form an adequate estimate of it, or sym-
pathize fully with the sufferer. "Each mind," says Foster, "possesses in its interior mansions a solemn, retired apartment, peculiarly its own, into which none but himself and the Deity can enter." See 1 Cor. 2: 11. A physical burden can be divided equally
between two individuals. But the cares and troubles that press
upon the spirit, though as real as the load that lies upon the back,
are not so tangible and divisible. Happily, however, there is one,
who can either remove the burden, or give us strength to bear it.

9. "*Guilt exposeth the foolish to mockery*," Boothr.—"*Fools scoff at a charge of
guilt*," French—"*Sin-offering mocks fools*," Stuart.

11. The house of the wicked shall be destroyed;
But the tabernacle of the upright shall flourish.

12. There is a way, which seemeth right to a man;
But the end thereof is the way of death.

13. Even by laughter the heart is made sad;
And the end of mirth itself is grief.

---

11. The antithesis in this couplet is very beautiful and impressive. The most substantial structure,—the *house* of the wicked,—though from its materials and construction, apparently adapted to permanency, shall, nevertheless, be destroyed. But the frail tenement—the tabernacle, tent, fragile and temporary structure of the righteous, though having the appearance of weakness and frailty, shall endure.

12. Self-deception in regard to the character of our conduct and the consequences which must result from it, is no uncommon thing in this fallen world. Many an act and course of procedure is justified by man, which God condemns and will punish. The way *seems* right to him whose vision is clouded by prejudice and sin; but nevertheless it is wrong; and the result accords not with the false opinion, but with the absolute truth of the case. It surely leads to death, and its issue proves that its direction was erroneous. See ch. 12: 15. 16: 25. *Way of death*—lit. *the ways of death,*—plural of intensity—the sure way of death.

13. A painful depression of spirits often succeeds immoderate joy, and mirth not unfrequently ends in sadness. In this mutable and uncertain state of being, the cup of joy is sometimes followed quickly by that of sorrow; while there is often concealed an aching heart under a smiling countenance. Laughter, indeed, is not always the effect of joy. Campbell, in his "Elegy of Love and Madness," thus speaks of the laugh of agony:

"Long slumb'ring vengeance wakes to better deeds.
He shrieks, he falls, the perjur'd lover bleeds!
Now the last laugh of agony is o'er,
And, pale in blood, he sleeps to wake no more."

It is a curious fact, that as a tear frequently expresses the highest joy which the human mind can receive, so a laugh seems at times to denote the severest agony of which the mind or the body is susceptible.

14. The backslider in heart shall be filled with his own ways ;
But the good man (*shall be satisfied*) from himself.
15. The simple (*man*) believeth every word ;
But the prudent (*man*) looketh well to his steps.
16. The wise (*man*) feareth and departeth from evil ;
But the fool is haughty and confident.

---

14. The ways in which the backslider goes are evil ways, and with the fruit of these, as a natural consequence and just punishment, he shall be filled   See ch. 1: 31. But the good man has a perennial spring of satisfaction in his own soul, which will preserve him from returning to the world in pursuit of its pleasures, from desire of its friendship, or from dread of its power. The second member is rendered by some, " But the good man will depart from him,"—i. e., from the paths of the backslider, or from his company. He will cease to associate with him while he continues in that sinful and dangerous state.

15. To believe every word of God is faith; to believe every word of man is credulity; and excessive credulity is a mark of folly. The simpleton, devoid of sound wisdom and discretion, listens eagerly to any suggestion which may be made, any opinion which may be expressed, and any adviser who may choose to control his actions. The prudent man, on the contrary, proceeds cautiously, examines before he trusts, and considers well before he adopts the opinions or advice of others. " Trust is a lovely thing; but it cannot stand, unless it has truth to lean upon. When its tender branch has been often pierced by a broken reed of falsehood, it pines away and dies of grief. In this world a man is obliged to be suspicious. Man suffers more from man than from the elements of nature, or the beasts of the field." (Arnott.)

16. The wise man fears the displeasure of God no less than the punishment of sin, and hence he avoids the occasion and appearance of evil. But the foolish are self-confident, inflated with pride, impatient of control, and regardless of consequences. The Hebrew verb מִתְעַבֵּר, *mithabber*, properly signifies in Hiph. *to overflow*, and *is applied* to waters overflowing their banks: then tropically, *to overflow* with anger, i. e., *to be wroth*. Also, *to overflow* with pride, i. e., to be haughty, arrogant and self-reliant, inflated with pride and

---

16. " *Transgresseth, and (yet) is confident*," Holden, Boothr., French.

17. (*He, who*), is soon angry, committeth folly ;
And a man of wicked devices is hated.

18. The simple inherit folly ;
But the prudent are crowned with knowledge.

19. The evil bow down before the good ;
And the wicked (*bow down*) at the gates of the
righteous.

20. The poor (*man*) is hated even by his own neighbor ;
But the friends of the rich are many.

---

impatient of control. The word in this form usually means *to be re-
venged,* and so it is rendered here in our authorized version. But it
is here opposed to the modest and humble course of the wise man,
and clearly means to be *haughty,* to *act haughtily.*

17. *Soon angry* is literally *short of nostrils,* and figuratively *short
of anger, quick tempered, irritable.* Sept. οξυθυμος. See v. 29.
The Hebrews, Greeks and Romans agree in representing the *nose* as
the seat of anger. "Ira furor brevis est." "Anger is a brief fury."
(Horace.) "Sed tamen, ira procul absit, cum qua nihil recte fieri,
nihil considerate potest." "But yet, let anger be far removed,
with which nothing can be rightly or considerately done." (Horace.)

18. *Folly* is the patrimony of fools. As men sow, so will they
reap. The prudent are crowned with knowledge as with a diadem.
This is what they diligently seek, and this they obtain as their reward or ornament. (יַפְתִּירוּ, Hiph. fut. intransitive of פָתַר.)

19. The evil are constrained to pay homage and respect to the
good, and often to acknowledge their superiority and to solicit their
favor. The second clause conveys the same sentiment as the first,
and differs from it only in being more specific.

20. The poor man, instead of being pitied, comforted and aided,
in consequence of his poverty, is often neglected and even despised
by his more highly favored and prosperous neighbor. But multi-
tudes pay court to the rich, and they never lack friends. The verb
to hate is here used in a somewhat qualified sense.

" Nil habet infelix paupertas durius in se
Quam quod rediculos homines facit."—*Juvenal.*

---

18. "*The prudent ardently seek knowledge,*" Dathe, Boothr.—"*take fast hold of,*"
Sept.—"*expect knowledge,*" Vulg.

21. He, who despiseth his neighbor, committeth sin;
But he, who hath pity on the poor,—happy is he.
22. Do they not err, who devise evil?
But mercy and truth are to those, who devise good.
23. In all labor there is profit;
But the talk of the lips (*tendeth*) only to penury.
24. The crown of the wise is their wealth;
But the elevation of fools is folly.

"Donec eris felix, multos numerabis amicos;
Nullus ad amissas ibit amicus opes."—*Ovid.*

21. *Happy is he*—emphatic repetition of the pronoun.

22. *To err* is in this place, *to wander* from the object and end proposed to one's self. The English verb is used in the sense of *wandering* in the Episcopal Prayer Book: "We have erred and strayed from thy ways like lost sheep." The aim and object of those who devise evil is the acquisition of wealth, honor or power; but in this they are generally disappointed. They miss their aim and fail in their efforts. On the contrary, such as desire good, shall meet with kindness and truthfulness from their fellow men, and thus will obtain the reward which they deserve for their good intentions. Sept. "They that go astray devise evil; but the good devise mercy and truth. The framers of evil do not understand mercy and truth; but compassion and faithfulness are with the framers of good." Some commentators render, *Do they not perish?* instead of *Do they not err?*

23. By *all labor* is here intended all lawful, well-directed industry as contrasted with idleness and empty talk. "Working without talking will make men rich; talking without working will make men poor." "Solomon," says Lord Bacon, "here separates the fruit of the labor of the tongue, and the labor of the hands: as if want was the revenue of the one and wealth the revenue of the other. For it commonly comes to pass, that they, who talk liberally, boast much, and promise mighty things, are beggared."

24. Riches constitute a crown, honor, and ornament to the wise. But the opulence, elevation, advancement of fools, only administer

---

22. "*Do they not miss their aim?*" Boothr.—"*Do they not miss their end?*" French.
24. "*The opulence of fools,*" Holden—"*the possession,*" Boothr.—"*the occupation,*" Sept.—"*the promotion,*" Noyes.

25. A true witness saveth lives;
But a deceitful (*witness*) uttereth lies:
26. In the fear of Jehovah is strong confidence;
And to his children there shall be a refuge.
27. The fear of Jehovah is a fountain of life,
To turn (*men*) from the snares of death.

---

to their folly, and render it the more conspicuous. The word אִוֶּלֶת, *ivveleth*, occurs twice in the second member of this verse, but evidently in different senses. Otherwise we must translate thus: " The folly of fools (the foolishness, E. V.) is folly;" which would be a mere truism of little significance, and unsuited to the character of this book. There would seem to be a paranomasia or play upon the two-fold signification of the word; it being first used in the sense of *precedence, elevation, advancement, promotion*, a meaning which it acquires from the root אָעַל, *ul;* and then in the more common sense of *folly*, a signification which it obtains from the root אָוַל, *aval.* Comp. v. 29.

25. *Lives*—i. e., the lives of the innocent who have been wrongfully accused. *Uttereth*—lit. *breathes forth*—implying habitual conduct.

26. *Fear—confidence.* " The words sound strangely. They are like that blessed paradox of Paul, 'When I am weak, then am I strong.' They are strange, indeed, but true. To fear God aright is to be delivered from all fear. 'His salvation is nigh them that fear him.' The fear which brings a sinner submissive and trustful to the sacrifice and righteousness of the substitute, is itself confidence." (Arnott.) *His children.*—The first clause of the verse is descriptive of a *person* who fears God, although he is not named, but only characterized. Hence, by his children is intended the children of him who exercises this fear. The pronominal affix in Hebrew sometimes refers to an antecedent or subject not expressly mentioned, but implied from the scope of the discourse. See for a similar construction ch. 19: 23. The reverential fear of God confers the greatest blessings not only on parents, but also on their children and posterity. Boothroyd supposes God's children to be meant, to whom he will afford his aid and protection.

27. See ch. 13: 14.

---

27. " *To depart from the snares,*" S. V., Stuart—" *to avoid the snares,*" Holden— " *by it men avoid (depart from) the snares,*" French, Noyes.

28. In a multitude of people is the king's honor;
But the want of subjects is the destruction of a prince.

29. He, who is slow to wrath, is of great understanding;
But (*he, who*) is of a hasty spirit, exalteth folly.

30. A tranquil mind is the life of the flesh;
But envy is the rottenness of the bones.

31. He, who oppresseth the poor, reproacheth his Maker;
But he, who hath mercy on the poor, honoreth him.

---

28. The chief glory, as well as safety of a ruler, consists not in his personal splendor, his palaces, treasures, or pomp, but in the abundance of happy and virtuous subjects. These he cannot have without good government, and such a government they will aid him to maintain.

29. *Of a hasty spirit*—lit. *short* (*hasty*) of spirit, i. e., impatient, irritable, prone to anger; the antithesis of *short of nostrils*, i. e., slow of anger. *Exalteth folly*—renders it conspicuous. See ch: 3: 35.

30. The phrase לֵב מַרְפֵּא, *leb marpe*, literally signifies a *heart of tranquility*, i. e., a tranquil, placid, mind. The second noun is no where translated "sound" in the common version, except in this place. Comp. ch. 15: 4, where the same word occurs in connexion with the tongue. Equanimity of temper and tranquility of mind are highly conducive to bodily health and long life. While envy, jealousy, fretfulness, anger, and other malignant and corroding passions, prey upon the spirits, and undermine the health, like some latent or chronic disease, which torments and consumes the body. Comp. ch. 12: 4.

31. He who oppresses the poor on account of his poverty, brings reproach and dishonor on God, who is alike the Creater of rich and poor, and ordains that the former should be the protector and friend, not the enemy and oppressor of the latter. Comp. ch. 22: 2. Job ?' '5. On the contrary, he who has mercy and compassion on the (ute and dependent, honors God.

"*A sound heart*," S. V., French, Boothr.—"*a quiet heart*," Noyes—"*a sooth- rt*," Stuart.

31. "*Who is kind to the needy*," Boothr , French.

32. The wicked (*man*) is driven away in his wickedness ;

But the righteous hath hope in his death.

33. Wisdom resteth in the heart of him who hath understanding ;

But (*that which*) is in the breast of fools is made known.

---

32. The wicked man *is driven away*—thrust away—suddenly removed from life in the midst of his wickedness. He is torn away from his only heaven here, with no joyous heaven beyond. The righteous man, on the contrary, when he dies, is inspired with a hope full of immortality—the comforting and sustaining expectation of happiness beyond the grave. When the Christian dies, he goes to what he loves, to his everlasting home, to his Saviour's bosom, to his rest, his crown, his eternal joy. The apothegm appears to furnish strong ground for believing that the knowledge, recognition and inspiring influence of the doctrine of a future state of rewards and punishment, obtained to a considerable extent among the Hebrews in the time of Solomon. "The peculiarities of the Hebrew proverb shine conspicuous in this specimen. The two arms of the sentence are nearly balanced, and move round a common centre. There is a mixture of similarity and difference which makes the meaning perspicuous and the expressions memorable. But if there is peculiar beauty in the words, there is a terrible sublimity in the thoughts, which the two balanced branches of this proverb hold in their hands. These two arms outstretched and opposite, direct the observer, by their piercing finger-points, to Death on this side, and Life on that—endless both. Looking this way, you read the doom of the wicked; that way, you descry the hope of the just." (Arnott.)

33. *Resteth*—i. e., quietly abideth, is not forward in displaying itself, but reserves itself for proper occasions. *That which, &c.*—i. e. folly. Comp. ch. 12: 23. 13: 16. 15: 2. 29: 11. *In the breast*—lit. *in the midst*, i. e., in the interior of fools. "He that is truly wise hides his treasure, so as not to boast of it, though he does not hide his talent, so as not to trade with it." (Henry.) *Is made known*—i. e. they rashly give utterance to their thoughts at all times. Sept. "But in the heart of fools it (wisdom) is not discerned." So Syr. and Arab.

34. Righteousness exalteth a people;
But sin is a reproach to nations.
35. The king's favor is towards a wise servant;
But his wrath is against him who causeth shame.

---

34. Exaltation imports advancement to a state of dignity and honor, power and influence, usefulness and happiness. The exaltation or real advancement of nations does not consist in their territorial acquisitions, their splendid victories, or their extended dominion; for in each of these particulars it may originate in fraud, be established by oppression, and productive of human misery. But it consists in their intellectual, moral, political, social and physical superiority. In all these respects the natural tendency and effect of righteousness, or conformity to the Divine law, is to elevate a people to the highest pitch of excellence, prosperity and happiness. Sin, on the contrary, is a reproach, a disgrace and dishonor to nations. It degrades as much as righteousness exalts both individuals and communities, and brings in its train calamities and misery.

CHAPTER XV.

1. A soft answer turneth away wrath;
But bitter words stir up anger.

---

1. Mild and gentle language has great power in allaying angry passions, reconciling differences, and restoring harmony between parties who are at variance. It is the best remedy for poor arguments. "The best defence," says Wogan, "as well as remedy against anger is meekness. There is an invincible charm in the mild looks and soft words of this pacific virtue, which shames, or tames the fiercest wrath. But anger opposed to anger, adds fuel to the flame, and rather enrages than allays its fury." A soft answer is the water to quench: bitter words are the oil to quicken and increase the fire in the human breast. Soft and soothing words give a double victory—over ourselves, and over our offended and enraged brother.

2. The tongue of the wise maketh knowledge pleasing;
But the mouth of fools poureth out foolishness.

3. The eyes of Jehovah are in every place,
Beholding the evil and the good.

4. A mild tongue is a tree of life;
But perverseness therein is a breaking of the spirit.

---

2. The wise man, in the communication of knowledge, is guided by discretion as to the time, the subject, the person addressed, and the manner in which he speaks. Hence what he communicates is not only instructive in itself, but is made pleasing, agreeable and attractive to others. But fools utter their crude and ill-digested thoughts, without consideration and without discretion. Hence they amount only to foolishness. (תֵּיטִיב, Hiph fut of נָטַב.—בְּיַ־עַ, Hiph. fut. of נָבַע.)

3. This is a proof passage (locus classicus) in support of the doctrine of the divine personality and omnipresence. Jehovah is every where and at all times present, observing both evil and good men, and is acquainted by actual inspection with all they think as well as with all they do. He sees both direct sins and secret services. A continual sense of the Divine omnipresence is the best and only sure preventive of vice, the strongest and most effectual incentive to virtue and holiness. This proverb stands opposed equally to atheism and pantheism. It recognizes a loving, intelligent Being, distinct from and independent of the world, which he created, and exercising a moral as well as natural government over that world.

4. The word here translated *mild*, and in our Standard Version *wholesome*, primarily signifies *healing*. Hence some translate the phrase, "the healing of the tongue," and "the healing medicine of the tongue." In this place, however, it appears to be employed rather in the sense of *gentle, mild*. See ch. 14: 30, where it occurs in the analogous sense of *tranquil, placid*, as applied to the mind. *A breaking of the spirit*—i. e. it causes bitterness and anguish of mind. "Hard words will not break the bones, but they may break the heart."

---

4. " *The healing of the tongue*," French—" *the healing medicine*," Holden—" *softness of tongue*," Stuart=" *breaketh the spirit*," Boothr.—" *afflicteth the spirit*," Holden " *a wounding of the spirit*," Noyes—" *a crushing of spirit*," Stuart.

5. A fool despiseth the instruction of his father;
But he, who regardeth reproof, will become prudent.

6. (*In*) the house of the righteous (*man*) is much
treasure;
But in the revenue of the wicked there is trouble.

7. The lips of the wise disperse knowledge;
But the heart of the foolish is not right.

8. The sacrifice of the wicked is an abomination to
Jehovah;
But the prayer of the upright is his delight.

9. The way of the wicked is an abomination to
Jehovah;
But him, who followeth after righteousness, he
loveth.

---

7. The Hebrew אֶל־כֵּאן, *al-ken*, is rendered *not so* in our E. V.
preceded by the supplied verb *docth*, i. e. does not scatter knowledge.
The phrase often has that meaning and is so translated here in the
Chald. and Vulg. But it appears to be susceptible of a more forcible meaning, and the parallelism seems to require it. Some supply
the verb "disperse" from the preceding member, and translate,
"The heart of the foolish *disperses* that which is not right," or
"sound," i. e. spreads abroad what is false, futile, or foolish. Others merely supply the substantive verb, and render as above.—"*is*
not right," i. e. is not in a right state, and therefore indisposed to
disseminate knowledge, or incapable of doing so. This construction is supported by the Sept. and Syr. verss. (יְזָרֶ, Piel fut. of
זָרָה.)

8. Man judges by acts—God, by principles. Hence the sacrificial offerings of the wicked, though they be part of God's own
appointed service, will in his register be found in the catalogue of
sins to be accounted for. "However costly sacrifices may be, yet
if offered by those who lead wicked lives, they are odious in the
sight of God; while the prayer alone of the good man, even though
unattended by any offering, is graciously accepted by him. Upon
those who had been led to set a high value on the outward observances of the Mosaic law, the spiritual character of this proverb
was calculated to produce a good effect." (French.) Comp. ch. 21:
27. 28: 9.

9. The sacrifice, the prayer, the way, or course of life, of the

10. A grievous correction (*shall be*) to him, who
forsaketh the way;
And he, who hateth reproof, shall die.

11. Sheol and destruction are before Jehovah;
How much more, then, the hearts of the children
of men.

12. The scoffer loveth not one, who reproveth him;
Nor will he go to the wise.

13. A merry heart maketh a cheerful countenance;
But by sorrow of heart the spirit is broken.

---

wicked, are all declared to be an abomination, i. e. odious and un-
acceptable to Jehovah, because He who looks at the heart, perceives
no sincerity or real humility in any of them.   If the heart be wrong
and the life, which is the sure index of the heart, be opposed to the
law of God, no external religious observances which the insincere
may perform, however proper in themselves, can be pleasing and
acceptable to Jehovah.

10. The adjective *grievous*, as appears from the parallelism, belongs to the subject, and not to the predicate, in this proverb, as in
our English version.   *The way*—viz. the way of rectitude—the right
path, appointed by God.   Vulg. "the way of life."

11. *Destruction* (*Abaddon*) is here put metonymically for the *place*
of destruction, and is a poetical equivalent of sheol. (Comp. Ps.
88: 12. 55: 23. Job 26: 6.)   The invisible world—the place of the
dead, is penetrated by the all-seeing eye of Jehovah: much more
then is he acquainted with the thoughts of man.

12. *Loveth not*—i. e. dislikes, abhors, hates, by the figure *litotes*.
See Ps. 119: 85.   The scoffer at sacred things dislikes his reprover,
because he dislikes the reproof; nor will he seek the society of the
wise and good, lest he should receive merited reproof for his skep-
ticism and misconduct.

13. *A merry heart*, (i. e. a glad, joyous, cheerful, happy state of
mind,) imparts a corresponding impress to the countenance, while
a sorrowful heart not only discovers itself in the countenance, but
depresses and breaks the spirit.

---

10. "*A sore affliction*," French, Noyes.

14. The heart of (*the man of*) understanding seeketh knowledge;
But the mouth of fools feedeth on folly.   .

15. All the days of the afflicted (*man*) are evil;
But a merry heart is a continual feast.

16. Better is a little, with the fear of Jehovah,
Than great riches, and trouble therewith.

17. Better is a dinner of herbs where love is,
Than a stalled ox, and hatred therewith.

---

14. The man who is possessed of an intelligent and teachable
mind, seeks diligently after knowledge. But folly is the very meat
and drink of fools. They delight in it as in the choicest viands.
(Instead of נָבוֹן, *understanding*, the Sept., Ar., Syr., Chald., and several MSS. read נָכוֹן, *uprightness*—"an upright heart." The reading
of the Keri פִּי, *the mouth*, constr. of פֶּה, in the singular number,
instead of the plur. פְּנֵי, (*faces*) in the text is supported by all the
ancient versions and many MSS. and rightly, for the verb which
follows it is singular.)

15. All the days of the afflicted man are painful, sad, and sorrowful (see ch. 25: 20); but a cheerful heart or disposition is a
source of constant enjoyment. The Vulg., Syr., Chald. and Symm.
read, "All the days of the *poor* are evil." Accordingly French
translates the couplet, "Though all the days of the poor man are
evil, yet he who is of a cheerful heart, hath a continual feast," i. e.
"Great as undoubtedly are the trials to which the poor man is exposed, yet he is not denied the luxury which inward peace, con-
tentment and cheerfulness of heart resulting from these, can bestow."

16. True piety, accompanied with but little of this world's
goods, is vastly more conducive to real and enduring happiness in
this world, than great riches without piety, accompanied by the
fears, perplexities, anxieties and vexations, which not unfrequently
attend on the possession and management of large estates.

17. Better is the most humble and scanty repast, where mutual
love prevails, than a banquet of the choicest delicacies accompanied with hatred and contention. "Better is it to have peace without plenty, than plenty without peace." "This is peculiarly applicable to the marriage state, in which an union, sweetened by mutual

18. A passionate man stirreth up contention;
But (*he, who*) is slow to anger, appeaseth strife.

19. The way of the sluggard is like a hedge of thorns;
But the way of the righteous is made smooth.

20. A wise son maketh a glad father;
But a foolish son despiseth his mother.

21. Folly is joy (*to him, who*) is void of understanding;
But a man of discernment walketh uprightly.

22. Without counsel purposes are disappointed;
But in the multitude of counsellors they are established.

---

affection and endearment, is far preferable to the greatest wealth, or the most splendid station, without the solace of love." (Holden.) Bread, fruits and vegetables, form the usual repasts of the masses of society, not only in Western Asia, but also in Southern Europe. The necessity, indeed, for daily animal food is not felt as it is in more northern latitudes. At the same time, animal food is highly prized in the East, though rarely met with except at the tables of the opulent.

19. The path of the sluggard is constantly beset with real or imaginary difficulties. There is always a lion in the way. On the contrary, the path of the upright man, who is industrious and diligent from principle, is made smooth, plain, free from obstructions and easy to travel. *Smooth* is literally *raised up*, like a highway.

20. "The brightest joys and bitterest tears flow from parents' hearts."

21. The man without understanding takes pleasure in doing foolish and wicked things. But the man of discernment and intelligence conducts himself uprightly, and finds his enjoyment in that course of conduct. (לֶכֶת, Kal inf. fem. of יָלַךְ.)

22. *Without counsel*—i. e., without mature deliberation and consultation, plans fail of being accomplished. Lit. *there is a frustration of purposes*, or plans. *They are established.*—Lit. *it* (*the purpose*) *shall stand.* (הָפֵר, Hiph. Inf. absolute of פּוּר.)

---

22. "*Plans come to nought*," Noyes—"*devices are frustrated*," French.

23. A man hath joy by the answer of his mouth ;
And a word in due season, how good it is.

24. The path of life to the wise (*man, leadeth*) upward ;
That he may depart from sheol beneath.

25. Jehovah will destroy the house of the proud ;
But he will establish the landmark of the widow.

26. The thoughts of the wicked are an abomination
to Jehovah ;
But (*the words*) of the pure are pleasant words.

---

23. *By the answer, &c.*—i. e. by giving good advice. *In due season.*—Lit. *in its season,* i. e. at an appropriate time. See ch. 25: 11.

24. The word *upward,* in the first member of the verse, is opposed to *sheol, downward* or *beneath.* Hence some commentators suppose that a prolonged and happy existence on earth is intended by
the former, and a short life and premature death by the latter.
Thus French : "the wise pursue a path insuring to them a continu-
ance of life and happiness, which, being directly opposed to the
path leading down to the grave, is said 'to lead upward.'" I am
persuaded, however, that it has a deeper and more evangelical significance. The path in which the truly wise man walks, conducts
upward and heavenward, and it terminates in the abode of the blest.
The way in which the ungodly walk, conducts downward and terminates in the regions of the miserable. The one is the path to
life, to spiritual life—spiritual happiness, both here and hereafter:
the other is the way to death—spiritual death, and ends in eternal
death.

25. By *house,* the household, or family occupying the house, is
tropically intended. Jehovah will destroy the household of such as
imagine themselves independent of Providence, and rely entirely on
their own strength, wisdom, or skill. But he will maintain the
right of the widow whose sole reliance is on the paternal care of
the Most High, against the oppression of unjust men. (יַפֵּח, Kal
fut. of נָסַח.)

26. *Pleasant words.*—i. e. suitable, becoming, and hence regarded
with favor by Jehovah. See ch. 16: 24. "How lightly do the mass
of men think of the responsibility of their thoughts, as if they were

---

24. "*So that he departs from the pit beneath,*" Noyes.

27. He, who is greedy of gain, troubleth his own house;
But he, who hateth gifts, shall live.

28. The heart of the righteous (*man*) studieth (*what*) to answer;
But the mouth of the wicked poureth out evil things.

29. Jehovah is far from the wicked;
But he heareth the prayer of the righteous.

30. (*As*) the light of the eyes rejoiceth the heart,
(*So*) a good report maketh the bones fat.

31. The ear, which hearkeneth to the reproof of life,
Shall abide among the wise.

---

their own, and they might indulge them without restraint or evil. But they are the seminal principles of sin. And as the cause virtually includes the effects, so do they contain, like the seed in its little body, all the after fruit. They are also the index of character. Watch their infinite variety—not so much those that are under the control of circumstances, or thrown up by the occasion, as the voluntary flow, following the habitual train of associations." (Bridges.) Plutarch describes the thoughts as "the indigenous fountain of evil."

27. He who is so greedy of gain as to be unscrupulous in regard to the means he employs for its attainment, often in the end brings disgrace and ruin upon himself and family. But he who hates gifts bestowed as bribes for the purpose of perverting right and justice, will prosper and confer honor and happiness on his household. Comp. ch. 11:29.

29. Jehovah is said to be *far from the wicked* when he does not regard their cry, nor afford them any relief or assistance when they call upon him. Comp. Ps. 18:41.

30. By *the light of the eyes* may be meant that which the eye sees, and by *a good report*, that which the ear hears. The sense would then be, as the objects which we behold by means of the eye afford pleasure to the mind, so does a good report among men cause inward gratification, and contribute to the health of the body.

31. By *the reproof of life*, is intended that salutary reproof and admonition of a friend, which, right and judicious in itself, and arising from good motives and intentions, is calculated to promote the happiness of its object.

32. He, who refuseth instruction, despiseth his own soul;

But he, who hearkeneth to reproof, getteth understanding.

33. The fear of Jehovah is the instruction of wisdom;
And before honor is humility.

---

32. See ch. 13. *Despiseth his own soul*—i. e. acts as though he valued it not. Comp. ch. 8: 36.

33. Wisdom's grand lesson is reverence for Jehovah, without which the first elements of true knowledge cannot be acquired. Comp. ch. 1: 7. 9: 10. But there is no true reverential fear of him without humility, arising from a deep sense of dependence and unworthiness. Such humility is the precursor of exaltation. "God exalts none but those who are truly humble," "He resists the proud, but gives grace to the humble." See Matt. 23: 12.

CHAPTER XVI.

1. The preparation of the heart (*belongeth*) to man;
But the answer of the tongue is from Jehovah.

2. All the ways of a man are pure in his own eyes;
But Jehovah weigheth the spirits.

---

1. The *preparation of the heart*—i. e. the purposes, plans, designs, formed in the mind. Man forms plans of action and determines the modes and means of accomplishing them; but the result is wholly with God, and we must look to him for the desired success. All our wisdom and ingenuity in contriving and executing, will be futile, unless his overruling providence favor us. "Man proposes, God disposes." Comp. v. 9. *The answer of the tongue* is the answer to that which the tongue utters—the answer of God to the voice of prayer.

2. The judgment which a man forms of himself is commonly partial, and often quite erroneous. But God always judges accord-

1. "*The deliberation of the heart in man, and the utterance of the tongue,*" Holden, Boothr.

3. Commit thy works to Jehovah ;
And thy purposes shall be established.
4. Jehovah hath made every thing for its end ;
Yea, even the wicked (*man*) for the day of evil.

---

ng to truth. Self-love usually renders a man blind to his own
faults; but Jehovah forms a perfectly accurate and just estimate of
men's hearts and true character. "Man will not believe that he is
what he is, till suitable temptations discover him to himself."

3. *Commit*—lit. *roll, devolve upon.* In all your undertakings seek
the approbation and blessing of Almighty God, and then cheerfully
and confidingly leave the result with him. Obey his will, follow
the teachings of his word, and the monitions of his spirit, and confide in his infinite wisdom; and he will grant success, so far as success may contribute to your best good: or else will give you patience
to bear disappointment in the spirit of the Gospel. (לֹּג Kal Imper.
of נָלַל.)

4. The word לְמַּעֲנֵהוּ, *lammaanehu*, has been generally regarded
by commentators as a compound preposition with the pronominal
affix attached, referring to Jehovah, and accordingly render it *for
himself*, i. e. for his own glory in the exercise and manifestation of
his infinite perfections. But though the sentiment is true, it does
not appear to be that which is intended to be conveyed in this passage. The word is regarded by others with more probability as a
noun, מַעֲנֶה, *maane*, in the apocopate form (מַעַן, *maan*,) with the
prefix preposition and the pronominal affix referring to *every thing*,
and here denoting *purpose, design, object, end, final cause.* The noun
etymologically signifies with the affix *its answer.* (See ch. 15: 23.
16: 1.) Here it imports tropically *that which corresponds to it,* or *is
filled to it.* Thus every thing is made in accordance with *its correspondence*, i. e. with the *end, design, purpose,* which it was intended to
accomplish. "God has ordained every thing to that which answers
or is suited to it, and the wicked he has ordained for the day of evil,
i. e. of punishment. There is not only a wise arrangement and
correspondence in good things, but also in evil things; for the evil
of punishment follows the evil of guilt; the evil day is appointed
for the evil doer." (Grotius.) When it is said in the text that God

---

4. "*For himself*," E. V., Holden—"*for his own purpose*," French—"*to serve his
design*," Boothr.—"*for its purpose*," Stuart.

15

5. Every one, (*who*) is proud in heart, is an abomination to Jehovah ;

(*Though*) hand (*be joined*) to hand, he shall not go
unpunished.

6. By mercy and truth iniquity is covered ;
And through the fear of Jehovah (*men*) depart from
evil.

7. When the ways of a man please Jehovah,
He maketh even his enemies to be at peace with
him.

8. Better is a little with righteousness,
Than great revenues without right.

---

made (or ordained) even the *wicked* for the *evil day*, the meaning is
not that God created men wicked, or made the wicked for the purpose of punishing them and rendering them miserable. This would
be an unjust reflection on the character of Jehovah, and inconsistent
with the plainest declarations of his word. But the idea intended
to be conveyed is, that he has so ordered events in his providence—
so established the connexion between cause and effect, antecedent
and consequent, that piety and uprightness will surely receive their
appropriate reward, while punishment will certainly follow the commission of sin, unless averted by timely repentance, implicit reliance on the Redeemer, and speedy reformation.

5. See ch. 11: 21.

6. The verb כִּפֶּר, *kaphar*, literally sig. *to cover, to cover up, to hide
from view*. Figuratively it denotes, 1. *to atone*, 2. *to pardon, to forgive*. It is here employed in the last sense. By *mercy and truth*
may be understood objectively the attributes of God known by those
names, and exercised towards men. The sense of the first clause
would then be, that by the mercy and truthfulness of God, displayed
in the performance of his promises, the transgressions of the peni-
tent sinner are forgiven. Comp. Ps. 32: 1. כָּסָה, *kasa.* see ch. 14:
22. Ps. 78: 38. 79: 9. Or the phrase may be taken subjectively of
man, as denoting mercy and truth exercised by good men towards
their fellow men. See ch 3: 2. 20: 28. The sense would then be,
that by the manifestation of kindness, compassion and truthfulness,
the divine favor may be propitiated and man's transgressions forgiven.

9. The heart of man deviseth his way;
But Jehovah directeth his steps.

10. A divine sentence is on the lips of the king;
His mouth transgresseth not in judgment.

11. A just balance and scales are (*the appointment*)
of Jehovah;
All the weights of the bag are his work.

---

9. Comp. ch. 20: 24. Ps. 37: 23. Jere. 10: 23.

10. The Hebrew word כֶּסֶם, *kesem*, sig. 1. *a lot*, 2. *divination*, 3.
an oracle, or *divine sentence*. The last appears to be its meaning in
this place. A divine sentence or sacred oracle of course implies a
righteous judicial decision. The scope of the maxim appears to be
to inspire respect for the judicial decisions of wise and upright
rulers and magistrates, who are supposed to be above the influence
of the ordinary motives for pronouncing a wrong, partial and unjust
judgment. The proverb in this verse and those in v. 12 and 13,
only indicate duty, right, *official obligation*, and not what is always
true in point of fact. So St. Paul says of the civil magistrate, that
"he is the minister of God to thee for good."

11. *Balance*. The Heb. word occurs here and in Isa. 40: 12,
where it is translated *scales* in E. V. Since in both instances it is
found in connexion with balances or scales, it would evidently seem
to belong to the apparatus for weighing. The translators of our
Standard Version supposed *weights* to be intended: but it more probably denotes the *rod* or *yard* from which the scales were suspended.
The derivation of the word פֶּלֶס, *Peles*, from פָּלַס, *Palas*, to *make
level*, or *even*, favors this view. The following noun is dual, and
evidently denotes the scales at the extremeties of the balance-rod.
Weights and measures were prescribed to the Hebrews by Jehovah
himself. See Lev. 19: 36. The word rendered *weights* properly signifies *stones*. The Hebrews used stones for their weights, and kept
them in bags. Just weights and scales are said to be the work or
appointment of Jehovah, because made by his direction; so that no
man could alter them without violating the divine law and incurring
the divine displeasure. See ch. 11: 1. 20: 10 Fraud in weights
and measures is a punishable offence among all civilized nations;

---

10. " *Mature counsel*," Boothr.—"*The sentence of a diviner*," French—"*Divination*," Vulg , Holden—"*an oracle*," Sept., Stuart.
11. " *The steel-yard and the balances*," Stuart.

12. The doing of wickedness is an abomination to kings ;
And the throne is established by righteousness.

13. Righteous lips are the delight of kings ;
And they love him, who speaketh right things.

14. The wrath of a king is (*like*) messengers of death ;
But a wise man will pacify it.

15. In the light of the king's countenance is life ;
And his favor is like a cloud (*bringing*) the latter rain.

16. How much better it is to get wisdom than fine gold !
And to get understanding is to be chosen rather than silver !

---

and in the East great severity is frequently exercised towards those who are detected in the perpetration of it. The comment of good old Fuller on this passage is apt and forcible. "The good merchant wrongs not the buyer in number, weight or measure. These are the landmarks of all trading, which must not be removed; for such cozenage were worse than open felony—first, because they rob a man of his purse, and never bid him stand; secondly, because highway thieves defy, but these pretend justice; thirdly, as much as lies in their power, they endeavor to make God accessory to their cozenage, deceiving by pretending his weights. For God is the principal clerk of the market: all the weights of the bag are his work."

12. *To kings*—i. e. to virtuous and upright kings, who are worthy of the name and dignity. (יִכֹּן, Niph. of כּוּן.)

14. The form of expression in the first clause of this verse doubtless originated in the customs of oriental despotism. Under such a government the king's displeasure is instantly followed by vengeance, without regard to forms of law. Comp. 1 Kg. 2: 5. Matt. 14: 10.

15. In Palestine, there are two rainy seasons in the course of the year. These are often called in Scripture the *former* and the *latter* rain. The first, which is the *autumnal* rain, begins in October, or early in November, and is so called because the Hebrews began their civil year about the time of the autumnal equinox. The second or spring rain, begins in April, just before the harvest, and is

17. The highway of the upright is to depart from evil ;
He, who keepeth his way, preserveth his soul.

18. Pride (*goeth*) before destruction ;
And a haughty spirit before a fall.

19. Better is it to be of an humble spirit with the lowly,
Than to divide the spoil with the proud.

20. He, who attendeth to the word, shall find good ;
And he, who trusteth in Jehovah,—happy is he !

21. The wise in heart shall be called prudent ;
And sweetness of lips increaseth learning.

---

indispensable to an abundant crop.   Hence the force and beauty of the comparison in the text.

17. A highway is a smooth and beaten path—a plain, safe and pleasant road to travel—contrasted with a by-way, which is but little travelled, rough, uneven, crooked, and unsafe. The upright in departing from evil choose such a highway—the way of holiness; and by keeping in that way, they are preserved from danger. The Septuagint adds: "He who receives instruction shall be in prosperity; and he who regards reproof shall be made wise. He who keeps his ways, preserves his own soul; and he who loves his life, will spare his mouth."

18. Ruin presses hard on the steps of pride and arrogance of spirit. Comp. ch. 11: 2. 18: 12.

20. The Hebrew word דָּבָר, *dabar*, sig. both *word* and *thing*. If the former be its meaning here, then the sentiment of the first member of the verse is, that he who attends or gives heed to the precepts of the word of God—the divine oracle—shall obtain success in his undertakings and pursuits. If the latter, then the sense is, that he, who conducts his affairs prudently and wisely, will be prospered. The Sept. version adopts the latter interpretation; but the parallelism favors the former

21. *Sweetness of lips* denotes *gentle* and *persuasive* language; the lips being put metonymically for what the lips express. Persuasive and winning language secures attention, and thus affords peculiar advantage for communicating knowledge.

15*

22. Understanding is a fountain of life to him who hath it;
But the instruction of fools is folly.

23. The heart of the wise (*man*) teacheth his mouth,
And addeth learning to his lips.

24. Pleasant words are (*like*) a honey-comb:
Sweet to the soul, and healing to the bones.

25. There is a way which seemeth right to a man;
But the end thereof is the way of death.

. 26. He, who laboreth, laboreth for himself;
For his mouth urgeth him on.

27. An ungodly man diggeth up mischief;
And on his lips there is a burning fire.

---

22. Whatever instruction fools undertake to give, will prove only foolishness. If they attempt to instruct others, they only make them like themselves. Some commentators invert the terms of the proposition in the last line. "It is folly to instruct fools," i. e. it is lost labor to endeavor to communicate knowledge to those who have no capacity or no disposition to receive it. Others render, "The chastisement of fools is their folly," i. e. folly brings its appropriate punishment with it.

23. The well-regulated mind of the wise man enables and disposes him to clothe his thoughts in appropriate, conciliatory, persuasive and discreet language, and to communicate knowledge pertinently, judiciously and successfully.

24. Agreeable and instructive discourse is both delightful and salutary. *Honey-comb* is put for *honey* by synecdoche of the container for the thing contained. The word *bones* is also put by the same figure for *body*.

25. See ch. 14: 12. We must not trust ourselves in a way or course of action which merely *seems* to be right; for appearances are often deceptive: but take the requisite pains to assure ourselves that it *is* right. *The way of death* is the way which leads to death.

27. An ungodly person (lit. *a man of Belial*) employs himself in devising and laboring diligently to find out some mischief. He digs

---

22. "*Wisdom to its possessor is a fountain of life*," Boothr.—"*Understanding is a spring of living water to its possessor*," French—"*is a well-spring of life*," Noyes, Stuart.   27. "*A flaming torch*," Boothr.

28. A perverse man spreadeth contention;
And a whisperer separateth friends.

29. A man of violence enticeth his neighbor:
And leadeth him into a way that is not good.

30. He shutteth his eyes to devise perverse things;
He biteth his lips, he bringeth evil to pass.

31. The hoary head is a crown of glory,
(*If*) it be found in the way of righteousness.

32. (*He, who*) is slow to anger is better than the mighty;
And he, who ruleth his spirit, than he, who taketh a city.

---

for it, as if delving in a mine for the precious metals. His tongue is a burning firebrand, full of bitterness and slander, with which to inflame the passions of others and spread-strife and contention through the community. Sept. "The perverse man carries perdition on his mouth. The foolish man diggeth up evils to himself; he treasures up fire on his lips." See James 3: 6.

29. *Not good*, i. e. into an evil way, by the figure *litotes.*

30. This verse describes the course adopted by the violent man when plotting mischief. He shuts his eyes, that his thoughts may be concentrated on the base scheme which he has devised; without being diverted by external objects. He bites his lips, as people in deep thought frequently do.

31. The hoary head is the aged man's honor (ch. 20: 29) and his claim for respect and deference. The Roman satirist intimates that the neglect of "rising up before the hoary head," was punishable with death. The reverence paid by the Lacedæmonians to old age is well known. (הִמָּצֵא, Niph. fut. of מָצָא.)

32. This proverb is identical with the well known line of Ovid: "Fortior est qui se quam qui fortissima mænia vincat." "Better is he who conquers himself than he who conquers the strongest walls." "In all ages," says Cicero, "fewer men are found, who conquer their own lusts, than that conquer an army of enemies." Seneca, writing to a friend, says, "If you wish to subject all things to yourself, subject yourself to reason. You will rule many, if reason rule you."

33. The lot is cast into the lap;
But the whole disposal thereof is from Jehovah.

33. *The lap*—viz. of the umpire,—the person appointed to decide. The lot is properly a casual event purposely applied to the determination of something doubtful. Among the Hebrews, the most important matters were frequently determined by lot. Officers were thus chosen—work determined—dwellings fixed—discoveries made, and contentions terminated. (See 1 Chron. 14: 5. Lu. 1: 9. Neh. 11: 1. 1 Sam. 14: 41. Prov. 18: 18.) This aphorism teaches that the decision of the lot is, like every thing else, under the control of Jehovah, although to human view the result may appear altogether casual and fortuitous. The following Greek proverb expresses the same thought under a similar trope. "The dice of Jupiter are always loaded; they fall as he wills."

CHAPTER XVII.

1. Better is a dry morsel and quietness therewith,
Than a house full of banquets with strife.

2. A wise servant will rule over a son, who causeth shame;
And share the inheritance with brothers.

1. The word rendered *banquets* properly signifies a *slaughtering*, 1. of men, 2. of beasts, whether for food or for sacrifice. Hence it may denote a *sacrifice, victim*, or by metonymy a *repast* or *banquet*, which last is plainly the meaning here. Thus the phrase "a house full of banquets," would sig. a house well supplied with provisions. The Hebrew is literally *banquets* of *strife*,—quarrelsome feasts—the limiting noun indicating, that the beasts were eaten with strife and contention, instead of harmony and love. Some expositors suppose that there is particular allusion to sacrificial feasts, or feasts which were customarily made from the remains of peace offerings. See ch. 7: 14.

1. "*Of feastings,*" Boothr —"*slaughtered beasts,*" Stuart—"*sacrificial banquets,*" Holden—"*sacrifices,*" S. V.—"*many good things and unjust sacrifices,*" Sept.

3. The crucible is for silver, and the furnace for gold;
But Jehovah is the searcher of hearts.

4. A wicked doer listeneth to false lips:
(*And*) a liar giveth ear to a wicked tongue.

5. He, who derideth the poor, reproacheth his
Maker;
And he, who rejoiceth at calamity, shall not go un-
punished.

6. Children's children are the crown of the aged;
And the glory of children are their fathers.

---

3. The art of man has invented means to test the purity of gold
and silver; but only Jehovah can explore the human heart. This
he claims as his prerogative. Nothing deceives him: nothing
escapes his all penetrating eye.

4. "The wicked listen with pleasure to those who utter scandal
and falsehood: and those addicted to the odious vice of lying lend
a willing ear to a malevolent tongue: both thereby gratify their malignity." "Were there no *publishers* of slander and calumny, there
would be no *receivers;* and were there none to *receive* them, there
would be none to *originate* them; and were there no *inventors, receivers* nor *propagators* of calumnies, how vastly would the peace of
society be promoted." In the Heb. text the second member expresses
the same thought substantially as the first. But the Septuagint and
other ancient versions read antithetically, "But a righteous man
listeneth not to false lips." (מֵרַע, Hiph. part. of רָעַע. מַאֲזִין=מֵזִין,
Hiph. part. of אָזַן)

5. To hold the poor in derision and contempt on account of their
poverty, or to rejoice at the calamities which befall others, is virtually to treat with contempt the providence and precepts of God.
"Why should I for a little difference in this one particular of
worldly wealth, despise my poor brother? When so many and great
things unite us, shall wealth only divide us? One sun shines on
both; one blood bought us both; one heaven will receive us both;
only he has not so much of earth as I, and possibly much more of
Christ. And why should I disdain him on earth, whom happily
the Lord will advance above me in heaven?" (Bp. Reynolds.)

6. The aged and their numerous descendants reflect mutual

---

5. "*Shall not be held guiltless.*" French—"*shall not be guiltless,*" Stuart.

7. Excellent speech becometh not a fool;
Much less do lying lips (*become*) a prince.

8. A gift is a precious stone in the eyes of him, who
taketh it;
Wherever it turneth, it prospereth.

9. He, who covereth an offence, seeketh love;
But he, who repeateth a matter, separateth friends.

---

honor and dignity upon each other. Comp. Ps. 127 and 128. Eccles. 3: 11. *Glory*—i. e. the ornament and pride.

7. *Excellent speech*—wise and learned discourse, would be incongruous and out of place in a fool. Much more inappropriate is
falsehood in a prince or ruler. "Heathen morality," says Bridges,
"from the lips of one of her wisest teachers (Plato) allowed the
lying lips of princes, because they governed for the public good.
'All others,' he adds, 'must abstain.' 'Qui nescit dissimulare,
nescit regnase.' 'He who knows not how to dissemble, knows not
how to reign,' has been not unfrequently a royal maxim. How
much more suitable and becoming was the remark of Louis IX. of
France—'If truth be banished from all the rest of the world, it
ought to be found in the breasts of princes.'"

8. The gift or present here alluded to is a *bribe* offered for the
purpose of obtaining influence or accomplishing some object. This
is regarded by the receiver as a precious stone—an object of great
value—and consequently held in high estimation. "A diamond
reflects a variety of lights, when viewed on this side or that. Turn
it how you please, it will never cease to reflect lustre; and this the
text calls *prospering* or *succeeding*. So of a bribe if accepted: it will
influence in many ways, even without a consciousness of its poison
on the part of the receiver. Turn he which way he will, the influence of it will follow him." (Stuart.)

9. To *cover an offence* is to forgive an offender: while the communication of the injurious act to others implies an unforgiving
spirit. The sentiment expressed in this verse is very beautiful.
"It shows a delight in the atmosphere of *love*—man's highest elevation in communion with God. It implies not the mere exercise of
love, where it is presented, but the searching—making opportunity
for it. A forbearing spirit is a fine manifestation of it. Our motives are often misconstrued. We meet in a world of selfishness
cold reserve, instead of glowing confidence. Prejudice builds a wall

10. A rebuke will sink deeper into a wise man,
Than a hundred stripes into a fool.

11. A rebellious (*man*) seeketh only evil;
Therefore a cruel messenger shall be sent against him.

12. Let a bear robbed of her whelps meet a man,
Rather than a fool in his folly.

13. He, who rewardeth evil for good,
Evil shall not depart from his house.

14. The beginning of strife is (*as*) when one letteth
out water;
Therefore cease from contention before it breaketh
out.

---

against Christian intercourse. Wounded pride would return unkindness with contempt. Resentment stirs up recrimination. Disappointment kindles morbid suspicion. Here is the noble field for
Christian victory; instead of resenting, to cover the transgression
with a mantle of love.—with that act of amnesty, by which we are
saved,—the most aggravated transgression—the most unprovoked
injuries—covered in eternal forgetfulness." (Bridges.)

10. A seasonable and appropriate rebuke, even when not accompanied by the slightest chastisement, will have more effect on a wise
man, than the severest corporeal punishment on a fool. (תֵּחַת, Kal
fut. of נָחַת.)

12. The female bear is remarkable for her intense attachment to
her young; and nothing can exceed her frantic rage, when they are
injured or killed. See Hos. 13: 8. Dreadful as it is to meet a bear
in such circumstances, it is more dangerous to meet a furious and
revengeful man while under the influence of his impetuous passions.
It is possible by the use of stratagem to escape the vengeance of the
incensed beast; but no consideration of interest or duty: no partial
gratification—can arrest the furious career, or divert the attention of
the man, who is rendered insane by passion. "Reason, degraded
and enslaved, lends all her remaining wisdom and energy to passion, and renders the fool more cruel and mischievous than the bear,
in proportion as he is superior in instinct."

14. *Breaketh out*—lit. *grows warm*, i. e. before anger is excited.
" As in breaking down the banks of a river the inundation, though

---

14. " *The commencement of strife is the letting out of water,*" Stuart.

15. He, who acquitteth the wicked (*man*), and he, who condemneth the just (*man*).

Even they both are an abomination to Jehovah.

16. Why is there a price in the hand of a fool to get wisdom,

When (*he hath*) no understanding.

17. A friend loveth at all times;

And a brother is born for adversity.

small at first, continues to increase till the whole country is over-flowed; so strife is trifling at its commencement: but if indulged, increases to insatiable animosity: therefore dismiss contention be-fore it becomes fierce and unappeasable." (Holden.) "One hot word," says Henry, "one peevish reflection, one angry demand, one spiteful contradiction, begets another, and that a third, and so on, till it proves like the cutting of a dam; when the water has got a little passage, it does itself widen the breach, bears down all before it, and there is then no stopping it, no reducing it."

16. The Hebrew word לֵב, *leb*, properly sig. *the heart;* but some-times is applied to the mind in the sense of *understanding, intelli-gence, wisdom.* Comp. ch. 7: 7. 9: 4. Job 9: 4. The sentiment here is, that wisdom cannot be obtained by money, where mental capacity is wanting. Riches cannot purchase brains. The verse may be rendered, 'Wherefore is there a price in the hand of a fool? To ac-quire wisdom? But he hath no heart (no capacity) for it."

17. True friendship is uniformly the same under all external circumstances. It is as sincere and warm in adversity as in pros-perity. The meaning of the second member is doubtful. Its im-port appears to be, that the true friend shows himself in a season of adversity to be even more than a friend. He acts the part of a brother. Thus Bp. Patrick: "A true friend becomes a brother in adversity. He was a friend before; this makes him a brother." Such a friend to the truly pious man is Christ. "Though solitary and unsupported and oppressed by sorrows unknown and undi-vided, I am not without joyful expectation. There is one friend who loveth at all times; a brother born for adversity—the help of the helpless, the hope of the hopeless, the strength of the weak, the riches of the poor, the peace of the disquieted, the companion of the

15. "*He who justifieth,*" E. V., Holden, Noyes, Stuart.
16. "*It is sense that is wanting,*" Noyes.

18. A man void of understanding, striketh hands, (*And*) becometh surety in the presence of his friend.

19. He, who loveth contention, loveth transgression; And he, who maketh high his gate, seeketh destruction.

20. The perverse in heart findeth no good; And he, who hath a double tongue, falleth into mischief.

---

desolate, the friend of the fatherless.   To him alone will I call, and he will raise me above my fears."   (Mrs. Hawkins.)   (יַיְלֶד, Niph. fut. of יָלַד.)

18. Among the Hebrews one person became surety for another by striking hands with the creditor in the presence of a mutual friend, who being a witness to the transaction, was competent to testify to it in a court of justice, if required.   This gave legality to the act and made it binding.   Witnesses to business transactions of importance were particularly necessary in ancient times, because contracts were rarely reduced to writing.   Parol testimony was consequently much more frequently appealed to, and more relied upon, than written.   Holden, however, supposes that *by his friend* is meant the person *to* whom or *for* whom one becomes surety.   While some others regard it as denoting the person for whose benefit the surety is given.

19. He who loves and seeks to promote contention and quarrels, is a lover of sin.   Sept. "He that loves sin, rejoices in fightings." So French and Noyes, "He who loveth offence, loveth quarrels." By *his gate* is intended the gate leading to his house or into his court-yard.   The proverb in its literal and proper sense, has reference to the custom which still prevails in the East, of making the archways in which the gates communicating with private dwellings were hung, very low, in order to prevent the marauding Bedouins from entering them on horseback for the purpose of harassing, and plundering the inhabitants.   The proverb, however, may and doubtless was, intended to be used allegorically, and then the phrase to make high his gate would denote pride and ostentation, and would be equivalent to the expression, "He carries his head too high."

20. The *perverse in heart*—see ch. 11: 20. .*Double tongue*—literally, one who *turns about with his tongue*, i. e. is versatile.

---

20. "*False tongue*," Noyes.

21. He, who begetteth a fool, it is a grief to him :
Yea, the father of a fool hath no joy.

22. A merry heart is a good medicine ;
But a broken spirit drieth up the bones.

23. A wicked (*man*) taketh a gift out of (*his*) bosom
To pervert the ways of justice.

24. Wisdom is present with him, who hath understanding ;
But the eyes of a fool are in the ends of the earth.

25. A foolish son is a grief to his father :
And bitterness to her who bore him.

26. Moreover to fine the righteous is not good ;
Nor to smite the noble for (*their*) rectitude.

27. He, who hath knowledge, spareth his words ;
And a man of understanding is of a quiet spirit.

---

22. Is *a good medicine*—i. e. is like a good medicine. Cheerfulness of mind doubtless exerts a beneficial influence, both in restoring the body to health, and in keeping off disease. A broken and
crushed spirit or sorrowful heart, on the contrary, tends to impair
the health; and causes the bodily frame to waste away. Sept. "A
glad heart promotes health." Gesenius, "A joyful heart maketh a
happy cure." The verse is parallel to ch. 12: 25. 14: 30. 15: 13.
also ch. 3: 8. 4: 22.

23. The Hebrews were accustomed to carry in their bosom their
purse, money, and other valuables. The expression appears to indicate the manner in which a bribe was sometimes given and received with a view to defeat the ends of justice. It was conveyed
in a furtive, stealthy and clandestine manner, from the bosom of the
briber to that of the judge. See ch. 21: 14.

24. While wisdom is *before the face* of the intelligent man—near at
hand, the fool looks far away for it, and is never able to find it.

26. *To fine*—such was and still is the practice in the regions of
oriental despotism. The Heb. verb sig. *to amerce, to impose a fine,*
(see Deut. 22: 19) and then generally *to punish.* Here the primary
and specific meaning appears to be the more appropriate. So Boothr.
French, Noyes, Gesenius.

27. The natural order of the words in the original favors the

---

26. " *To punish,*" S. V., Holden, Stuart, Sept.
27. " *Of a forbearing spirit,*" Holden—" *of a cool spirit,*" Boothr., Noyes, Stuart.

28. Even a fool, when he is silent, is accounted
wise;
And he, who shutteth his lips, is (*accounted*) intelligent.

---

rendering given to this verse by some translators. "He who spareth his words is imbued with knowledge; and he who is of a quiet
spirit is a man of understanding." This may possibly be the
meaning; but the received translation gives a sense altogether preferable. The adj. וְקַר, *vequad*, which is the textual and preferable
reading, signifies tropically, *cool, quiet, calm*. The Keri reads,
יְקַר, *yequad, precious, excellent*, which is followed in E. V.

CHAPTER XVIII.

1. He, who separateth himself (*from others*), seeketh his (*own*) desire;
He is offended at all sound wisdom.

---

1. This difficult verse has been interpreted by some commentators in a *good* sense, and by others in a *bad* sense. 1. in a good
sense. Holden paraphrases thus: "He who separates himself from
sinners, seeks wisdom, the object of his desire; he deals not in folly,
but in all sound wisdom." Durell: "The contemplative man seeketh that which is desirable," &c. Hodgson: "A retired man pursueth the researches he delighteth in," &c. T. Scott: "According
to desire, he that is separate seeketh; and he engageth in all concerns." In explanation of the verse Dr. Scott remarks: "Whatever
a man earnestly desires he seeks after, and secludes himself from
other avocations, that he may not be interrupted in the diligent pursuit of it. Thus it is in all kinds of business and learning: none
excel, but those who desire to excel, and who separate themselves,
that they may have leisure to pursue their favorite object.—A man
has a strong desire to be wise, and this induces him to avoid vain
company, diversions, trifling studies, and needless engagements,
that he may have leisure and retirement to examine things to the
bottom." Aben Ezra transposes the terms in the first member, and
paraphrases thus: "He who seeks wisdom as an object of his ear-

2. A fool hath no delight in understanding,
But (*rather*) in revealing his (*own*) heart.

3. When a wicked (*man*) cometh, (*then*) cometh also
contempt;
And with dishonor (*cometh*) reproach.

4. The words of a man's mouth are deep waters;
The fountain of wisdom is a gushing stream.

---

nest desire, separates himself or departs from his native place and
country, leaves his relations, and travels through various and dis-
tant-regions in pursuit of it." This view of the meaning, however,
though favored by our English version, is at variance with the ancient versions, and irreconcilable with the parallel clause. Sept. "A
man who means to separate from friends seeks excuses; but at all
times he is liable to reproach." 2. The verb rendered *is offended*
and in E. V. "intermeddled with," is never used in Kal conj., and
is found in Hithp. conj. only in this book, where it uniformly signifies *to be angry, to be offended, to grow warm*, &c. in strife. See Prov.
17: 14. 20: 3. Accordingly the majority of interpreters understand
the first clause in a *bad* sense. The separation spoken of would
seem to import a withdrawal in a great measure from the society of
one's fellow-men, and from all communion of intercourse and interest with them. It may indicate the *misanthrope*, who having been
disappointed in his expectations in life, and decceived in his too
favorable estimate of men, withdraws in disgust from the society of
others and lives only for and to himself. Or it may describe *the
proud and haughty rich man*, who, puffed up with the idea of his own
importance and superiority, withdraws from intercourse and familiarity with those around him, who are less favored in the possession
of worldly wealth than himself, and treats them with neglect and
affected contempt. Such an one seeks only the gratification of his
own desires, and the accomplishment of his own selfish ends. Boothroyd thinks the *Opinionist* is intended—one who having formed an
overweening estimate of his own talents and attainments, thinks no
one right but himself, and scornfully rejects the opinions and advice
of others. Bennett translates: "To pursue voluptuousness man
seeketh privacy; but in pursuit of wisdom he maketh a display."

4. The words of a wise and discreet man are here represented

---

2. " *His own mind*," French, Noyes—"*the thoughts of his heart*," Boothr.
3. " *And with ignominy*," E. V., Holden—"*with baseness*," Noyes—"*with public
disgrace*," Boothr.

5. It is not good to accept the person of the wicked,
(*So as*) to overthrow the righteous in judgment.

6. A fool's lips enter into contention,
And his mouth calleth for blows.

7. A fool's mouth is his destruction;
And his lips are the snare of his soul.

8. The words of a tale-bearer are like dainties,
For they go down into the chambers of the body.

9. Moreover he, who is slothful in his work,
Is brother to the spendthrift.

---

under the similitude of deep waters as opposed to a shallow stream. They are deep because they express profound thoughts and are replete with knowledge. They are called in the parallel clause "the fountain of wisdom," because they proceed from a mind richly stored with knowledge; just as in ch. 10: 11, the mouth of the righteous is called "a fountain of life."

5. The original rendered *to accept the person*, literally signifies *to lift up the face*, i. e. to show partiality towards any one—to take part with any one—to be biassed in legal decisions by the worldly rank or wealth of the parties at issue, or swayed by other improper influences. (Comp. Ps. 82: 2.) The proverb appears to be specially directed against the venality of judges, which is very common under the despotic governments of the East. It is founded on the Mosaic law (Lev. 19: 15. Deut. 1: 17. 16: 19), which forbids any respect of persons in judicial proceedings. (Comp. ch. 24: 23.)

6. *Calleth for blows*—merits chastisements.

8. This proverb appears to be intended as a caution against slander and detraction, which are so eagerly listened to, swallowed with so much avidity and delight, and remembered and repeated with so much apparent satisfaction by those to whom they are communicated. The *body*—lit. *belly*, put by synecdoche for the body. *Dainties*—dainty morsels. So Shultens, Gesenius, French, Noyes, from the Arabic. (מִתְלַהֲמִים, Hithp part. of לָהַם, not used in Kal.)

9. *Spendthrift*—lit. *waster of wasting*, i. e. a waster, spendthrift, prodigal. Idleness is as bad as wastefulness: they both lead to poverty and ruin.

---

8. "*Like sportive ones*," Stuart—"*like wounds*," E. V., Holden.

10. The name of Jehovah is a strong tower ;
The righteous (*man*) runneth into it, and is safe.

11. The rich man's wealth is (*his*) strong city ;
And like a high wall, in his own conceit.

12. Before destruction the heart of a man is haughty;
And before honor is humility.

13. He, who returneth an answer, before he hath
heard (*a cause*),
It is folly and shame to him.

14. The spirit of a man will sustain his infirmity ;
But who shall sustain the wounded spirit ?

---

10. The *name* of Jehovah is a Hebrew periphrasis for *Jehovah himself*. (Comp. Ps. 20: 1.)   The Heb. verb translated *is safe*, properly sig. *is elevated*, or *exalted*, and so it is here rendered by Sept. Vulg. Chald. Aqui. Sym. and Theod., i. e. elevated to a place of safety.   The elevation of a fort or tower above the surrounding country was a circumstance which particularly in ancient times greatly conduced to safety.   Protection therefore was the consequence of repairing to it.

11. This proverb expresses the influence which riches often exert over the possessor, in inspiring self-confidence and self-esteem. They are to him like a fortified city and high walls, under the protection of which he feels secure.   "The rich, instead of looking to Jehovah for protection, trust in their riches,—which are a high wall in their own imagination, but not so in reality." (Stuart.)   A similar proverb occurs in ch. 10: 15, but in a different relation and in a different sense.

12. Comp. ch. 16: 18.   Pride is the forerunner of calamity, mortification and destruction; while humility is the precursor of honorable distinction.

13. "Answer not before thou hast heard the cause; neither interrupt men in the midst of their talk."   Ecclus. 11: 8.

14. *Infirmity* relates to the body; a *wounded spirit* to the mind. A lofty and resolute spirit, especially if it be coupled with a firm and steadfast reliance on divine providence, will sustain a man under all outward afflictions and bodily sufferings; will carry him

---

10. "*Tower of strength*," Hebr., French, Stuart.
11. "*His own imagination*," French.

15. The heart of the prudent (*man*) getteth knowledge ;
And the ear of the wise seeketh knowledge.

16. A man's gift maketh room for him,
And bringeth him into the presence of the great.

17. (*He, who*) first (*pleadeth*) his cause, (*seemeth*) just ;
But his opponent cometh, and searcheth him through.

- -

undaunted and resolute through fire and blood, through perils by land and perils by sea, through disappointments, misfortunes and calamities, through conflicts and dangers the most appalling, and it may even nerve him to meet death itself in its most dreaded forms with composure. But the wretchedness and misery attendant on the broken and crushed spirit—the afflicted soul itself—who can sustain? The latter clause of the verse may be understood not merely of a wounded conscience—a mind smitten with a sense of guilt and with remorse; but of a wounded spirit in general— wounded, dejected and depressed by sorrow, unkindness, ingratitude, injustice, or other outward affliction, the spirit of a man will alone enable him to sustain; but when the spirit itself is stricken and falters: if a wound is inflicted on the heart, what is to be done? The form of the question implies that there can be no help from within. Physically a man cannot support himself; nor can the spirit of man receive adequate support through its own powers. It is only the Father of our spirits who can heal the wounds of the spirit. The soul then must look up for adequate support to the great physician of souls, "who healeth the stricken in heart, and bindeth up their wounds." Ps. 147: 3. (יְכַלְכֵּל, Pilpel fut. of כּוּל. יְשֻׁאֶנָּה, Niph. fut. of שֵׂא, with pronominal affix.)

17. The man who first pleads his own cause or that of his client, may make out an apparently equitable case, and seem clearly to have justice and right on his side. But his opponent afterwards shows the other side of the case in dispute, and puts to the test of a rigid cross-examination the truth of his allegations *Audi alteram partem* is an equitable and safe rule in every question; and the apothegm in the text is peculiarly important to judges and jurors, as a caution against making up their minds in a case on trial, till they have heard the evidence and pleadings on both sides. In common life great injustice is often done to individuals by the credit

18. The lot causeth contention to cease,
And parteth asunder the mighty.

19. A brother offended is (*harder to be won*) than a
strong city ;
And the contentions (*of such*) are like the bars of a
castle.

20. With the fruit of a man's mouth shall his belly
be satisfied ;
He shall be filled with the produce of his lips.

21. Death and life are in the power of the tongue;
And those, who love it, shall eat the fruit thereof.

---

which is given to one-sided statements and prejudiced representa-
tions. *His opponent*—Heb. his neighbor, fellow. ὁ πλησίον.
Here an opponent in a trial is evidently intended. So Boothroyd,
Noyes.

18. The Hebrews in the time of Solomon, it would seem, when
disagreements and litigations arose among them, were accustomed
to appeal to the lot, which was regarded as giving the decision of
Jehovah, and in nearly every case, where reason cannot decide between the conflicting claims of different parties, recourse is still had
in the East to the lot. *The mighty*—i. e. the powerful and fierce con-
testants or litigants. The lot parts these asunder by putting an
end to the dispute.

19. Quarrels between near relatives are proverbially more difficult to settle than those, which arise among comparative strangers.
It is harder to adjust their differences than to take a fortified city;
and their stubborn minds resist all endeavors to bend them to a cor-
dial reconciliation, like the iron bars of a castle.

"Acerrima ferme proximorum odia sunt."—*Tacitus.*
"Hatred between the nearest relations is the deepest."

Castle.—The Heb. אַרְמוֹן, *armon*, commonly signifies *palace;* but
here it is evidently used in the sense of *castle,* or *citadel.*

20. *The fruit of a man's mouth,* and *the produce of his lips,* are
equivalent metaphorical expressions employed to denote the words
which he utters. "The body is nourished by food; the mind by
words; both by the ministry of the mouth." (Comp. ch. 13: 2. 14:
14. Matt. 12: 37.)

21. A man may utter that, which will destroy human life, or
what will preserve it. This is sometimes eminently the case when

22. He who findeth a (*good*) wife, findeth a good (*thing*);
And obtaineth favor from Jehovah.

23. The poor (*man*) useth entreaty;
But the rich (*man*) answereth roughly.

24. A man of (*many*) associates will be ruined;
Yet, there is a friend, who sticketh closer than a brother.

bearing testimony in a court of justice, where the verdict depends on the testimony of the witnesses. The proverb is also true in a subjective as well as objective sense. Men may not only say what will be prejudicial or useful to others, but what will have a reflex influence on themselves, and either benefit or corrupt their own souls. (See ch. 10: 19. Comp. also ch. 21: 23)

22. The qualifying adjective is not expressed before the emphatic word *wife* in the original, but is unquestionably implied. It is found in the Sept. Syr. Vulg. and Arab. versions. It is not unusual for the sacred writers to employ a noun without any modifying adjunct when goodness and excellence, or the opposite, are evidently intended in the mind of the writer. The accessary idea becomes a material part of the meaning in such a case. Thus *name* in ch. 22: 1, is put for *good name; way* in ch. 15: 10, for a *good*, or *right way; answer*, ch. 15: 23, for a *just* and *proper answer; king*, ch. 16: 10, for *a wise* and *virtuous king.* So *man* for *a wicked man*, ch. 21: 8; *fool* for *rich fool*, ch. 19: 1. "He that hath married a wife, who is truly an helpmate for him, hath met with an excellent blessing; and ought thankfully to acknowledge the singular favor of God in guiding his mind to make so happy a choice." (Bp. Patrick.) Comp. ch. 19: 14. 31: 10. The Sept. adds, "He who puts away a good wife, puts away a good thing, and he who keeps an adulteress is foolish and ungodly."

23. The necessities of the poor often render them importunate; while the independent condition of the rich is apt to make them arrogant, haughty, overbearing, and insolent.

24. The great consumption of time occasioned by having a large circle of intimate associates,—time often spent with them to the neglect and consequent injury of business; and especially the expensive style of living, induced thereby, often prove ruinous to

22. "*Findeth a blessing,*" French, Noyes.

men. (Comp. ch. 21: 17.) At the same time, the tie of true friendship is often stronger than that of natural affection. Our English version renders the verb in the first clause of the verse, "Must show himself friendly." Boothroyd translates the clause thus: "A man by being friendly, shall have friends." To justify either of these renderings, we must derive the verb הִתְרֹעֵעַ, *hithroca*, from רֵעַ, *rea*, *a friend*. But this last word comes from the root רָעָה, and from such a root we cannot analogically obtain the Hithpolel form of the text. It must therefore come from the verb רָעַע, *raa*, which occurs in this conjugation in Isaiah 24: 19, where it plainly signifies *to be broken in pieces;* and hence from the nature of the subject, it must signify in this place, *will be ruined*, or reflexively, *will destroy* or *ruin himself.* So Gesenius, Holden, French, Noyes. Prof. Stuart thinks this a stronger expression than the verb will bear, and therefore renders it, "will show himself as base;" and the sentiment which he deduces from the proverb, is this: "the man who professes to regard every body as a special friend (the phrase *a man of friends*, signifying, as he thinks, 'a man who professes to regard everybody as his *friend*,') must bring on himself the imputation of false profession and base designs. Yet there is another and a real kind of friendship, the opposite of this: and it sometimes rises higher than that which even a brother ordinarily exhibits."

CHAPTER XIX.

1. Better is the poor (*man*), who walketh in his integrity,
Than (*he, who*) is perverse with his lips, and is a fool.

---

1. Poverty is never a disgrace except when the consequence of misconduct; and when adorned with true and godly sincerity, it is even honorable. By *fool* is here evidently intended a *rich fool*, as the antithesis requires. The Vulgate expresses the sense accurately: "than the rich man who is perverse with his lips." Comp. the parallel passage, ch. 28: 6, where "rich" is substituted for "fool."

---

1. "*Than he who is perverse in his ways, though rich*," Boothr., Holden.

2. Moreover, for the soul to be without knowledge,
is not good ;
And he, who hasteneth with his feet, will make a
false step.

3. The foolishness of man perverteth his way ;
And his heart fretteth against Jehovah.

4. Wealth maketh many friends ;
But the poor (*man*) is separated from his neighbor.

5. A false witness shall not go unpunished ;
And he, who speaketh lies, shall not escape.

6. Many court the favor of the prince ;
And every one is a friend to him who giveth gifts.

7. All the brothers of the poor (*man*) hate him ;
How much more do his friends go far from him ;
He followeth (*them with*) words ;—they regard not.

Syr. "Better is the poor man who walks in his integrity, than the
rich, whose ways are perverse." The Chald. and Arab. vss. and
some MSS. also read "ways" instead of "lips." *Perverse*—i. e. deceitful, lying, false. If perverse with his lips, then of course in his
heart and conduct.

2. The verb חָטָא, *chata*, in the second clause of this verse properly signifies *to miss*, viz. the mark, and is spoken of an archer or
slinger, (see Judg. 20: 16): also as here of the feet, *to miss*, to *make
a false step;* then figuratively *to sin, to err.* The proverb is allegorical, and used of one who commits mistakes and falls into trouble,
misfortune, and sin, in consequence of acting ignorantly, rashly,
precipitately, and without due consideration.

3. The evils which men bring upon themselves by their misconduct, they are prone to charge upon God. This propensity is alluded
to by St. James, when he says, "Let no man when he is tempted
say, he is tempted of God," &c. James 1: 13. Such conduct is as
foolish as it is wicked.

4. *Is separated*—i. e. is deserted by his neighbor. He who ought
to be his friend, stands aloof from him. See ch. 14: 20.

6. *Court the favor*—lit. *rub* or *smooth the face*, i. e. caress, flatter,
court.

7. *Brothers*, put for near relatives generally. The verb *to hate* is

---

2. "*Sinneth*," E. V., Boothr.—"*erreth*," Holden—"*stumbleth*," Noyes—"*goeth
astray*," Stuart.

8. He, who getteth wisdom, loveth his own soul;
He, who keepeth understanding, shall find good.

9. A false witness shall not go unpunished;
And he, who uttereth lies, shall perish.

10. Luxury is not seemly for a fool;
Much less is it for a servant to rule over princes.

11. The understanding of a man maketh him slow
to anger;
And it is his glory to pass over an offence.

12. A king's wrath is like the roaring of a lion;
But his favor is like dew upon the grass.

---

here used in a comparative and not an absolute sense. They love
less than they in duty are bound to do. When the poor man applies
for assistance to his pretended friends, they turn away with cold
indifference and neglect. He follows them with earnest appeals, but
they refuse to listen to his entreaties and expostulations.

> "His familiars to his buried fortunes
> Slink all away; leave all their false vows with him,
> Like empty purses picked; and his poor self
> A dedicated beggar to the air,
> With his disease of all shunn'd poverty,
> Walks like contempt alone."—*Shakspeare.*

> "Donec eris felix, multos numerabis amicos,
> Tempora si fuerint nubila, solus eris."—*Ovid.*

8. *His own soul*—i. e. himself. He who acts with a proper and
commendable regard to his own best interests and highest enjoyment.

10. Comp. ch. 26: 1, 8. 30: 22.

11. A man who is possessed of good common sense and a well-
regulated mind, will not allow himself to be easily provoked, but
will endeavor to suppress any rising resentment, and readily overlook an offence.

12. The monarch of the land is here compared to the monarch
of the forest. The roaring of the lion is so terrible, that all other
animals in a wild state are said to flee away in consternation at the
sound. Similar to this in the terror it inspires is a despot's wrath.
On the contrary, his favor is grateful and refreshing like dew upon
the grass, which in Eastern countries especially is exceedingly copious.

13. A foolish son is a calamity to his father;
And the contentions of a wife are a continual dropping.

14. Houses and wealth are an inheritance from
fathers;
But a prudent wife is from Jehovah.

15. Slothfulness casteth into a deep sleep;
And an idle person shall suffer hunger.

16. He, who keepeth the commandment, keepeth
his life;
But he, who neglecteth his ways, shall die.

17. He, who hath pity on the poor, lendeth to Jehovah;
And that, which he hath given, He will repay him.

---

13. The contentions of a quarrelsome wife are here compared to
the constant droppings of rain from the eaves of a house. By their
frequent occurrence, as well as from their vexatious character, they
become exceedingly annoying and destructive of the peace and comfort of a family. Comp. ch. 27: 15. Geier quotes the following proverb of the Illyrians: "There is no necessity for him to go to war,
who has a smoking house, a dropping roof, or a contentious wife;
for he has war in his own house."

14. Splendid mansions and extensive estates are often acquired
by hereditary right; and though these are in a certain sense the
gift of God, yet a prudent and discreet wife is more especially from
the Lord. She is a more valuable possession than wealth, and her
influence for good is infinitely more potent and enduring. Comp.
ch. 18: 22.

16. He who keeps the commandments of Jehovah (see ch. 13: 13)
adopts the best course for preserving and prolonging his temporal
life, and the sure means of saving his immortal soul. But he who
is regardless of his conduct and cares neither for human nor divine
law, renders himself obnoxious to death both corporeal and spiritual.
The verb *to keep* is here employed in two different senses by the
figure antanaclasis; first in the sense of *to observe, to obey*, and then
in the sense of *to preserve, to save. Keepeth his life*—i. e. himself, including both body and soul.

17

18. Correct thy son, while there is hope,
And let not thy soul desire his death.

19. A man of violent anger will suffer punishment;
For if thou deliver him, yet thou mayest do it again.

20. Hear counsel, and receive instruction;
That thou mayest be wise in thy latter end.

21. Many are the devices in a man's heart;
Nevertheless the counsel of Jehovah shall stand.

22. That, which maketh a man esteemed is his kindness;
But a poor man is better than a man of falsehood.

23. The fear of Jehovah (*tendeth*) to life,
And (*he, who hath it*), shall abide satisfied;
He shall not be visited with evil.

24. A slothful man hideth his hand in the dish;
And will not so much as bring it to his mouth again.

---

18. *While there is hope.*—Before he becomes too old to be chastized,
or his habits become too firmly fixed to be overcome. How many
children are ruined by the indulgence of parents and their neglect
to administer proper correction seasonably. Comp. ch. 25: 13, 14.
His death.—The Hebrew word translated *his death* is a verb Hiph.
Inf. constr. with affix from מוּת, *muth, to die.* The clause may therefore be rendered, "Let not thy soul desire to *slay* him," i. e. do not
correct him with too great severity, but with due moderation. So
Vulg. and Aquila.

19. A man of irascible and ungovernable temper is always getting into difficulty, and if you help him out of one trouble, it will
not be long before his violent temper will involve him in another.

24. This proverb furnishes a forcible illustration of the paralysis
of sloth. The modern orientals use neither knives nor forks in eating, and spoons are used only for liquids. The same custom prevailed in ancient times, as is evident not only from the indications
of ancient literature, but also from the representations of banquets,
in all of which, whether Egyptian, Grecian, Roman or Syrian, the
guests are exhibited as taking their food from the dish with their
fingers Comp. Matt. 26: 23. It was considered vulgar and coarse,
however, to introduce much of the hand into the dish; the proper
mode being to gather and take up only what the fingers could hold.

25. Smite a scoffer, and the simple will become prudent;
Reprove (*a man*) of understanding, and he will discern knowledge.
28. An ungodly witness scoffeth at justice;
And the mouth of the wicked devoureth iniquity.
29. Judgments are prepared for scoffers;
And blows for the back of fools.

Here the sluggard is described as guilty, from sheer indolence, of the gross indecorum of plunging and hiding his hand in the dish, in order to take as much as possible, rather than be at the trouble of repeating the operation; and even then, although he might feel the cravings of hunger, it is irksome to him to raise the hand to the mouth. See ch. 26: 15. The English version, following the Sept. and Syr. translates צַלַּחַת, *tzallachath*, here and in the parallel passage by *bosom*, instead of *dish*, while in 2 Kgs. 21: 23, it renders it *dish*. The latter signification is so appropriate here and so amply confirmed by Hebrew usage and Oriental customs, that it has been adopted by all modern interpreters.

25. See ch. 15: 5, (תָּכֶּה, Hiph. fut. of נָכָה. הוֹכִיחַ, Hiph. Imp. of יָכַח.)

CHAPTER XX.

1. Wine is a mocker, strong drink a brawler;
And every one, who is led astray thereby, is not wise.

---

1. This proverb is intended to describe the deleterious effects resulting from the habitual use of intoxicating drinks. The juice of the grape, properly used, is numbered among the blessings which the God of nature has bestowed upon men. But like every earthly blessing, it may be, and often is abused to gratify a depraved appetite, and then becomes a curse, instead of a blessing. The Hebrew word שֵׁכָר, *sekar*, from which our English word *cider* comes, denotes a beverage made of fruits other than grapes, such as dates, &c. The epithet *strong* in our English version is not intended to indicate that

2. The dread of a king is like the roaring of a lion ;
He, who enrageth him, sinneth (*against*) himself.

3. It is an honor to a man to cease from strife ;
But every fool is contentious.

4. The sluggard will not plow in autumn ;
Therefore he shall beg in harvest, and have nothing.

---

the fermented liquor in question was stronger or more inebriating
than grape wine; for none of the fruits of Palestine yielded a juice
more potent and intoxicating than grapes. It is employed for the
want of a better term, simply to distinguish it from grape wine,
in connexion with which it is generally found. Distilled liquors
were of course unknown at that early period. The proverb, however, is evidently applicable to intoxicating liquors of every description. *Is not wise*—i. e. is a fool, by the figure litotes.

2. The phrase *dread of a king* denotes the terror and alarm which
an enraged king in despotic governments inspires in others, who
have rendered themselves obnoxious to his wrath. Comp. ch. 19:
12. *Sinneth against himself.*—He only injures himself and is sure
to be the sufferer.

3. *To cease from strife*—lit. the *abstaining from strife.* Comp. ch.
17: 14. (שֶׁבֶת, a seghodate noun from the root שָׁבַת, *to cease.*)

4. *In autumn.*—This is the proper meaning of the noun חֹרֶף,
choreph, from חָרַף, *charaph, to pluck, to pull, to gather.* It denotes the
season for gathering. In Syria the farmers commence plowing their
land about the last of September and sow their earliest wheat about
the middle of October. This rendering therefore corresponds with
facts, as well as with the etymology of the word. So Gesenius,
Mercer, &c. The Vulg. Sym. and Eng. Ver. render "by reason of
the *cold,*" but this is an interpretation rather than a translation.
The word never signifies cold, and is never elsewhere so translated.
Holden, Booth., Stuart, Marg. Reading—"*winter.*" It often includes the winter season, and is used with "summer" to represent
the whole year. The sluggard, in consequence of his indolence,
allows the proper season for plowing his land to pass unimproved.
Hence he fails of a harvest and is compelled to depend on charity
for the supply of his wants. Sept. "The sluggard when reproached
is not ashamed: so also he who borrows corn in harvest."

5. Counsel in the heart of man is (*like*) deep water;
But a man of understanding will draw it out.

6. Most men will proclaim, each his own goodness;
But a faithful man who can find?

7. He, who walketh in his integrity, is a righteous
(*man;*)
Happy (*will*) his children (*be*) after him.

8. A king, who sitteth on the throne of judgment,
Scattereth all evil with his eyes.

9. Who can say, " I have made my heart clean;
I have purified myself from sin?"

---

5. Deep water is difficult to be sounded; or rather water in a
deep well is hard to reach: so counsel in the heart of man, or his
secret purpose, it may be very difficult to ascertain. Yet a wise,
discerning, and skillful man will at length arrive at its import. He
will draw it out from its depths, as water is drawn out of a deep
well with a bucket, till at last the bottom is reached.

6. The interrogative form in the second member is not intended
to indicate that no one absolutely can be found, who comes up to
his professions of kindness, and is truly faithful under all circumstances; but that it is rare to meet with such. Comp. ch. 19: 22.

8. *A king*—i e. a pious and upright king. *All evil*—the Hebrew
word רַע, *ra*, may be taken either in an abstract or concrete sense.
If the former is intended, then the meaning is, that a king, who
acts as a king should do, and as a wise and righteous king will do,
will exert his power to banish as much as possible all evil, every
thing which is base, wicked and corrupting, from his dominions.
If the latter is intended, then the sense is, that such a king will
expel from his kingdom or severely punish all wicked persons, so
as effectually to put a stop to their iniquity. The difference is not
material, and as the former virtually includes the latter sense, it is
here preferred as the more comprehensive. The image of scattering
is here taken from the winnowing of grain. The phrase *with his
eyes* would seem to indicate the diligence with which he scrutinizes
and inquires into the wickedness which may exist in his dominions.

9. No man living can say with truth that he is free from sinful
propensities or from actual transgressions. "There is not a just

8. " *Scattereth all the wicked like chaff*," French, Noyes.

17*

10. Diverse weights and diverse measures,
Both these are an abomination to Jehovah.

11. Even a child maketh himself known by his doings,
Whether his (*future*) conduct .(*will be*) pure and
upright.

12. The hearing ear, and the seeing eye—
Jehovah hath made even both of them.

---

man on earth that doeth good and sinneth not." The interrogative
form is equivalent to a strong negation.

10. *Diverse weights, &c.*—literally, *a stone and a stone, an ephah
and an ephah.* The repetition of the nouns in this case denotes not
plurality, but diversity. Light weights and heavy weights, and
measures of different sizes, one of the proper size, and another too
large or too small according to circumstances; one set to buy with,
and another to sell with. See ch. 11: 1. The Ephah was a dry
measure, holding about 1 1-9 bushels English.

11. By observing the actions of a child, or the conduct, pursuits
and even diversions of a youth, an accurate judgment may often be
formed, in regard to his future character and course of life. "The
boy is father to the man." Some commentators suppose the meaning of the proverb to be, that the child by his conduct develops his
present character. "His work will indicate whether he is well or
ill inclined; for early in life is the disposition disclosed." (Stuart.)
"Let parents watch their children's early habits, temper, doings.
Generally the discerning eye will mark something in the budding
of the young tree, by which the tree in maturity may be known.
The child will tell what the man will be. No wise parent will pass
over little faults, as if it was only a child doing childish things.
Every thing should be looked at as an index of the secret principles,
and the work or word judged by the principle. If a child be deceitful, quarrelsome, obstinate, rebellious, selfish, how can we help
trembling for his growth? A docile, truth loving, obedient, generous child—how joyous is the prospect of the blossom and fruit from
this hopeful budding! From the childhood of Samuel, Timothy,
much more of the Saviour, we could not but anticipate what the
manhood would be. The early purity and right principles promised
abundant and most blessed fruit. (Bridges.)

---

11. "*Will dissemble in his doings*," Holden, Boothr.

13. Love not sleep, lest thou come to poverty;
Open thine eyes, and thou shalt be satisfied with bread.

14. ("*It is*) bad!" ("*it is*) bad!" saith the buyer;
But when he hath gone his way, then he boasteth.

15. There is gold, and an abundance of pearls;
But the lips of knowledge are the precious casket.

16. Take his garment who is surety (*for*) a stranger:
Yea, take a pledge from him, who is bound for strangers.

17. The bread of deceit is sweet to a man;
But afterwards his mouth will be filled with gravel.

---

14. The buyer disparages an article which he wishes to purchase, till he has succeeded in reducing the price to the lowest terms; and then he goes away and boasts of his advantageous bargain. It is a thing of daily occurrence for men to underrate the commodity they desire to purchase, in order to obtain it for less than its actual value; and on the other hand, to magnify the excellence of an article which they wish to sell, beyond its intrinsic or marketable value, in order to obtain for it more than it is worth. While one is bent on buying cheap, the other is equally bent on selling dear. The one decries unjustly: the other praises unduly.

15. Gold and jewels laid up in the repositories of the affluent are both abundant and valuable. But "the pearl of great price"—the saving knowledge of religious truth possessed and communicated by the pious man is both more rare and more precious than these.

16. "In this precept we are exhorted not to trust any one, who inconsiderately makes himself responsible for a stranger, but to obtain from him immediate and adequate security." (French.) See ch. 27: 13. Instead of the textual reading נָכְרִים, *nakrim, strangers,* the Masorites have placed in the margin the keri נָכְרִיָּה, *nakreya, strange woman,* and have pointed the text accordingly. This reading is followed in Eng. ver. and by some of the early interpreters. But the textual reading is that of all known Hebrew MSS. and is represented in the Latin Vulgate. There is much more authority for changing the reading in ch. 27: 13, to make it conform to this, than to change this, in order to make it conform to that.

17. By "bread of deceit," is meant food obtained by fraud and deception, or other dishonest means. This may be pleasant at the time, but is sure to be followed by painful and vexatious conse-

18. Purposes are established by counsel;
Therefore with wise counsel make war.

19. He, who goeth about (*as*) a tale-bearer, revealeth secrets;
Therefore associate not with one, who keepeth his
lips open.

20. He, who curseth his father or his mother—
His lamp shall be put out in midnight darkness.

21. A possession (*may be*) gotten hastily at the first;
But the end thereof will not be blessed.

22. Say not thou, " I will repay evil;"
But wait on Jehovah, and he will help thee.

23. Diverse weights are an abomination to Jehovah;
And deceitful balances are not good.

---

quences. The figure in the second member may allude to the practice among some nations of punishing malefactors by mixing gravel
with their bread.

19. "Hic niger est; hunc tu, Romane, caveto," was the warning
of the Roman satirist against the tattler. See ch. 11: 13.

20. The phrase *in midnight darkness* is literally *in the very eye-
ball* (pupil) *of darkness*, i. e. in the thickest darkness—the darkness
which prevails at midnight. It is an intensive expression. See ch.
7: 9. The sense is—Such an one shall have no comfort to cheer
him in the season of adversity, when he most needs it; while, on
the contrary, to the upright there ariseth light in the midst of the
deepest adversity.

21. The word translated *possession* commonly signifies *inheritance*;
but here and in Eccles. 7: 11, it is evidently employed in the more
general sense of *possession* or *wealth*. As wealth acquired by honest
means is not to be condemned, whether obtained suddenly by for-
tunate speculation, or by the slower and surer process of laudable,
patient and persevering industry, the allusion in the proverb must
be to property acquired suddenly by unlawful and questionable
means; by dishonest extortion, avarice or rapine. (Instead of the
textual reading, מְבֻחֶלֶת, the Keri has מְבֹהֶלֶת, Pual part. of בָּהַל,
which is supported by the parallel passage, ch. 28: 22, by all the
ancient versions and by many MSS)

23. *Deceitful*—i. e. false, and therefore calculated and designed
to deceive. See v. 10. ch. 11: 1. 16: 11.

24. The steps of a man (*are directed*) by Jehovah;
How, then, can a man understand his own ways?

25. The man is ensnared, who rashly utters sacred
words;
And then, after vows, maketh inquiry.

26. A wise king scattereth the wicked,
And bringeth the wheel over them.

27. The spirit of a man is the lamp of Jehovah;
Which searcheth all the chambers of the body.

28. Mercy and truth preserve the king;
And his throne is upheld by mercy.

29. The glory of young men is their strength;
And the ornament of old men is the gray head.

---

25. To *utter sacred words* is to make a solemn vow or promise, in
which the name of Jehovah is invoked under a curse. The proverb
is designed to administer a timely caution against contracting the
obligation of a vow, before making proper inquiry in regard to the
consequences.

26. See v. 8. The wheel here alluded to is the wheel of the
threshing wain or sledge,—an agricultural instrument used in the
East to separate the grain from the straw. It had wheels with iron
teeth or edges, like a saw; the axle was armed with iron teeth or
serrated wheels throughout. It moved on three rollers armed also
in like manner to cut the straw. Some suppose the royal sceptre to
be intended, which in the East, is said to have been often made in
the shape of a wheel.

27. Under the term *spirit* are here included the intellectual principle and the moral faculty, which have been implanted in man by
his Maker, and by means of which he is enabled to reflect upon
and estimate the moral character of his own thoughts, motives and
actions.

28. *Preserve*—i. e. guard and protect the king. Mercy and
truthfulness, or fidelity, are qualities which make the throne of a
king stable and secure, because they will insure the attachment and
support of the people.

29. Every stage of life has its peculiar honor and privilege.
Comp. ch. 14: 31. " Youth," says Jermin, " is the glory of nature,
and strength is the glory of youth. Old age is the majestic beauty

30. The stripes of a wound are a cleansing from evil;
Yea, the strokes (*which reach*) to the chambers of the body.

---

of nature, and the gray head is the majestic beauty, which nature has given to old age."

20. *Stripes*—See Ex. 21: 25. Isa. 1: 6. 53: 5. The scars or marks of a wound, or wounding stripes (i. e. stripes which cause wounds), in other words an appropriate corporeal punishment judicially inflicted in the way of penalty for crime, is often an effectual means of reclaiming a vicious man.

CHAPTER XXI.

1. The king's heart is in the hand of Jehovah (*as*) streams of water;
He turneth it wheresoever he pleaseth.
2. All the ways of a man are right in his own eyes;
But Jehovah weigheth the hearts.
3. To do justice and judgment
Is more acceptable to Jehovah than sacrifices.

---

1. In the comparison here drawn there is allusion to the practice common among gardeners and agriculturists, especially in Eastern countries, of directing the course of brooks and constructing artificial canals, or water-sluices, for the purpose of irrigating the soil. "As these fertilizing rivulets, the work of art, are conducted forwards and backwards, to the right hand or the left, diverted or stopped, at the will of him who manages them; so is the heart of kings, and by parity of reasoning, of the rich and mighty of the earth, swayed at the sovereign disposal of the Lord of all creatures. He, by the course of his providence and by the inward promptings of his Spirit, can turn the enriching tide of their bounty in any direction he sees fit, whether to bless the poor with bread, or to supply the means of salvation to the destitute." (Bush.) (יַטֶּנּוּ, Hiph. fut. of נָטָה.)

3. See 1 Sam. 15: 22. Hos. 6: 6. Mic. 6: 7, 8.

4. The lofty look—the proud heart—
(*Yea*) the lamp of the wicked is sin.

5. The purposes of the diligent (*tend*) only to plen-
teousness ;   .
But (*those*) of every one who is hasty, only to want.

6. The getting of treasures by a lying tongue,
Is (*like*) a fleeting vapor to those who seek death.

7. The violence of the wicked shall sweep them
away ;
Because they refuse to do justice.

8. The way of the guilty man is perverse ;
But (*as for*) the pure, his conduct is upright.

---

4. *The lofty look*—lit. *loftiness of eyes*—a sign or token of pride
and superciliousness. The noun נֵר, *nir*, is most probably pointed
incorrectly for נֵר, *ner*, *lamp*, or *light*, from the verb נוּר, *nur*, to *shine*.
So all the ancient versions and many manuscripts. The word
נִיר, *nir*, (from the verb נִיר, *to plough*, *to break up with the plough*, *to
till*,) properly sig. *fallow ground*, or *tilled land*, rather than the act of
ploughing, as in Eng. Vers. (see ch. 13: 23), and moreover, it never
elsewhere occurs defectively written.

5. The *diligent* man is usually in this book contrasted with the
slothful, but here with the *hasty*. "Haste has much of *diligence* in
its temperament: but as indolence is its defect, this is its excess,
its undisciplined impulse. The hand too often goes before, and acts
without, the judgment." (Bridges.) The man who is in haste to
become rich, engages in hazardous enterprises and rash speculations; or undertakes more than he is capable of managing; and
hence his schemes frequently result in disappointment and mortification, if not in crime and utter ruin.

6. Treasures may be got by falsehood and deception. But like
a fleeting vapor they rapidly pass away from those, who, by resort-
ing to such fraudulent and deceptive means to acquire wealth, show
that they seek their own destruction.

7. Comp. Ps. 7: 16. 34: 21. 140: 1. (יְגוֹרֵם, Kal fut. of גָּרַר, with
ו fulcrum and pronominal affix.)

8. (וָזָר, an adjective from וָזַר, found in the Arab. and signifying
guilty, laden with guilt. The earlier commentators supposed it to be

9. It is better to dwell in the corner of the house-top,
Than with a contentious woman even (*in*) a large
house.

10. The soul of the wicked (*man*) desireth evil;
Even his neighbor findeth no favor in his eyes.

11. When the scoffer is punished, the simple is
made wise;
And when the wise (*man*) is instructed, he receiveth
knowledge.

---

the participial adj. of זוּר, *strange*, with the copulative ו conjoined,
חֲבַכְבַּן, *crooked, perverse*, is an adj. from the Pealal form of the verb
חָבַן.)

9. The roofs of the houses in the East were anciently, and still
continue to be built flat and properly guarded by a parapet. It was
customary to occupy these for retirement, air, exercise, and in some
instances, for sleep; for which purpose little closets, like arbors,
made of slight materials, were constructed. Comp. 2 Sam. 11: 2.
The phrase בֵּית חָבֶר, *beth chaber*, literally sig. *a house of association*,
society or *fellowship*, which may mean a *large, spacious house*—one sufficiently extensive to accommodate several families; or it may denote a *common house*, or *house in common*, i. e. a house occupied in
common by several families (so Sept. and Vulg.); or it may import
a house in which one is compelled to associate with its inmates.
See v. 19, 4 ch. 25: 24. The sentiment appears to be, that it is better to live solitary and alone in the corner of the house-top, where
peace and quietness reign, though subjected to many inconveniences
and discomforts, than even in a large and commodious house, where
you are continually subjected to the annoyance and vexation of a
contentious and brawling woman.

10. This is a caution against having any close intimacy or connexion with a wicked and unprincipled man, since he will spare
neither friend nor foe who may stand in his way. (אִוְּתָה, Piel Perf.
3d pers. sing. fem. of אָוָה. יֻחַן, Hoph. fut. of חָנַן.)

11. Comp. ch. 19: 25, where a similar sentiment is expressed.
Sept. "When an intemperate man is punished, the simple become
wiser: and a wise man understanding, will receive knowledge."

12. The Righteous (*One*) considereth the house of
the wicked ;
He casteth the wicked headlong into evil.

13. He, who stoppeth his ears against the cry of the
poor—
Even he shall cry aloud, but shall not be answered.

14. A gift in secret pacifieth anger ;
And a bribe in the bosom, strong wrath.

15. It is joy to the righteous to do justice ;
But destruction (*shall be*) to the workers of iniquity.

16. The man, who wandereth from the way of understanding,
Shall dwell in the assembly of the shades.

17. He, who loveth pleasure (*will be*) a poor man ;
And, he who loveth wine and oil, shall not be rich.

---

12. The subject of the first member may be either the righteous
one, i. e. Jehovah; or the righteous *man*. Accordingly some commentators, taking "righteous man" in the sense of a righteous *judge*
or magistrate, interpret the couplet thus: 'The righteous magistrate
carefully searches the houses of wicked men, in order to detect and
punish their crimes.' Others make righteous *man* the subject of the
first clause, and *God* the subject of the second. So Eng. Vers. "The
righteous *man* wisely considereth the house of the wicked; *but God*
overthroweth the wicked for *their* wickedness." There would seem,
however, to be no sufficient reason for regarding the subject of the
second member as different from that of the first; and if so, then
the predicate of the second member would indicate clearly that God
is the subject of both. The sense is, that Jehovah takes cognizance
of the household or family of the wicked, and will ultimately inflict upon them the punishment their sinful conduct deserves.

13. *Even he*—emphatic; even the very same.

14. *In secret*—i. e. offered or bestowed in private. Comp. ch. 17:
8, 23. 18: 16.

16. *The shades*—i. e. the dead,—in the abode of departed spirits.

17. Convivial pleasure—festive joy—is particularly alluded to.
The fast liver who spends his time and money in the gratification

---

13. "*Shall not be heard*," E. V., Holden, Boothr.
14. "*A reward*," E. V., Holden, Boothr.—"*a present*," Noyes.

18. The wicked (*man shall be*) a ransom for the righteous;
And the transgressor, for the upright.

19. It is better to dwell in a desert-land,
Than with a contentious and passionate woman.

20. Precious treasure and oil are in the dwelling of the wise;
But the foolish man devoureth them.

21. He, who followeth after righteousness and mercy,
Shall find life, righteousness, and honor.

22. A wise (*man*) scaleth the city of the mighty;
And casteth down the strength of its confidence.

23. He, who keepeth his mouth and his tongue;
Keepeth his soul from trouble.

---

of his appetite, may expect to die a poor man. Wine and oil constituted a customary part of feasts among the inhabitants of Palestine; hence they are frequently named in Scripture as the representatives of all those delicacies and luxuries in which those indulged who were addicted to a voluptuous life. "The greatest pleasure," says Cyprian, "is to have conquered pleasure: nor is there any greater victory, than that which is gained over our own appetites."

19. Comp. v. 9. The picture here drawn of the misery caused by domestic dissention is even stronger than in the parallel passage.

20. By *precious treasure* is intended here *valuable stores of all kinds*, and not simply money. The wise man, by industry, forethought, and prudent management, provides and lays up in store for future as well as present use, an adequate supply of the necessaries and comforts of life. On the contrary, the foolish and improvident man, makes no provision for the future, but squanders or consumes as he goes, all he earns, for the gratification of the present moment.

21. Comp. Matt. 5: 6. Rom. 9: 30, 31. 1 Cor. 14: 1. 1 Thess. 5: 15. 1 Tim. 6: 11. 2 Tim, 2: 22. Heb. 12: 14.

22. *Strength*—i. e. the strength of the city in which the mighty confide. So Sept., Holden, Noyes. Wisdom is more efficacious than force. The proverb may be regarded as a parabolic rendering of the maxim announced by Lord Bacon, that "knowledge is power." Comp. Eccles. 7: 19. 9: 14, 18.

24. (*As for*) the proud (*and*) haughty (*man*)—scoffer is his name;
He acts with the insolence of pride.

25. The desire of the sluggard killeth him;
Because his hands refuse to labor.

26. All the day long, he coveteth eagerly;
But the righteous giveth and withholdeth not.

27. The sacrifice of the wicked is an abomination;
How much more (*when*) he bringeth it with an evil design.

28. A false witness shall perish;
But the man, who hath heard, shall always speak.

29. The wicked man hardeneth his face;
But the upright (*man*) directeth his ways.

30. Wisdom is nothing, and understanding is nothing;
And counsel is nothing against Jehovah.

---

25. "The slothful man makes no adequate effort to satisfy his desires, and they are consequently a continual torment to him." Comp. ch. 13: 4, 12.

27. This is a repetition of the proverb in ch. 15: 8, but with increased intensity. The religious performances and sacrifices of the wicked cannot under any circumstances be acceptable to the searcher of hearts, because they spring not from love to him, or a true desire to promote his glory. But especially abhorrent to him are such acts when hypocritically performed for the purpose of accomplishing some selfish end.

28. A person who falsely certifies to that of which he is ignorant, shall be severely punished for his audacity and perjury. On the contrary, the faithful, conscientious and upright witness, who testifies only what he knows from personal observation, will always be respected, and implicit reliance placed on his testimony.

29. The wicked man displays at all times the utmost assurance, and never thinks of blushing at his vices and wrong-doings. But the upright man carefully regulates his conduct by the divine law. (Instead of יָכִין, the Keri reads יָבִין, *understandeth his way*, with which the Sept. agrees. But the textual reading is the more significant, and is supported by the Vulg. Syr. Chald. Aquila and Sym.)

81. The horse is prepared for the day of battle;
But the victory is from Jehovah.

---

31. *Victory*—see 2 Sam. 19: 2. 23: 10, 12. So marginal reading.
Comp. Ps. 33: 17. 20: 7.

CHAPTER XXII.

1. A (*good*) name is to be chosen rather than great
riches;
(*And*) kind favor is better than gold and silver.
2. The rich and the poor meet together;
Jehovah is the maker of them all.

---

1. The accessory idea of *good* is evidently implied in the word
name, and the qualifying adjective is accordingly expressed in the
Sept. Vulg. and Chald. as it is also in our Eng. Vers. See ch. 18:
22. Comp. Eccles. 7: 1. A good reputation, founded on a virtuous
and pious character, adds greatly to one's usefulness and influence,
and gives authority to reproof, counsel and example. Hence it is
truly described as a possession of more value both to the possessor
and the community than riches. At the same time it should be acquired and maintained in the exercise of a good conscience. "Two
things there are," says Augustine, "whereof every man should be
specially chary and tender,—his conscience and his credit. But
that of his conscience must be his first care; this of his name and
credit must be content to come in the second place. Let him first
be sure to guard his conscience well, and then may he have a due
regard to his name also. Let it be his first care to secure all within,
by making his peace with God and in his own breast. That done,
but not before, let him look abroad if he will, and cast about as
well as he can, to strengthen his reputation with and before the
world."

2. The rich and the poor are in the world promiscuously mingled
together, differing materially in their outward condition, but on a

---

31. "*Safety*," E. V., Holden, French—"*deliverance*," Stuart.

3. The prudent (*man*) seeth the evil and hideth himself;

Bnt the simple pass on and are punished.

4. The reward of humility, (*and*) of the fear of Jehovah,

Is riches and honor, and life.

5. Thorns (*and*) snares are in the way of the perverse (*man*);

But he, who regardeth his life, will be far from them.

6. Train up a child in the way he should go,

And when he is old, he will not depart from it.

---

perfect equality as to origin, natural rights and both physical and spiritual wants. They constitute, therefore, one universal brotherhood. Each class has its appropriate lot, sphere, and duties. And as the two are mutually dependent, so they may be mutually helpful and beneficial. Reciprocal kindness, forbearance and good will, are consequently the obvious duty of all.

3. The same proverb occurs in ch. 27: 12.

4. *Reward*—Comp. Ps. 19: 11. So marginal reading.

5. *Thorns and snares* are here metaphorical expressions for pains, troubles, calamities and sorrows. These lie in the path of the perverse man. But the good man, mindful of his safety and happiness, will avoid that path and consequently escape those evils and sufferings. For this use of the verb *regardeth* see ch. 13: 18. 15: 5. Ps. 31: 6.

6. The phrase *in the way he should go*, is literally *according to his way*. This ambiguous expression may mean, 1. "in that manner of life which he ought to lead,"—i. e: in that course of conduct which his duty to God, to his fellow beings and to himself requires. Or 2. "in that mode of life which he is destined to lead." According to this interpretation the meaning is, educate a child for that particular sphere in life in which he is expected to move, and for that particular pursuit which he is expected to follow. Or 3. "According to the bent of his disposition, inclinations and capacity." The first interpretation, which is the one most commonly received,

---

6. "*Instruct a child with respect to his way*," French—"*Train up a child according to his way*," Stuart.

7. The rich (*man*) ruleth over the poor;
And the borrower is servant to the lender.

8. He, who soweth iniquity, shall reap calamity;
And the rod of his anger shall be broken.

9. He, who hath a bountiful eye, shall be blessed;
For he giveth of his bread to the poor.

10. Cast out the scoffer, and contention will depart;
Yea, strife and reproach will cease.

11. He, who loveth purity of heart,
His lips are kindness, (*and*) the king is his friend.

12. The eyes of Jehovah watch over knowledge;
But he overthroweth the words of the transgressor.

13. The sluggard saith, ("*There is*) a lion without;
"I shall be slain in the streets."

14. The mouth of strange women is a deep pit;
He, who is abhorred by Jehovah, shall fall therein.

---

is to be preferred, because it accords best with the connexion and with the general scope of the book and of Scripture.

8. The meaning of the second clause is, that the vicious man shall be deprived of the means of venting his anger or insolence on others.

9. By *a bountiful eye* is intended figuratively a charitable and humane disposition, just as an *evil eye* denotes an envious and malignant disposition. See ch. 23: 6. 28: 22. Deut. 15: 9.

12. *Knowledge* is the abstract for the concrete—*the knowing*, or the man of knowledge—in opposition to false pretenders. Jehovah watches over so as effectually to protect the intelligent, wise and good; but he brings to nought the deceitful and pernicious counsel of the wicked.

13. No excuse is too improbable and absurd for the sluggard to offer in justification of his slothfulness and indolence. See ch. 26: 13.

---

8. "*The rod of his insolence shall perish*," Stuart.

11. "*Jehovah loveth holy hearts*," Sept.—"*Jehovah loveth the pure in heart*," Boothr.="*for the grace of his lips*," Eng. Ver., French—"*grace is upon his lips*," Noyes.

15. Folly is bound up in the heart of a child ;

(*But*) the rod of correction will drive it far from him.

16. He, who oppresseth the poor (*man*) to enrich himself,

And he, who giveth to the rich, (*will*) surely (*come*) to want.

---

16. He who oppresses the poor man in order to aggrandize himself, or who bestows gifts on the rich in order to receive a greater benefit in return, will be disappointed in his expectations and at length come to want: for the motives by which he is actuated are not such as God approves or will bless. Luther renders the verse: "He that oppresseth the poor to increase his own estate, giveth to the rich only to impoverish himself."

PART III.

CHAPTER XXII, 17.—XXIV. 34.

CHAPTER XXII. 17-21.

[SOLOMON RESUMES HIS EXHORTATION TO THE STUDY AND PURSUIT OF
TRUE WISDOM, AND AGAIN POINTS OUT THE ADVANTAGE WHICH
IS SURE TO RESULT FROM A REGARD TO ITS PRECEPTS.]

17. Incline thine ear, and hear the words of the
wise,
And apply thy heart to my instruction.
18. For (*it will be*) a pleasant thing, if thou keep
them within thee;
(*If*) they be altogether established on thy lips:
19. That thy trust may be in Jehovah,
I have this day made (*them*) known to thee, even to
thee.
20. Have I not written to thee before
Concerning counsel and knowledge?
21. To make thee know the certainty of the words
of truth;
That thou mayest return words of truth to those
who send thee?

17, 18. (הַט, Hiph. imper. apoc. of נָטָה. הָשִׁית, Kal fut. 2d pers.
sing. used for the Imperative. הוֹרַעְתִּיךָ, Hiph. fut. of יָרַע, with
pron. affix.)

CHAPTER XXII. 22.—XXIV. 22.

[OTHER PROVERBS, MAXIMS, AND EXHORTATIONS.]

22. Rob not the poor (*man*), because he is poor;
Nor oppress the afflicted in the gate.
23. For Jehovah will plead their cause;
And spoil of life those, who have spoiled them.
24. Make no friendship with a passionate man;
And associate not with a man (*prone*) to wrath:
25. Lest thou learn his ways;
And get a snare to thy soul.
26. Be not thou (*one*) of those, who strike hands—
Of those, who are sureties for debts;
27. When thou hast nothing (*with which*) to pay,
Why should (*thy creditor*) take thy bed from under
thee?

---

22. The rich and powerful often think that they may oppress
and defraud the poor with impunity. But that very poverty, which
is their misfortune rather than their fault, furnishes a sufficient reason why they should be treated with kindness and lenity. It was
near the gates of walled towns, that the courts were anciently held
and judicial trials prosecuted, because they were places of chief resort, and also afforded the best accommodation in regard to room,
convenience of access, &c. See Amos 5: 15. Job 5: 4. note on ch.
1: 21.

23. This verse is connected with the preceding. It declares
that God, as the righteous judge, advocate and protector of the poor
and oppressed, will defend them and avenge their wrongs by punishing their oppressors.

27. Every thing, except necessary clothing, could be taken for
debt among the Hebrews, even to the bed. This among us is regarded as an indispensible article, of which a man should not be
deprived by legal process. But in Palestine, a bed for the most
part is merely a coverlet or piece of carpet, and it could be easily
replaced by something else, which would answer the same purpose

---

27. "*Why should thy bed be taken?*" Holden, Boothr., French, Noyes.

28. Remove not the ancient landmark,
Which thy fathers have set.
29. Seest thou a man diligent in his business?
He shall stand before kings;
He shall not stand before mean (*men*).

---

in that warm climate. Still it is probable, from the particular mention of it here, that it was usually the last thing which the creditor exacted from his debtor. If so, then the general import of the second clause is, 'Why should you, by becoming surety for another, render yourself liable to be stripped of every thing which you possess?'

28. See Deut. 19: 14. 27: 17. The boundary of an inherited estate was peculiarly sacred in the estimation of the Hebrews, because it marked the portion allotted to them by the special gift and appointment of Jehovah. Even among the Heathen, who respected the rights of personal property, the landmark was held in so great veneration, that it was deified and worshipped as a god, to whom there was appropriated an annual festival. In an allegorical sense, the proverb has been understood to apply to hasty and unnecessary changes and innovations in respect to established customs, laws, institutions, manners and religion. (תַּסֵּג, Hiph. fut. of נָסַג, used in the sense of the Imperative.)

29. A diligent attention to one's particular vocation will generally insure success and advancement. To *stand before kings* is an idiomatic expression denoting to attract the attention and enjoy the friendship and patronage of the chief rulers of the nation. *Mean* —the original word properly sig. *dark*; hence figuratively, *obscure*, *mean*, *ignoble*.

CHAPTER XXIII.

1. When thou sittest down to eat with a ruler,
Consider well in whose presence (*thou art*);

---

1. The ancient manner of eating at meals was in a sitting posture. But when luxury and effeminacy began to prevail, seats were

1. "*What is before thee*," E. Ver., Holden, Stuart, Sept., Syr., Chald.

2. And put a knife to thy throat;
If thou art a man given to appetite.

3. Be not desirous of his dainties;
For they are deceitful food.

4. Labor not to become rich;
Cease from thy own wisdom.

5. Wilt thou let thine eyes pursue that (*which*) is not?
For (*riches*) certainly make for themselves wings,
And fly. away, as an eagle toward heaven.

6. Eat thou not the bread (*of him, who hath*) an evil
eye;
And desire not his dainty food.

---

exchanged for couches (κλιναι), and the people took their food in a
recumbent posture.

2. *Put a knife to thy throat*, is an allegorical expression denoting
'restrain thy appetite,' and do not indulge in excess and intemperance, either in eating or drinking, not only from self-respect and a
sense of propriety, but from the apprehension of degrading yourself in the estimation of your superiors and incurring their ill will
and contempt.

> "Reges dicuntur multis urgere concullis,
>   Et torquere mero quem perspixisse laborent
>   Amicitiæ dignus."—*Horace.*

"Certain kings are said to ply with frequent bumpers, and by the
strength of wine to make trial of, a man, when they are sedulous to
know, whether he is worthy of their friendship or not." (שָׁמְתָ, Kal
perf. 2d pers. sing. of שׂוּם.)

3. The luxuries and delicacies of the affluent have often proved
a snare to the sensuous. Sensual pleasure has tarnished many a
Christian profession. "God gives us a body to feed, not to pamper;
to be the servant, not the master of the soul. To go as near as we
can to the bounds of intemperance is to be in imminent danger of
exceeding."

5. *Pursue*—lit. *fly towards—which is not*—i. e. which has no permanent existence, but is perishable, transient and evanescent. See
Matt. 6: 20.

6. The phrase *evil eye* is here used in a metaphorical sense to
denote an *envious, covetous, sordid, avaricious,* or *malignant* disposition. Comp. ch. 22: 9.

7. For as he thinketh in his heart, so is he:
He saith to thee, " Eat and drink :"
'But his heart is not with thee.

8. The morsel, (*which*) thou hast eaten, thou shalt
vomit up ;
And thou wilt have thrown away thy pleasant words.

9. Speak not in the hearing of a fool ;
For he will despise the wisdom of thy words.

10. Remove not the ancient landmark ;
And enter not into the fields of the fatherless.

11. For their avenger is mighty ;
He will plead their cause against thee.

12. Apply thy heart to instruction ;
And thine ears to the words of knowledge.

---

7. A man's real character depends upon the state of his mind, upon the ordinary tenor of his thoughts, his motives of action, and affections. The words which he utters do not necessarily exhibit this. These may or may not be the true exponents of his feelings, disposition and intentions. They may or may not indicate what is really passing within him. They may be sincere, or they may be hypocritical and deceptive. Jehovah, however, looks at the heart, and knows the cherished thoughts of a man, and judges of the character by them. The verb שָׁעַר, *shaar*, occurs no where else, and different significations have been assigned to it by lexicographers and critics. Sept. "hair," (שֵׂעָר.) Chald. "gate," (שַׁעַר.) The signification attached to it in Eng. Vers. *to think*, is that of the cognate Chaldee verb, שְׂעַר, which appears to be its true meaning.

8. A discovery of the hypocrit's insincerity will produce disgust and regret that you should have thrown away kind words upon a worthless man. (תְּקִיאֶנָּה, Hiph. fut. of קֹוא.)

9. *Hearing*—lit. *ears*—" Cast not your pearls before swine."

10. See ch. 22: 25. *Enter not*—do not invade or take possession of the orphan's field by enlarging the bounds of thy own, with a view to defraud him of his rightful possessions.

11. The *avenger* of the fatherless,—the vindicator and defender of their cause, is Jehovah. See ch. 22: 28. *Jehovah* is expressed in the Sept. and Arab.

---

11. " *Defend their cause*," French.

13. Withhold not correction from a child ;
For (*if*) thou chastise him with a rod, he will not die.
14. Chastise thou him with the rod,
And thou shalt deliver his soul from sheol.
15. My son, if thy heart be wise,
My heart, even mine, will rejoice.
16. Yea, my reins will exult,
When thy lips shall speak right things.
17. Let not thy heart envy sinners ;
But (*live thou*) in the fear of Jehovah all the day
long.
18. For surely there is a reward ;
And thy expectation shall not be cut off.
19. Hear thou, my son, and be wise ;
And guide thy heart in the (*right*) way.

13. If seasonable correction, tempered with discretion, be administered to a child for wrong doing, he will be likely to profit by
it, and thus escape the disgrace, misery and ruin consequent upon
an unsubdued will and a vicious course of life. See ch. 19: 18.
(תַכֶּנּוּ, Hiph. fut. of נָכָה.)

18. Ungodly men may enjoy temporary prosperity in this world,
as the fruit of their dishonesty, fraud, extortion, or other crimes;
but that is all which they will get; and this will soon terminate,
and be succeeded by a misery which will know no end. But for
those, who live in the fear of Jehovah,—who persevere in the path of
piety and virtue, whatever may be their present outward condition,
there is in reversion a sure, stable, enduring reward. It can hardly
be doubted that there is allusion in this verse to a *future* reward
consequent upon integrity and uprightness of conduct—a recompense in a future state and world.

19. *Way* is here put elliptically and emphatically either for the
" way of understanding" (see ch. 9: 6) or for the "right way."
The latter is preferable on account of its greater simplicity. There
is a similar expression in Terence: " Te oro, Dave, ut redeas jam in
viam." "I entreat you, Davius, to return now into the way;"—
where the limiting adj. "right" must be supplied to complete the
sense.

19

20. Be not among wine-bibbers ;—
Among those, who are prodigal of flesh for themselves.

21. For the drunkard and the glutton shall come to
poverty ;
And drowsiness shall clothe (*a man*) with rags.

22. Hearken to thy father, who begat thee ;
And despise not thy mother when she is old.

23. Buy the truth and sell it not ;
(*Yea buy*) wisdom, and instruction, and understanding.

24. The father of a righteous (*man*) shall greatly
rejoice ;
And he, who begetteth a wise (*child*), shall have joy
in him.

---

20. The full force of the expression *prodigal of flesh*, i. e. great
eaters, gluttons, cannot be felt except in a country like Palestine,
where animal food does not enter into the ordinary diet of the people, and where it is esteemed a great luxury, and as such is indulged in to excess, when it can be had. Comp. ch. 15: 17. *For
themselves*—i. e. for their own gratification. Some render the clause
" who are prodigal of their flesh," i. e. who are wasting their bodies
in sensual indulgence. But the connexion both here and in v. 21,
and Deut. 21: 20, would indicate that gluttons are intended.

22. *Despise not*—i. e. by figure litotes, pay to thy mother in her
venerable old age all that honor and respect which are her due.
Some commentators take the particle כִּי, *ki*, in a causal sense, and
render " because she is old," i. e. as if, on account of her advanced
age, she were incapable of giving suitable advice.

23. No sacrifice should be deemed too great for the attainment
of divine truth; for it is more valuable and precious than all other
acquisitions combined. And when attained, no allurements should
tempt us to part with it, or to deviate into the path which she forbids. Comp. ch. 4: 7–9.

24. (The textual reading should be pointed יָנוּל גִּיל, instead of
גּוֹל יָנִיל. But the Keri has גִּיל יָגִיל. Both forms are used, but the

---

25. Let thy father and thy mother be glad ;
Yea, let her, who bore thee, rejoice.
26. My son, give me thy heart.
And let thine eyes observe my ways.

latter is more common. יׁלֵד reads in the Keri וְיׁלֵד, which is right:
while the ו before יִשְׂמַח in the text is properly dropped in the Keri.)

26. Solomon would seem here to rise above himself, and to speak
in the name and person of Divine Wisdom. For no one but Jehovah
can claim the gift of the heart—the work of his own hands. *My
son*—" Such is the relationship which God acknowledges; including
every blessing which he can give, and all the obedience that he can
claim. No obedience can be without the believing and practical
acknowledgment of this filial relation. *My son*—not a stranger—
not an enemy—not a slave—but a son; invited to return. Many
are the claimants for the *heart*. Heaven and hell contend for it.
The world with its riches, honors and pleasures, and science with
its more plausible charms—cries, 'Give me thy heart.' Nay, even
Satan dares to put in a loud and urgent plea—'If thou wilt worship
me, all shall be thine.' The loving Father calls—'My son, give
me thy heart.' The answer too often is,—'I have no heart for God.
It is engaged to the world.' An honor indeed he puts upon his creatures, in condescending to receive as a *gift* what is his most rightful
debt, and what he might at any moment command for himself. But
his call wakens his child to recollection and conscious dependence.
It is the striving with his child's will. It is the test of his child's
obedience. Indeed happiness is bound up in this gracious command. For what else can fill the aching void within, but 'the love
of God shed abroad in the heart by the Holy Ghost.' Created objects only seem to widen the chasm. The heart, wilfully remaining
at a moral distance from God, can find its home only in a land of
illusive shadows. It grasps nothing solidly; while its incessant
conflict with conscience is 'the troubled sea, which cannot rest.'
God will not abate one atom of his full requisitions. He asks not
for magnificent temples, costly sacrifices, pompous ceremonials, but
for the spiritual worship of the heart. He demands—not the hands,
the feet, the tongue, the ears, but that which is the moving principle of all the members—*the heart* Give that:—it is all he desires.
Withhold it:—nothing is given." (Bridges.) (הֵנָה, Kal imperative
of רֵהַן. הַרְצֶנָה. The text should be pointed תִּרְצֶינָה=תִּרְצֶנָה,
Kal fut. of רָצָה, *to rejoice, to take pleasure.* So Symm. The Keri has

27. For a harlot is a deep ditch ;
And a strange woman, a narrow pit.

28. She also lieth in wait like a robber ;
And increaseth the transgressors among men.

29. Who hath woe? Who hath sorrow?
Who hath contentions? Who hath anxiety?
Who hath wounds without cause? Who hath red-
ness of eyes?

30. They who tarry long at the wine ;
They who go about to seek mixed wine.

31. Look not thou on the wine when it is red ;
When it sparkleth in the cup ;—
When it goeth down smoothly.

32. In the end it will bite like a serpent,
And sting like an adder.

33. Thine eyes will look on strange women,
And thy heart will utter perverse things.

34. Yea, thou shalt be as one, who lieth down in
the midst of the sea ;
As one, who lieth down on the top of a mast.

תִּצְרֶנָה, from נָצַר, *to observe.* So Sept. Arab. Chald. Syr. and Vulg.
Either makes good sense.)

30. *Mixed wine.* This expression undoubtedly here sig. *spiced,
drugged, medicated* wine, the intoxicating power of which is increased
by the infusion of drugs and spices. It was a common practice
with habitual drunkards to use wine of this description, but not of
the people generally. Comp. ch. 9: 2, where a different article is
intended by the phrase.

31. *Red wine* is said to be more esteemed in the East than white
wine. Some render the Hebrew word *turbid. When it sparkleth, &c.*
is literally, "When it gives its eye in the cup;"—figuratively, *spar-
kles, bubbles. Smoothly* is literally *evenly,* i. e. without roughness or
harshness. Vulg. *blande.* The property here alluded to is called
by wine drinkers *mellowness.* (תֵּרָא, Kal fut. apoc. of רָאָה. The
textual reading כִּים, *pure,* makes no sense. The Keri בְּכֹס, *cup,* is
undoubtedly the true reading.)

34. The drunkard is here represented as surrounded by danger,

35. " They smote me,—(*but*) I felt no pain ;
" They beat me,—(*but*) I knew it not;
" When I wake up, I will seek it again."

---

and yet insensible to his perilous situation; as a reckless mariner reposing in a frail bark in the midst of a rolling, tempestuous sea, (lit. in the heart of the sea); or as a sea-boy sleeping soundly in unconscious security at the mast-head in imminent peril of his life

35. The drunkard is here represented as soliloquising and employing language corresponding to his stupid and insensible condition. He declares that he felt not the ill usage and hard blows which he received in consequence of his intoxication; and then avows it as his fixed determination, instead of reforming, to resort again, as soon as he can sufficiently rouse himself, to the intoxicating cup.

CHAPTER XXIV. 1–22.

1. Be not thou envious of wicked men,
Nor desire to be with them.

2. For their heart studieth violence,
And their lips talk of mischief.

3. By wisdom is a house builded,
And by understanding it is established.

4. Yea, by knowledge shall the chambers be filled
With all precious and pleasant treasures.

5. A wise man is strong;
Yea, a man of knowledge increaseth strength.

6. For with wise counsel thou shalt make war for thyself;
And in the multitude of counsellors there is safety.

---

5. " Knowledge is power.", Comp. Eccles. 9: 14–16.

6. Comp. ch. 20: 18. *For thyself*—i. e. for thy own advantage—with success.

7. Wisdom is too high for a fool:
He openeth not his mouth at the gate.
8. He who deviseth to do evil,
Shall be called a mischievous person.
9. The thought of folly is sin;
And the scoffer is an abomination to men.
10. Dost thou faint in the day of adversity?
(*Let*) adversity (*give*) thee strength.

7. *At the gate.* He is incapable of advocating his own cause in a court of justice. (רָאכִית. The aleph is an epenthetic fulcrum— רָמֹות, from רוּם.)

9. *The thought of folly.*—The expression answers most probably to the phrase *evil thoughts* (διαλογισμοι πονηροι) in the New Test. (Matt. 15: 19. Mark 7: 21. James 2: 4.) *Sin*—i. e. sinful—abstract for concrete. Thoughts as well as actions possess a moral character, so far as they may be voluntary; and in a great many instances, a man is as accountable for his thoughts, as for his words and deeds. The thought is the source and spring of the act; therefore God regards it as the act, and holds us responsible for it.

10. *To faint* here denotes to be discouraged—to become disheartened. This precept is an exhortation to bear misfortunes and calamity with fortitude and equanimity. Adversity instead of depressing, should stimulate to renewed exertion and increased activity. The proverb corresponds to the Latin precept: "Ne cede malis, sed contra audentior ito." "Do not yield to evils, but, on the contrary, go on the more boldly." Some render the second member, "In the season of adversity put forth thy strength." "In the season of adversity there is the greatest necessity for showing strength of mind, and steady resolution, grounded, as they can only be with effect, upon the reverence and love of God." (French.) Gesenius regards צַר, *tzar*, in this place as an adjective instead of a noun, and renders the clause, "straightened will be thy strength," i. e. limited, small, feeble, as in our Eng. Vers. Stuart makes it a verb from צָרַר, *tzarar*, Kal perf. to the same purport. According to this interpretation, the aphorism is intended to teach that man has no trial of his moral strength—in other words, does not know his weakness—till he is brought into trouble.

10. '*Dost thou faint in the day of calamity?* *In calamity put forth thy strength.*" French.

· 11. Dost thou forbear to deliver (*those who are*) led away to death?

And (*those who are*) tottering to the slaughter?

12. Dost thou say, "Behold, we know not this (*man*)?"

Will not He who weigheth hearts, observe (*it*)?

Yea, He who keepeth thy soul, knoweth (*it*).

And He will render to (*every*) man according to his work.

13. (*As*) thou eatest honey, my son, because it is good;

And the droppings (*of the honey-comb*) because they are sweet to thy taste;

14. So (*let*) the knowledge of wisdom (*be*) to thy soul;

If thou find (*it*), then there shall be a (*future*) reward,

And thy expectation shall not be cut off.

---

11. When a criminal was anciently led to execution, a crier went before, who proclaimed the crime of which he had been convicted, and called upon any one who could say any thing in behalf of the condemned culprit, to come forward; in which case, he was led back to the tribunal, and the cause was re-heard. The passage contains an implied exhortation to assist the unfortunate, succor the distressed and vindicate the cause of the innocent, when about to suffer unjust punishment.

12. This verse is intimately connected with the preceding. The ignorance here professed with regard to the accused party, must be supposed to be in a great degree, voluntary and feigned—the evidence of criminal indifference to the cause of injured innocence.

13, 14. The 13th verse forms the protasis and the 14th the apodosis of the comparison. Hence the correlative *as* is supplied in the first to correspond with *so* expressed in the second. The verb אָכַל, *ekol*, in v. 13, is in the imperative mood, but it must evidently be understood in a permissive sense. *Droppings*—Comp. ch. 5: 3. *Taste*—literally *palate*. Comp. ch 23: 18, where the same phraseology occurs as in v. 14, and with the same signification; also ch. 24: 20.

15. Lie not in wait, O wicked (*man*) against the dwelling of the righteous ;
Nor despoil his resting-place.

16. For the righteous (*man*) may fall seven times,
Yet will he rise again ;
But the wicked shall be overwhelmed with evil.

17. Rejoice not when thy enemy falleth ;
And let not thy heart be glad, when he stumbleth.

18. Lest Jehovah see (*it*), and it displease him ;
And He turn away his anger from him.

19. Fret not thyself because of evil (*men*) ;
Nor be thou envious of the wicked.

20. For there shall be no (*future*) reward to the evil (*man*) ;
The lamp of the wicked shall be put out.

21. My son, fear Jehovah and the king ;
(*And*) associate not with those who are given to change.

22. For their calamity shall rise up suddenly,
And their ruin, (*proceeding*) from both, in a moment.

---

16. *Seven times*—i. e. frequently. The context shows that the reference here is not to moral lapses, but to outward misfortune. Comp. Ps. 34: 18. 37: 26.

18. Many commentators suppose an ellipsis of עָלֶיךָ, *aleka, to thee*, at the end of this verse. If this be correct, then the sense is, ' Lest Jehovah be displeased and turn away the calamities of thy enemy from him upon thee, in just punishment for thy hard heartedness.' So Bp. Coverdale. "Lest the Lord be angry and turn his wrath from him to thee."

21. By *those who are given to change* is intended disorganizers and disturbers of the peace of the community and of the church, who delight in political revolutions, social disorder and hurtful agitation, or in religious innovations, novelties and dissentions.

22. *From both*—viz. from Jehovah and the king. Literally, *the ruin* (or destruction) *of them both,—in a moment*—literally, *who knoweth?* as in Eng. Vers., i. e. who knows when or how it will come?

CHAPTER XXIV. 23–34.

[OTHER PROVERBS.]

23. These are (*the words*) of the wise:
It is not good to have respect of persons in judgment.

24. He who saith to the wicked (*man*), "Thou art righteous";
Him shall the people curse; nations shall abhor him.

25. But to those who rebuke (*him*) shall be delight;
And the blessing of the good shall come upon them.

26. (*Every man*) will kiss the lips (*of him*),
Who giveth a righteous sentence.

27. Prepare thy work without,
And make it ready in thy field;
Then afterwards thou mayest build thy house.

28. Be not a witness against thy neighbor without cause;
For wilt thou deceive with thy lips?

29. Say not, " I will do to him as he hath done to me:
" I will render to the man according to his work."

---

23. See ch. 18: 5. (הַכֵּר, Hiph. infin. of נָכַר.)

24. This verse is intimately connected with the preceding. In this, as in that, there is particular allusion to a judge who, influenced by unworthy and improper motives, pronounces an unjust decision in favor of the wicked, and acquits the guilty.

26. To *kiss the lips* is a phrase here used figuratively to express reverence and esteem—the kiss being a symbolical act denoting affection and respect.

27. Order is a primary law of nature. Before you commence to build a house, collect and prepare the necessary materials. Observe the same rule in respect to every undertaking.

29. Solomon again, as in ch. 20: 22, earnestly dissuades men from taking upon themselves to revenge their own wrongs.

30. I went by the field of the sluggard;
And by the vineyard of the man void of understanding.

31. And behold! it was all grown over with thorns;
Thistles covered the face of the ground;
And its stone-wall was broken down.

32. When I saw (*this*), I considered (*it*) well;
I looked on it, and received instruction.

33. " A little sleep; a little slumber;
" A little folding of the hands to rest."

34. So shall thy poverty come upon thee, (*like*) a
robber;
And thy want, as an armed man!

-----

30. The cultivation of the vine appears to have been, in the earliest times, very general in Palestine, and the grape furnished the
husbandman with his principal means of support. Hence a state
of material prosperity is described by every one dwelling "under
his own vine and fig tree." (1 Kgs. 4: 25.) And, on the other hand,
the miseries of famine are represented as the consequence of a failure of the grape and fig crop. (Jer. 8: 13.)

PART IV.

CHAPTER XXV.—XXIX.

[PROVERBS OF SOLOMON COLLECTED BY ORDER OF KING HEZEKIAH.]

CHAPTER XXV.

1. These are the proverbs of Solomon, which the men of Hezekiah, king of Judah, collected.

2. It is the glory of God to conceal a thing;
But the honor of kings is to search out a matter.

---

1. *The men of Hezekiah* are those whom Hezekiah appointed to make the collection of proverbs which follows. These are called in the Sept. the "friends" of Hezekiah. *Collected.*—The verb here employed (עתק, *athaq*,) may indicate that the persons in question *copied* or *transcribed* from some MSS. of Solomon proverbs which had not before been collated and published; or, that they collected and reduced to writing such proverbs as had been orally circulated before, and were ascribed to the king of Israel.

2. "The counsels, designs and operations of God are inscrutable, (Deut. 29: 29. Rom. 11: 33, 34,) and man can only adore with reverent humility that which is so far above his reach. It, therefore, redounds to the glory of God that his ways are inscrutable, and, as it were, concealed; but it is honorable for kings to search out vice, in order to punish it, virtue, in order to reward it, and truth, in order to promulgate it." (Holden.)   Comp. Isa. 45: 15.

3. (*As*) the heavens for height, and the earth for depth,
(*So*) is the heart of kings unsearchable.

4. Take away the dross from the silver,
And there will come forth a vessel for the refiner.

5. Take away the wicked from the presence of the king,
And his throne will be established in righteousness.

6. Display not thyself in the presence of the king,
And stand not in the place of great men.

7. For better is it that one should say to thee—
"Come up hither,"
Than that thou shouldst be put lower.
In the presence of the prince, whom thine eyes behold.

8. Go not forth hastily to contention.
Lest (*thou know not*) what to do in the end thereof.
When thy neighbor hath put thee to shame.

9. Plead thy cause with thy neighbor;
But reveal not the secrets of another.

10. Lest he, who heareth it, reproach thee,
And thy infamy depart not from thee.

11. (*As*) golden fruit in baskets of silver.
(*So*) is a word spoken at the proper time.

---

3. As in despotic governments the king is responsible to no one for his designs or acts, he need not communicate his intentions to others, either for counsel, sympathy, or support. If he chooses to keep his own secrets, he can do so with perfect impunity.

7. Comp. our Lord's parable, Lu. 14: 8–10. Matth. 23: 12. *That one*, i. e. that he, who has been deputed to arrange the guests at table, should say, &c.

11. Although the expression "apples of gold in pictures of silver," in our Eng. Vers. is very beautiful, the meaning conveyed by

6. "*Arrogate not honor*," Holden—"*honor not thyself*," Boothr.—"*affect not grandeur*," French.

11. "*A word fitly spoken in its season is like apples of gold in curiously wrought baskets of silver*," Holden—"*Like apples of gold among figures of silver*," Boothr., Noyes—"*among picture-work of silver*," Suart.

12. (*As*) an ear-ring of gold, and an ornament of fine gold,
  (*So*) is a wise reprover to an attentive ear.

it is not very clear. The Sept. renders the clause, "an apple of gold in a sardine (cornelian) collar." Vulg. "Apples of gold in beds of silver." Stuart supposes the comparison to refer to a garment of precious stuff, on which was embroidered golden apples among picture work of silver. It seems most probable that it refers to some kind of fruit resembling gold in its rich yellow color, just as we speak of the golden harvest. The fruit intended could hardly have been the *apple*, because the apples of the Levant are extremely poor, and uninviting both in their appearance and taste. It is different with the *orange*; but the climate of Palestine is not favorable to the cultivation of that delicious and beautiful fruit; and it is neither abundant, nor very good. That variety of lemon called *citron*, on the contrary, attains its highest perfection in that country, is very abundant and highly esteemed. This, according to the consentient testimony of Jewish writers and the probability of the case, is the fruit here intended, and always to be understood by the Hebrew word here translated in our Eng. Vers. "apple." As it is not entirely certain, however, that this is the specific article intended, I have preferred to employ a general term. By the Heb. word מַשְׂכִּיּוֹת, *mashphioth*, is here most probably intended ornamental baskets made of silver net-work, in which beautiful and delicious fruits were served up, particularly at royal banquets, and through the elegant texture of which the fruit was set off to the best advantage. The comparison teaches that an agreeable medium greatly enhances the attractiveness of truth: that appropriate words, uttered at a fitting time, are sure to be acceptable and effective. *The proper time*—i. e. seasonably, opportunely. The Margin reads, "upon his (its) wheels," i. e. with celerity, quickly. But אָפְנָיו, *aphunav*, would come more naturally as a segholate noun from אֹפֶן, *ophen*, *time*, *season*, than from אוֹפָן, *ophan*, *a wheel*, and it makes better sense. This rendering is supported also by the Vulg. Arabic and Symm. Comp. ch. 15: 13.

12. "So far from disliking the person who properly reproves him for his misconduct, a man of teachable and good disposition will esteem such an one as much as if he had presented him with any valuable ornament. (French.) See Ps. 141: 5.

13. (*As*) the cold of snow in the time of harvest,
(*So*) is a faithful messenger to those who send him;
For he refresheth the soul of his masters.

14. (*As*) clouds and wind without rain,
(*So*) is the man who boasteth of a deceitful gift.

15. By long forbearance is a prince appeased:
And a soft tongue breaketh the bone.

16. Hast thou found honey? eat (*only*) what is sufficient;
Lest thou be surfeited with it, and vomit it up.

13. Snow was used in ancient times where it could be had, as ice is among us, for cooling wines and other drinks during the summer season. The Greeks and Romans derived the custom from the Asiatics. Plutarch describes the manner in which they preserved the snow for this purpose, by covering it with straw and coarse cloths. They had their snow-houses, as we have our ice-houses. Snow was deemed preferable to ice, because it was thought that drinks cooled with snow were more agreeable and refreshing than those in which ice was put. Snow packed away in a mass consolidates into an ice colder and less easily melted than common ice. Mount Hermon was always covered with snow, and consequently furnished an abundant supply to the inhabitants of the adjacent country; whence it was frequently carried to Tyre. The promptness, fidelity and alacrity of the faithful messenger, affords to his employers, satisfaction and gratification, as the cooling properties of snow are grateful and refreshing in the hot season of the year.

14. Clouds and wind, when unaccompanied with refreshing showers, disappoint expectation. In like manner, he who promises to make valuable presents, and boasts of what he is going to do, but fails to fulfil his promises, disappoints the reasonable expectations of him to whom these promises are made. It is bad to promise and deceive: it is far worse to promise with the intention to deceive.

15. *Breaketh the bone* is a vivid image descriptive of the power which mildness, gentleness and forbearance have in overcoming obstinacy and allaying irritation of feeling. A bone is a hard substance; but hard as it is, a soft tongue—mild, persuasive language, has power to break it.

16. In ch. 24: 13, Solomon invites us to eat honey. Here, how-

17. Let thy foot be seldom in the house of thy neighbor;
Lest he become weary of thee, and (*then*) hate thee.

18. (*Like*) a war-club, and a sword, and a sharp-pointed arrow,
Is the man, who beareth false witness against his neighbor.

19. (*Like*) a broken tooth and a dislocated foot,
Is confidence in a perfidious man in the time of trouble.

20. (*As*) he, who taketh off a garment in cold weather;
(*And as*) vinegar (*poured*) upon natron,
(*So*) is he, who singeth songs to (*one of*) a heavy heart.

---

ever, he evidently designs to impose a restraint on the appetite,—only what is sufficient being opposed to an excessive and hurtful indulgence. This aphorism is doubtless intended to inculcate temperance and moderation in the enjoyment of earthly and sensuous pleasures of every kind. (הֲקֵאתוֹ, Hiph. preter. 2d per. with suffix קִיא.)

17, This rule illustrates some of our own proverbs, which have lost nothing of their significance by traditional usage,. "Too much of a good thing," "Familiarity breeds contempt," &c.

19. A broken tooth and dislocated foot produce pain, uneasiness, irritation and inconvenience. Similar effects result from misplaced confidence in a pretended but faithless friend.

20. *Natron*—or *soda*, Heb. נֶתֶר, *nether*, Sept. and Symm. νετρον, Vulg. *nitrum.* The Hebrew word occurs only twice in the Old Test. viz. here and in Jere. 2: 22, and in both places it is translated in our Eng. Vers. *nitre.* But the *natron, natrum, nitrum* or *nitre* of the ancients, was not the substance now denominated *nitre* or *saltpetre;* for this is a neutral salt (nitrate of potash) and hence will not effervesce with an acid, like vinegar. It was the native mineral alkali, (not the vegetable alkali, which is called *Borith* (בֹּרִית), *soap,* Jere. 2: 22. Matt. 3: 2.) denominated by chemists the *sesqui-carbonate of soda,* which violently effervesces when vinegar or any strong acid is poured upon it. It is found native in some parts of Syria and the

21. If thine enemy hunger, give him bread to eat ;
And if he thirst, give him water to drink.
22. For thou wilt heap coals of fire on his head ;
And Jehovah shall reward thee.

East, and especially in Egypt, from whence it is exported, and
serves, when mixed with oil, as soap to the present day in the East.
The meaning of the proverb is, that, as an acid poured upon an
alkaline substance, so is the singing of merry songs to one of a
heavy heart. It is untimely, inappropriate, incongruous, unsuitable, and so far from cheering, or soothing, it only irritates the mind
and wounds and disturbs the feelings of the afflicted person, thus
aggravating instead of relieving his grief. *Vinegar.*—This word
should here and elsewhere when it occurs in the Scriptures, be understood in its strictly etymological sense, of *sour wine*, (from the
French *vin, wine and aigre, sour,*) used by the poorer people of the
East as a common beverage.

21, 22. These verses, with the exception of the last clause in v.
22, are quoted verbatim by St. Paul from the Sept. version. (See
Rom. 12: 21. Comp. also Matt. 5: 43, 44.) Such a quotation by an
inspired Apostle, not only attests the divine inspiration and authority of this book, but clearly shows that the same rule of duty
as it regards the treatment which we are to manifest towards our
enemies, is found in both Testaments. The law of love is not set
forth more spiritually or comprehensively in any single precept of
our Saviour or his Apostles, than it is in this passage. There is
some difference of opinion among Commentators in regard to the
import of the figurative expression, "to heap coals of fire on the
head." That the idea of *pain* is involved in it, all are agreed. The
Oriental style which abounds in strong expressions, contains many
kindred forms of speech, in which this idea is prominent. Thus
the Arabians say, "he roasted my heart," or "he kindled a fire in
my heart," meaning that he inflicted pain. In Pirke Ar. the phrase
"coals of the wise," is equivalent to "cutting jests which give
pain." In 4 Ezra 16: 54, occurs the following passage, "Coals of
fire shall burn on the head of him, who denies that he has sinned
against God." But the question arises, is the pain caused by *shame*
and contrition for misconduct here intended ? Or is it the anguish
arising from the punishment incurred for misconduct? 1. Several
of the Greek fathers, and most of the early modern commentators,
regard the figure as employed in reference to the *burning, consum-*

23. (*As*) the north wind bringeth forth rain,
So a backbiting tongue, an angry countenance.

24. It is better to dwell in the corner of the house-
top,
Than with a contentious woman in a large house.

25. (*As*) cold water to a thirsty soul,
So is good news from a far country.

26. (*As*) a troubled fountain and a corrupted spring,
(*So*) is a righteous man falling down before the
wicked.

---

ing, *destructive* power of living coals, and view it as emblematical
of the punitive vengeance of God inflicted on the wicked. Such
is the import of the expression in Ps. 140: 10. Ezek. 10: 2. 4 Ezra
16: 54. According to this interpretation, the meaning of the proverb is, 'If, notwithstanding your kindness, your enemy perseveres
in his hatred and injurious treatment of you, you will by these acts
of kindness, greatly aggravate his just doom, while you will receive
the reward appropriate to your forgiving and benevolent disposition' 2. Nearly all the later commentators, however, regard the
language as an image, not of the consuming, but of the *melting*
power of coals. The metaphor is supposed to be taken from the
fusing of metals in a crucible by means of hot burning coals. According to this view, the meaning is, 'Thou shalt inflict upon him
a sensible pain, yet not to harm him, but to melt down and dissolve
his enmity—to fill him with a tormenting yet salutary sense of
shame, at his misconduct, and soften his hard heart to contrition
and kindness.' The latter interpretation is preferable, because most
consonant with the context both here and in Romans, and also with
the whole tenor of the Gospel.

23. *Bringeth forth.*—This is the marginal rendering of the verb,
and is required by the parallelism. It is also the rendering of all
the ancient versions except the Vulg. and Symm.; and of nearly all
modern commentators. The same verb is implied in the second
clause.

26. *A troubled fountain* is a fountain or cistern stirred up, and
rendered feculent, turbid and unfit for use. Such a spring or body
of water disappoints the expectations of the thirsty traveller, and
fills him with grief. So it is a disappointment and grief to the
pious man to witness the virtuous and good oppressed or ruined by
the unprincipled and corrupt.

20*

27. (*As*) it is not good to eat much honey,
(*So*) the searching after one's own glory is wearisome.

28. A man who (*hath*) no rule over his own·spirit,
Is (*like*) a city that is broken down and without walls.

27. See v. 16. Honey was far more important as an article of
food formerly than it is at present. Then there was no sugar manufactured, and consequently honey was extensively used in the
place of it. The noun כָּבוֹד, *kabod,* here occurs in the same connexion in two different senses by figure antanaclasis, as in ch. 14:
24; first in the sense of *glory, honor;* and then adjectively in the
sense of *weighty, burdensome, wearisome,* (from כָּבֵד, *kabed, to be
weighty, troublesome, wearisome, burdensome.*) An imperfect imitation
of the line in English so as to preserve the assonance would be,
"The search of weighty things is weighty,"—the term *weighty* being taken in the first case in the sense of *important,* and in the sec
ond, in the sense of *heavy, burdensome, wearisome.* So Bp. Coverdale: "Like as it is not good to eat much honey, even so he that
will search out high things, it shall be too heavy for him." *One's
own glory*—literally, *their own glory,* i. e. honor, reputation.

28. Self-government is the most important and at the same time
the most difficult to be acquired, of all governments. "The man
who has no command over his passions, especially over his anger,
lies open to the assault of every invader; any one may exasperate
and torment him, and rob him of his comfort, his peace, and his
reason at pleasure; every temptation seduces him into sin; and the
most trifling concerns involve him in the most serious contests."
(Scott.)

27. " *But to search their own glory is glorious,*" Holden—" *So the contempt of honor
is from honor,*" Boothr.

CHAPTER XXVI.

1. As snow in summer, and as rain in harvest,
So honor is not becoming to a fool.

1. Rain in Palestine is confined principally to the autumnal and

2. As the sparrow in wandering, as the swallow 'in flying,
So a curse (*uttered*) without cause, shall not come.

3. A whip for the horse, a bridle for the ass,
And a rod for the back of fools.

4. Answer not a fool according to his folly;
Lest thou also become like him.

5. Answer a fool according to his folly;
Lest he become wise in his own eyes.

---

winter months. It rarely falls in harvest time, when it is regarded as not only unseasonable, but as exceedingly inconvenient and injurious, since it interrupts the labors of the reaper and damages the crop. So it is unsuitable and out of place to bestow that respect and honor which are justly due to the wise and good, upon one who by his folly or his wickedness, or both combined, shows that he is entirely unworthy of them. Comp. v. 8.

2. As the sparrow and the swallow in their rapid flight quickly disappear, so is it with a causeless curse. Pronounced without reason, it will fail to take effect; it will not hit the mark; it will not reach the injured party, but pass swiftly away without leaving a trace behind. (Instead of לֹא, *not*, the Keri reads לוֹ, "shall come upon him," viz. upon the fool who utters it. But the textual reading suits the comparison much better.)

3. A rod is as appropriate for the correction of fools, as a whip is for the horse or a bridle for the ass. Comp. ch. 10: 13. 19: 29, see Ps. 32: 9.

4, 5. The opposite directions given in these two precepts are supposed by some commentators to indicate the course which a man should pursue towards the same individual at different times and under different circumstances. Thus: ' Answer not a fool, &c., when he is in a passion, cr intoxicated with liquor; for in that case, you will be guilty of the folly of "casting pearls before swine." But answer a fool, &c., when he is calm and sober, and in a proper state of mind to be benefitted by what you say to him, then is the time to convince him of the folly and impropriety of his conduct.' But the majority of interpreters adopt a more probable and satisfactory mode of reconciling the apparently conflicting proverbs. They interpret the phrase *according to* in different senses. In ver. 4, the Hebrew particle *Kaph* is understood to denote *similitude*. Answer

6. He, who sendeth a message by the hand of a fool,
Cutteth off the feet, and drinketh damage.

7. (*As*) the legs of a lame (*man*) are weak,
So is a proverb in the mouth of fools.

8. As the binding of a stone in a sling;
So is he, who giveth honor to a fool.

---

not a fool *in the manner* of his folly, i. e. with folly similar to his,
by saying silly or passionate or scurrilous things, as he does; for
this would but convert a wise man into a fool. "If a fool boast of
himself, do not answer him by boasting of thyself. If he rail and
talk passionately, do not thou rail and talk passionately too. If he
tell one great lie, do not thou tell another to match it. If he calum
niate thy friend, do not answer him in his own language, lest thou
be like him." (Henry.) In ver. 5, the same particle is understood
to denote *fitness* and *propriety*. 'Answer a fool in the manner which
his folly deserves and demands,' so as to expose it, and convince
the author of it, that he may be profited by the rebuke.

. 6. He who sends a message to another by a fool, so far as any
benefit may be expected from it, does the same as if he were to cut
off the messenger's feet; and besides, in consequence of his impru-
dence in employing an incompetent and untrustworthy person, he
suffers positive damage by having his message delayed, misappre-
hended or perverted. The phrase to *drink damage*, sig. metaphori-
cally to *suffer injury*. Gesenius renders the verse thus: "He cutteth
off (his own) feet; he drinketh damage, who sendeth a message by
the hand of a fool." So Dr. Scott: "He who employs an ignorant
and worthless man in any important business, as it were, cuts off
his own feet, puts himself to much pain, disables himself, and re-
tards his affairs; and he can expect nothing but disappointment,
vexation, and damage in abundance, as the recompense of his folly."

7. (דַּלְיוּ, Kal perf. of דָּלַל, probably put for דָּלְלוּ=. It might
as to form be more easily made from דָּלָה, Piel. But the signification is that of Kal, and properly belongs there, unless we suppose
the Piel to be used in the same sense.)

. 8. To bind a stone to a sling, and then expect it to do execution,
would be preposterous in the extreme. Not less so is it to confer
honor on a fool, and expect good to result from it, either to him, or

8. "*Like the putting into a purse a stone of the heap*," French—'*As he who puts a
purse of gems upon a heap of stones*," Noyes.

9. (*As*) a thorn branch taken up by the hand of a drunkard,
So is a proverb in the mouth of fools.

10. (*As*) an arrow that woundeth every one,
(*So*) is he, who hireth a fool, and he who hireth way-farers.

11. As a dog returneth to his vomit,
(*So*) a fool repeateth his folly.

---

to any one else. The marginal reading, " putteth a precious stone in a heap of stones," is preferred by several commentators. According to this rendering the meaning would be, that the value of honor bestowed on a fool is lost, like a precious stone covered up in a promiscuous heap of rubbish. The rendering in the text is supported by the Sept. and Syr.

9. A thorn-branch in the hand of a drunkard is sure to inflict injury on him, and may probably do harm to others; so a fool's words will be very apt to injure both himself and others.

10. The Hebrew text of this verse is uncertain, and the meaning of nearly every word is doubtful. The words רַב, *rab*, מְחוֹלֵל, *mecholel*, and שֹׂכֵר, *soker*, have various significations, and neither the context nor the construction clearly indicates their import in this place. The word רַב, *rab*, properly signifies *much, many*; then, *large, great*, from which comes the substantive meaning, *chief, master*. These are its ordinary significations. But in Job 16: 3, the plural רַבָּיו, *rabbiv*, is rendered by all the ancient versions, "his (God's) arrows," from the secondary meaning of the verb רָבַב, *ra bab, to shoot*. That signification is appropriate here, and it is accordingly so rendered by Stuart. The import of the proverb appears to be, that a man, in transacting any important business, should employ those to assist him, who are known to be capable and well acquainted with it, and not unknown, ignorant, incompetent and irresponsible persons. The employment of the latter is like an arrow which, if poisoned, may seriously wound those who handle it, as well as those against whom it is sent.

11. As a dog repeatedly eats the filthy food which produces

---

10. "*The great God that formed all things, both rewardeth the fool, and rewardeth the transgressors*," E. V., Holden " *A great man terrifieth every one when he hireth fools—when he hireth transgressors*," French—" *A master brings every thing to pass; but i e who hires fools hires way-fairers*," Noyes.

12. Seest thou a man wise in his own eyes?
There is more hope of a fool than of him.

13. The sluggard saith, "There is a lion in the way;
"There is a lion in the street."

14. (*As*) the door turneth upon its hinge,
So (*doth*) the sluggard, upon his bed.

15. The sluggard hideth his hand in the dish;
It is wearisome to him to raise it to his mouth.

16. The sluggard is wiser in his own eyes,
Than seven men, who can render a reason.

17. (*As*) he, who layeth hold on the ears of a dog,
(*So*) is he, who, passing by, becomes engaged in a
quarrel not his own.

18. As one, who feigneth himself mad,—
Who casteth about darts, arrows, and death;

---

loathing and vomiting, so the fool repeats his nonsense.   Comp.
2 Pet. 2: 22.

14. Doors anciently turned upon vertical pivots,—hinges not
being then in use, nor are they used in Syria at the present day.
As the door moves *on* but not *from* its hinge or pivot, so the sluggard
moves *on* but not *from* his bed.   He lies on one side till he is weary
of that, and then turns to the other, but still is in his bed.   (תִכּוֹב,
Kal fut. of כָּבַב, Chaldee form.)

16. The sluggard can offer more plausible arguments to justify
his disgraceful conduct, than many wise and good men can present
in favor of a correct course of action.   There is a lion in the streets;
it is too hot or too cold; too wet or too dry; too early or too late;
time enough yet, or the opportunity has passed by: and so on *ad in-
finitum*.   The number *seven* is equivalent to *many*—a definite being
put for an indefinite number.

17. The irritable and savage disposition of the dog is the foundation of this beautiful proverb.   He who seizes a dog by the ears,
voluntarily and unnecessarily exposes himself to personal injury.
Dogs in the East are very wild and ferocious.   He who, a mere
passer by and uninterested spectator, warmly eng
with which he has no particular concern, will hav
of his folly.

19. So is the man, who deceiveth his neighbor.
And saith, "Am I not in sport?"

20. Where there is no wood, the fire goeth out;
So where there is no tale-bearer, contention ceaseth.

21. As a coal to burning coals, and wood to fire,
So is a contentious man for kindling strife.

22. The words of a tale-bearer are like dainties;
And they go down to the chambers of the body.

23. (*As*) drossy silver, spread over an earthen vessel,
(*So*) are warm lips with an evil heart.

24. He, who hateth, dissembleth with his lips;
And layeth up deceit within him.

25. When he speaketh fair, trust him not;
For seven abominations are in his heart.

26. (*His*) hatred is covered by deceit;
(*But*) his wickedness shall be disclosed before the
congregation.

27. He, who diggeth a pit, shall fall therein;
And he, who rolleth a stone, it will return upon him.

28. A lying tongue hateth (*those, who have been*)
crushed by it;
And a flattering mouth worketh ruin.

---

22. See ch. 18: 8. 20: 30.

23. An earthen vessel covered over or glazed with drossy silver
is made to appear valuable, while it is really worthless. So ardent
lips, giving warm kisses, that seem to indicate much affection, if
connected with disguised indifference or aversion, are worthless.

24. A secret enemy often endeavors to deceive him whom he hates,
by practising the grossest dissimulation, and professing great friendship.

28. "Proprium humani ingenii est, odisse quos læseris." *Tacitus.*
"It is common for men to hate those whom they have injured," because
the injurious person is conscious of having done a wrong which he
is unwilling to confess, and for which he knows that he has justly
incurred the displeasure and enmity of the injured party. This
adage is applicable not only to sins of the tongue, but to other offences likewise. Sept. "A lying tongue hateth truth." Some render the adj. דַּךְ, *dak*, transitively:—"a lying tongue hateth those
who chastise it."

CHAPTER XXVII.

1. Boast not thyself of to-morrow.;
For thou knowest not what a day may bring forth.
2. Let another praise thee, and not thy own mouth ;
A stranger, and not thy own lips.
3. Stone is heavy and sand weighty ;
But the wrath of a fool is heavier than both of them.
4. Wrath is cruel, and anger impetuous ;
But who is able to stand before jealousy ?

---

1. Events are figuratively described as brought forth from the womb of time. See James 4: 13, 14. "Quid sit futurum cras, fuge quærere." "Avoid inquiring what may happen to-morrow." All attempts to pry into the future are as fruitless as they are foolish. Improve the present hour, which is all you can call your own.

2. "Praise," says Jermer, "is a comely garment But though thou dost thyself wear it, another must put it on, or else it will never sit well about thee. Praise is sweet music; but it is never tuneable in thy own mouth. If it cometh from the mouth of another, it soundeth most tuneable in the ears of all that hear it. Praise is a rich treasure; but it will never make thee rich, unless another tell the same."

3. "Ira furor brevis est animorum; rege, qui, nisi paret,
     Imperat, hunc frænis; hunc tu compisce catena." *Horace.*
"Anger is a brief fury of mind; govern that with reins, which unless it obeys, rules; do you confine it with chains." The word *heavy* is here employed first in a literal and then in a moral sense; by the figure antanaclasis, as in Matt. 8: 22, ."Let the dead bury their dead."

4. The primary and common signification of קִנְאָה, *qira*, is *jealousy*, and it is so rendered twenty-five times in our Eng. Version. See also ch. 6: 29, and the margin in this place. In some places, however, it expresses more exactly the notion of *envy*, which is indeed the same passion as jealousy, though the object and occasion are different. (See ch. 14: 30. Eccles. 9: 6.) If that be the meaning here, then the following story related by Rabbi Levi, will illustrate the text. To two persons " a certain king promised to grant whatever they should ask, and double to him who asked last. The cov-

5. Better is open reproof,
Than love kept concealed.

6. Faithful are the wounds of a friend;
But the kisses of an enemy are deceitful.

7. The full soul loathes the droppings (*of the honey-comb*);
But to the hungry soul every bitter thing is sweet.

8. As a bird, that wandereth from her nest,
So is a man, that wandereth from his place.

9. (*As*) oil and perfume rejoice the heart,
So (*doth*) the sweetness of one's friend (*which springs*)
from the counsel of the soul.

etous man would not ask first, because he hoped for the double portion; nor would the envious, that he might not benefit the other. But at length he requested that *one* of his eyes might be taken out, in order to deprive his companion of *both*."

7. *Soul* is put for person by synecdoche. For *droppings, &c.*, see ch. 24: 13. "The pampered glutton loathes even luxurious food; but he who is really hungry, will eat even indifferent food with a high relish."

8 The bird that forsakes its nest, leaves the place where it has found shelter, warmth, repose, and safety; and exposes itself to hardship and dangers. So every man has his proper place in society, in which he may be comfortable, respected and useful. But when from discontent with his situation, from love of change, from an inordinate and misguided ambition, or allured by some visionary prospect of advantage, a man abandons his accustomed occupation and home and friends, he is very likely to exchange imaginary for real disquietudes, and to fall into temptation and a snare, destructive to his usefulness, comfort and happiness, and perhaps to his innocence.

9. Oil and perfumes were formerly, and are still very much used in the East, where a dry atmosphere and enervating climate render the emollient nature of the one, and the gentle stimulus of the other, exceedingly grateful, refreshing and invigorating. So is the sweetness, tenderness or comity of one's friend, which springs from sincere regard.

9. "*So agreeable is the counsel of a person to a friend,*" Durell; Boothr.—"*But the sweetness of a friend is above scented wood,*" French—"*Sweet, too, is a man's friend by hearty counsel,*" Noyes.

10. Thy own friend, and thy father's friend forsake
not ;
Into the house of thy brother enter not in the day
of thy calamity ;
Better is a friend near, than a brother far off.

11. Be wise, my son, and make my heart glad ;
That I may give an answer to him who reproacheth
me.

12. The prudent (*man*) seeth the evil, and hideth
himself ;
But the simple pass on and are punished.

13. Take his garment, who is surety for a stranger ;
Yea, take a pledge from him, who is bound for
strangers.

14. He, who, rising early, with a loud voice blesseth a friend,
To him it shall be accounted a curse. -

15. A continual dropping on a rainy day,
And a contentious woman are alike.

---

10. In adversity the ties of consanguinity are not always to be
depended upon. It is only long-tried friends who can be confidently relied upon in such circumstances. Distance is apt to produce indifference even among relations. Hence a true friend near
at hand is more available and beneficial than a brother far away.

11. *Reproacheth me*—viz. with want of care for my child on account of his unworthy conduct.

13. *Strangers.* The plural is the reading of several MSS. and
is supported by the Sept. and Vulg. Comp. ch. 20: 16.

14. Extravagant and ill-timed praise and flattery are calculated
to awaken the suspicion of insincerity and hypocrisy. The fawn-
ing sycophant, from his very vehemence and apparent earnestness,
will be suspected of being actuated by sinister and selfish motives.
There is an Italian proverb, " He who praises you more than he is
wont to do, either *has* deceived you, or is *about* to do it."

15. "Such rains as we have had," says Dr. Thompson, " thoroughly soak through the flat earthen roofs of these mountain houses,
and the water descends in numberless leaks all over the room. This
continual dropping—tuk, tuk—all day and all night, is the most

16. He, who can restrain her, may restrain the
wind,

And (*conceal*) the oil on his right hand (*which*) proclaimeth (*itself*).

17. (*As*) iron sharpeneth iron,

So a man sharpeneth the countenance of his friend.

18. (*As*) he, who keepeth the fig-tree, shall eat the
fruit thereof;

(*So*) he, who regardeth his master, shall be honored.

19. As in water face (*answereth*) to face;

So (*doth*) the heart of man to man.

---

annoying thing in the world, unless it be the ceaseless clatter of a
contentious woman."   (נִשְׁתָּוָה, Nithpael part. of שָׁוָה.)

16. By *oil* in the text is intended *fragrant oil*, which makes its
presence known by its agreeable odor.

17. As iron is polished and sharpened by the friction of iron, so
a man by agreeable and instructive conversation and cheerful social
intercourse, exhilerates the spirits of his friend, enlivens his countenance, and quickens and invigorates his mental faculties. The
proverb is illustrative of the enlivening and improving influence of
friendly and intelligent society.   (יָחַד is regarded by Gesenius as
the Kal fut. of חָדַד, put for יֵחַד, and יֵחַד, in the second clause as
the Hiph. fut. of the same verb formed after the Chaldee manner for
יְחַד.   Others, however, suppose a root חָדָה, with the same signification, and both words in the Hiph. fut. apoc. the kamets in the
first being inserted merely on account of the Athnach.)

18. The cultivation of the fig-tree in Palestine was a profitable
labor, and the fruit was regarded as of great value and importance.
Proper attention to it therefore fitly illustrates the general reward of
fidelity in the relations of life.

19. As there is an exact resemblance and correspondence between
the face of a man and its reflected image in water, so there is a resemblance between one man's heart and another's. The same physical, intellectual, moral and emotional nature is possessed by both

---

16. "*He that hideth her hideth the wind*," E. V., Holden—"*He that would hide
her, may as soon hide the wind*," Boothr.="*Or the right-hand ointment, which discovers itself*," Boothr.—"*And conceal the fragrant oil, which is upon his right hand*,"
French—"*And his right hand cometh upon oil*," Stuart.

20. Sheol and destruction are never satisfied ;
So the eyes of man are never satisfied.

21. (*As*) the crucible for silver, and the furnace for
gold ;
So is a man (*proved*) by the praise bestowed upon
him.

22. If thou shouldst beat a fool in a mortar,
In the midst of crushed wheat, with a pestle ;
His foolishness will not depart from him.

23. Be diligent to know the state of thy flock ;
And look well to thy herds.

24. For riches (*will*) not (*continue*) forever ;
Not even a crown (*endureth*) from generation to
generation.

25. The grass appeareth, and the tender herbage
showeth itself ;
And the herbs of the mountains are gathered.

---

in common; the same appetites, passions, desires, hopes, fears, affections and sympathies exist in all, and the same infirmities, pre-
disposition and liability to sin are found in all. Hence we may
often rightly judge others by ourselves, and ourselves by others.
"A man," says Lord Bacon, "may see *himself* while he looks upon
other men, as well as *know* other men, by considering his own inclinations." Water poured into a vessel is the only looking-glass
in use among many Eastern nations to this day. Castellio and
others translate the couplet thus: "As water represents the face to
the face; so does the heart, the man to the man," i. e. a man's heart
discloses to himself his own moral character, as the water by reflection represents accurately his face.

20. Insatiableness is here and in ch. 30: 16, described as characteristic of sheol—the invisible world personified. Comp. Isa. 5:
14. (Instead of the textual reading אֲבֵדָה, the Keri has אֲבַדּוֹן, as
in ch. 15: 11.)

21. A crucible or refining pot will bring out the pure silver, and
a furnace, the pure gold. In like manner the effect produced by
praise upon a man is to develope his real character.

23–27. The design of the writer in these verses is to encourage
strict attention to business, first, on the ground that the wealth we

26. The lambs are for clothing,
And the goats are the price of thy field;

27. Yea, (*there will be*) goat's milk enough for thy food,
For the food of thy household,
And (*for*) the sustenance of thy maidens.

---

may possess we hold by an uncertain tenure, and we may be deprived of it, and left in a state of destitution at a time of life when riches are most necessary to our comfort; secondly, because diligence in our vocation will insure an ample remuneration. The illustration is drawn, as we might expect, from pastoral life, since the Hebrews were chiefly employed in agricultural and pastoral occupations. The small cattle of the Hebrews consisted of *sheep* and *goats*, which usually pastured together. Hence the Hebrew noun צֹאן, *tzon*, often includes both. Goats were formerly, as they are still, highly esteemed in the East, particularly for their milk. This is sweet and of an agreeable flavor, and forms a large part of the diet of the people in that part of the world; though cow's milk is also used during a portion of the year.

CHAPTER XXVIII.

1. The wicked flee when no one pursueth;
But the righteous are bold as a lion.

2. Because of the rebellion of a land, many are its rulers;
But by a man of understanding (*and*) knowledge (*its*) stability shall be prolonged.

---

1. Fear makes men cowards; but conscious rectitude inspires confidence and courage. Fearless as the king of the forest, the righteous dare to do anything but offend God. The fear of him drowns every other fear. The boldness and courage of the lion in facing his enemy are proverbial.

2. The generic signification of פֶּשַׁע, *pesha*, is *transgression* of law, *sin*, *trespass*. The specific meaning in this place, as the context

21*

3. A poor man who oppresseth the needy,
Is (*like*) a sweeping rain, which leaveth no food.

4. Those, who forsake the law, praise the wicked ;
But such as keep the law, contend with them.

5. Evil men understand not justice ;
But those, who seek Jehovah, understand every
(*thing*).

6. Better is the poor (*man*), who walketh in his uprightness ;
Than (*he, who*) is perverse (*in his*) ways, though he
(*be*) rich.

7. He, who keepeth the law, is a wise son ;
But he, who delighteth in prodigals, shameth his
father.

---

shows, is *rebellion.* When a people rebel against the constituted
authority of the country, and set at defiance its law, they generally
become victims to the tyranny of many rulers, who rob and plunder them for the accomplishment of their ambitious ends. Whereas
under the administration of a wise, intelligent and virtuous prince,
whose character is revered, and whose authority is respected, the
integrity of a nation is preserved, and its stability and prosperity
established and perpetuated. The Arabs have a current anecdote
of a wise man, who used this imprecation upon his enemies, " May
God multiply your sheiks,"—a fearful malediction.

3. By a *poor man* is here supposed to be intended a ruler, raised
from a condition of poverty and obscurity to one of power and authority. Such a person, instead of sympathising with the poor, as
we should naturally expect, is very apt to abuse his power by becoming overbearing, insolent, and oppressive toward them. Just as
a sweeping rain, instead of fertilizing the ground, causes the destruction of the crops. In Eastern countries obscure men are often
raised to a position of eminence and power, and not unfrequently
avail themselves of the opportunity thus afforded to rob without
mercy the industrious poor of the fruits of their labor.

5. *Every thing*—i. e. every thing pertaining to justice and equity.
The universal term should be limited by the subject. So πανÏα,
in Jas. 2: 20.

8. He, who increaseth his wealth by usurious gain,
Gathereth it for him, who is kind to the poor.

9. He, who turneth away his ear from hearing the
law ;
Even his prayer (*will be*) an abomination.

10. He, who causeth the righteous to go astray in
an evil way ;
Shall himself fall into his own pit ;
But the upright shall inherit good.

11. The rich man is wise in his own eyes,
But the poor (*man*) possessed of understanding,
searcheth him out.

12. When the righteous rejoice, there is great glory ;
But when the wicked rise, men hide themselves.

13. He, who covereth his sins, shall not prosper ;
But he, who confesseth and forsaketh them, shall
find mercy.

14. Happy is the man who feareth always ;
But he, who hardeneth his heart, shall fall into mischief.

---

8. *Usurious gain.*—The two words נֶשֶׁךְ, *neshek*, and תַּרְבִּית, *tir-
bith*, signify *interest* for money loaned. When the two are used in
connexion as here, they are either employed in an intensive sense
and import *interest*, or else by Hendiadys, the one performs the office
of a modifying adjective to the other, as in the version. See ch.
13: 22. Lev. 25: 35–37, Job 27: 17.

12. When the righteous rejoice in the possession of power and
influence, which they may exercise for the benefit of the community,
then the dignity and honor of the state are maintained, and prosperity abounds. But when the wicked rise to power, good men re-
tire from public life, either from disgust or from regard to their per
sonal comfort or safety. See v. 28.

. " When vice prevails, and impious men bear rule,
" The post of honor is a private station."—*Cato.*

13. *Covereth*—i. e. either conceals his sins from observation or
extenuates them, and persists in the commission of them. Comp.
Ps. 32: 3–5. " Concealment of sin exempts not men from punishment by a Being who knows all things; confession and repentance
are indispensible to the obtaining of mercy." (Stuart.)

15. (*As*) a roaring lion, and a hungry bear;
(*So*) is a wicked ruler over a needy people.

16. A prince void of understanding, is a great oppressor;
But he, who hateth extortion, shall prolong (*his*) days.

17. A man oppressed with life's blood,
Will flee to the pit, that he may not be taken.

18. He, who walketh uprightly, shall be safe;
But (*he, who*) is perverse in (*his*) ways, shall fall at once.

19. He, who tilleth his land, shall have bread enough;
But he, who followeth after vain (*persons*), shall have poverty enough.

20. A faithful man aboundeth in blessings;
But he, who hasteneth to be rich, shall not go unpunished.

21. To have respect of persons is not good;
Even for a piece of bread that man will transgress.

---

17. *Oppressed with life's blood*—i. e. with the guilt of having shed human blood. *Pit*—i. e. the grave. He will rush on to self-destruction rather than fall into the hands of the avenger of blood.

18. The path of integrity and uprightness is ever the path of safety, as well as of peace. *At once*—i. e. suddenly, unexpectedly, and irrecoverably.

19. This couplet literally rendered reads thus: "He who tilleth his land shall be *satisfied* with bread; but he who followeth vain (persons) shall be *satisfied* with poverty." Comp. ch. 12: 11. The assonance is preserved in the translation we have given, after Noyes.

20. *Faithful man*—i. e. a man faithful to his promises and obligations—faithful to the trusts confided to him and in all the relations of life. *Hasteneth to be rich*—viz. by dishonesty, fraud, violence or oppression, instead of steady industry and fidelity. "No one who is just ever becomes rich quickly," says Mariander.

21. Comp. ch. 18: 5. Ezek. 13: 19.

22. A man of an evil eye, hasteneth to be rich,
And considereth not that poverty shall come upon him.

23. He, who reproveth a man, will afterwards find more favor,
Than he, who flattereth with his tongue.

24. He, who stealeth from his father or his mother,
And saith ' It is no harm !'
Is a (*fit*) companion for a robber.

25. He, who is of a haughty spirit, stirreth up contention ;
But he, who trusteth in Jehovah, shall have abundance.

26. He, who trusteth in his own heart, is a fool ;
But he, who walketh wisely, shall be delivered.

27. He, who giveth to the poor, shall not want ;
But he, who hideth his eyes, shall have many curses.

28. When the wicked rise, men hide themselves ;
But when they perish, the righteous increase.

---

27. *Hideth his eyes*—i. e. turns away from distress and poverty, and refuses to bestow relief. Comp. ch. 11: 25.

CHAPTER XXIX.

1. A man who, being often reproved, hardeneth (*his*) neck,
Shall suddenly be destroyed, and that without remedy.

---

1. *A man—reproved*—lit. *a man of reproofs,*—plural intensive. Comp. Isa. 53: 3. *To harden* or make stiff, *the neck*, is to be perverse, self-willed, refractory, obstinate and contumacious The metaphor is taken from stubborn and refractory bullocks, who do not submit quietly to the yoke.

2. When the righteous increase, the people rejoice;
But when a wicked (*man*) beareth rule, the people
mourn.

3. The man, who loveth wisdom, rejoiceth his father;
But he, who delighteth in harlots, spendeth (*his*)
wealth.

4. A king by justice establisheth the land;
But a man, who (*receiveth*) gifts, overthroweth it.

5. A man, who flattereth his neighbor,
Spreadeth a net for his feet.

6. In the transgression of a wicked man there is a
snare;
But the righteous shall sing and rejoice.

7. A righteous (*man*) considereth the cause of the
poor;
But the wicked will not understand knowledge.

8. Scóffers kindle a city into a flame;
But wise (*men*) turn away wrath:

9. (*When*) a wise man contendeth with a fool;
Whether he be angry or laugh, (*there will be*) no
rest.

---

2. See ch. 28: 28. (יֵאָנַח, Niph. fut. reflexive—*bemoan themselves.*
Instead of the singular רָשָׁע, several MSS. and all the versions read
רְשָׁעִים, plural.)

4. *Who receiveth gifts*—lit. *a man of gifts*, i. e. who loves gifts,
and gladly accepts them as bribes for partiality and injustice. Such
a ruler will soon ruin his country.

7. This proverb doubtless has special reference to judicial proceedings. An upright judge considers the cause of the poor, sees
that his case is properly heard and justice administered to him; but
a wicked judge will not take the trouble to become acquainted with
the merits of a poor man's case; for he cares not whether justice is
done him or not.

9. The second memb   his proverb is ambiguous. The subject of the proposition i   oe either the *wise man*, or the *fool*. If

---

2. "*Are in authority.*" E. V., Boothr., Holden, Noyes.

10. Blood-thirsty men hate the upright (*man*) ;
But the righteous seek (*to preserve*) his life.

11. A fool uttereth all his mind ;
But a wise (*man*) keepeth it back.

12. If a ruler hearkeneth to false reports,
All his servants (*will be*) wicked.

13. The poor (*man*) and the oppressor meet together ;
Jehovah enlighteneth the eyes of them both.

---

the former, then the sense is, When a wise man contends or disputes with a fool, whether he takes a serious or jocular way of dealing with him; whether he be severe or pleasant, there will be no
end of the controversy; the fool will go on answering, objecting,
excusing, &c., and persist in having the last word. If the latter be
the subject, then the sense is, When a wise man contends with a
fool, the latter will at one time be moved with rage, at another, with
scornful laughter; but there will be no cessation of his contention.

10. The expression *to seek the life* of any one, is commonly employed in a bad sense in the Old Test., as signifying *to endeavor to
destroy the life*. But there is very little doubt that it is here employed in a good sense; and to avoid the *equivoque*, the verb *to preserve* is supplied. Comp. Ps· 142: 5.

11. The word רוּחַ, *ruach, mind, spirit*, may here be employed to
denote the seat of the affections and passions—the emotional rather
than the intellectual part of man, as in ch. 25: 28, and be put specifically for *anger*. Accordingly some translate the verse, " A fool
lets out (or displays) all his anger; but a wise man restrains it,"—
i. e. keeps his anger within proper bounds.

12. " As the judge of the people is himself, so are his officers;
and what manner of man the ruler of the city is, such are all that
dwell therein." Ecclus. 10: 2.

13. Parallel passage, ch. 22: 2. Comp. also ch. 14: 31. James 2:
6. By *enlightening the eyes* is meant making them sparkle with life
and intelligence. Jehovah is the common father and benefactor of
all. "He makes his sun to rise on the evil and on the good." (Matt.
5: 45.) Both are equally dependent on him, and both are under his
supervision and control. Common wants compel both the rich and
the poor to mingle together. Their common brotherhood demands
from them mutual justice, kindness and forbearance.

14. The king who faithfully judgeth the poor:—
His throne shall be established forever.

15. The rod and reproof give wisdom;
But a neglected child bringeth shame to his mother.

16. When the wicked increase, transgression increaseth;
But the righteous shall witness their fall.

17. Correct thy son, and he will give thee comfort;
Yea, he will give delight to thy soul.

18. Where there is no vision, the people become dissolute;
But he, who keepeth the law,—happy is he.

19. A servant will not be corrected by words;
Although he may understand, yet he will not answer.

20. Seest thou a man hasty in his words?
There is more hope of a fool than of him.

21. He, who bringeth up his servant delicately from childhood,
Will have him become (as) a son at the last.

22. A passionate man stirreth up strife;
And a furious man aboundeth in transgression.

23. The pride of a man shall bring him low;
But (he, who) is of an humble spirit, shall obtain honor.

24. He, who shareth with a thief, hateth his own life;
He heareth the curse, yet he will not confess.

---

18. By *vision* is probably intended religious instruction, divine communication, with particular allusion to the teaching of inspired prophets and holy men, under the Jewish dispensation. But of course the proverb admits of a much wider application.

19. Sept. "A stubborn servant." Sometimes more than words of argument and persuasion is necessary to secure the prompt obedience of unprincipled servants and dependants. The servants in early times were generally the property of their masters, for the time being, who claimed and exercised the right of chastising them. *Not answer*—viz. by *doing* what is commanded.

24. He who shares the plunder with a thief, exposes himself to

25. The fear of man bringeth a snare;
But he, who trusteth in Jehovah, shall be safe.

26. Many seek the favor of a ruler;
But the right of a man (*cometh*) from Jehovah.

27. A wicked man is the abomination of the just;
And the upright in (*his*) way, is the abomination
of the wicked.

---

a like punishment. In doing this, he acts in such a manner as to
lead one to infer, that he esteems his own life of little value. By
the *curse* is intended the adjuration or imprecation denounced against
him who should conceal a theft to which he was privy. See Lev.
5: 1, and Comp. Judges 17: 2.

25, Comp. John 12: 43. Luke 12: 4, 5.

26. *Favor*—lit. *the face.* This proverb may denote that the judicial sentence which the ruler gives respecting any man's cause depends upon God, who controls the dispositions and wills of rulers
as he pleases. See ch. 16: 33. 21: 1. Or, that while many repair
to rulers, in order to obtain their favor by flattery, it is God only ·
who will and can do perfect justice to all. Or, more generally, that
every man's condition and success in life depend more upon the
favor of God than upon the favor of rulers.

27. Comp. 2 Cor. 6: 14. Ecclus. 13: 17.

---

26. " *The sentence of a man*," Boothr., French—" *every man's judgment*," Noyes.

22

PART V.

CHAPTER XXX. 1–33.

1. The words of Agur, the son of Jakeh; the divine sayings of that man unto Ithiel,—even unto Ithiel and Ucal.

2. Truly I am more stupid than (*any*) man;
Nor have I the understanding of a man.

---

1. It is evident that Jakeh, Ithiel, and Ucal, were regarded by the Chaldee and Syriac translators, and by the Masoretic interpunctists, as *proper names;* and so they have been regarded by nearly all modern commentators. It is equally manifest that they were not so regarded by the translators of the Septuagint and Vulgate, but merely as appellatives; and yet it is impossible to learn from either of them any thing satisfactory concerning their import. Prof. Stuart, after Kitzig and Bertheau, by changing the vocalization, renders the verse thus: "The words of Agur, the son of her who was obeyed in Massa, Thus spake the man: I have toiled for God, I have toiled for God, and have ceased." The repetition of Ithiel is wanting in some MSS. of Kennicott and De Rossi, and is possibly an interpolation. Some of the earlier commentators suppose that Agur is an enigmatical name for Solomon, and Jakeh for David. Others have imagined that Ithiel and Ucal denote Christ. But there is no foundation whatever for these conjectures. Who the persons here mentioned were, we have no means of determining. It would seem that they were the friends or pupils of Agur, but when or where they flourished cannot be ascertained.

2. This is undoubtedly the language of unaffected humility, springing from a consciousness of moral and intellectual deficiencies. Like Amos, Agur was not a professed and educated prophet, nor the

3. For I have not learned wisdom ;
Nor am I skilled in the knowledge of the Most
Holy.

4. Who hath ascended into heaven, or descended ?
Who hath gathered the wind in his fists ?
Who hath bound up the waters (*as*) in a garment ?
Who hath established all the ends of the earth ?
What is his name ? and what is his son's name ?
Tell me, if thou knowest !

5. Every word of God is pure ;
He is a shield to those who put their trust in him.

6. Add not thou to his words ;
Lest he reprove thee, and thou be found a liar.

7. Two (*things*) do I desire of thee, (*O God !*) ;
Withhold (*them*) not from me, before I die !

8. Remove far from me vanity and lies ;
Give me neither poverty nor riches ;
Feed me with food sufficient for me.

---

son of a prophet; yet the Lord taught him to utter divine, instructive, and weighty truths.

4. The design of the questions here propounded, is to impress
the reader with the idea of man's ignorance and impotence, as contrasted with the infinitude of knowledge and power in the Most
High. (Comp. Rom. 11: 34. Job 36: 23. John 3: 13.) Some of the
Church fathers, and not a few modern commentators, understand by
his name that of the first person in the Godhead, and by his *son's*
name, that of the second person. The Septuagint reads *sons* or
children in the plural. *If thou knowest*—lit. *since thou knowest*. This
is doubtless spoken by Agur ironically.

5, 6. Comp. Ps. 12: 6. 119: 140.—Deut 4: 2. 12: 32.

8. The prayer of Agur is brief; but very comprehensive.
" Though little is said, yet that little is fraught with matter, framed
in its proper order. Spiritual blessings occupy the first place; temporal blessings are secondary, and in subserviency to them."
Riches—All are ready enough to pray against poverty. But to de-
precate *riches*—"Oh ! deliver me from this muck-rake;" as Interpreter said to Christian in Pilgrim's Progress;—"that prayer has
lain by, till it is almost rusty." *Food sufficient for me*—lit. *the bread*

9. Lest I be full and deny (*thee*);
And say, ' Who is Jehovah ?'
Or, lest I become poor and steal,
And swear falsely by the name of my God.
10. Accuse not a servant to his master;
Lest he curse thee, and thou be found guilty.

---

of my portion, or *allowance.* There is a remarkable coincidence between the prayer of Agur and several petitions of the Lord's Prayer.

9. "It is a question," says Dr. South, "whether the piety, or the prudence of this prayer be greater." "Agur was well persuaded of the temptations incident to these two opposite conditions—the vanity and lies belonging to riches, the discontent and occasion of sin, which are the snares of poverty. Yet he does not pray absolutely against these states—only submissively. It is the prayer of his choice—the desire of his heart, that God would graciously exempt him from both, and bless him with a middle condition. Nor does he ask this for the indulgence of the flesh. He deprecates not the trouble, anxieties, and responsibilities, of riches, which might betoken an indolent, self-pleasing spirit; nor the miseries and sufferings of poverty. But he cries for deliverance from the snares of each condition.—Let me not be rich, 'lest I be full and deny thee.' Let me not be poor, 'lest I steal and take the name of God in vain.'" (Bridges.) "The sum and substance of Agur's prayer," says Holden, "is, O Lord, remove from me all sin and error, all falsehood and deception; give me neither a superfluity, nor a deficiency of those things which befit my station, but a competency adapted to my rank and condition of life; lest if I have more than enough, my heart may be tempted, through luxury or the pride of wealth, to forget thee; or lest, if I have not a sufficiency, I should be induced to steal, or to arraign the equity of the divine government, and profane the name of my God, by perjury and blasphemy." Comp. Deut. 8: 11, 12, 14, 17.

10. The condition of a slave was miserable at the best, and to add misery to misery by false accusation, is under any circumstances, most cruel and barbarous. The scope of the proverb is, Exercise due caution and discretion in accusing a servant to his master, lest he in return revile and curse you, and you be found guilty of making a false accusation, and suffer the consequences.

11. There is a generation that curse their father,
And do not bless their mother.

12. There is a generation who are pure in their own eyes,
And (*yet*) are not washed from their filthiness.

13. There is a generation, how lofty are their eyes!
And their eye-lids are lifted up!

14. There is a generation whose teeth are (*like*) swords;
And whose jaw-teeth are (*like*) knives,
To devour the poor from off the earth,
And the needy from (*among*) men.

15. The horse-leech hath two daughters;
" Give !" "Give !" (*are their names*).
There are three (*things*) that are never satisfied;
(*Yea*) four that never say, " It is enough !"

---

11. The Heb. word דור, *dor*, sig. in this place generation in the sense of a particular race or class of men. *Do not bless.*—This expression is equivalent to *curse* in the parallel member, by figure litotes.

13. The lifting up of the eyes and eye-brows is a physiognomical mark of pride, superciliousness and insolence. Comp. ch. 6: 17. 21: 4.

14. Teeth, as here, are frequently employed in Scripture as the symbols of cruelty.

15. The עֲלוּקָה, *aluqa*, is supposed by Prof. Stuart to be the *Vampire* or *Ghole* of Arabian superstition—an imaginary spectre, which in the ancient popular mythology is described as sucking with insatiable avidity human blood. But the word likewise denotes the *leech*, *the horse-leech* or *blood-sucker*, in Arabic, Syriac and Chaldee, and is so rendered here in the Sept. and Vulg. This signification accords with the context, and is almost universally adopted by modern commentators Horace, speaking of the mad poet says:

" But, if he seize you, then the torture dread;
" He fastens on you, till he reads you dead.
" And, like a leech, voracious of his food,
" Quits not his cruel hold, till gorged with blood."

---

15. " *Who cry, Give, Give !*" French—" *who are ever crying*," Boothr.

16. Sheol and the barren-womb,
The earth, that is not filled with water,
And fire that never saith, "It is enough!"

17. The eye that mocketh at a father,—
And despiseth obedience to a mother,—
The ravens of the valley shall pick it out,
And the young eagles shall devour it.

18. There are three (*things*) which are too wonderful for me,
Yea, four which I do not understand:—

19. The way of an eagle in the air;
The way of a serpent on a rock;

The *two daughters* may be merely a figurative mode of expressing the insatiable desire and constant craving of the leech for blood. Or, it may be a figurative description of the two lips of the leech, which are most regularly formed, as the external parts of its complex mouth. In the second clause of the verse there is generally supposed to be an ellipsis, which most commentators supply by inserting the word *crying*, or its equivalent, thus making the words *give, give*, the language of the two daughters, expressive of their earnest desire. But Noyes and Stuart, with more probability, regard the words *give, give*, as significant proper names bestowed on these two daughters, and indicative of their character and habits.

17. The eye is the first and favorite part attacked by birds of prey. This is seen in the case of numerous bodies, which various Eastern superstitions caused to be exposed to birds and beasts of prey. Not only do the ravens, which feed on carrion, commence their repast by picking out the eyes of the dead animal, whose carcass they have found; but eagles and falcons, which take living prey, when the game is large and powerful, aim their strokes at the eye, which, instinct teaches them is the readiest way of disabling their victims. "The crow shall one day pick out thy eyes," is a common imprecation in the East.

18. The cause of wonder in respect to the four things enumerated in the following verse does not lie in the things themselves, for they are common and familiar events; but in the impossibility of tracing the way or track once gone over by them, of which no sign or impression is left.

19. "As when a bird hath flown through the air, there is no

The way of a ship in the midst of the sea ;
The way of a man with a maid.

20. Such is the way of an adulterous woman,
She eateth, and wipeth her mouth,
And saith, "I have done no wickedness."

21. Under three (*things*) the land is disquieted ;
Yea, under four, it cannot bear up:—

22. Under a servant, when he reigneth,
And a fool, when he is filled with food.

token of her way to be found, but the light air, being heated with
the strokes of her wings and parted with the violent noise and motion of them, is passed through, and therein afterwards no sign
where she went is to be found." Wisd. 5: 11. "As a ship that
passeth over the waves of the water, which when it is gone by, the
trace thereof cannot be found, neither the pathway of the keel in
the waves " Wisd. 5: 10. *In the midst*—lit. *in the heart.* Comp. 23:
34. *The way of a man, &c.*—If the present Masoretic text be correct, then there is allusion here to clandestine amours. But one
MS. of De Rossi reads בְּעַלוּמָיו, *Bealumav, in his youth,* instead of
בְּעַלְמָה, *Bealma, with a maid,* or *virgin ;* and this is the reading of
the Syr. and Arab versions: the Septuagint and Vulgate also have
in youth. According to this rendering, the allusion is probably to
the secret and imperceptible manner in which one advances from
the feebleness, mental and bodily, of childhood, to the strength and
stature of manhood. This reading is preferred by Shultens and
Boothroyd; though the received text is followed by most commentators, as giving a sense more in accordance with the context.

20. *Such*—i. e. equally inscrutable and difficult to be traced. As
a man who has been eating; and being desirous to conceal the fact,
carefully wipes his mouth; so the adulterous woman removes all
external indications of her guilt, and then has the audacity to say,
"I have done no wickedness."

21. The four things here referred to were such as were deemed
by the proverbialist odious and intolerable incongruities. The idea
conveyed here by the word שְׂאֵת, *sheeth,* (contracted from שְׂאֵת, fem.
Infin. of נָשָׂא,) is that of *bearing up* under the weight of a heavy
pressure.

22. It sometimes happens under the despotic governments of the
East, that servants or slaves become rulers. When that is the case,

23. Under an odious (*woman*) when she getteth married;
And a handmaid, when she hath dispossessed her mistress.

24. There are four small (*things*) on the earth;
Yet are they exceedingly wise:—

25. The ants are a race not strong;
Yet they prepare their food in the summer.

26. The conies are a race not mighty;
Yet they make their houses in the rocks.

---

they are usually the most insolent, imperious, cruel and tyrannical of masters. There is a German proverb, "No razor shaves closer than when a boor becomes master." "Asperius nihil est humili, cum surgit in altum."—*Claudian*.

23. *Odious*, or *hateful*; one who is deservedly hated for her unamiable and tyrannical disposition. *Dispossessed*.—The verb ירש *yarash*, signifies not only *to possess* and *to inherit*, or *become heir to*, but to *dispossess*, to *drive out*. Accordingly the Sept. Syr., and several modern commentators render the clause, "And a handmaid when she hath dispossessed (or supplanted) her mistress," i. e. succeeds to the place of her mistress by marrying her master. So Gesenius. The four things mentioned in vs. 22 and 23, are evidently regarded by the writer as *odious incongruities*.

24. *Exceedingly wis*—lit. *wise made wise* (the last word being Part. Pual.): consequently if the *wise* are made still *wiser*, then they become very wise. The animals here alluded to, rank among the smaller and weaker tribes of terrestrial creatures; yet their activity, forethought, dexterity, and ingenuity, seem to have given occasion to the gnomic sayings which follow.

25. Are *not strong*—i. e. are weak and feeble. Hence the Arabians say contemptuously of a man who has become weak and infirm, "he is feebler than the ant." Comp. ch. 6: 8.

26. *Conies*.—The Hebrew word שפן, *shaphan*, occurs in several other places in the Old Test. (Lev. 11: 5. Deut. 14: 7. Ps. 104: 18.) and is uniformly translated in our Eng. Vers. after the Jewish Rab-

23. "*When she becometh heir to*" French, Noyes, Suart.
24. "*Yet do they possess the greatest wisdom*," Boothr.—"*are they wise-instructed in wisdom*," French, Noyes
26 "*The jerboas*," Noyes, French, Boothr.—"*mountain mice*," Tremellius, Stuart.

27. The locusts have no king;
Yet do they all go forth in bands.
28. The lizard taketh hold with its hands;
And is in the palaces of kings.

---

bies, *the Coney* or *Rabbit*. The Sept. in these places has χοιρο-
γρυλλοις, *hedge hog*. It is hardly probable that the Rabbit is
meant, because that is not an Asiatic animal, nor does it seek a
rocky habitation. The Shaphan is supposed by many commentators to be the Arabian *jerboa* or mountain-rat—the *mus*, or *dipus jacu-
lus* of Linnæus. But it is now generally regarded in scientific
zoology as one of the genus *Hyrax*, distinguished by the specific
name of *Syrian*, (*Hyrax Syriacus*) which is a small animal like a
marmot, found in Lebanon, Palestine, Arabia Petra, Upper Egypt
and Abyssinia, and is correctly described by Saadias, and by Bruce.
It is about the size, figure and brownish color of the Rabbit, with
long hind legs adapted to leaping, but is of a clumsier structure
than that quadruped. It is without a tail and has long bristly hairs,
scattered over the general fur. As to its ears, which are small and
roundish, instead of long, like the rabbit, its feet and snout, it re-
sembles the hedge-hog. From the structure of its feet, which are
round and of a soft, pulpy, tender substance, it cannot dig, and
hence is not fitted to dwell in burrows, like the rabbit, but in the
clefts of the rocks. It lives in families, is timid, lively, and quick
to retreat at the approach of danger; and hence is difficult to capture. In its habits it is gregarious, and feeds on grain, fruits and
vegetables. *Daman*, or *Gaman*, is the Syrian name of this animal;
the Arabs call it *Wabr* (Wabber), and the Abyssinians *Ashkoko*.
The rendering *Conies* in the text is retained simply because more
familiar to our ears.

27 *Bands*—i. e. formed into divisions or companies. like soldiers
under their respective leaders. That the locusts thus march spontaneously without a king or chief-leader to direct their movements,
is a proof of their instinctive sagacity. The head of the column,
when the insect army is not tossed and scattered by the wind, which
often happens, is directed by their voracious appetite for food; and
the rest follow in long succession under the influence of the same
instinct; but the devastations they commit, are as methodical and
complete, as if they acted under the strictest discipline.

28. The *house-lizard* and not the spider, is now generally under
stood to be the meaning of the word שְׂמָמִית, *shemameth*; for, though

29. There are three (*things*) which excel in step,
Yea, four are stately in their gate: —

30. The lion, the strongest among beasts;
Which turneth not away from any one;

31. The greyhound, and the he-goat;
And a king, against whom no one can stand.

32. If thou hast been foolish in lifting up thyself;
Yea, if thou hast devised mischief;
(*Lay*) thy hand on thy mouth.

33. For (*as*) the pressing of milk bringeth forth cheese;
And the pressing of the nose bringeth forth blood;
So the pressing of anger bringeth forth contention.

---

several ancient writers have ascribed fingers to the spider, not one
has honored her with hands. The ancient poet, on the contrary,
has represented the spider as saying, "I have no hands, but all
things are done by my feet." The small house-lizard is very common in Palestine, and, having the power of supporting itself by its
feet upon the walls and ceilings of houses, it gets into every kind
of dwelling in pursuit of its prey. Its principal food is spiders
and flies, and these it springs upon and grasps with both its pre
hensibles, as if they were hands.

31. The *greyhound.*—The Hebrew phrase literally sig. *compressed
of loins*, or *one, girded as to his loins*. Some render it *the loin-girded
war-horse*, and regard it as an epithet descriptive of the war-horse
ornamented and equipped for war, with girths and buckles, capari-
soned for battle. Others make it refer to the *Zebra*; but this animal
does not inhabit Palestine. The ancient versions (Sept. Syr. Vulg.
and Chald.) translate it *cock*. Our English vers. has *greyhound*, and
this seems most probably to be the animal intended.

32. *Lay thy hand, &c.*—lit *hand to mouth*, i. e. be silent. Comp.
Job 21: 5. 40: 4. Mic. 7: 16.

33. *For*—causal particle—*because* if you persevere in your folly
and wickedness, you will only provoke the wrath of your enemies.
Cheese.—The usual sig. of חֶמְאָה, *chema*, is *thick, curdled milk*, distinguished from חָלָב, *chalab*, which denotes *new milk*. Here it would
seem to be employed in the sense of cheese, and not butter, as in
our Eng. vers., for the noun מִיץ, *mitz*, sig. *pressing, pressure*, (from
מִיץ, *to press*,) and milk subjected to pressure, becomes cheese. *Pressing of anger*—lit. *of the nostrils*—a caution against the hasty expression of anger, and the utterance of provoking language.

PART VI.

CHAPTER XXXI. 1–9.

[THE ADVICE OF A QUEEN MOTHER TO HER ROYAL SON.—CAUTION AGAINST INCONTINENCE AND INTEMPERANCE.—MONITIONS RESPECTING THE ADMINISTRATION OF JUSTICE, AND THE VINDICATION OF THE OPPRESSED.]

1. The words of King Lemuel, even the divine sayings which his mother taught him.

2. "What, O my Son! and what, O Son of my womb!

" Yea, what, O Son of my vows, (*shall I say to thee?*)

3. " Give not thy strength to women,

" Nor thy ways to (*that which*) destroyeth kings.

4. " It is not for kings, O Lemuel!

" It is not for kings to drink wine,

" And for princes to desire strong drink.

---

2. There is evidently a lacuna at the end of the second clause of this verse, and the ellipsis must be supplied, as is done in the version, in order to render the sentence complete and intelligible. The repetition denotes earnestness.

3. *Strength.*—The Heb. word חַיִל, *chayil*, sig. *wealth*, as well as strength, and it is so rendered in this place by the Sept. Vulg. and several modern commentators. But mental and bodily vigor would seem to be the more appropriate meaning here. Sensuality and debauchery are productive of the most mischievous effects. They pervert the conscience, harden the heart, consume the property, enervate the body and mind, and impair the constitution, destroy the character, bring on premature old age and death, and finally, ruin the soul forever,

5. " Lest they drink and forget the law,
" And pervert the cause of any of the oppressed.

6. " Give strong drink to him who is ready to perish;
" And wine to the sad of heart.

7. " Let him drink, and forget his poverty,
" And remember his misery no more.

8. " Open thy mouth for the dumb;—
" In the cause of every orphan.

9. " Open thy mouth; judge righteously,
" And defend the cause of the poor and needy."

---

6. Let the wealthy, instead of freely indulging themselves in the habitual use of wine and other stimulating and intoxicating drinks, unnecessary, if not positively injurious to those who are in health, bestow them, as an act of kindness and charity, upon such as are about to die, or who are borne down by poverty, sickness, excessive grief, or other misfortune. The Jews say that on this passage was founded the custom of giving a stupifying draught, composed of wine and frankincense, to criminals, who were about to suffer capital punishment, so as to render them less sensitive to pain. See Matth. 27: 34. Ma. 15: 23.

8. *The dumb*—speak in behalf of one figuratively dumb, i. e. one who is incapable of advocating his own cause. *Every orphan*—lit. *of all the children of bereavement.*

CHAPTER XXXI. 10–31.

[AN ACROSTIC EULOGY ON THE PRUDENT, ECONOMICAL, INDUSTRIOUS
AND THRIFTY HOUSE-WIFE.]

10. Who can find a virtuous wife?
For her worth is far above pearls.

---

10. This alphabetical poem on the domestic virtues of a good wife, was probably written, either by the mother of King Lemuel, or by the King himself. It consists of twenty-two verses, beginning with the first letter of the Hebrew alphabet, and proceeding

11. The heart of her husband trusteth in her;
And he will not lack gain.

12. She will do him good and not evil,
All the days of his life.

13. She seeketh wool and flax;
And worketh willingly with her hands.

---

in consecutive order, through it to the last verse. On account of
this arrangement it is called by Doederlein the golden A, B, C, for
wives; and Matthew Henry denominates it "the looking-glass for
ladies, into which they should look, and by which they should dress
themselves." This artistic form of composition seems to have been
much admired by the Hebrews, and was frequently adopted, we
may presume, for the purpose of assisting the memory of the reader,
as well as displaying the ingenuity of the author. A *virtuous wife*
is literally a *woman of strength, or energy.* *Strength* is used tropically for moral and mental power,—integrity, capability, piety and
virtue. See ch. 12: 4.

11. The first item in the catalogue of good qualities here enumerated, is the rarest of all. The oriental husband, in a large majority of instances, does by no means feel confident that his wife
can be trusted, and that she will always consult his benefit and not
his injury. Hence, he commonly keeps a watch over her, and
places every valuable article under lock and key. He trusts more
in hired guards and iron locks than in his wife. "This," says Dr.
Thompson, "is mainly owing to two things; bad education and
the want of love, both grievous sins against her, and committed
by her lord and master. She is kept in ignorance, and is married
off without regard to the affections of her heart; and how can it be
expected that the husband can safely trust in a wife thus trained
and thus obtained?"

13. The lovely character of the faithful and devoted house-wife
is here drawn according to the usages and customs of ancient times.-
Whatever changes in this respect may have since taken place, the
general principles and virtues here described are of universal application. "In the state of society to which this description belongs, every kind of drapery for the person, the tent, or the house,
is manufactured at home by the women, who make it a matter of

---

11. "*Shall not want domestic wealth.*" Holden—"*is in no want of household substance,*" French—"*of his property he will not be deprived,*" Boothr.

14. She is like the ships of a merchant ;
She bringeth her food from afar.

15. She riseth while it is yet night,
And giveth food to her household,
And a portion to her maidens.

16. She considereth upon a field and buyeth it ;
With the fruit of her hands, she planteth a vineyard.

17. She girdeth her loins with strength,
And strengtheneth her arms.

18. She perceiveth that her traffic is profitable ;
Her lamp goeth not out by night.

---

pride to be able to boast, that their husbands and children are entirely clad by the labor of their hands, and the man's robe clings
the more sweetly to him,—is warmer in the cold and cooler in the
heat from his knowledge of the dear hands by which every thread
has been prepared." (Kitto.) The valley of the Nile produced
flax in great abundance in the time of Solomon, which was imported into Palestine, and spun and woven into cloth by the Hebrew women.

15. "The Orientals generally rise very early in the morning.
"To be up with the sun," is not in the East regarded as early
rising. Every one who is not prevented by infirmity, or sickness,
from the ruler to the meanest of his subjects, is usually up and
dressed by the morning dawn; and even in royal courts, the most
important public business is transacted at a very early hour. The
women almost invariably rise even sooner than the men, often a
good while before day; especially when to their numerous duties
of domestic engagement, is added the manufacture of stuffs for
household use or sale, giving them incessant occupation, and leaving the day too short for their labors." (Kitto.) *A portion*—i. e. an
allotted portion of food.

17. The phrase *to gird the loins* is here used tropically, as appears from the adjunct *with strength*. It represents her as active
and energetic, putting forth all her strength, and doing what she
undertakes with all her might. The expression is drawn from the
custom of wearing loose, flowing garments which required to be
girded close about the body, before undertaking any active or laborious employment.

19. She putteth forth her hands to the spindle,
And her hands hold fast the distaff.

20. She stretcheth out her hand to the poor;
Yea, she reacheth forth her hands to the needy.

21. She is not afraid for her household on account
of the snow;
For all her household are clothed in scarlet.

21. *In scarlet*—i. e in garments of scarlet color. If this be the
true interpretation, then the idea intended to be conveyed must be,
that her family is not only protected from the cold of winter by
comfortable garments, but splendidly arrayed. Comp. 2 Sam. 1: 24.
Scarlet and purple tapestry and embroidery, are still the favorite
colors and patterns of oriental taste.   The word שָׁנִים, *shanim*, rendered *scarlet*, denotes a deep red or rich crimson;—that shade of
color, which we now denominate scarlet, was unknown at the time
our English Version was made.   This color was obtained from the
Cocus ilicis of Linnæus, an insect found in Spain and other countries bordering on the Mediterranean Sea.   It was greatly in request
among the ancients, who obtained from it a dye somewhat resembling that which is now obtained from the *Coccus cacle*, or the
Cochineal insect, which belongs to the same genus.   The worm
itself was called in Hebrew הוֹלֵע, *tola*.   It was the female of this
remarkable insect that was employed in producing this color, and
though supplanted in a great measure by the Cochineal, it is still
used for the purpose in India and Persia.   It attains the size and
form of a pea, is of a violet-black color, and covered with a whitish
powder.   It adheres to the leaves of plants, chiefly various species
of the oak, especially the *quercus coccifera*, or kerme oak. and so
closely does it resemble grains, that its insect nature was not generally known for many centuries.   Since there is no connexion, or
very little, between the color of a garment and its power of defence
against cold, many commentators have translated the word שָׁנִים,
shanim, *double garments*, or *garments of a double texture*, from the root
שָׁנָה, *shana*, *to repeat*, Sept. δισσας χλαίνας, Vulg. *vestite duplicili-
bus.*   So Margin. and Coverdale's English Version.   "All her
household folks are doubly clothed."   If this be the meaning of the
word, then the sense is, that she provides thick, warm and comfortable garments for the use of her family in winter.   But though
the Hebrew word will etymologically bear this construction, it no
where else is used in that sense in the Old Testament.   There is

22. She maketh for herself coverlets;
Her clothing is fine linen and purple.
23. Her husband is known in the gates,
When he sitteth among the elders of the land.
24. She maketh linen (*garments*) and selleth (*them*);
And she delivereth girdles to the merchants.

---

the same want of support from the *usus loquendi* of the Old Testament in reference to the rendering *double-dyed* ($\delta\iota\beta\acute{\alpha}\varphi o\iota$) given to it by some commentators. Besides, only purple garments were dyed twice, never those dyed with coccus.

22. *Coverlets*—see ch. 7: 16. By שֵׁשׁ, *shesh*, is meant either *fine cotton*, or *fine linen*, most probably the latter; but not *silk*, as in our Eng. Vers., for this elegant article of luxury is supposed not to have been in use among the Hebrews in the time of Solomon. Indeed, the silkworm was unknown beyond the territory of China, of which country it is a native, till the reign of Justinian. (See Gibbon's Rome, ch. 40.) *Purple*—i. e. purple cloth. (Comp. Ezek. 27: 16. Jer. 10: 9.) Sept. $\pi o\rho\varphi\acute{\upsilon}\rho\alpha$, Vulg. *purpura*. The purple color here mentioned, was no doubt obtained, like the far-famed Tyrian purple, from the juice of certain species of shell-fish found on the Eastern shores of the Mediterranean Sea. The juice of the entire fish was not used, but only a little of its liquor called the flower, contained in a white vein or vessel in the neck. This color was extensively employed in religious worship among both the Jews and Gentiles. It was ultimately superseded by the use of indigo, cochineal, &c., from which a cheaper and finer purple is obtained, free from that disagreeable odor which attended that which was derived from shell fish.

23. To *sit among the elders*, imports to exercise the functions of a magistrate, who occupied a seat by the gates of the city for the purpose of hearing and determining causes. The implication is that the husband is indebted at least in part to the wife's industry, frugality and general good management, for the high social and official position which he occupies in the community.

24. The use of girdles in the East is universal with both sexes, not only on account of the loose outer vestments, which it is employed to confine about the person; but also in consequence of the general impression that the girdle greatly contributes to the strength of the loins as a support, around which it is twisted tightly in

25. Strong and beautiful is her clothing;
And she rejoiceth at the days which are to come.

26. She openeth her mouth with wisdom;
And the law of kindness is on her tongue.

27. She looketh well to the ways of her household;
And she eateth not the bread of idleness.

28. Her children rise up, and call her blessed;
Her husband, and he praiseth her,—(*saying*)

29. "Many daughters have done virtuously;
"But thou excellest them all!"

30. Gracefulness is deceptive, and beauty, vain;
(*But*) a woman who feareth Jehovah, shall be praised.

31. Give her according to the fruit of her hands;
And let her works praise her in the gates!

---

many a circling fold. Being always in demand, it is an important article of domestic manufacture. Girdles were sometimes of so fine and rich a texture as to be considered a valuable present. Those worn at present by people of rank in the East, are sometimes made entirely of silk superbly adorned with gold and silver. *Merchants* —literally Canaanites. The Canaanites were celebrated merchants' and hence the term came to be used for merchants in general.

30. *Gracefulness.*—The Heb. word חֵן, *hen*, here subjectively denotes *gracefulness*, loveliness, personal charms; not objectively the *favor* conferred on another in consequence of possessing these qualities. All such personal attractions are fleeting, evanescent, unreliable and unsatisfying; but true piety is as enduring as eternity. She, therefore, should receive as she deserves, constant praise, whose conduct is guided by the pure and never-failing principles of true religion.

31. *Give her, &c.*—Let her receive the honor, which her virtues merit, in the most public assemblies of the people.

ERRATA.

The reader is requested to correct the following errata:

Page xxxviii. of Introduction, 7th line from the bottom, for "preparation" read "preposition."

Page xxix. 21st line from the top, for "have" read "has."

Page xxxiii. 15th line from the top, for "where" read "when."

Page 93, 18th line from the top, for "mean" read "to be meant."

Page 189, 16th line from the top, for "from the eaves," read "through the roof," see ch. 27: 15, note.

Page 260, 11th line from the top, del. "themselves."